The Langdon Trilogy Book 3

I0637979

A Second Revolution

An American Civil Rights Story

C. James Gilbert

Mechanicsburg, Pennsylvania USA

Published by Sunbury Press, Inc.
Mechanicsburg, Pennsylvania

www.sunburypress.com

For information about special discounts for bulk purchases, please contact Sunbury Press Orders Dept. at (855) 338-8359 or orders@sunburypress.com.

To request one of our authors for speaking engagements or book signings, please contact Sunbury Press Publicity Dept. at publicity@sunburypress.com.

ISBN: 978-1-62006-828-1 (Trade paperback)
ISBN: 978-1-62006-829-8 (Mobipocket)

Library of Congress Control Number: 2017931390

FIRST SUNBURY PRESS EDITION: March 2017

Product of the United States of America
0 1 1 2 3 5 8 13 21 34 55

Set in Bookman Old Style
Designed by Crystal Devine
Cover by Terry Kennedy
Edited by Jennifer Cappello

Continue the Enlightenment!

Dedication

To those whose passion is the written word; to those whose dream is to one day see before their name the word, "author" . . . I affectionately dedicate this book.

Acknowledgments

I would like to express my deepest gratitude to Lawrence Knorr and Sunbury Press for the privilege of calling myself an author.

Special thanks to my editor, Jennifer Cappello, who has for the third time now, given me her dedication and her expertise.

I would like to thank Terry Kennedy for the fine job he has done on the book's cover.

I would also like to thank Crystal Devine for her diligent effort in the design of this book.

ONE

The Promise

Jim Langdon was having a very restless night to say the least; it was only five months since the deaths of his parents. As fate would have it, his mother and father both departed within a matter of hours of one another leaving a unique void in Jim's life that almost nothing could fill.

As he lay in bed beside his sleeping wife, Elizabeth, and while he labored to lie still, his mind wandered; mostly through the past, a direction taken in league with the memory of his mother and father. He was the third generation to own Langdon Plantation, a twenty-five hundred acre cotton plantation located twenty miles south of Macon, Georgia.

But the plantation was not the only thing he inherited from his parents. He was given the belief that all people, regardless of race, are equal and should be treated as such. When Jim's grandfather, John, owned the plantation, it was worked by slaves. That was when the change in Langdon family history first began. Jim's father, James—also Jim's real name—was very much against slavery, and rightfully so. It became a serious issue between Jim's father and grandfather.

So Jim's father decided to take matters into his own hands, leaving home when the Civil War broke out, but not to fight for the South as he had led his family to believe. Instead he began helping slaves escape to Canada, later joining the Union army and remaining in Union blue until the end of the war.

One thing Jim had learned in his lifetime: Racism is not inherent; it is taught, and the same is true of anti-racism. His father had been a very direct and permanent influence in his life; that is to say that Jim was a lot like his father. Many points of view were shared, especially that no man should have domain over another; slavery and discrimination were wrong.

1

Speaking metaphorically, the final line of his father's will bequeathed to Jim the hatred of the Ku Klux Klan. He'd inherited a feud of sorts that had commenced in 1866 when the white supremacists discovered that Jim's father had served the Union during the war. Jim could remember many confrontations with the Klan, several resulting in loss of life. Through it all, his father did everything in his power, which went as high as his involvement in the state Senate, to bring about the destruction of slavery and establish equality for the black race.

Shortly after the war he had partnered with a few white men and a number of former slaves to stand together and fight against the Klan and the southern bureaucracy, which was determined to keep the Negroes from ever taking their rightful place in society. His father gave black friends all the land they could farm in exchange for no more than a fair share of the crops. He built housing for them, educated their children, and created a safe haven for all who lived there.

At the time of James' death, Jim promised his father that he would continue the fight until the former slaves were given the same rights as white Americans. He was now 57 years of age and could truthfully say that the dispute over civil rights had been going on throughout his entire life.

He rolled to his side and stared toward the window while Elizabeth snored quietly. Suddenly he noticed a glint of light in the night sky. The light was not still such as that from a beacon, but rather it had movement; a flickering effect. He rose very slowly so as not to disturb his wife and then took a half dozen steps to the window. In the meadow, just on the other side of the big barn, stood a cross, fully engulfed in flames.

Jim watched the spectacle feeling very melancholy but experiencing no fear; no sense of alarm. It was just a calling card left by the Klan, an act that had been repeated many times beginning shortly after the passing of his parents. It was a reminder that the Klan knew what the residents of Langdon Plantation stood for and that they were the enemy. The burning crosses were just a petty form of intimidation.

2

In the late 1800s the Ku Klux Klan had all but died out, but in 1915, near Atlanta, Georgia, a revival of the Klan was organized by white Protestant nativists. The fire was fueled by Thomas Dixon's 1905 book, *The Clansmen*, and a film made by D. W. Griffith titled, *Birth of a Nation*. In addition to their anti-black doctrine, the Klan now condemned organized labor, Roman Catholics, Jews, and foreigners.

A burning cross was adopted as the Klan's new emblem, and the entire country became a stage for their membership rallies, marches, and parades.

The days of armed confrontation between the Klan and the men of Langdon Plantation were gone. Due to the cunning of Jim's father, the Klan was handed numerous defeats including the arrest, prosecution, and execution of their Exalted Cyclops for the crime of murder in 1869. Of course both sides suffered losses; several graves in the Langdon family cemetery were proof of that. And Jim would never forget that he was not an only child by choice but by an accident involving his pregnant mother—an accident caused by members of the Klan.

It was now the spring of 1919, and all that had taken place in the past had shaped Jim's future. It would be his personal mission to continue his father's altruistic struggle to see a terrible injustice come to an end. But it was in no way thrust upon him, rather it was something he had become a part of while growing up, actively joining his father after graduation from college; together they had worked tirelessly until his father's death. And, like his father, he was not alone.

Jim's son, John, who lived in a house he built on Langdon Plantation with his wife, Abbey, and their two children, now accompanied him on speaking tours as they worked to gain support for civil rights. They closely followed newspapers for stories of racial upheaval, in many cases traveling to the scene to get involved and to use the incident as a podium from which to get the attention of the people.

"Jim?" He hadn't noticed that Elizabeth stopped snoring and had reached out to find him gone. He went over to her side of the bed and sat down on the edge of it.

"I'm sorry, my dear. I woke up and I couldn't get back to sleep. I didn't want to disturb you."

"Are you thinking about Mother and Father?"

"Yes, I guess I am. Of course there are other concerns."

"I understand, Jim, I know how deeply you put yourself into the crusade. Surely you know that I am right there with you."

"I do know that, and it makes it so much easier that we have each other for support. It must sound like a cliché to say that I know just how Father felt, but darned if it isn't the truth. Mother was always there for him too."

"Well, cheer up. Tomorrow many of your family members will be here in remembrance of your parents, and you will see your aunt Kate. You seldom get to see her."

"You're right, and that means I'd better get some rest."

Without mentioning the cross burning, Jim got back into bed, kissed his wife, and went back to sleep.

The following morning at around eleven, Aunt Kate and Uncle Bradford arrived all the way from Columbus, Georgia. Bradford was a railroad engineer, a wealthy man. They had made the drive in Bradford's Pierce-Arrow 5-Passenger Touring Car. The couple had three sons, Matthew, Thomas, and Charles. All three were in their twenties, married with children, and officers in the army. They all drove in for the day with their families. Jim seldom saw his aunt Kate, and his cousins even less frequently.

Aunt Ashton and Uncle Jeremy lived in a home they built up the hill behind the plantation house. Uncle Jeremy had come to the plantation as a young man, looking for a chance to sharecrop. He became a close personal friend of Jim's father and ended up as a member of the family.

Aunt Ashton and Uncle Jeremy had two daughters, Madeline and Emma. Madeline lived in California with her husband, Andrew; the couple had no children. Andrew had made his fortune in the timber industry.

Emma never married and still lived at home. She was a very quiet woman whose only interests in life were writing poetry and growing flowers.

Jim's son, John, his wife, Abbey, and their two children—their son, William, twelve, and their daughter, Julia, nine years of age—were also in attendance.

4

A beautiful memorial service was held at the family cemetery for his parents with Reverend Archibald P. Whittaker from Macon, officiating. After the lovely repast that followed, the women and girls made themselves comfortable in the parlor and the men and boys took to the veranda to catch up on family news and discuss topics of interest.

"So, Charles," Jim said to his nephew. "I apologize in advance for asking you to remember things I know you'd rather forget, just having put a terrible world war behind you. But I have to know what it was like for the black soldiers. I've read all of the newspapers about the battles and the terrible losses, but to know what happened inside the ranks, you have to talk to a soldier."

"You surely needn't apologize for asking, Uncle Jim. I understand about your work, and I am in total agreement with it, by the way. It is long overdue for the people of this country to defeat their bigotry and pull together as a people and a nation."

"Very nicely put, Charles. I know it would make my father mighty happy to hear you say that."

"There is no one in this family who doesn't agree with you, Uncle Jim," said his nephew, Thomas. "We all know that slavery was wrong, and the only thing that makes it worse is the continuation of racism and discrimination. We all feel that our family's history has been so darkened by the memory of slavery on this plantation that we wholeheartedly support the work that you and John do to help those people who have known degradation for so long. The people of this nation must understand that we are all equal under God, and if we are all equal under God, no man has the right or power to dispute it."

"We can *all* tell you what the war was like for the black man, Uncle Jim," said Charles. "Even though they had a different motive this time, they were just as eager to fight for America as they were when the Civil War broke out. In 1861, they wanted to fight for their freedom. This time they wanted to fight for their new country and for the government that had won them their freedom. You probably know that by the end of the war, some 350,000 black men had joined the US Army."

"Yes, I have heard that," said Jim. "They have always done their share, beginning with the revolution of the eighteenth century. The one positive good for the black man in the revolution: if he fought and survived, his reward was oftentimes his freedom. Please continue with your story, Charles."

"Regardless of their patriotism, the army is still segregated, and the white officers in charge of the black troops were not fond of giving guns to them nor were they happy about training them to use the weapons. And, as it was in the Civil War, most of the black units were relegated to support roles and did not see any action."

"Yes, Charles, it is history repeating itself. My father told me stories about black units like the 54th Massachusetts and how they longed for a chance to face the Confederates. When they finally got their chance they performed superbly. Why did they need to prove themselves all over again?"

"I suppose the old wars are eventually forgotten, but prejudice cannot be defeated by war. It was passing to the next generation even during the time when white men and black men were dying on the same battlefields. When the Americans finally got to France, the allied commanders were badly in need of soldiers. They had the officers to lead them, but they were begging for troops. The American commander, General John Pershing, did not want to send his white soldiers into combat until they were ready, nor did he want to dismantle any of his units. To solve the problem he sent his black units to the allied commanders."

"Did they see action then?" asked Jim.

"I heard that the allies assigned them to the toughest, most dangerous missions they could find."

"Not much respect or gratitude there," said Jim. "I can't imagine volunteering my life for a country who wouldn't even acknowledge the sacrifice."

"Nor can I, Uncle," said Charles. "And sacrifice they did. One infantry regiment, the 369th, known as the Harlem Hellfighters, once spent six months on the front line. That was longer than any American unit ever spent in that position. By the end of the war, one hundred seventy-one soldiers from the 369th were awarded the Legion of Merit."

"To interject another positive note," Thomas said. "Things *are* improving as time goes by, Uncle Jim, although I concede that the steps are small and progress is very slow. But the army is further ahead in race relations than the other branches of the service. The Marines will not take black men at all, and the navy will only use them for menial tasks. However, by the end of the war, black men in the army had served in artillery, signal, cavalry, medical, infantry, and engineering units, also serving as chaplains, truck drivers, surveyors, chemists, and intelligence officers."

After sitting quietly and listening the whole time, Matthew spoke his mind. "It's true that things are slowly changing, Charles, but in the meantime the status quo is still robbing these brave men of the thing that they deserve the most, and that is appreciation from their fellow man. Just someone to say, 'you were needed and you were there, thank you.'"

"I read a story of a black soldier by the name of Corporal Freddie Stowers, who was in the 371st regiment. He was transferred to the 157th French Army Division. He was killed on September 28, 1918, as he was leading his company during the attack on hill 188, Champagne Marne Sector, France. During the battle the Germans suddenly stopped shooting and starting climbing to the top of the trench with their hands in the air. Thinking the enemy was surrendering, the Americans stopped shooting as well. When Stowers and his men got to within a hundred meters of the trench line the Germans jumped back into the trench and began firing at the unsuspecting Americans. Half of Stowers' company was shot down. Into the face of certain death, Stowers crawled forward, inspiring his men to follow. Shot twice, Corporal Stowers kept moving and fighting until death took him out of the battle that was eventually won by his comrades. I heard that Corporal Stowers was nominated for the Congressional Medal of Honor. I wonder if his family will ever see it."

"I wonder too," said Jim. "This whole country is in a period of evolution and has been since the outbreak of the Civil War. Since then it has been one costly event after another. First the war, then an assassinated president,

7

then the dreadful period of Reconstruction, and now we are mired in a great racial struggle still primarily instigated by the descendants of those who are to blame for letting all of this happen. Maybe someday there will come a time for acknowledgment and responsibility."

"That sums it up pretty well, Uncle Jim," said Charles. "Things are no different in the army than on the home front, but the world will be a much different place if the evolution is ever complete. We are all aware of the migration that's going on and has been for the last six years."

"Yes," Jim replied. "Many black families are leaving the South. Some are moving west but even more are moving north to cities like Pittsburgh, New York, and Chicago, bringing new influence and culture to the inner city. They really have no choice; they are looking for a new beginning, a chance to leave the oppression of the South and the sharecropping way of life, which saw them always in debt and buried in hopelessness. In addition, the justice system in the South refuses to protect them equally under the law; vigilante mob violence is rampant. Race riots are breaking out everywhere; the Ku Klux Klan is operating in 27 states, and Jim Crow is stronger than ever."

"It is definitely a work in progress, Father," said John. "Sometimes it appears as though the hatred is subsiding. Other times it seems that we'll never see it end. All we can do is accept the challenge and stay the course."

"We have certainly learned that it is the only way, haven't we, son?"

"Yes, Father, both from our own experiences and from the example that Grandfather left for us to follow."

At that moment, the front door opened and the women poured out onto the veranda. That ended the men's conversation, but Jim felt a sense of relief. He had not intended to spend the family's entire visit talking about unpleasant subjects. It was helpful to learn all he could about racism, why it existed, who had the most power to make changes, and how the power could be persuaded to act.

But he fully understood, as did his father, that authority could only accomplish so much because there are those who reject authority and continue to spread their harmful influence throughout the population. This weakens the efforts of the anti-racism movement and puts fear into the hearts of those who may be inclined to say a kind word on behalf of the black race.

Sadly, too many people let others do their thinking for them. What, Jim wondered, would the world be like if everyone acted according to their own feelings? Would pacifism suddenly rise to the top and stifle the voices that perpetuate unfounded hatred? But he knew that to gain ground it would be necessary to change the thinking of the people; small groups or one at a time perhaps, but reach them, enlighten them, and drive the demon out once and for all.

The remainder of the evening was spent most pleasantly; Jim thrived on the support and good wishes of his family. By the time the sun had dropped behind the mountain, everyone had drifted from the veranda to the sharecroppers' quarters to pass some time with black friends and neighbors who worked on the plantation. Jim began circulating through the crowd laughing and talking to so many good people, all of whom he cared for as if they were family.

It was easy to understand why his father had so loved the life of peace and mutual respect he had established in his twenty-five hundred acre world. Perhaps even heaven was not so much of an adjustment for him.

Eventually, someone had to be the first to say that it was getting late and time to be leaving for home. In the old days, Aunt Kate, Uncle Bradford, and their family would have rested the night before traveling. But with the new age of the automobile, even Columbus was only a few hours away. The last to leave were Aunt Ashton and Uncle Jeremy, but Jim did not see Emma anywhere.

"Is Emma still here, Aunt Ashton? I didn't see her after we left the veranda."

"She went up to the house a couple of hours ago, Jim. She said she was tired. I hope that's all that there is to it."

"What do you mean?"

"You know how she is," said Uncle Jeremy. "We love her dearly but she *is* a bit of a star gazer. We have always

9

hoped that she would eventually find more common interests in life, but she is content just keeping constant company with her poems and her flowers. We try not to worry, but she is middle age now, and we are afraid she will end up alone. Talking about it always ends with your aunt and me feeling like we are prying."

"I see your point, but things can always change," said Jim with an optimistic tone.

"We'll keep praying for her," said Aunt Ashton.

"As will I. Good night," Jim replied.

As he made his way to the house, Jim pondered the question of what might be bothering his cousin, Emma. She had always been a very serious person; even as a child she did not frolic as her peers did. But she was always amiable and cooperative. Aside from her parents, she had always seemed most fond of Elizabeth. But lately, for maybe six months or so, Emma seemed withdrawn and moody. Jim stopped on the veranda, sat down on the swing, and said a prayer for Emma. Then he went inside for the night.

TWO

Charleston

By the time Jim had taken control of the plantation at the end of 1918, the whole operation had become so efficient due to competent management that he seldom had to get involved in routine matters. There were qualified people overseeing every stage of the planting, cultivating, harvesting, and shipping processes. Jim took care of the accounting, and that was about the extent of his responsibilities.

However, early in May he sent a telegram to a Mr. Byron Hutchinson of Charleston for the purpose of setting up a meeting to discuss the better use of commercial fertilizers. Jim would pass along the information to his foremen and let them decide if changes were necessary. He would ask John to go with him; they had not been to Charleston in years.

Plans were made; the trip was set; Jim and John would arrive in Charleston by train on the afternoon of May tenth. The three and a half hour trip was uneventful but passed quite pleasantly in stimulating conversation as father and son immersed themselves in their usual topic: the civil rights movement in America.

"I was reading another story in the *Atlanta Journal* a few days ago about two black men who were lynched somewhere in Mississippi; they were soldiers returning from the army, still in uniform," said John.

"I read that story too, John. It is difficult to consider this a civilized country. How anyone can murder a man because his skin is black—especially after that man risked his life for his country—is beyond me. The hatred is ever present; it never goes away. There is no need for effrontery or instigation from the black man. His appearance is enough to bring about confrontation. Prepare yourself and try to maintain your calm, John. You'll likely see plenty of examples in Charleston."

11

When father and son left the train at the station, they took a trolley car over to the Charleston Hotel, which was adjacent to Marion Square. As they rode in silence, each man pointed out many of the signs they saw that designated "Whites only," or "Colored only." In addition, there were all the humiliating advertisements using Negro caricatures. It was not that it was anything new to them, it was simply something that served as an unpleasant reminder that they lived in a segregated country.

When they reached the hotel, they climbed down from the trolley, but before they could retrieve their baggage, a black porter hurried out to take them inside. The man stood in ridged silence until Jim had signed the register, then he picked up the bags, which were more than he could easily carry, and started up the stairs. Both Jim and John wanted to lend a hand but thought better of it for fear of getting the porter in trouble; it wouldn't have taken more.

When they reached the room, the porter put the bags down, opened the door, handed Jim the key, then stood back so the two men could enter. Then he carried the bags in and asked where he should put them.

"Please put them on the bed, and thank you," said Jim. Then he handed the porter a generous tip for which the servant profusely thanked him. He bowed again and again as he backed out into the hallway and closed the door.

"Amazing," said Jim. John did not respond because he knew to what his father was referring. The black people had been put in their place, and for the most part, they stayed there. It angered them both to see such behavior, but they had become accustomed to biting their tongues and trying to control their feelings rather than making matters worse.

At six thirty that evening, they walked over to King Street to a fashionable restaurant called Rita's Southern Fare. They were to meet with Mr. Hutchinson at seven o'clock for dinner. A table had been reserved for the meeting; the two men were seated, served refreshments, and informed that their host would arrive shortly.

It was just after seven when Mr. Hutchinson entered the restaurant out of breath, a look of panic on his face.

"Forgive my tardiness, gentlemen," he said as he took his seat. "There is trouble up the street. I heard gunshots!"

"Gunshots?" said Jim.

"Yes, down by the Palace Poolroom. I saw a swarm of Blue Jackets up there."

"What are Blue Jackets?" John asked.

"They are sailors from the Naval Training Camp here in Charleston. Maybe they were called out for some reason. One thing's for sure, there must be . . ."

Mr. Hutchinson's voice trailed off as the sound of gunfire could now be heard from inside the restaurant. Jim got up from the table and went over to the large front window, followed by John, Mr. Hutchinson, and other patrons whose meals had been disturbed by the sound of violence. The window afforded a perfect view up King Street, where a mob of sailors and a few white civilians could be seen moving slowly toward Marion Square.

Some of the mob members went into a place called the Dixie Shooting Gallery, while others disappeared into a barbershop that Mr. Hutchinson said was owned by a local black man. In a matter of minutes, more gunshots could be heard coming from the shooting gallery; several black men came running out into the street through a gauntlet of clubs and stones wielded by the growing mob. A chair came crashing through the front window of the barbershop then smoke began to pour from the doorway. The barber and two of his patrons came out through the smoke with sailors on their heels. The barber was shot in the back and collapsed in the street.

"My God!" said Jim. "Where is the law in this town? Why is this rampage allowed to continue?"

"Don't be too concerned, Mr. Langdon," said Byron Hutchinson. "The sailors can take care of themselves. I'm sure that Mayor Hyde will send for the Marines at the naval base if it gets out of hand."

At that moment a black man was dragged off of a trolley car by two white men who proceeded to beat him with clubs while one of the barbershop patrons was shot in the head.

"Have you taken leave of your senses, Hutchinson?" said John. "There is murder being committed before your very eyes, and you haven't deemed the situation to be out of hand?"

Mr. Hutchinson eyed John and his father wistfully, as did several other men in the restaurant. "Just exactly which side of this little fracas are you on, gentlemen?"

"Which side? The side who is not responsible for this criminal outrage!"

"And would that be the black side or the white side?" snarled one of the other men.

"I am sure I don't know who started it," Jim replied. "But I can sure as hell see what is going on now."

"Why don't you explain to us what's going on, mister," said a rotund man with breadcrumbs clinging to his coal black beard.

The crowd in the restaurant began to move in and around Jim and his son. Jim sensed that danger was imminent. He had not forgotten about the sentiment toward anyone with white skin who would stand up for the black race, but he would never pretend or fail to be himself to placate those whose ignorance was exceeded only by their stupidity.

"I see people being beaten and killed indiscriminately because the law is manipulated and trampled on by men who are so narrow-minded that they must have been raised wearing blinders. I see men committing criminal acts against the Constitution of this country; a Constitution which states that all men are created equal under God. I see wrongdoing that you cannot make right by your callously idiotic Jim Crow laws. Those black men out there are people and deserve to be treated as such the same as you do!"

"Well, you're quite a pipe organ for the niggers, aren't you, Langdon?" said Hutchinson. "I don't know how you've managed to live in Georgia all these years without getting strung up, but I guess that's Georgia's problem. The thing you two nigger lovers need to do is get out of Charleston and out of South Carolina altogether before we dip you in tar so you won't be mistaken again for a white man. Let's throw them out of here, men!"

Before Jim and John could get to the door, a half dozen angry vigilantes grabbed them, picked them up off their feet, and carried them to the entrance. Byron Hutchinson opened the door, and the two men were literally thrown through the doorway and into the street. John got to his feet quickly and helped his father up.

The violence outside was still spreading. Another black man was shot down in Marion Square; Jim and John made their way back to the Charleston Hotel. Jim was limping badly by the time they got there. The desk clerk noticed their disarray and a bloody scrape on John's forehead.

"Good grief, gentlemen," he said. "Were you caught up in the mayhem?"

"No," Jim quickly replied. "May we have our key please?"

The desk clerk handed over the key and watched after them as they climbed the stairs to the second floor. Once in the room, Jim stretched out on the bed while John poured water into the basin on the washstand.

"Are you all right, Father?" John asked.

"I think so. I landed on my right side, and my hip is a bit sore, but I don't think it's serious. Your head is bleeding, John. You need a bandage."

"I'll be fine, Father. It's just a scratch. I'm more concerned about what is going on outside. How many more will be killed until this is over?"

"It's bad, son, real bad. I can't believe the mayor of this town isn't doing anything about this; if for no other reason, so that no whites are injured—you'd think he'd show concern for that. Surely the black population isn't going to take this without reprisals. There are about 80,000 people living in Charleston, and more than half of them are black."

"Perhaps the Marines have been called like Hutchinson mentioned. I seem to be hearing more gunshots than before."

"Yes, it sounds like a full-scale riot. I despise this feeling of helplessness, but I think the best thing we can do is to get out of Charleston as quickly as possible. Unfortunately, John, we won't be able to get a train until morning."

"But we weren't able to eat, Father. We'll have to have something."

"And we will, John. We'll wait until after dark, then we'll get something at the closest place we can find."

At nine o'clock p.m., darkness had fallen over the city, but gunshots could still be heard in the distance. "I think we should go out carefully and quietly and see if we can get a bite to eat before it gets any later," said Jim. "Hopefully the desk clerk can be of some help."

The two men left their room and went down to the front desk. They were glad to see that the lobby was empty. To their great surprise, the night clerk was sitting in a chair behind the desk, snoring quietly. John tapped the tiny service bell and the snoring stopped.

"Can I help you, gentlemen?" he asked with a yawn.

"I can see your dining room is closed; could you direct us to the closest place where we might get something to eat?" Jim asked.

"Yes, and the closest place would be the wise choice tonight. The Marines are out there putting down the disturbance; the town is under martial law, but I heard that there are local blacks aiming sniper fire at anybody wearing a uniform. They might even take a shot at *anything* white," the man said with a wry smile.

"Pardon me for saying so, but you don't seem particularly vexed by the whole situation," said Jim.

"Well, it's nothing new really, except that the blacks never put up this much of a counter attack before; the ignorant bastards. I keep telling folks that it doesn't matter to me, but one of these days the blacks are going to get tired of being kicked around, and there is more of them than there are of us."

"And what do your fellow townspeople say in reply?" John asked.

"They say the niggers are too damn dull in the brains to know where to wipe themselves let alone fight back against their superiors. But maybe after tonight they'll think I might be right," said the clerk with a look of satisfaction on his face.

In a completely disgusted tone of voice Jim said, "Where did you say we might get something to eat?"

With Jim's irritation going completely unnoticed, the clerk replied, "Oh yes, just up the street is a tavern called the Cottonwood. It's right next to Mason's Funeral Parlor. You can get a good steak and a stiff drink, and that would be a good combination right now."

"It certainly would," Jim answered. "Thank you for the information."

The clerk went back to his chair; Jim and John went out the front door and then stopped to take a good look up and down the street. There was very little activity in either direction, but an occasional gunshot could still be heard in other parts of town.

The tavern was not far nor was it very busy; a table in a dimly lit corner offered itself to them. The place was quiet; from inside the tavern no one would ever know there was such trouble going on somewhere in the confines of Charleston. Both men ordered plenty to eat as they had grown quite hungry after the long wait. When they had finished they went back outside and checked the street again before starting back to the hotel.

As they made their way, the near quiet on the street was suddenly interrupted by the sound of someone running down the sidewalk on the other side. By the illumination of the street lights, they saw a young black man getting all the speed that he could from his flying feet. Nearly falling, he stopped unexpectedly, took a quick look behind him, and then disappeared into the darkness between two houses.

About a half minute later, two white men, one carrying a coiled rope, came running down the street and stopped just a few feet past the opening where the young black man had entered. Looking anxiously all around, then noticing Jim and John, they started to cross the street. Without a word, Jim began waving his right arm emphatically in the direction of Marion Square. One man raised his arm in reply and then the two of them took off down the street at a brisk pace.

Without hesitation, Jim looked at his son and said, "Let's go." They hurried across the street and stood near the opening, peering into the darkness between the houses.

"Do you think he is still in there?" asked John.

17

"It's hard to say," Jim replied. "I don't know if this gap goes straight through or if it is blocked off in the back."

"My guess is that it goes straight through," said John. "If the young man is a local he probably knows the town well, and it is unlikely that he would allow himself to be trapped."

"You have a very good point, son. On the other hand, when someone panics they usually lose their ability to think clearly, especially if they don't have much time to think. Maybe getting off the street was the only move that seemed logical."

"Well, I know how we can find out, Father."

"I am with you, son. Let's see if we can help this young man."

Side by side they walked slowly between the two houses. It was too dark to see much of anything, so they let their ears act for their eyes. After walking perhaps twenty-five feet, they could hear loud breathing. The sound was of a quick tempo coming from deep within the chest of a terrified human being. Jim reached out a hand and touched John's arm to stop him in his tracks.

"Do not be afraid, young man," said Jim into the darkness. "My son and I are friendly, and we want to help you."

At first there was no reply; only more heavy breathing. Jim repeated their intentions, and finally the young man spoke. "Who is you and why is you lookin' to get mixed up in this? I can tell by your voice that you ain't black."

"You are quite right. My son and I are not black. But that has no meaning to us. Our belief is that all people are the same, and we do not stand with those who discriminate against another man because of the color of his skin. My son and I are visitors to Charleston, and I guess you could say that we got caught up in the trouble that broke out tonight. We were across the street when those two men chased you in here, and I waved to them to indicate that we saw you continue on toward Marion Square."

"Why would you do that?"

"To mislead them, of course."

"Well I reckon I don't understand every word you said but I am mighty obliged to you for not givin' me away."

"We'd like to do more than that if we can," said John.

"Is you the son?"

"That's right. Can you tell my father and I why those men were chasing you?"

"It ain't hard to explain. Them two is white, and I'm a nigger."

"No," said Jim. "That isn't what you are. You are a human being, as good as and equal to anyone else, white or black."

"Never heard that come out of no white man's mouth before, and that's for sure."

"I guess that is sad but true, young man. But my son and I, among others, would like to see that change. Someday all people will be treated the same if we just keep working on it."

"Gonna take a long, long time."

"You're probably right, but for now I am more concerned with your safety. Where do you live?" Jim asked.

"In an empty hog shed on the edge of town when the weather ain't fit. When it's dry I most times sleep in the woods."

"What about family?"

"Ain't no one left now that my daddy got killed. He was hung for stealin' a chicken cause he couldn't find work and he was hungry. I ain't too sure he did steal that chicken, but it don't matter now. Sayin' he stole it is as good a reason as any to hang a nigger I reckon."

"So then you are all alone?" John asked.

"Just me and an old hound I shares the hog shed with. We ain't kin though. We just share the hog shed."

"I have a plan to smuggle you into our hotel room," said Jim. "We are on the second floor in the back, and our window provides a wonderful view of another building. There are no windows in that end of it, and an alley runs in between. We can hoist you up to our room without being seen."

"Do you have a rope?" asked the young black man.

"No, but we'll tie the bed sheets together if necessary. Let's get out of here now and get to the hotel."

"I feel mighty scared about trustin' you, mister."

"I don't blame you," said Jim. "But you have to. If we meant to do you harm we would have given you up to the men who were chasing you."

"I reckon you would have. All right, what do you want me to do?"

"Make sure the street is quiet, then get to the alley behind the hotel and wait. We'll open our window and drop the line. Grab a hold of it and hold on tight. Give us a few minutes' head start, and be careful."

"Yes suh."

Jim and John walked out toward the street, stopped before walking into the light of the streetlamp, and checked the scene. Everything appeared to be quiet; only a few people could be seen, and they were not close enough to pose a threat. Quickly but calmly they made their way to the hotel, and in a matter of minutes John closed the door to the room behind them.

After removing the bed sheets and tying them together, Jim opened the window and lowered the makeshift rope to the ground. There was very little light in the alley, but it was enough for him to see their new acquaintance when he walked around the corner of the building and grabbed hold of it. The young man didn't weigh much, and in no time Jim was pulling him through the window.

For the first time, Jim and John got a good look at the young fugitive, and he in turn cast a curious eye over his benefactors. Not much more than a boy, the thin fellow had the look of someone who was not afforded the luxury of regular meals. His clothing was ragged and foul smelling; his expression was one of trepidation.

"Now that we can relax a bit, what is your name?" Jim asked.

"Name's Regis Poe."

"I'm happy to meet you, Regis. You can call me Jim, and this is my son, John."

"Hello, Regis," said John. "It certainly has not been a good night in Charleston has it?"

"Worse than most, but it don't pass for surprisin'."

"How do you mean?"

"I mean if you is black you can always expect trouble. Seems like black *is* trouble. Been that way long as I can recollect. Reckon it always will be."

"Why were those men chasing you, Regis?" Jim asked.

"One of them I don't even know. Other one saw me takin' scraps outta his garbage barrel a couple times so now he says I be a thief like my daddy. Says I oughtta be hung, and one day he's gonna do it. It don't add up to sense. He just hates me cause I be a nigger. That's all it is."

"I told you, Regis—"

"Yes suh, I knows. I am a human being. That's what you say. It don't change nothin' round here. I have to watch out for that man all the time. He will sure 'nuff hang me if he can catch me. I don't much leave the woods or the hog shed after dark. I feels safer in the light. But I was out tonight, and he saw me, and I near didn't get away this time. He'll get me for sho . . . he'll get me."

"Why don't you leave Charleston?" said John.

"Where I'm gonna go? I reckon I can starve or get myself hung some other place same as I can here. Least I got places to hide in Charleston 'less that man catches up with me."

John looked at his father, and it was plain to see that they were sharing the same thought. Jim nodded to his son, and then John said, "Regis, how would you like to go someplace where you don't have to worry about having food or clothing or a place to live? How would you like to go someplace where you'll have friends who will look out for you and you won't have to worry about that man chasing you anymore?"

The young man looked back and forth at the two men who had saved his life and then he said, "I reckon I'd have to see this place 'fore I'd believe it."

"There is such a place," said Jim. "And we can take you there. We own a large plantation in Georgia, and we have many black friends there that are like family to us. They work on the plantation, and we pay them well for their labor. You can have a good life, Regis, and you'll be part of that family. How does that sound?"

"I guess I can't believe it, but it sure gets me to wishin'."

"Wishes can come true," said Jim. "And when we leave tomorrow, you'll be coming with us."

"I reckon I won't sleep much tonight for thinkin' about it."

"Why don't we all try to get some sleep so the morning will come quicker," said John.

Jim and John put the sheets back on the beds and then took an extra blanket and pillow and made Regis as comfortable as they could. The following morning they were all up by seven a.m., anxious to leave Charleston.

"First we have to get some food for everyone," Jim told his son. "Go down to the dining room and get plenty of eggs, bacon, bread, and coffee. Bring some milk too. After breakfast I'll go out and get Regis some decent clothes, then we'll get to the train station. There is a train leaving at ten thirty, and we're going to be on it."

When John got back with the food, they spread the feast out on a small oak table and then helped themselves. Neither Jim nor John ever saw anyone eat as much or enjoy himself as thoroughly as Regis did. Surely the poor soul never had such a meal in his life. John had gotten enough food for four hungry people but when they were finished, everything was gone.

While John and Regis retied the sheets into a rope, Jim went out to get the young man some clothes. He returned with a new shirt, jacket, trousers, a pair of shoes, and a pair of socks—even a straw hat. Then John sneaked him down to the bathroom in the hall and stood guard outside while Regis took a badly needed bath and got dressed. When he was finished John sneaked him back to the room.

"You look wonderful, Regis!" Jim exclaimed when he saw the young man. "I hardly recognize you!"

"I never did feel any better than this my whole life, Mr. Jim." Jim was beside himself, as was John. Regis was so excited; his joy gave them a satisfaction that they had not known for quite some time. They knew that Regis would have such a good future on the plantation, and they could not wait to get him there.

"I don't know how to say thanks well enough for all this, Mr. Jim, Mr. John. It don't seem right this happenin' to me. I didn't believe when you first told it to me, but I is sho believin' it now."

"Well if you are ready, Regis, let's get you out of here and over to the station. When we lower you to the ground, go out to the street and wait by the front of the hotel. We'll need a few minutes to straighten up in here, and then we'll get checked out and meet you outside."

"I'll be waitin', Mr. Jim."

When all was ready, Jim checked the alley. It was very quiet. The whole town seemed surprisingly quiet considering what had happened the night before. Seeing no one in the alley, Regis positioned himself on the windowsill facing inward, took hold of the end of the sheet, and then Jim slowly lowered him to the ground. Jim pulled the rope up, then they gathered their things and went downstairs to the front desk.

About fifteen minutes later, the two men walked out of the hotel; to their astonishment, Regis was nowhere in sight. They looked up and down the street, but that was just a natural reaction because there had been no misunderstanding. Regis should have been in plain sight.

"Where could he be, Father?" said John.

"I don't know, John," answered his father in a worried voice. "I don't know, but you can be sure he didn't change his mind about going with us. Let's check the alley."

They walked to the back of the hotel and looked both ways but saw nothing. Then Jim's eyes fixed on something lying in the middle of the alley about fifty feet away. He set his bags down, let out a groan, and started walking slowly toward the object. John followed at a short distance as if he were hypnotized, moving involuntarily. When Jim reached the little straw hat lying in the alley he bent over and picked it up. There was no mistake; it was the one he'd given to Regis. He continued down the alley, looking everywhere for what he was so afraid he would find.

When he came to a rundown horse stable with its doors ajar on the right side of the alley he suddenly stopped, turned slowly, and let out an audible gasp. There, hanging from a crossbeam by a leather strap, was that poor, abused young man whose life they had so badly wanted to change. In the space of fifteen minutes the chance had been taken away forever. The poor boy was naked, stripped of the new clothes he had been so proud of. How could it have happened? Was it by the hand of the man who had been chasing him the night before? Jim would never know. He barely noticed John standing by his side in tears until John took him by the arm.

"My heart feels like it's in pieces, Father," he said.

"If it is possible to hate a man I've never met, I guess that is how I feel," Jim replied. "Let us do what little we can, son."

Jim turned away and walked back up the alley with John still holding him by the arm. Jim picked up his bags and then the two of them walked out to the street. When they reached Mason's Funeral Parlor, Jim led the way inside. A tall lanky man wearing a well-worn suit and showing a crooked set of teeth came from behind a heavy black curtain.

"Can I help you, gentlemen?" he asked.

John had never seen his father in so much emotional pain before, but mired in his own shock he understood just how his father felt and he understood why the man tried to spit out the bitterness through the spoken word when he replied, "Do you bury *niggers* in this town?"

"Every chance we get," said the miserable bastard.

"How much?"

"Five dollars will cover it."

Jim laid down the money, told him where to find the body, put his hand on John's shoulder, and headed for the door. They ignored the trolley and walked the whole way to the train station. When they finally boarded and settled in their seats, Jim leaned back and wept without shame until he drifted off to sleep. John sat quietly staring out the window; he did not disturb his father until they reached the station in Macon.

THREE

Emma

When Elizabeth and Abbey met their husbands at the train station in Macon, it did not require their women's intuition to know that something was terribly wrong. Not only could they read the moods of the men, but they couldn't help noticing the nasty scrape on John's forehead. But they also knew their men well enough to understand that it was one of those things that would come out when they were ready to talk about it and not before. So they did their best to carry on in a cheerful manner and be content with having Jim and John home again.

That evening they all had dinner together, and afterward, as they relaxed in the parlor, Jim told Elizabeth and Abbey what had happened in Charleston.

"Have you read today's *Atlanta Journal*?" Jim asked Elizabeth.

"No, actually I haven't. It is lying on the kitchen table still folded. Shall I get it for you?"

"No, dear, I'll read it later. It probably carries a story of the riot in Charleston."

"Riot?" said Abbey.

"Yes, and we were witness to a large part of it. We were in a restaurant called Rita's Southern Fare, just about to have dinner with Mr. Hutchinson, when we heard gunshots from across the street. We watched as a mob of sailors from the Charleston Naval Base and some white citizens worked their way down the street destroying black businesses and beating and killing black men. We don't know how many were injured or killed, but the violence went on until early this morning."

"How awful," said Elizabeth.

"Oh dear," said Abbey. "Is that how you got the injury to your forehead, John?"

"Yes, but it wasn't in the riot. It was after a difference of opinion with our Mr. Hutchinson. No need to go into detail. Needless to say, it is the usual payment when you side with the black race."

"Were you hurt as well, Jim?" asked Elizabeth with deep concern in her voice.

"I had a bit of a limp afterward, but I'm all right now."

"It makes me sad, my dear husband."

"It breaks my heart as well. There is a propaganda movement going on in this country; it started a few years ago. The black race is intentionally being maligned and demonized. It started with that film, *The Birth of a Nation*, back in 1915, which portrayed the black man as being unintelligent and unable to curb his sexual lust for white women. It also portrayed the Klan as a heroic force. I have heard that it was very instrumental in bringing about the inception of the second era Klan at Stone Mountain, Georgia the same year. This is being done to reinforce the Jim Crow laws. Everywhere you look, especially in the larger towns and cities like Charleston, you see those Negro caricatures; anything the white racist can do to make the black man look stupid, lazy, untrustworthy, and just plain subhuman."

At that point, John proceeded to tell the women the story of Regis Poe. When he finished, all four of them were in tears.

"I have to believe that the murderer or murderers were the two men whom we saw chasing Regis the night before," said Jim "They must have kept a watch on the area because it was the last place they had seen him. Or perhaps I was not careful enough and someone saw him sneaking out of a hotel for whites only. We wanted so much to bring him here, and he wanted so much to come. I will see him in my dreams for the rest of my life."

"It has been a long and difficult day, Jim," said Elizabeth. "I think it is time to rest."

As all were in agreement, the two couples exchanged a pleasant good night, and then John and Abbey walked home.

The following morning, Jim was in his office when he heard someone knocking. Then he heard Elizabeth in the hallway followed by her pleasant greeting when she opened the front door. It was Aunt Ashton and Uncle Jeremy. As they entered the house and then the parlor, Jim took his attention away from his work and went out to greet them.

"Good morning to all," said Jim. "Have you had coffee yet?"

"Plenty, thank you," said Aunt Ashton. "We need to talk to you and Elizabeth."

"Certainly, please make yourselves comfortable."

His aunt and uncle took seats, and then Aunt Ashton immediately came to the point.

"Emma is pregnant," she said. The expression on Jim and Elizabeth's faces clearly revealed their surprise.

"I know," Aunt Ashton continued. "We were more than a little shocked when we found out, for a number of reasons. Apparently it happened about six months ago; she never said a word. The only reason we know now is because she can't hide it any longer. If she could have had her way I don't think she would ever have told us. Another concern is that Emma is close to forty years old."

"She also refuses to tell us who the father is or the *reason* for not telling us his name," said Uncle Jeremy. "You know that she has always been, well, different. She is intelligent, she has no disabilities, but she marches to her own tune. Quite honestly, I have to say that I never even knew she noticed men let alone had any interest in them. Ashton and I always hoped that she *would* find someone someday. We don't want her to end up alone. We want to find a way to be happy for her, but we can't, not like this."

"I can certainly understand how you feel," said Jim. "Why do you suppose she won't tell you who the father is?"

"I don't know," said Aunt Ashton, "But I *can* tell you that she is afraid of something. She was almost hysterical when I pressed her for details. You also realize that, at her age, she doesn't have to oblige us at all. She is a grown woman, and we have no right or authority to demand to know anything."

"Yes, I understand," Jim replied.

"Would you mind if I spoke to her?" asked Elizabeth.

"Oh, Elizabeth, I would be most grateful if you would. You know that Emma likes you very much. Maybe she would be more comfortable talking to you. It is certainly worth a try."

"Then I will come up this afternoon."

"We appreciate it, Elizabeth," said Uncle Jeremy. "Ashton and I will make ourselves scarce so it will be just the two of you. We have to make a trip to Macon anyway."

That afternoon around one o'clock, Elizabeth heard Uncle Jeremy's Model T Ford going by the house toward the main road. She fixed a pot of tea and a plate of freshly made cookies then she went up the hill to call on Emma. She had to knock three times before the door was slowly, almost reluctantly opened by Jim's timid cousin.

"Hello, Emma," said Elizabeth. "I hope I'm not disturbing you. I brought tea and cookies. I thought we could visit awhile."

"I suppose that would be all right," Emma replied. She stepped back so that her guest could enter and then led the way to a sitting room just off the kitchen. She offered Elizabeth a chair and then went into the kitchen for cups and saucers. When she returned, they helped themselves to the tea and cookies then began to talk. Elizabeth noticed that Emma seemed a bit uneasy, and she was unsure about how to broach the touchy subject. Fortunately, Emma helped her out by doing it for her.

"I think I can guess why you're here," she said. "Mother and Father told you that I am pregnant didn't they?"

"Yes, Emma, they did. You know that they love you very much, and they are ever so concerned about you, as we all are."

"All?"

"Yes, your parents, Jim, and I. No one else knows."

"I guess I am grateful for that although I don't know why. Something like this is too big to keep a secret forever."

"Why would you want to do that, Emma?"

"I have my reasons, and they are very good reasons. I just feel that this is something that I have to work out for myself; I don't know how, but I have to. I love my parents, Elizabeth, and I am extremely fond of you, Jim, John, and Abbey. But if you knew why I feel I must keep silent, I am sure you would understand."

"I have no doubt of that, Emma, but the one thing that you are overlooking is the trust that we have in this family.

By confiding in us, you will be doing no harm to yourself or the man whom you are protecting. If there is no way to solve your problem without causing hurt to you or him then it will go no further."

"I suppose I never thought of it that way. I must admit, it would be a great relief to unburden myself a little. But what will everyone think of me, and will they understand? I am not ashamed of the baby I am carrying, and I care very much for its father, but this is not the way that these things are normally or acceptably done."

"I promise you, Emma, you will have our support."

Elizabeth was very pleased with the way the conversation was going. Emma seemed to relax a little; she was beginning to take to heart the assurance of the love and trust the family was extending to her.

But then she grew quiet, almost sullen. She set her cup down, got to her feet, and started pacing the floor. Then she said, "Elizabeth, I know that everyone thinks of me as a bit odd. It's not that I've heard things, but that I can see that other people are different from me as they can see that I am different from them. The problem is that the group I am in is much smaller. It seems that the world is partial to uniformity, and if you don't fit in then you are odd. I don't think that too many people ever understood my simple nature, and that perhaps it takes less to please me than it does others."

Elizabeth was very moved by Emma's words. She had never heard Emma express herself in such a revealing way before. And she couldn't deny that there was a lot of truth to what she said. As much as Emma's own parents loved her, even *they* had used the word different when referring to their daughter; and in those terms, different could very easily be translated to odd.

"I understand, Emma," said Elizabeth. "And I have to tell you that I now have a much deeper appreciation for your right to think and feel the way that makes life comfortable for you. I have never heard you express yourself in such an intimate way before, and it makes me very happy that you shared it with me."

Emma smiled. "I feel a very close bond with you as well. It is a lot like the way that sisters feel about each other. Sometimes it really hurts that Madeline lives so far away. But I must tell you that if my secret is unearthed, what people will think of me, and I mean people outside of the family, may complicate matters."

"I believe that all of us must trust you too, Emma. We must trust you to make the right decision concerning this situation. Aside from that, all we can do is to let you know that we are here for you in any way that you might need us."

"I thank you for that, Elizabeth, and I appreciate your coming to see me. I feel much better, and I know now that I must make my decision considering both sides of how I might handle this instead of barring the door against what might prove to be a better way. Please allow me a little time to think things over again. I wouldn't mind if you tell Mother and Father about our talk; I know they are worried about me. Somehow I couldn't bring myself to open up to them. I guess they will forgive me."

"I think you can be sure of that."

Elizabeth got up to leave. The two women hugged each other like sisters, and then they parted.

When Elizabeth returned home, Jim was anxiously waiting. She told him about her promising conversation with Emma, which inspired him to take his wife in his arms and tell her once again how much he loved her. Arriving home from Macon, Aunt Ashton and Uncle Jeremy stopped by to see how Elizabeth's visit with Emma had gone. They too were very pleased and very grateful to hear the good news.

"I was only too happy to help," Elizabeth told them. "She needs a little time to collect herself I think, but I believe that she will let us help her."

"I hope and pray that she does," said Aunt Ashton. "I want to get home and see her, but I won't bring up the subject unless she does. We will give her time to come to us now."

The following morning, Jim and Elizabeth prepared to make their usual Friday shopping trip to Macon for dry goods and a visit to the local market. While Elizabeth wrote out her list, Jim went out to the barn to bring the automobile to the driveway in front of the house.

The country was still in transition from the horse and wagon to the mechanized mode of travel—a changeover that would take quite awhile to complete. It was still a time when affordability was the deciding factor between horses or autos, not to mention the percentage of folks who did not trust the newfangled world and chose to rely on what *they* considered reliable. But rural people such as himself still had horses in spite of the usefulness of the automobile.

Jim remembered suggesting that his father should purchase an automobile but the man had simply said, "They are nice, but they are noisy." But Jim realized that the time had come for certain changes to be made, especially with a plantation to run. Machines, to an extent, had also become part of the way the work was done. Six months earlier, several Price Campbell cotton pickers had been purchased, which saved a great deal of time compared to picking cotton by hand.

When Elizabeth was ready they headed down the road, bouncing along on a surface not perfectly suited to the horseless carriage. With an internal combustion engine that delivered 12.7 horsepower to the rear wheels, a top speed of 45 miles per hour could be reached. But considering the condition of most roads, a cruising speed of 30 miles per hour was recommended.

As they were driving down a long straight stretch in the road, Jim's attention reached out to a crossroad about a quarter mile away. On the road to the right, a horse and rider waited just off the main road. Jim kept expecting the rider to move on, but he stood his ground as if he wanted to see who was in the oncoming automobile. When they were no more than twenty-five yards from the intersection, the man on the horse suddenly moved his animal out into the middle of the road causing Jim to brake hard to avoid a collision.

After quickly making sure that Elizabeth was all right, he set the automobile's parking brake and hastily got out. As he began voicing his disapproval, Jim recognized the man was none other than Jared Sykes, the only son of Bernard Sykes—the man who owned the plantation next to his. Bernard was an old man now and had been a neighbor to Langdon Plantation for as long as Jim could remember. But he was a neighbor who was never neighborly, at least not to Jim's father or his family. Like most everyone else in Bibb County, he hated the Langdons because of their kindness and compassion toward the slaves, and later, the former slaves.

The Sykes family had a history of affiliation with the Klan, and the border lines between the two plantations had always been strictly observed. As Jim approached Jared he could plainly see by the look on his face that this would be a typical encounter.

"I won't even ask what your reason is for pulling such a stupid stunt, Jared, but if my wife had been injured because of it you would not still be sitting upright in that saddle."

"Well now, that raises a question with only one way to get an answer doesn't it?"

"Considering what could have happened, I am ready to oblige if that's what you want," Jim replied.

"As tempting as that is, I guess it will have to wait," said Jared. "I have something else on my mind right now. I've been waiting for months for a chance meeting like this."

"Then say what's on your mind, and be damn quick about it."

"The law is what's on my mind, mister."

"What in the hell are you talking about?" Jim shouted.

"I'm talking about nigger law! I'm talking about Jim Crow! I don't give a damn about that dirty black sanctuary you live on, and neither does most of the people around here. Those tar-colored friends of yours are subject to the law no matter where they live."

"Are you making an accusation against one of my friends?" Jim asked. "If you are, I'd like to know what it is."

"Maybe not one of your friends; maybe one of your cousin Emma's friends."

Jim was confused. He didn't know what Jared was raving about, and he certainly didn't know what it had to do with Emma.

"You can play innocent with me if you want to," Jared continued. "But I saw it with my own eyes. That damn

32

nigger, Willis Tyson, was over at the fence line up on the hill, and he was talking to your cousin, Emma. I saw him doing it, and I could lynch that son of a bitch just for that."

Jared's charge took Jim completely by surprise. He knew that Willis Tyson worked on the Sykes plantation, but he didn't know that Willis had ever spoken to Emma. Jim was definitely at a disadvantage in this conversation, and he had no idea how to respond. So he decided to see what else he could find out.

"When did you see the two of them talking?" he asked.

"It was last spring," Jared answered. "I was looking for Willis, and when I couldn't find him in his shack I saddled up and started covering the plantation, and I found him talking over the fence to your cousin. If that bastard wasn't such a hard worker I swear I'd have strung him up to the nearest tree. Instead I rode over to the fence and I took my rope and put it around his neck. Then I told the both of them if I ever caught them together again, the buzzards would be picking at that nigger's eyes. Emma took off running, screaming her head off the whole way down the hill. I worked that nigger over with a willow branch and he lit out for his shack."

Thoughts were swimming through Jim's head; thoughts about his cousin, her pregnancy, and why she was so terrified. But he wasn't about to do or say anything other than to convince Jared that everything he had said was news to him.

"I didn't know anything about this, Jared, but as far as I'm concerned, it's none of my business, and it's certainly none of yours."

"That's about what I expected from you. You people don't object to anything those black animals do. But you're wrong about one thing: it is my business because it's against the law for one of those bucks to even make eye contact with a white woman, and you know it. So you'd better warn your cousin, and she'd better have more sense than Tyson because it doesn't matter who starts the interaction between them. If she doesn't want to get him hung she better keep her distance."

"You've spread your misguided gospel enough for one day, Jared, so why don't you go now and find someone else to irritate. Oh and, Jared, the next time you get in my way like you did a little while ago, we're going to find the answer to that question."

Jared said no more except for the profanity he muttered under his breath, and then he turned his horse around and spurred the animal down the road. Jim went back to the automobile and got behind the wheel. One look at Elizabeth told him that she had heard most of the conversation he'd had with Jared. All she said was, "I wonder."

"I wonder too," he replied.

FOUR

Emma's Story

Initially, neither Jim nor Elizabeth mentioned the meeting with Jared Sykes to anyone. They were hoping that Emma would soon come forward and bring everything out in the open. It did not seem prudent to worry Aunt Ashton and Uncle Jeremy any further in the meantime. But after two weeks had gone by, Jim and Elizabeth took to worrying themselves.

Then one afternoon, Jim was in the barn tending to his favorite saddle horse when he heard someone come up behind him. When he turned around, much to his surprise, he saw Willis Tyson standing there with his hat in his hand.

"Mr. Langdon? I'm not sure you know me, sir, but my name is Willis Tyson."

"I *do* know you, Willis. That is to say that I know who you are even though we've never met." Jim held out his hand, Willis tentatively shook it. Jim Crow allowed such a gesture as long as the white man initiated it. It was unlawful for a black man to extend his hand first. It was obvious that Willis knew the rules, which made it even more surprising that he would risk his life by having a conversation with Emma. Jim's curiosity was mounting even higher. He could also see that Willis was very nervous, so he tried to ease the tension.

"Jim Crow has no place on this plantation, Willis. In truth, it has no place anywhere except in the minds of ignorant people."

"Thank you, sir. I have heard as much from many black folks around here, but it isn't easy to forget my place just because I walked onto your property. I couldn't let it cause me to be careless when I walk off again."

"I understand," said Jim. "You express yourself very well, Willis. Have you had some education?"

"Yes, sir, I have had some. I can read pretty well, and I can work a little with numbers. I was not born a slave, and

35

I thank God for that. But my parents were slaves, and they were not able to teach me very much. I was able to get my hands on some old school books, and I worked at teaching myself. I heard that President Abraham Lincoln did much the same thing."

"He certainly did. You are more than welcome here, Willis, but I have to tell you that it could get you into a lot of trouble if Jared Sykes finds it out."

"Yes, sir, I know that. But he went to Atlanta this morning, and he won't be back until tomorrow sometime. That's why I came down."

"In that case, what can I do for you?"

"Well, sir, I'm worried about Miss Emma. I don't want to say much more than that, and if you have talked to Jared then I guess you know some of the story anyway."

"Yes, I did talk to him. He stopped me on the road a couple weeks ago, and he told me that he saw you up at the fence line with Emma. He also told me what he did that day, and that was about it. I told him that it was none of my business and none of his."

"I could say that there is more, Mr. Langdon, but I won't explain. I respect Miss Emma, and if she wants to tell her family anything I must wait for her to do it. I'm just worried about her because I never got a chance to talk to her since the day that Jared saw us at the fence line. She was very upset, and I wanted to tell her that I am sorry. But I know that I can't see her again because it might bring more hurt to her."

"I don't think that you are the one who should be apologizing, Willis. I don't think that you did anything wrong. And I *know* that seeing her again could do *you* harm."

"Thank you, sir. Would you please tell her that I hope that she will be all right?"

Jim thought for a long moment before answering because he was not sure that what had suddenly entered his mind should actually come out through his mouth. Then, after a quick but meaningful prayer he said, "I have a better idea, Willis, and there is no more opportune time than now. Come with me."

He took Willis over to the house, introduced him to Elizabeth, and told her to keep him company for a little bit.

He walked out the back door and headed up the hill to Aunt Ashton's house. A short time later Jim returned with Aunt Ashton, Uncle Jeremy, and Emma. He took them into the parlor, having told them nothing and thinking to himself how terrible he was going to feel if his plan ended in disaster.

When Emma saw Willis, she stopped and emitted a quiet gasp; Willis immediately stood up. Aunt Ashton and Uncle Jeremy felt the intensity of the moment; they stood quietly and waited. After what seemed like eternity, Emma said, "Willis, I can't believe you're really here. I am happy and frightened at the same time."

"I am sorry if you are not comfortable, Miss Emma. I did not mean for that to happen. I just wanted to know if you were all right."

"You needn't be sorry, Willis. For the first time, I think maybe I *will* be all right. There is so much that has to be explained, and I suddenly feel that I am ready to do that. Please, everyone, sit down."

Without a word, seats were taken. Emma stood in the middle of the room dressed in a loose fitting frock, and she started talking. She was steady and sincere, and yet her voice made her sound as if she were in a trance, speaking pure truth from deep inside her heart, truth without guilt or shame.

"I have learned through my steadfast belief in God that we all have the same basic purpose in this life. I believe that we are all here to love God, to be loved by God, and to follow a pursuit which allows us to express love in our own way. I was born a humble creature; someone who finds adoration in the simplest things in creation. My heart is content with a deep blue sky, a spring flower, or a book filled with poetic lines. To others I seemed different; perhaps odd. But I did not want for anything more than what I had.

"Long ago I found a place up on the hill beneath a huge black walnut tree. It was a place of peace, a place of contentment. I found love beneath that tree; a kind of love that I could understand; the kind that was infinite. I was alone, but I could feel a presence; it was the presence of God.

37

"Then one day my refuge was compromised. My calm was shattered by something that I couldn't understand. My tree stands near the fence that separates our land from the next plantation. I was there one beautiful day early in March; I read from one of my books. Suddenly I was startled by a sound just beyond the fence. I looked up to see a man named Jared; he was watching me. He asked me to come to the fence; he said he wanted to talk to me. I hesitated, but then I did as he asked because it was a request from one of God's creations.

"But as I stood before him he reached out and touched my arm. I didn't feel comfortable with it. I backed away but then he apologized so I moved toward him again. This time he touched my breast, and I knew that his way was not what God intended. When I went back to the tree and refused to return, Jared spoke to me in a very harsh way. He called me ugly names and he continued until I got up and went home. Later he came to the fence line a second time, and following that, a third. After that I didn't go back for weeks.

"I missed that place so much that I finally ventured back near the middle of May. I was sitting with my back to the fence when I heard footsteps. I was afraid to turn around. When I found the courage I looked over my shoulder and saw Willis standing by the fence. I greeted him politely, and he returned the same to me, but even though I saw something quite different in his eyes than I had seen in Jared's, I was troubled that he might ask me to come near. Instead he begged forgiveness for intruding and turned to leave. But for some reason that I could not understand, I wanted him to stay and I told him so. I could see that he was fearful; he knew it wasn't allowed.

"I was drawn to him not knowing why, but at some point I realized that the two of us had been talking by the fence for hours. When he told me he had to be going I asked him to come back again and made him promise to do so. Soon we were meeting every day, and I began to feel that something very different and very special was happening to me. I didn't know it then, but it was love—only it was not the same as I felt for the flowers and the poetry and my solace beneath the huge tree.

"What happened next, is to me, a wonder that will transcend all the joys I have ever known in my life. Almost spiritually rather than physically, Willis and I, under the huge black walnut tree, related to one another in a way such as could not be expressed in any language on earth. It was kind, it was gentle, and it was the summation of all that God created, which is good. It was not, in fact, until that night before I fell asleep that I was struck by the realization that we had made love.

"It was the next day that Jared came by and saw Willis talking to me. He flew into a terrible rage, and he swore he would kill Willis if he ever caught him talking to me again. I was devastated by Jared's brutality, and I ran away. I promised myself I would never say a word about what had happened to anyone, and I knew I could never see Willis again. That was until I realized that I . . ."

Then Emma walked over and stood in front of Willis. She grabbed the material of her loose frock on each side and pulled it tight so that her swollen belly was obvious to him. He stood up, put his hands on her shoulders and said, "Oh, Emma, I had no idea. This fills me with such happiness and at the same time scares me so when I think of what could happen to you and to this child because of it."

"I have the same fear, Willis," she replied. "Except that I fear for you and not for myself." Then she looked at her family and said, "Now you can understand the reason for my silence. And in spite of my reason, I realize now that I have been a fool. I regret nothing that has happened, but I never meant to hurt anyone. I understand now that even if I do whatever it takes to protect Willis, when this child is born, it will be scorned, and I will be branded. There will be no place we can live in peace; not even here."

Ashton and Jeremy left their seats, went to their daughter, and took her by the hand.

"In our eyes, you did nothing wrong," said Jeremy.

"Your father is right, Emma," Ashton added. "We love you, and we always will. We will find an answer to the problems; all of us together will find an answer."

"I will be part of this, Mrs. Todd," said Willis. "Even if it should mean my life, I will not turn my back on Emma or my child."

"I never contemplated otherwise, Willis," Ashton assured him. "If it is your desire to marry our daughter you will be welcomed into our family. Emma needs you, which means that we all need you."

"I am very grateful for your words, Mrs. Todd. I am grateful to all of you. Meaning no offense, I cannot tell you how difficult it is to believe that there are white people who feel as all of you do, especially in the South."

"No offense taken, Willis," said Jeremy. "How would it be possible for you to feel any differently? Now, I think we should all sit down and discuss what we must."

Everyone took their seats; Jeremy was the first to offer a suggestion.

"As much as it tears at me to say it, Emma was quite right when she said that there would be no peace living here or anywhere in the South. My thoughts tell me that Willis should take her to California. There is family in California; Madeline and Andrew."

"I can see the reason in your thinking, Jeremy," said Ashton. "But California is not without Jim Crow segregation; even the Klan has a following there. California is not only prejudiced against blacks, but Asians as well. We know this from Madeline's letters. There *are* many black people in California, especially in Los Angeles, but I fear that a black and white couple with a child would not be accepted there any more than they would be here."

"I guess you're right," Jeremy conceded.

"I would like to offer a suggestion, if I may," said Jim. "I remember many stories my father used to tell me about the time when he was helping slaves to escape the plantation to freedom. His first thought was to get them out of the South; to take them north of the Mason Dixon Line. But he quickly found out that as long as they were in this country there was no assurance that they would remain free. He learned that slave catchers were operating as far north as Boston. Without any rights whatsoever, even a black man whose master may have chosen to free him still had no real defense against being returned to slavery. That was when he knew that he would have to get them out of the United States and into Canada."

"So then, Canada is the perfect solution, Jim?" asked Uncle Jeremy.

"I believe that it is, yes. I believe that Willis and Emma could live there, raise a family, and be happy."

Everyone was silent for a time. As much as they wanted this mixed race couple to live long and prosper, equal to swallowing castor oil was the understanding that they would, in effect, have to live in exile in order to do so. It was true that Emma's own sister lived far away in California, but she did it by choice and not because of fear of repercussions for her life's decisions.

"I think," said Aunt Ashton, "that the facts are pretty simple and very clear. And as much as my daughter means to me, I know that she must live her own life. I realize that this is her decision and Willis' decision to make, and I will support them no matter what they do. So I ask you, Emma, and you, Willis, what are your wishes?"

The couple looked at each other, and with not a word, but simply with a simultaneous nod, they made their declaration. Then to the family, Emma said, "We have made a commitment, entering into it with full knowledge of the responsibilities and consequences," said Emma. "We will live our lives in Canada if that is what it takes, and no two people on earth ever benefited so much from the support and caring of their family."

"Then it is settled," said Uncle Jeremy. "It will take some time and planning, but when all is ready, your mother and I will travel to Canada with you and Willis, see that you get settled, and stay for a while; at least long enough to see our grandchild born."

"If I may, please," said Willis. "There is one more thing we wish to do, and the sooner the better. Emma and I would like to be married very quietly here with all of you so that you may bear witness to our dedication and love for each other."

A lively cheer resounded through the parlor as a fitting end, driving away the melancholy spirit that had so recently pervaded the Langdon family. If they could not destroy prejudice, they would at least do whatever necessary to keep it from restraining their liberties or forbidding them to live as they saw fit.

With a great deal of caution, the family kept their guarded secret from the outside world, except for a Macon preacher who reluctantly performed the service in exchange for a hefty donation from Jeremy and Ashton. A month after Emma told her amazing story, she was married to the love of her life and on her way to Canada with her husband and her parents.

A week later, Jim and Elizabeth were sitting in the parlor, late on a Sunday afternoon, when they heard the sound of automobiles coming up the driveway. They got up and went outside to the veranda. There were two autos: one held four men, two of whom Jim recognized; the other was driven by the sheriff of Macon, and seated beside him was Jim's old nemesis, Jared Sykes. All of the men disembarked; Jared and the sheriff walked up to the bottom step of the veranda while the other four stood behind them in support. In Jared's right hand he carried his calling card: a coil of rope.

"Good afternoon, Sheriff," said Jim. "What brings you out this way?"

Before he could answer, Jared held the rope up in a menacing manner and said, "Where is he, Langdon? Where is Willis Tyson?"

This time, before *Jim* could answer, the sheriff spoke his peace.

"I know you, Jim, and I know the color of your politics and it spites me to say that it is mostly black, if you get my meaning. But you can't circumvent the law this time. Jared here has accused Tyson of breaking the law by directly consorting with a white woman—your cousin, Emma."

"That happened months ago, Sheriff."

"That doesn't mean a thing," shouted Jared. "I saw it happen, and I can bring a charge any time I want."

"He's right, Jim," said the sheriff. "Now tell me if you know where he is."

With an overwhelming sense of genuine pleasure Jim replied, "By now, Canada." The lynch mob stood dumbfounded; Jared looked as though he might explode.

"I'm not sure I believe you," said the sheriff.

"I don't really care if you believe me or not," Jim replied. "And there is something else I don't care if you believe or not. Willis and Emma were married in this very house over a week ago, and immediately afterward, they left for Canada with Emma's parents."

Jared was incensed. He turned away, walked over to the sheriff's auto, and pounded his fist down on the hood leaving a serious dent.

"That's my auto, Jared!" the sheriff shouted.

"Damn your auto, Sheriff!" the outraged man shouted back. "Did you hear what he said?"

"I heard him, but it doesn't help matters to put a dent in my auto."

"You're right about that, Sheriff," said Jim. "Unless you're willing to invade Canada, there is nothing that will help you punish an innocent man. This is a free country, and that goes for everyone no matter what color they are, whether you and your kind agree with it or not. But since you don't, my cousin and her husband had no choice but to go where they will be out of your reach forever. Canada is where they've gone, and Canada is where they will raise their soon-to-be-born child."

"Child!" Jared screamed. Then he walked over to the sheriff's auto again and raised his fist into the air. But before he could bring it down, the sheriff hurried over, grabbed his arm, and said, "If you pound my auto again I'm going to arrest you for damaging city property."

Jared walked back to the bottom of the steps and began to unleash a barrage of profanity, racial slurs, and personal insults. Jim had already had enough of the intrusion from the unwanted visitors, and when Jared opened his foul mouth in front of his wife, he could take no more. He marched himself down the steps and stood in front of the miscreant.

"My cousin married a good man and a better man than you will ever be. Emma told us about your crude, unwanted advances, and now you have no choice except to stack your jealously on top of your crimes against humanity. But at this moment, if you open your vulgar mouth again in front of my wife, I'll put a dent in your head to match the one you put in the sheriff's auto." Then Jim looked at the sheriff and said, "Take this trash and get off my property. You have no business here."

The sheriff walked over to Jared, took him by the arm, and led him to the automobile. A minute later, both vehicles were rolling down the driveway. Jim rejoined Elizabeth on the veranda, and then they went back inside.

"You know," said Jim. "If this entire situation with Emma was written up in a diary and that diary was found by someone a hundred or so years from now, I believe that the reader would say, 'It is unbelievable what the black race had to contend with in the Jim Crow South.'"

FIVE

The Crusaders

One morning in mid-June 1922, Jim was reading the local paper when John came in to go over his report on the planting season. In Georgia, the season runs from February to June; upland cotton is the variety that is planted.

"Good morning, John," Jim called to his son. "I'm glad you're here."

"Hello, Father. I knew you would be anxious for this report so I came over as soon as I was finished. The planting should be complete by the end of the week."

"That's fine, son, and I did want to hear your report, but actually there is something else of greater importance on my mind."

"I see, well, let me pull up a chair and you can tell me about it."

Having heard John arrive, Elizabeth brought a fresh pot of coffee to Jim's office, and then she left, closing the door behind her so the men could concentrate on their work.

"Of course you know, John, about your grandfather's involvement in the Georgia General Assembly; his idea was to introduce a bill for equal rights and then push it through the political process."

"I know that he worked very hard in that endeavor. In spite of the bill failing to pass, I believe that Grandfather *did* crack the surface of racism. I believe that he created some awareness and perhaps changed a few people's way of thinking."

"I think you are exactly right, John. However, I also realize now that my dear father's heart may have been a bit larger than his vision. I was right there with him, and at the time, I too was completely caught up in the idea of an equal rights bill, a move that might grant the black race the constitutional rights and protection that they so clearly deserve. But I think that in our zeal, we overlooked the fact that political change is a dreadfully slow process and that moving people in the right direction is tantamount to moving a mountain."

"What is your point, Father?"

"Well, as you know, in 1863, President Lincoln initiated the Emancipation Proclamation in order to take the first step, a huge step, which was to secure freedom for these oppressed people. It was a move that was predicated on the victorious outcome of the war. Having accomplished this, it should have been obvious that it would be quite some time before another significant success could be realized."

"I think I understand, Father. You are saying that we should concentrate our efforts on removing one brick at a time as opposed to trying to tear down the entire wall."

"Precisely. Now, in your opinion, what is happening in this country that we should most be focusing our attention on?"

Without a moment's hesitation John replied, "The unlawful killing of innocent people."

"You read my mind, son. The unlawful killing of innocent people; the lynchings. This outrageous injustice must stop. The people of this country have got to see that the innocent suffer along with the guilty by the effects of mob violence. These mobs have assaulted prisons and courtrooms to apprehend and murder incarcerated persons who have already been sentenced. The authorities offer little or no resistance to these perpetrators; they are completely unrestrained. The members of such mobs are seldom arrested and put on trial in spite of the fact that they go to no trouble to hide their identity and operate without benefit of the cloak of darkness. Very few of these murderers have ever been punished. The loyal residents of this country must endure the disgrace of the nation brought about by these horrible acts of violence. The disrespect of our courts and lawful procedures must be halted, and the people, especially women and children, must not be traumatized by the public spectacle of the burning of human beings."

"What you're saying does make a very good argument, Father. And if this violence goes unchecked because of the racist point of view—that blacks are subhuman and warrant no protection—then I would like to point out that it is not only black people who are being lynched. I read somewhere that three thousand four hundred and sixty-five people have been lynched between 1889 and the present. While it is true that eighty-eight percent of those people were black, the white percentage also has the potential to grow. The point is: if you allow violence to get out of hand, there is no limit to how far it will spread."

"That is perfectly true, John. This terrible problem should be the concern of every man and woman in this country. It seems that at this time, a very strong platform exists from which to present this argument."

"So what do you propose, Father?"

"At the present time, there is an anti-lynching bill making its way through channels, and I would like for us to jump on the bandwagon. Four years ago, Leonidas C. Dyer, a congressman from St. Louis, first introduced to the US House of Representatives the Dyer Anti-Lynching Bill. The purpose of the bill is to bring punitive action against state and county authorities who do not preclude lynching. It is Dyer's hope that the bill might also bring about the end of the practice entirely. This bill is sponsored by the NAACP. Last year, at a speaking engagement in Birmingham, Alabama, President Harding announced *his* support for the bill. I also read that the bill was quickly passed by a large majority in the House of Representatives."

"How can we most effectively help this cause, Father?"

"Fundraising," Jim replied. "We must devise a way to raise money to support the bill. I got the idea from this morning's paper. There is a story here about Mary Talbert, who is the president of the National Association of Colored Women. She has just founded an organization of women who call themselves the Anti-Lynching Crusaders, whose mission it is to eradicate lynching and to support Congressman Dyer's bill. Their slogan is, 'A Million Women United to Stop Lynching.' Their hope is that they can find one million women who will donate at least one dollar to support the campaign. This money will go to the NAACP. I propose that we help them add to their coffers."

"That's an excellent idea, Father. Is there anything else we can do?"

"There most certainly is. Ms. Talbert's formula is a mixture of publicity, political promotion of the bill, fundraising, and prayer. I don't know about political promotion but we can raise money, and we can definitely pray. We can also get your mother and Abbey to help with that."

"I know that Mother and Abbey will do anything they can to help," said John. "We can also count on William and Julia. How do we get started?"

"We will embark on a campaign of our own. First we need a slogan; something to make our cause recognizable wherever we go."

"Yes," said John, "And I think I have an idea. I am inspired by something you said earlier. All the patriotic Americans have to endure the disgrace cast over the nation by the rampant violence of the lynch mobs. I think our slogan should be, 'Take Pride in America: Stop the Violence.'"

Jim turned the idea over in his mind for a moment and then said, "I like it, John, in fact, I think it says it all. We will have a banner made for the slogan and placards to put outside of the places where we are holding our rallies to help draw a crowd. Notices will be put in the papers with dates and times in the cities we plan to visit."

"Good, Father, and with the planting nearly complete, we can recruit some of our black friends to go with us. We can have them pass through the crowd and collect donations while you and I take turns speaking. I considered suggesting that we afford our black friends an opportunity to speak but I am afraid that it might jeopardize our mission, not to mention their safety. We must not be too obvious. We will let it be known that we are acting in support of the Dyer Anti-Lynching Bill."

"I applaud your wisdom, son."

"Thank you, Father."

"I think we are just about set, John. I believe we can be very successful; I don't see any obvious problems because, as I said, this should concern everyone. When I worked with your grandfather, campaigning for equal rights, we battled the bigots all along the way, but ending violence should appeal to the majority and not the minority comprised of the lawless who perpetrate these violent acts. The money we collect will be turned over to the Anti-Lynching Crusaders—a fact that never need be revealed lest our efforts become misconstrued. We want to end the violence for the sake of all people but if we're pegged as supporters of only the black race, unfortunately we will not be as well received."

"I will ask for volunteers this week; I should think two or three will be enough," said John.

"And I will set to work on the banner, the placards, and anything else we'll need. Then I will work out a schedule, make arrangements in the targeted cities for a place to hold our rallies, and contact the newspapers. Explain everything to Abbey, and I will have a talk with your mother. We may be gone for at least a month or two, so prepare accordingly."

"I will do that, Father. I should be getting to the field office now. I will keep in touch with you about our plans. If you need me to help with anything else, just let me know."

"I will do that, son. Good day to you."

By the end of the week, Jim was able to report the completion of the banner and the placards they would need to set up at all the rally points. He had also made an itinerary for the trip. They would start out in Atlanta, the closest large city, then they would head north and make ten more stops on the way to their final destination, which was Washington DC. There, the money they collected would be turned over at the headquarters of the NAACP.

Information had been sent to the *Atlanta Journal* and the *Atlanta Constitution* so that word of the rally would precede them. Jim did likewise for all ten cities on the itinerary. Finally, he sent the notice to the *Macon Telegraph*, hoping that a few local people might make the relatively short journey to Atlanta to attend the rally there.

On the twenty-fifth of June, Jim, John, and two men who lived and worked on Langdon Plantation, were packed and ready for what they hoped would be a very worthwhile journey. Out of the many who volunteered to go with the Langdons, John chose Samuel Pratt and Darius Freeman. Both were single black men in their late twenties; both men grew up on Langdon Plantation and were educated there. It was all John could do to convince his fifteen-year-old son, William, that he would be more help at home than on the road.

At nine o'clock a.m., the self-appointed crusaders took the road to Atlanta, and by twelve thirty p.m. they had arrived at the Piedmont Hotel on the corner of Luckie and Peachtree Streets.

"If you will wait here, John, I will go in and get someone to help with our bags; we'll get checked in and then we'll take Samuel and Darius to the McKay Hotel on Auburn Avenue and get rooms for them; the hotel is owned by a black man. I have to speak to a Mr. Miles Nelson and tell him we are here and ask him to show me where we are to set up for this evening's rally."

"Are you sure that Samuel and Darius will be allowed in here to help with the rally, Father?"

"Yes, Atlanta may be segregated, but they have no problem with Negroes in their whites only businesses as long as the Negroes are working. I have already told Mr. Nelson that Samuel and Darius will be helping us."

Jim went into the hotel, located the front desk, and asked where he could find Mr. Nelson. The desk clerk sent a young black bellboy to find him. When the hotel manager appeared, Jim introduced himself, which brought a look of bewilderment to Mr. Nelson's face.

"I'm afraid I am confused," said Mr. Nelson. "I was informed that you had canceled your rally here in Atlanta."

"I must say that I am confused as well," Jim replied. "I made arrangements about a week ago to use one of your parlors for this evening."

"Indeed you did, sir, and your reservation was in place until yesterday. A man came in at about nine o'clock a.m., claiming to be a colleague of yours. He said that your trip had been delayed and I would receive a new time and date for your visit in the near future."

"Did he give you a name?" Jim asked.

"Yes, he said his name was—I believe it was, yes—his name was James Kemp. Do you know him?"

"I do not," said Jim.

"I guess I'm not surprised," said the hotel manager.

"I am sure I don't know anything about this or about the mysterious Mr. Kemp who was here yesterday, Mr. Nelson, but we came here all the way from Macon expecting to begin our rally schedule in this hotel tonight. Is there nothing you can do to help?"

"I'm afraid not, Mr. Langdon. This happens to be a very busy week in Atlanta, and even if it were not terribly busy, I doubt there would be anything I could do on such short notice. You might try one of our local churches as an alternate location. I would think a cause such as yours would be of interest to them."

"You may be right, Mr. Nelson, and I appreciate the suggestion. Which is the closest church in the area?"

"The First Baptist Church is at the southeast corner of Peachtree and Cain Streets. I believe it is the closest."

"Could I use your telephone?" Jim asked.

"Of course, it's the least I can do to make up for your trouble. Please come with me."

Jim went with Mr. Nelson, placed his call, and by a stroke of luck, not only reached the pastor but was granted permission to hold the rally at the church. "Thank you so much," he told the hotel manager. "If anyone comes in tonight looking for the rally, would you please direct them to the church?"

"I will instruct my staff to do so."

Jim went back out to the auto with a bellboy in tow and apologized for keeping everyone waiting. He explained what had happened and then said to John, "I hate to say it, but I have a bad feeling about this. I have no idea who might have done this, but I'll bet his name isn't James Kemp."

"Do you think it was someone from Bibb County who knows us?" John asked.

"It would certainly make sense. Our family has made many enemies in Georgia over the years, and a stunt like this is definitely not the work of a friend; consequently, thinking it might be someone who knows us does not narrow down the possibilities. But there could be many

other people who do not approve of an anti-lynching bill
and would love to disrupt what we are trying to do."

"So what do we do, Father?"

"We go on with our business and keep our wits about
us. I will get our bags into the hotel with the help of the
bellboy. You take Samuel and Darius to the McKay. The
rally starts at eight o'clock p.m.; the men should be at the
church by six o'clock to get set up."

"Very good, Father. I will be back shortly."

That evening at eight o'clock p.m., Jim and John were
behind the podium in the front of the church, but there
were no more than two dozen people in attendance. With
only a couple of placards outside to catch the interest of
passersby and a few more people sent over from the hotel,
the Langdons were really feeling the sting of the despicable
trick that had been played on them.

At the end of the oratory, Samuel and Darius passed
through the miniscule crowd and collected what they
could. But fifty dollars from their first stop—in a city the
size of Atlanta—was disconcerting at best. All they could do
was get a night's rest and then head northeast toward their
next stop, which was Columbia, South Carolina.

Jim had never believed in premonitions but for some
reason he felt like they were being followed as the Model T
rolled along the road to Columbia. He said as much to
John, Samuel, and Darius, but none of them shared his
feeling. He hoped that three against one was enough to
make his suspicions unfounded.

The next rally, an outdoor venue, was to be held at the
Colonia Hotel at 1614 Hampton Street. The grounds
surrounding the hotel were dotted with southern magnolia,
white oak, sweet gum, and American holly trees. The
centerpiece was a beautiful fountain encircled with flower
gardens adorned with passion flowers, azaleas, hydrangea
bushes, and a soft pink flower called the confederate rose.

Jim and John took a room at the hotel, but Samuel
and Darius were relegated to a boarding house in the
Negro section of the city. At three o'clock p.m., the rally got
under way. In contrast to their lack of success in Atlanta,
the gathering totaled nearly five hundred people, and the

money that was collected averaged a little over five dollars per person. Jim had a satisfactory chuckle to himself when he thought about the hunch he had entertained earlier that day.

That evening the four of them enjoyed a delectable repast at the same establishment, except that they had to sit in color-appropriate sections. It irked Jim and his son so much that they expressed to one another a desire to ignore the law and go sit with Samuel and Darius. But they knew that it would only cause trouble, and having had such a good turnout at the rally it was decided that they should cut their losses.

When morning came, Jim awoke in high spirits. He was anxious to get on the road to Greenville, South Carolina; all the disappointment in Atlanta had vanished. Bags in hand, he met John in the hallway, and then they went down to the front desk to check out. To save time, Samuel and Darius were to walk to the hotel; a breakfast stop would be made before leaving the city.

Jim and John were chattering like jaybirds as they walked outside to a beautiful morning and headed around the hotel to where the automobile was parked. But when they reached the coal black Model T, it was immediately apparent that someone had used a sharp object to puncture and flatten all four tires. Jim was acrimonious, not only because of the damage to the tires and the inconvenience it caused, but worst of all, he was sure he'd been right about being followed.

"I don't know who or why, John," he said, "but someone is deliberately poisoning our well."

"I certainly can't argue, Father. It is clear that those tires were intentionally damaged. I also agree that someone followed us here. They might have learned that we would be in Atlanta from the notice in the *Macon Telegraph*, but our entire trip was not publicized. If the same person who canceled our rally in Atlanta flattened those tires then we are being stalked without a doubt."

"We are certainly going to assume that at this point. We don't know if it is someone acting alone or if he might have help, and we don't know if physical harm should be expected or if the intention is just to make our trip as difficult as possible."

"Well," said John. "So far the culprit or culprits are doing a fine job of that. I wonder what will be next."

"I don't know, but right now I need to find a garage and get a new set of tires."

Jim went into the hotel and telephoned the nearest garage. In a short time a burly man with grease-blackened hands showed up and began jacking up the automobile, setting blocks under the axles, and removing the wheels.

When Samuel and Darius reached the Colonia Hotel, they too were a bit uneasy about the run of bad luck that had befallen them. "I don't want to add to our worries," Samuel told Jim and John, "but walking over here this morning Darius and I think we saw the same automobile pass us two or three times. Maybe it's nothing, maybe the driver was lost or something, but he went past us pretty slowly. Then we remembered that the same thing happened the night we were walking to the church in Atlanta. We are pretty sure it's the same auto because it has a real big crack in the back window like the one in Atlanta did. But we still didn't think a lot of it until we got here and saw what happened to your tires."

"That's right," said Darius. "Adding this to what happened in Atlanta does make a man wonder."

"I understand how you feel," said Jim. "John and I feel the same way. Did either of you get a good look at the man in this auto?"

"Yes, I sure did, but I didn't recognize him," said Darius; Samuel's answer was the same.

"And you're sure he was alone each time?" John asked.

"Yes," said Samuel. "He was alone."

"If this suspicious person is paying close attention to Samuel and Darius, that would give us even more reason to believe that we are being followed," said John.

"Yes," Jim agreed. "If we are being watched then it's certain that all four of us have been seen together. I don't like this at all; he seems to be watching every move we make. As soon as the mechanic returns with the wheels we'll head for Greenville. We'll see how far our pursuer is willing to go."

Much to everyone's surprise, the rally in Greenville turned out to be monetarily successful—and even more surprising, nothing at all went wrong. Charlotte, North Carolina was next on the tour; on the way, no one seemed to want to talk about the absence of their mysterious nemesis. Each man was more inclined to bow to superstition.

The rally in Charlotte began in a promising way; the social hall they rented held about six hundred people, and every seat was taken. But while Jim was speaking to the crowd, a white man dressed in a cheap suit and a dilapidated top hat started to heckle him. Jim tried to ignore the man, but he became louder and louder to the point of being completely disruptive.

"Sir," said Jim. "Is there some problem that can easily be settled so that the other people in this hall can hear me speak?"

"I don't like your preaching against the lynch laws we have here in the South. You must be a damn Yankee."

"Well, I haven't heard that phrase in quite a while, but as it happens I am from Georgia, and if you aren't happy with my oratory you are free to leave rather than listen to it."

"Are you telling me to leave?"

"It's just a suggestion, friend," said Jim.

"I go where I want to go, and I don't leave until I'm ready. And I don't have any nigger-loving friends in Georgia or anyplace else. So if you don't want me here then you'd best come down here and remove me yourself."

"If you will look at our banner, sir, you will see that non-violence is what this rally is all about. Are you not a supporter of peace?"

"We'll have peace as soon as the niggers and all their friends, like you, are gone."

"That will never be," said Jim. "So why don't you make it easy on yourself and try to accept the fact that people of every race, creed, and religion have the same right to be here as you do."

Ordinarily Jim would have tried to reason with the man, but he knew that it would be a waste of time. The troublemaker was just that, and no amount of reason would satisfy him.

"I can accept it all right," he said. "And this is how I do it."

The man suddenly pulled a small revolver from his breast pocket and started firing it into the air. Frightened people got up and started pushing each other to get to the exits. The miscreant was quickly subdued by an off-duty policeman, but by the time he was dragged away most of the crowd was gone. In the end, the rally realized only one hundred and ten dollars; a serious disappointment to the distraught crusaders.

"So he is back," Jim said to the others as they left the hall.

"What do you mean, Father?" John asked.

"I mean that I am willing to bet the one hundred and ten dollars we raised that the troublemaker in the hall tonight was put there by the man who is trailing us. I have no proof, but I don't need any. We were not bothered in Greenville, which was to make us think the harassment had ended. Whether we thought so or not is debatable, but it makes me very angry the way this scoundrel is toying with us. I had never before laid eyes on that man in the hall tonight, and I do not believe that his interference was a coincidence. Also, an anti-lynching law is good for white people the same as black, so why the racial inferences from someone who doesn't know us? I tell you he was put up to that stunt by whoever is following us. I want so badly to turn the tables on this villain, but how do we do it?"

"We have to set a trap for him," said Samuel. "I think I have an idea, Jim. We believe that this man is following us, and there just isn't any other way he could have ended up in every city we've visited. If he *does* have a grudge against us then he's most likely from around home like you and John were thinking, and he got on our trail in Atlanta by reading the notice in the Macon newspaper. After Atlanta, he just followed us to the next city, right to the hotel where you and John figure to stay. Then he can find out where the rally will be held by looking for the notice in the local paper. After that, he knows just how much time he has to plan whatever mischief he chooses."

"I would say that so far you have everything pretty well figured out," said Jim.

"By now he has to think that we have gotten wary. But as long as we just drive straight to our next stop as we have been, without doing anything different, he may still be bold enough to trail us right to the next hotel. Once we get there he may be more cautious, expecting that we might be as well—perhaps having our automobile guarded, for example."

"Then what do we do?" John asked.

"The next step will have to come with a bit of luck. I'm guessing that each time we reach the next hotel, this man stops nearby and watches until you or your father takes me and Darius to *our* hotel. The pattern has been the same in every city, and I'm sure he is aware of that. Then he follows so he can keep track of all of us. Maybe he has a reason for doing that too."

"You might be right," said Jim. "Maybe he has a grand finale planned for all of us."

"Yes sir, maybe, and that's why we need luck on our side. When we get to the next stop, Darius and I will very carefully scout the area while you and John are checking in. If we can spot him, maybe there is a way that we can get on *his* trail."

"I think I have the answer to that," said Jim. "Let's move on to Greensboro. I can't wait to find out."

Everyone was in a different frame of mind during the ride to Greensboro. Jim and John were constantly checking the side view mirrors; Samuel and Darius kept watch out the rear window to see who might be following. The road was busy, and there were several automobiles keeping pace with them; each man wondered if any had a cracked rear window. As they neared the O'Henry Hotel, Jim explained his ending to the plan.

"John and I will carry our bags into the hotel and check in. Samuel, you and Darius go the whole way around the outside of the building and make your way out to the street so that you will be headed back toward the hotel entrance from the other direction. If our man is out there, he probably won't be far from the entrance. If you spot him, retrace your steps back around the hotel as quickly as possible and meet us at the front door. Be just as careful as you can, my friends, because if he is there and anything goes wrong, we probably won't get another chance. If you see him, I will call for a taxi, and with any luck, when our man pulls away to follow you fellows, I will follow him in the taxi."

When they arrived, Samuel and Darius started off around the hotel; Jim and John signed the register, asked the desk clerk where accommodations could be found for their friends, then waited anxiously for them to return. Excitement peaked in Jim and John when they saw the two black men waving to them from the portico. They hurried outside, but before they could ask the question, Samuel blurted out the answer. "We were right! By God and by thunder the same automobile with the crack in the rear window is just up the street!"

"Are you certain he didn't see you?" Jim asked.

"Yes, sir," Darius replied. "There is a hedgerow along the sidewalk that's almost six feet high. Samuel and I could see through the narrow gaps in the branches, and he wouldn't have noticed us anyway because his eyes were fixed on his side mirror. He's just waiting for us to lead him to the place where Samuel and I will stay. We even saw the side of his face well enough to recognize him, right, Samuel?"

"That's right. It's the same automobile and the same man we saw in Atlanta and Columbia."

"This is wonderful," said Jim. "It ends in Greensboro. All right, let's hope our devoted foe doesn't get impatient. I'll call for a taxi, and as soon as it arrives we're going to find out who James Kemp *really* is."

It took nearly twenty-five minutes for the taxi to reach the hotel. Anxiety replaced excitement and they all prayed silently that the man who had dogged their tracks for three hundred and forty odd miles was still waiting.

"Here we go, John," said Jim. "Head down to the Calder Hotel, and don't pay any attention to what's behind you. It is six blocks down, turn right onto Willow Street, and the hotel is on the left. As soon as you get started down the street I'll have the taxi driver move to the end of the driveway. If I see the auto in question pull out when you pass, I will instruct the driver from there." To Samuel and Darius he said, "John and I will pick you up for dinner about six p.m."

Jim got into the taxi and at the precise moment he said, "Pull your taxi out to the street and then stop."

When John had gone a little less than a block, a vehicle pulled away from the curb and started after him. "Go," said Jim. "Follow that auto that just pulled out. Don't get too close, but stay behind him."

The taxi driver eyed Jim carefully out of the corner of his eye but he said nothing and did what he was told. From the distance at which they followed, Jim could plainly see the telltale crack in the rear window. When John made the turn onto Willow Street, the auto behind him turned the corner but immediately pulled to the curb. Jim instructed the taxi driver to pull over about a hundred feet down from Willow Street.

Approximately ten minutes went by until the suspect apparently decided he had seen all he needed to. He pulled from the curb, made a U-turn on Willow, and then started down the street past the taxi.

"Follow that auto," he told the driver. Eight blocks and several minutes later, the vehicle they were following turned into Gott's Hotel. Jim had the taxi driver pull to the curb beneath a big maple tree and stop. Jim's vantage point was excellent, and when he finally got a look at his tormentor, he could not help saying, "Well I'll be damned."

"I beg your pardon," said the taxi driver.

"Never mind," Jim replied. Many questions were answered and many things fell into place when he recognized the man: it was Jared Sykes. Jim was intimately familiar with Jared's kind, and he knew that the man was a very vindictive sort. But he still could not believe that hatred could run so deep as to make a man go to such great lengths to even a score. When Jared retrieved two bags from his automobile and carried them into the hotel, Jim said to the driver, "Go back to the O'Henry."

When Jim returned to the hotel, John was waiting in their room.

"It's Jared Sykes," he told his son.

"That certainly explains a lot," said John in a dismal tone of voice. "I'm not surprised, just disgusted."

"It struck me the same way, son. Now we know who we're dealing with, and tonight after the rally we will deal with him in person."

"How do you want to handle this, Father?"

"By taking him to the edge and teaching him a lesson that he will never forget."

At ten-thirty that night, after an uneventful evening at the rally, everyone got into Jim's auto, and they headed to Gott's Hotel. After driving through the parking lot to make sure that Jared's vehicle was there, he parked in the shadows as far from the building as he could. Then John got out and walked to the front entrance with Samuel and Darius accompanying him as far as the door. There they waited while John entered the hotel to lure their quarry outside. A few minutes later he came out the front door and said, "He's on his way, fellows, get ready." Then he hurried over to join his father. Fortunately, all was very quiet around the hotel, and the parking lot was nearly full of autos, which offered a lot of cover for their actions.

Jim and John were sitting in the front seat quietly watching when Samuel and Darius assisted Jared to the auto blindfolded, and gagged, then lifted him into the back seat. Then Samuel got in and sat on one side of the prisoner; Darius went around and got in to sit on the other side.

Jim waited for a few minutes, observing the area very carefully to determine whether or not their kidnapping had stirred up any attention. When all remained quiet, Jim drove out to the street and headed south. No one spoke; each man was preoccupied with his own thoughts. Jared too made little or no sound; he sat stiff and still in the back seat, breathing very heavily. Jim figured that when he came out of the hotel and was grabbed, gagged, and blindfolded by two muscular black men, his own conscience told him that he had every reason to be afraid.

Five miles outside Greensboro, Jim turned off the road onto a narrow path that led back into the woods. After about a hundred yards they came to a small clearing; Jim stopped and shut the motor off but kept the headlights lit.

"Everyone stay here for a few minutes," he said, and then he got out and assembled a small pile of dead wood in the middle of an area where the ground was bare. Then he gathered handfuls of last year's leaves and packed them under the wood. Finally he lit the leaves on fire, and in a few minutes there was a nice bright campfire burning.

Jim walked over to the automobile, turned off the headlights, and said, "Samuel, you and Darius take him over to the fire and wait." Then he rummaged around in the back of the automobile until he located some heavy rope that he kept in the vehicle. Lastly, he tied a noose in the end of the rope and said, "Come on, John."

Samuel and Darius watched, a bit startled, as Jim took out a knife, cut two feet of rope from the end, and tied Jared's hands behind his back. But when he took some slack rope and tossed it up and over the stout limb of a tree ten feet from the fire, the two black men looked at each other with fear on their faces.

It nearly brought about a breaking point when Jim put the noose around Jared's neck, took the other end of the rope, and put some tension on it. By this time, Jared was whimpering audibly and his knees were trembling uncontrollably. Then Jim said, "Samuel, remove the blindfold and then the gag." Samuel did as he was told. When the blindfold came off, the look in Jared's eyes was as wild as a cornered animal's. When the gag was pulled from his mouth . . .

"Langdon!" he gasped. "What are you going to do to me?"

"Don't you know, Jared?" said Jim. "I would think that you've been to enough of these events to recognize them by now. Sorry we don't have a cross to burn the way you Klansmen do, but there just wasn't time to make one.".

"You can't do this, Langdon! I'm a white man!"

"I'm sorry but I don't differentiate between colors when it comes to lynching. I say, what's good for one is good for all, don't you agree? White men get lynched now and then too, you know. The only difference is that the lynch mob might at least find a real reason for doing it. But when it comes to the black man, well, if there isn't a reason the mob will invent one, and all too often the color of his skin will do."

"I beg you not to do this, Langdon. I'll do anything you say, but please don't hang me."

"It would just be so difficult to back down right now, Jared. I've been dealing with people like you all my life, as did my father, and neither one of us could ever get your kind to understand that God created all humans, white, black, or whatever. And no one has the right or the power to tell another that they are a lesser species and should be treated as such. I guess I've just gotten so tired of it all that I figure it's time to come around to your way of thinking."

"What about the law?" the condemned man screamed.

"Why should the law work for you when there are many citizens that the law refuses to work for?"

At that point, Jared was sobbing without restraint as he pleaded for mercy. Samuel and Darius looked over at John who stood stone-faced by the fire.

Jim walked over to Jared and stood so close that his wrath, his spittle, and his fiery eyes threatened to scorch the terrified man's face.

"Maybe now you can understand why my son, our black brothers, and I have tried so hard in our lives, in our hearts, and by making this journey, to do something to try to put a stop to the lynchings that happen almost daily in this country. Maybe you can understand how unjust, how horrible, and how inhumane it is! How does it feel to be on the other side, Jared? How does it feel to be standing with a rope around your neck, between two strong black men who could hoist you off your feet, and without pity watch you choke to death?"

Jared was physically drained. He wept loud and lively, expressing guilt, shame, and remorse.

"It is you who has been sabotaging our trip isn't it?" Jim asked.

"Yes," said Jared, without hesitation. "I did it all," he said through the tears. "I read about it in the paper, and I followed you from place to place. I canceled your rally in Atlanta, I ruined your tires, and I hired the man in Charlotte to disrupt your speech. I did it, and I am sorry. I apologize for everything I did; even for the day I came to your place with the sheriff, intending to hang Willis Tyson. I *was* jealous of him like you said. I liked your cousin, Emma, but I didn't know how to treat *her* right either."

The campfire was beginning to die out. Jim went over to the automobile and turned on the headlights. Then he walked back to Jared, took the noose from around his neck, and untied his hands.

Jared looked up at Jim and said, "You aren't going to hang me?"

"No, I'm not. I guess I'll have to settle for hoping that you will live a different life from now on. I'll never get used to racial hatred or the lengths to which a man who is fueled by it will go. But maybe if I can change just one man's way of thinking, it is worth the effort."

"You have, Jim," Jared cried. "I swear to God you've changed my mind forever."

"Time will tell," Jim replied. "Let's go, John; come on Samuel, Darius."

The four men walked to the auto and got inside. Jim stepped back out of the vehicle and said, "You can walk back to Greensboro, Jared. You can think about this evening on the way, and maybe you'll be grateful knowing that black men as well as white men were willing to spare your life when they could have so easily and so unjustly taken it."

Then Jim resumed his place, put the auto in reverse, and backed out of the woods leaving the rope hanging from the tree and Jared still weeping quietly in near darkness.

A mile up the road, John broke the silence. "I'll say one thing without fear of contradiction, Father. You said you were going to take him to the edge and you couldn't have done a better job if you practiced for a month."

"Darius and I feel like we were taken to the edge ourselves," said Samuel.

"I am sorry about that, fellows," said Jim. "I wanted everything to seem as real as possible and you both helped a great deal with accomplishing that."

"Do you think that man will really change?" asked Darius.

"Time will tell," said Jim.

From Greensboro, the crusaders drove to Winston-Salem, and from that point on, they had no more trouble.

By the time they had finished their trip in Washington DC, nearly fifteen thousand dollars had been collected from well-wishers and supporters of the Dyer Anti-Lynching Bill. The money was personally handed over to the executive secretary of the NAACP, Mr. James Weldon Johnson.

Although the passage of the bill through the House of Representatives was by a healthy majority, due to filibusters by the White Southern Democratic Block, the bill failed to reach a vote in the Senate in 1922.

SIX

One Step Forward, Two Steps Back

With the perpetual passing of time comes inevitable changes because the world never stands still; progress never sleeps. Of course, under that account are recorded the gains and losses, attempts and failures, joys and sorrows.

John's son, William, had left for school in New York to study business, following in the footsteps of his father and his grandfather. At age fifteen, William's sister, Julia, a child prodigy with the violin, was also in New York City attending the Juilliard Graduate School, established in October of 1924.

Jim's cousin, Emma, and her husband, Willis, were living very happily in Canada with their two-year-old son, Nicolas. They had escaped the segregated South, which would not have allowed their marriage or the rights and freedoms promised them by the US Constitution.

In late January 1925, Aunt Ashton and Uncle Jeremy made the long journey to visit their daughter and her family. But as they were making their way home on the train, the locomotive derailed due to a defective wheel bearing and they perished in the crash along with the other one hundred and twenty-five people on board. Their remains were brought home and interred in the family cemetery on Langdon Plantation. Their passing was a terrible blow to Jim. His aunt Kate, who attended the funeral with her husband, Bradford, was now his last direct link to his parents.

The failure of the anti-lynching bill had also been a blow. The NAACP was relentless in their execution of a public awareness program, which may have brought about an over-all decline in lynchings. But until legislation was passed and laws were instituted, there would be no serious reduction of incidents, especially in the more violent states like Georgia, Alabama, and Mississippi.

Although Jim was well aware of the fact that the president of the United States was not the whole federal government and did not wield absolute power, he was still grateful that a man like Calvin Coolidge held that office. Due to Coolidge's beliefs and opinions, the Klan's influence was waning. Coolidge appointed no known Klan members to office, but he did appoint several black Americans. He continuously called for legislation that would outlaw lynchings.

Included in his first State of the Union Address were remarks in favor of African Americans; he said that protecting their rights was a public and private duty. In a commencement speech he had made at Washington DC's Howard University on June 26, 1924, Coolidge thanked and praised African Americans for their contributions to US society, their advances in education, and their willingness to serve as soldiers in the Great World War, all while carrying the burden of discrimination and prejudices at home.

In the spring of 1926, Jim sat down with John to discuss the progress of the civil rights movement and to look for new ways in which they might be able to get involved.

"As you know, John, your grandfather had a vision, but he knew that once the slaves gained their freedom it would still be a long time before they would enjoy the rights of equality. But I sometimes wonder if he understood just how much of a struggle it would be. It is easier for you and me to see what he went through because it is history. He could not know what we would face because it was in the future. Your grandfather witnessed slavery; I was too young to remember it now. He lived through and participated in the war that changed all that. I guess my point is that he probably felt that beyond freedom lay a hard road ahead but that *he* had seen the roughest part."

"I feel your frustration, Father, and it is only natural. I am sure that Grandfather experienced the same. But I guess we need to follow the example given us by the African Americans themselves, which is to stay the course. That is what I have seen them doing for as long as I can remember. They refuse to give up; they refuse to take the place in which the white man believes they belong. And I know that I speak for you when I say we will not give up on them as long as they do not give up on themselves."

"That was very eloquently put, John, and of course, you are right. The war of independence for this nation was a long and difficult struggle, which tried the stamina of many good men. How often it must have seemed that giving up was the only recourse. But determination will win the day, and our black brethren show no shortage of that."

"No, they don't. But there is something that they need just as much, Father, and that is good leadership. An army without competent leaders is like a ship without a rudder; it can find no direction. Of course leaders can sometimes have different opinions, which can also divide a camp and weaken it before the enemy."

"Yes, John, a leader has to consider many things and then choose the path that will bring about the most advantageous result. There have been many black activists in the past, and as time goes by there will be many more. Each generation has those individuals who will step forward regardless of the risks; those who will lead if others will follow. But as you've said, it can be counter-productive if they disagree."

"There are a number of them who stand out in my mind," said John. "In the nineteenth century there was a female journalist by the name of Ida B. Wells. It seems that through her experiences she adopted the belief in an eye for an eye. She documented lynchings and found that, contrary to popular belief, most blacks were not lynched for criminal acts as the white hordes claimed, but rather it was to punish or control blacks who competed with whites. A pamphlet was published by Ms. Wells in 1892, titled, *Southern Horrors: Lynch Law in All Its Phases*. The raping of white women was the reason for which many lynchings were carried out. She established that southerners used rape as their pretext for the lynchings to conceal the true reason: black economic progress. This not only endangered the white man's pockets but their notions of black inferiority as well."

"Very interesting," said Jim. "What was her solution?"

"Her message was that a Winchester rifle should be in every black home to provide the protection the law refused to supply. When the aggressive white man understands that he has as great a chance as his black victim of being killed, he will have much more respect for the black American's way of life. The longer the black man continues to give in, cower, and beg, the more he will be outraged, disrespected, and lynched."

"I cannot disagree with her logic," said Jim. "However, violence begets violence, which is the objectionable practice in the first place. But when your enemy forces it to be the last resort, perhaps it will stem the tide quicker than anything else. How ironic is it that violence may be the only way to stop violence."

"For a contrasting point of view, you look to Booker T. Washington," said John. "As you know, he was an educator, author, orator, and civil rights activist. He was also the most famous black man in America from 1895 until his death in 1915. He believed that black people should stay in the South because the whites needed them to do the jobs that no one else would do. He told them to learn skills that would make them become important. I suppose he had a point as well because so many blacks have left the South in the Great Migration that states such as Georgia, Florida, Tennessee, and Alabama are in jeopardy of losing their leading industries."

"But the blacks are anxious to leave because they want better jobs and better education for their children, not to mention escaping a culture of lynching violence," said Jim.

"Well, Mr. Washington had opposition; many black people felt that he was submitting to Jim Crow. The famous writer, W.E.B. Du Bois, renounced Washington's philosophy insisting that black Americans be given nothing less than equal rights. Washington felt that he had no choice except to strike a bargain; to trade political rights and voting rights for economic rights."

"So you have here a passive and an aggressive point of view," Jim replied. "Which do you suppose would take longer to get results?"

"I would say the passive, Father. I would have to lean toward Ms. Wells' advice; except that I would be sure the people understand that violence is only to be used in one's own defense. Otherwise, they will only be helping the white racists substantiate their case against them."

"I think," said Jim, "that what the black citizens are in
need of most right now is fair treatment in the courts. It
seems that Ms. Wells' message has had the desired effect;
case in point, the riot we witnessed in Charleston. I read a
full account of that incident, which confirmed what we
were told by the desk clerk at our hotel. Local blacks did
fight back that night, and were, for the most part,
exonerated. At the insistence of the NAACP and the
Interdenominational Minister's Union, the navy punished
some of the sailors who started the trouble and
compensated black businesses for damages. They also sent
resolutions to Charleston's mayor, Tristtram Hyde, asking
for improvements in sanitation, housing, black policemen,
and an interracial committee to avoid future incidents. The
resolutions did produce some results; however, it is a
popular belief that Mayor Hyde acquiesced to these
requests because the city's population is predominately
black."

"So the blacks in Charleston had a great advantage in
that situation because they outnumbered white citizens.
They also dispelled the myth that all blacks are docile and
complacent. I would even venture to say that the riot may
have brought about civil rights activity in Charleston. And
still . . . blacks are being lynched by the hundreds. One
step forward, two steps back," said John.

"Again, I believe what the black citizens need most
right now is fair treatment in the courts. Punishing the
wrongdoers and making them understand that they *will be*
punished for their actions is the only way to stop the
lynchings."

"What do you have in mind, Father?"

"I propose that we retain a black lawyer, the best one
that we can find. Through him we will provide legal help for
as many falsely accused African Americans as we can. We
will use newspapers and any other publications that are
available to notify black people in Georgia who need legal
help; we will provide contact information for our lawyer.
Surely we can only hope to scratch the surface, but the
more cases that are won, the more that will be able to be
won. Perhaps precedents will be set that can be used by

other lawyers. We will focus on those individuals who cannot afford legal representation."

"Do you have someone in mind?"

"As a matter of fact, I do. A lawyer by the name of Scipio Africanus Jones. He is a well-known litigator who lives in Little Rock, Arkansas. His experience is very impressive; he has been admitted to the State Supreme Court, United States District Court, United States Supreme Court, and the United States Court of Appeals."

"He sounds like an excellent choice, Father. How will you contact him?"

"I will write to him tonight."

One week later, in the middle of May, Jim was sitting on the veranda on a Saturday evening when Elizabeth came out to find him.

"Would you mind if I sit with you, Jim?"

"I would only mind if you didn't," he replied.

She took a seat beside him on the swing and said, "I am concerned about you, my dear husband."

"Oh? Well, I don't want you to have cause for concern," he said as he put his arm around her. "What's on your mind?"

"I would like to see you get a little rest."

"But that's what I'm doing now."

"No, I don't mean siting down at the end of the day. I want you to take some time and relax; maybe have a little recreation. You've been under a lot of stress the last several years. What with your trip to Charleston, the fundraising tour, the passing of Aunt Ashton and Uncle Jeremy, besides your responsibility of helping John oversee this plantation, I think you should get away for a little while."

"It's funny you should say that, Elizabeth, because I was actually thinking the same thing."

"You were?"

"I was. I want to show you something." Jim reached over to the end of the swing and picked up a copy of *Life Magazine*, which he had been reading before Elizabeth came out. He opened it to a page that he had marked and said, "Look at this. Read the story headline."

"The Harlem Renaissance," she read aloud. "What is this all about, Jim?"

"Harlem is a large neighborhood in the northern section of Manhattan, New York. It was originally a Dutch village organized in 1658, named for the city of Haarlem in the Netherlands. In 1915, it was an upscale white community. But due to the Great Migration, black people moved into the area in droves, and by 1924, it had become the black mecca; a place where black arts and culture have grown in spite of Jim Crow."

"It certainly sounds like a unique neighborhood," said Elizabeth.

"It isn't like anywhere else in America. It is the first place in this country where the African Americans can be themselves; showcase their talents in art, literature, and music. That's how it came to be known as the Harlem Renaissance. According to this article, the races can mingle there in ways they can't anywhere else. I want to go there and see this for myself."

"It sounds wonderful, Jim. When can we leave?"

"Just as soon as I can make a few arrangements; how about Sunday?"

"That doesn't give me much time to pack, but I'll make it. I'm so excited, Jim. We haven't done anything like this in a long time."

"Too long, I think. Pack enough clothes to last a week."

On Sunday afternoon, John drove his parents to Macon to catch the train. After they'd boarded and the train pulled out of the station, Jim showed Elizabeth the part of his personality that she loved so much and had seen so little of for a very long time. He was full of anticipation and as talkative as a child on his way to the circus.

When the train pulled into Union Station, the couple relieved the porter of their bags, disembarked, and hailed a taxi. The driver loaded the bags into the automobile and took them to the Hotel Theresa at the corner of 7th Avenue and 125th Street.

It was eight thirty a.m. when Jim and Elizabeth left the hotel after an elegant breakfast. Their first ambition was to conduct their own walking tour around the large

71

neighborhood, just to take in the sights. It was so different from Georgia—almost like another world: the big city hustle and bustle, thriving business and residential communities. And nearly all of it owned and inhabited by African Americans. The black people they met, whether it was in a café, a bookstore, or along the street, were happy, pleasant, and helpful with any questions the white couple had.

If only, thought Jim, all the white people living in the South could see this perfectly content and cultured neighborhood, they would have to admit that the black man, left to his own devices, could forge a society that was every bit as sophisticated and deserving of respect as their own. Seeing with his own eyes what they were able to accomplish, away from the degradation, racism, and violence of the South, only served to reinforce Jim's resolve to do anything possible to help the black race realize absolute equality.

Jim and Elizabeth stayed for a week, and in their own words, did everything. They visited the art galleries of sculptor Augusta Savage and painter and graphic artist Aaron Douglas. They saw the Black Birds starring Florence Mills perform a series of musical reviews at the Alhambra Theater, and they saw the Aldridge Players do a sequence of plays at the Harlem Library Little Theater. At the Cotton Club they enjoyed the legends of jazz, such as Duke Ellington, Cab Calloway, and the dynamic voice of Bessie Smith, who was known as "Empress of the Blues."

But they saved the best for last; the highlight of their trip was the evening that they spent at Happy Rhone's Black and White Club at the corner of 143rd Street and Lenox Avenue. The club, one of the first of its kind, was run by Arthur "Happy" Rhone and featured waitresses, music, and floor shows. However, the best thing about the club: it was integrated.

How wonderful it was for Jim and Elizabeth to watch the people, both black and white, laughing, dancing, enjoying, and mingling with each other the way the Good Lord had always hoped it would be. It was a wonderful time, and when it was over, Jim could not help but feel a bit melancholy when he thought about going back down south, even if it *was* home.

The following morning he bought a souvenir on the way to the train station: a copy of the *New Negro* published in 1925, in New York by Albert and Charles Boni. An anthology of fiction, poetry, and essays on African American art and literature, the book featured writers such as James Weldon Johnson and Langston Hughes.

On the train headed for Macon, Jim and Elizabeth talked about the week in Harlem, recounting their experiences as if they were trying to live them over again.

"You know," said Elizabeth. "I feel as though a new appreciation, a new era has been established. In a barrier once thought impervious, cracks are appearing, and seeping through are drops of a new social order."

"I believe that you're right," said Jim. "However, in order to thwart disappointment we must remember that the barrier has not been broken, but only cracked. In any case, I am glad we took this trip, and I am glad that we saw a near perfect world for a short time."

John was waiting at the station in Macon when the train from New York pulled in. It was a glad reunion, especially with so much to talk about. His parents regaled him with stories of their wonderful visit; John said he would like to take Abbey there sometime. When the fire beneath the exciting trip had burned out, John brought them up to date on what had happened at home the past week. "You received a letter from the lawyer in Arkansas, Mr. Scipio Africanus Jones; it came two days ago."

"That's good news," said Jim. "I hope he can join us."

"So do I, Father, but as you said, we can only hope to scratch the surface by helping as many blacks find justice as we can. I'm afraid the problem we'll have is that most of the lynchings are done by lawless mobs on the spur of the moment, giving the victim no chance to plead their case in a courtroom. There is no way to take justice to a lonely spot along an empty road in the middle of the night."

"Your point is well taken, son, but the same would be true if we had anti-lynching laws. If state law enforcement in the South will not uphold the law or punish the guilty then what good is the law? And if anyone who ignores a law against lynching is caught for committing such a crime, the federal government could only prosecute for a civil rights violation if the blacks were protected under civil rights laws, which they are not; and if they were, the punishment would not be as severe as it would be if the violator was prosecuted for murder. The word 'law' seems to be such an ambiguous term."

"You are right, of course, Father. Part of our work is living with the frustration of human ignorance. I forget that sometimes. Trying to destroy racism is like trying to empty the ocean with a teacup. I apologize for my mood, Father, and Mother. It's just that while you were seeing the impossible dream trying to come true in Harlem, a black man and his twelve-year-old son were lynched a few miles outside Macon last Wednesday night. No one seems to know who did it, and yet the rumor that's circulating is the victims were caught with a cow; the animal was supposedly stolen from a farmer named Joseph McCoy. McCoy took the cow; the bodies were cut down by family members and buried; that was the end of it."

All his father could say was, "Unbelievable."

"One step forward, two steps back," said his mother.

After a night of little sleep, Jim got up, poured a cup of coffee, and went into his office. The letter from Scipio Jones was on his desk. Not at all to Jim's surprise, was the fact that Mr. Jones, so laden with other responsibilities, would not be able to take on any additional cases. However, he was good enough to recommend another lawyer—a young protégé of his who had been working with him for the past two years.

The man's name was Jerome Tomkins, a married man with no children who would gladly relocate to Georgia and accept the assignment Jim had described in his letter. He need only reply with interest in the proposal, and Mr. Tomkins would provide notification of his plan as to when Jim could expect him and his wife to arrive in Macon. It would likely be within six weeks of receiving confirmation.

Elizabeth came in to see if he wanted more coffee; Jim showed her the letter.

"It looks like we'll be getting some new neighbors," she said.

"Yes," said Jim. "In fact, that gives me a wonderful idea. I would like Mr. Tomkins to be close by so that we can communicate easily, and my first thought was to offer him the hospitality of our home. But the word neighbor gives me a much better notion. Due to Aunt Ashton and Uncle Jeremy's untimely passing, their house on the hill sits empty. Madeline lives in California with her family and has no use for it. Emma is not likely to ever return here to live with her family. I will write to both of them, and if they are willing to sell, I will buy the house from Emma and Madeline; Mr. Tomkins and his wife can live there. The house has plenty of room should they want to start a family of their own, and our lawyer would be just a short walk away."

"It's an excellent idea, Jim. I will write the letters if you like."

"Yes, thank you, I would."

It took weeks before Jim could arrange to buy the house left behind by his aunt and uncle. But when the sale was complete, Mr. Tomkins was notified that his future lay in Georgia, and on a Monday morning in the middle of August 1926, the attorney and his wife arrived in Macon.

Jim and Elizabeth met them at the station and introduced themselves to Mr. Tomkins and his wife, Esther. It would be another week before the couple's furnishings arrived from Arkansas; in the meantime they would stay with Jim and Elizabeth.

On the way to the plantation, the four of them got acquainted. Of course Jim could not read Elizabeth's mind but in *his* opinion, Esther was very congenial; Jerome seemed reserved and aloof. In spite of first impressions, dinner at the Langdon house that evening was pleasant enough. After dinner, they took their future neighbors up the hill to the house where they would be living to show them around. Esther was very pleased with the house, but once again, Jerome did not have a lot to say.

After an extensive tour, Jim suggested they go back to their house to acquaint Mr. and Mrs. Tomkins with their temporary accommodations. But Jerome told his wife to go along with the Langdons and that he would be along shortly. Not wanting to show any surprise or annoyance, Jim said that he would be happy to escort the ladies back to the house.

Halfway down the hill, Esther stopped and said, "Please, Jim, Elizabeth, don't be offended by my husband's demeanor. He has had his share of difficulties growing up in Arkansas seeing friends and relatives hurt or destroyed by racial violence. His own father was lynched, and his mother took her life because of it. I grew up in Pennsylvania so I never saw the mistreatment of blacks that Jerome did, at least, not until I moved to Arkansas with him. Jerome got his bachelor's degree at the University of Pittsburgh and then attended law school there for three years; that's where we met."

"You were a student too?" Jim asked.

"Yes, I went there in 1922 to study nursing. Jerome was in his second year of law school by then. He graduated *cum laude* in 1924. He had always planned to go back to Arkansas, sit for the bar there, and practice in his home state. I always thought that I had a very deep desire to become a nurse, but when Jerome was ready to move home to Arkansas, I couldn't bear to be left behind. I knew I could finish my education there. We went back together and were married even before he passed his bar exam. After that he worked under Mr. Jones for two years, and he learned well. When your letter arrived, Mr. Jones told Jerome that this could be a great opportunity for him in spite of the fact that he hated to see Jerome leave."

"I assure you that this *is* a great opportunity, Esther," said Jim. "I want you and Jerome to stay for just as long as you both are happy here. There will be no shortage of work for your husband, and he will be a real asset to this community."

"I am so glad to hear it, Jim. We made some good memories together in Arkansas, and I hope we can make some here. If you can be a little patient with him, I know we can all be friends. He wants this position very badly. The minute you agreed to hire him in Mr. Jones' place, he immediately filed a petition for reciprocity so that he can practice law in Georgia."

"Please don't worry, Esther," said Jim. "We are already friends, and as time goes by, we will become very good friends."

"Very good friends," Elizabeth echoed.

When they reached the house, the three of them sat down on the veranda and waited for Jerome. He was not far behind them; after climbing the steps he took a long look from the vantage point of the veranda and then said, "You have a beautiful plantation here, Jim. I noticed that quite a few black people live in the dormitories out back. Are all of your workers black?"

"All of them, Jerome. Some have built their own houses down the road about five miles where the field office, the new plantation school, and the cotton fields are located. But they are not just workers, they are all partners. Each man helps to work the land, and they are paid weekly wages and a percentage of the crop when it is harvested. The wives take care of the homes, and the children spend their time playing and getting an education. Every family that has come here has started out living in the dormitories. Within two years, they can afford a house of their own, which will sit on a piece of land they will have earned as part of their partnership."

"So you pay them wages, a percentage of the crop, educate their children, and give them a parcel of land on which to build a house?"

"That's correct," Jim answered.

"That's very interesting. I know we have details to discuss, Jim, but it *has* been a long day; I'm sure that Esther is weary. Could you show us where we can freshen up before going to bed?"

"I will be happy to show you," said Elizabeth.

"Thank you. Then we will say goodnight, Jim. After a good night's sleep I will look forward to speaking with you again."

"Until morning, Jerome. Goodnight, Esther."

When Elizabeth had taken the guests into the house, Jim mused a bit about the future and how much the hiring of a lawyer might help some very unfortunate people. But no matter what kind of plan Jim came up with, it never seemed to be enough. Like his father, he knew he couldn't help everyone who needed it; it just wasn't possible.

Jim was up just after daybreak the following morning; he quietly made his way to the kitchen, not wanting to disturb Jerome and Esther. To his surprise, they were already having coffee with Elizabeth when he walked in.

"Good morning, everyone. I had no idea that I was the last one up."

"I think the quiet woke us," said Jerome with a smile. "We are used to a little more noise in the city, and I think the absence of it turned out to be a disturbance."

"I see what you mean. I guess any change takes some getting used to. Jerome, how would you like to bring your coffee out to the veranda? We can talk for a while and give the ladies a chance to do the same."

"I think that's an excellent idea, Jim"

The men took their cups outside and made themselves comfortable. Before Jim could begin the conversation, Jerome said, "I want to apologize for yesterday. I know that I was not as pleasant as I should have been. I feel that I should explain."

"It isn't necessary for me, Jerome, but I will listen anytime you wish to speak."

"I guess that is part of my point, Jim. Even though I arrived only yesterday, I can already see that I have been guilty of something that I criticize others for: labeling people. I won't go into the reasons, but I have always believed that all white people are alike. It was a little better in Pittsburgh where I attended school, but the feeling of not being equal was still there. But I can see in you and your wife that the white race is not all alike, and maybe I'd have learned that earlier if I had only given *them* a chance. You treat us the way all people want to be treated, and I know that your intentions are genuine."

"My faith in God is very strong, Jerome, and I try to live my life according to His guidance."

"But it's more than that, Jim. A lot of people believe in God, but they aren't all able to overcome grudges or prejudices. The way you conduct yourself is the way you really feel inside; it's who you are. Last night, when I walked down from the house on the hill alone, I stopped and talked with some of the people who live in the dormitories. They told me a lot about your family and about the history of Langdon Plantation. Many of those people are second generation; they grew up here; their parents knew your parents. Apparently, they were very fine people."

"They certainly were fine people. When my father took over the plantation, he had just come home from the war after having fought on the side of the Union. Once that information got out, he was hated by almost every white person in Bibb County. The local merchants wouldn't do business with him, and the local Ku Klux Klan harassed him constantly. They tried to drive him out, but he wouldn't leave. Instead, he partnered with three white men and a couple dozen former slaves to work this plantation and to protect one another. My father started all of this: the housing, the school, and the fair treatment of his fellow man. I carry on his will, and someday my son will follow, and his son after him."

"It is a moving story, Jim. I want you to know that I am very happy to be here, and I know that Esther is too. Now let's talk about what I can do to help."

The two of them talked for hours about offering legal help to the black population in Georgia. Jerome agreed that they could only do so much but that they would do everything possible. At length, John came over with William, who was on summer vacation from school. Jim introduced his son and grandson to Jerome, and the conversation went on until noon.

A week later, the Tomkins' furniture arrived by truck from Arkansas and they settled into the house formerly owned by Jim's aunt and uncle. Two days after that, Jerome was on his way to Atlanta to try his first case; Jim went with him to watch.

An elderly black man named Tyrone Pike had been caught coming out of a restroom that was for whites only. According to the accused, he was not able to read and had asked a white man for help in finding a restroom for coloreds. Tyrone went where he was directed, but when he came out, he was accosted by two policemen who beat him and put him in jail.

The trial only lasted for a few hours, and in the end, Jerome was able to obtain Tyrone's release. As always, the judge who heard the case was white, and as usual, the jury consisted completely of white men. Jerome argued that the charges should be dropped because the jury included no African Americans and, therefore, prosecution was discriminatory and unconstitutional. He was also able to make a point that his client could not read, and the white man who sent him to the wrong restroom was responsible for the incident—and most likely sent a black man to a white's only restroom intentionally.

Jim congratulated Jerome on a successful beginning, but Jerome was quick to point out that the charge was a relatively simple one and that cases involving more serious charges would not be nearly as easy to win. Still, Jim thought the lawyer had shown good form, greatly honed skills, and a very professional presence in the courtroom.

However, simple or not, Jerome had gotten noticed, and word of the black lawyer from Macon spread quickly. It wasn't long before letters requesting legal representation began to pour in from all over the state. Jim gave Jerome complete control over his practice, which resulted in his own choosing of the clients he most wanted to represent. These decisions were based solely upon the severity of the charge. He gave priority to those who were in the direst of straits.

With every victory, Jim became better able to absorb defeat. He was able to feel that the enemies of justice and equality were weakening, albeit ever so slightly. The memories of his visit to Harlem also helped to carry him further along without becoming so discouraged.

Then, in the beginning of autumn in 1929, he chanced to discover another issue of *Life Magazine*. Within the pages of the publication he discovered another article about Harlem, New York.

Once again, Jim's calm was shattered as he read the story about the decline of the milk and honey lifestyle that African Americans in one small part of the country had finally gotten to enjoy. He read about the once carefree citizens now besieged by the pressure of high rents, unemployment, and racist practices. He could only hope, now that the movement had begun—the movement of the *New Negro*—that the seed would remain, even if only to lay dormant for a time until it could begin again. "One step forward, two steps back," said Jim.

SEVEN

Black Depression

On October 29, 1929, the stock market on Wall Street crashed, throwing the whole country into a panic. The roaring twenties came to an abrupt halt, and a deep economic depression ensued.

When Jim Langdon read the news in the paper, he did not panic, but he also did not delay taking action. He did not invest in the stock market; he invested his money in Langdon Plantation. However, he was a man who did not have complete trust in banks, and financial trouble, especially on a large scale, made him wary. Consequently, he was one of the first to close his accounts at the bank in Macon and put his liquid assets in a safe at the house.

Jim also realized that the country would be tightening its belt as it slipped deeper into the Depression and that the African Americans would suffer far more than the whites. He also knew that the conditions for blacks would be even worse in the South. He knew that they were already being pushed out of the menial jobs they once held. As the group of Americans who were the last hired and the first fired, blacks actually entered the Depression before white Americans did.

It was time for Jim and his family to discuss the future and what steps they might take to provide for and protect themselves and all of their black friends who worked on the plantation. On Christmas Eve 1929, everyone took a seat in the parlor, including William, a recent college graduate, and Julia, who had just completed a European tour with the New York Philharmonic Orchestra.

"It seems that a whole new trial is facing this nation, and it will affect nearly every American family's ability to support itself," said Jim. "The culprit behind this catastrophic turn of events is greed. When people find themselves in a comfortable state of living, you would think that they would be content. But for many, that will never be enough. Consequently, for the last ten years, stock prices have been going up; many people thought they would keep climbing, and the enticement of fast money compelled them to invest their money, sometimes beyond their means. Even banks got in on the action by speculating with depositors' funds."

"In other words, they were gambling all they had," said John.

"Exactly," Jim replied. "The banks, combined with the private investors, stand to lose millions and millions of dollars. I have already closed all accounts at the bank and suggest, John, that you and Abbey do the same immediately. There is no telling how long this depression might last, but you can be sure it will take quite some time before the country is able to come back from a financial disaster of this magnitude. Our concern now is to plan well for the future and to keep our heads above water."

"As you know, Father, the price of cotton is now eighteen cents a pound and will most likely drop further before this thing is over. My first suggestion would be to discontinue all purchases of any kind unless they are absolutely necessary. For example, the new machinery we were planning to buy this year for planting and harvesting. It is cheaper to make repairs on what we already have than to replace it."

"I agree with that idea, John. I will talk to all the men after the holidays and recommend that we all take a little less in cash and crop until this crisis blows over. Hopefully we can extend our means far enough to ride out the storm."

"I think that you are both on the right track," said William, "but right after the holidays I would like to take a closer look at our financial situation. I may have a few more suggestions we can benefit from."

"A second look is always a good idea, William," said Jim.

"I guess all the ladies can do is to let the men figure it out," said Julia.

"There is one more thing that you can do, Julia," said Jim.

"What is that, Grandfather?"

"Entertain us with your violin."

"I thought you'd never ask," she replied with a smile.

"Splendid. Now, let us not forget what day this is and prepare to celebrate a Merry Christmas."

As 1930 made its debut, the belt tightening was well under way at Langdon Plantation. There was no need for any great alarm, and Jim intended to keep it that way. Like all Americans, it was a priority for him to stay as informed as possible by reading the newspapers and listening to all the reports on the radio.

By February of 1930, the prime interest rate was cut from six percent to four percent by the Federal Reserve. With a major purchase of US securities, the money supply was expanded. But the federal government was not putting much money into the economy.

The Depression became the chief topic of conversation; nearly every evening after dinner, Jim and Elizabeth would sit in the parlor and ruminate about the situation.

"There is a lot in the paper about the state of affairs in this country, and none of it is encouraging," he told her. "Here is a depressing article in which Treasury Secretary Andrew Mellon announces that the Federal Reserve will stand by as the market works itself out: 'Liquidate labor, liquidate stocks, and liquidate real estate . . . values will be adjusted and enterprising people will pick up the wreck from less competent people.' Like it or not, I realize that money is the foundation of human existence, and many people are worrying themselves to death trying to figure out how to recoup their lost fortunes. But in a time like this, I think the most important thing is to worry about *all* people having what they need to survive."

"I support you in that thought, Jim. I lie awake at night and try not to imagine how many poverty-stricken people have little or nothing to eat. I am talking about those families who had very little before this economic depression began. The unemployment rate is up to 8.9 percent and getting higher all the time. Without work, there is no way for people to help themselves."

"Of course I am concerned about everyone too; I would not turn anyone away from my door if they were starving. But with discrimination and persecution already hanging over their heads like a pall, African Americans are being crushed at the bottom of the barrel. Most federal aid goes to needy whites, and there isn't much of that to begin with. Even after the Great Migration, many blacks still live in the Jim Crow South. And let's not forget that Washington DC is a Jim Crow city. I know that jobs are hard to come by, even for a white man, but at least he doesn't have to risk his life just for asking for one. And if he has a job, no one will try to kill him to create a vacancy."

"I'm afraid that things will get worse before they get better," said Elizabeth.

"I fear that very same thing. All we can do for now is to wait and pray," Jim replied.

In March, President Hoover announced that the worst was over and the economy would show improvement within sixty days. Few took his optimism seriously and most chided the president for making such a weak attempt to placate the population who knew that nothing on such a large scale could possibly turn around that quickly.

In June, Jim read in the paper about the Smoot-Hawley Tariff Act, which Congress had just passed, raising duties in an effort to protect American manufacturing against foreign competition. But the tariff increase did not do much to help the American economy, and by the end of the year he read that the first US bank had failed.

Early in April, the following year, Jim called John and William into the office.

"In spite of everything, we are holding our own," said William. "Cotton prices have dropped a couple more cents per pound, but we have a reserve of fertilizer and seed, which means we won't have to make a buy for a while."

"Well, Father, I can certainly report that all the men are in good spirits in spite of the situation; they are just glad to have what they need to get by," John added.

"I never doubted their support, John. They are good men, and they know that *we* are here for them. We'll all get through this because we believe in one another."

"The articles in the newspapers offer little encouragement," said John. "Sometimes I wonder why I

read them. You definitely did the right thing when you
closed all the accounts at the bank last year. Of course,
Abbey and I followed suit. People are now flocking to the
banks, trying to withdraw their money. I wonder how many
banks will close this year."

"I don't know, but I am hoping that the president is
defeated in next year's election. I have been reading a lot
about the governor of New York, Franklin Roosevelt. I think
he would make a good president. I see him as a man who
can get the country moving again. The only reason I might
feel otherwise is that Roosevelt contracted polio in 1921.
Can a man with that serious a disability handle such a
position?"

"He'd have to have the heart of a lion I would think,"
said John.

"I agree with you," Jim replied. "In October of 1924, he
went to Warm Springs because it seems that warm water
does the most to ease his pain. I remember a story the
Atlanta Journal did about Roosevelt being there."

"Where is Warm Springs, Father?"

"Sixty miles south of Atlanta. It was a spa town
because of its consistent eighty-eight degree mineral spring
water. Roosevelt actually bought the resort and the
seventeen hundred acre farm surrounding it in 1927."

"He must really believe it can help him," said John.
"Maybe he *does* have the heart of a lion."

"He may have, but in any case, the Langdons have
always been Republicans and Roosevelt is a Democrat.
However, I do not stand on ceremony. If he should be the
man for the job then so be it."

Suddenly there was a knock at the office door, and
Elizabeth entered the room.

"I am sorry to interrupt, gentlemen, but there is
someone here to see you."

"Who might that be, dear?" said Jim.

"Well, try not to fall from your chair, but its Jared
Sykes."

Jim had never told Elizabeth about the trouble Jared
had caused during the fundraising trip to support the Dyer
Anti-Lynching Bill. He saw no reason to share such an
unpleasant story. But she knew about the trouble Jared

had caused for Emma and Willis and therefore assumed that Jim would be wary of his presence.

"Please have him come in, Elizabeth."

She left the room, and a few minutes later there was another knock at the door.

"Come in," said Jim.

Jared opened the door, walked in, and stood in front of Jim's desk. John pointed to a vacant chair and said, "Sit down, Jared."

"Thank you, John. And thank you, Jim, for seeing me."

"You're welcome, Jared. This is my grandson, William."

"William," said Jared, nodding his head.

"Welcome, Jared," William replied.

"I must admit, I am surprised to see you," Jim remarked.

"I can certainly understand that, and I want to say right off that I hold no grudge against you, and I hope that you bear me no malice as well. I really am sorry for all the trouble I caused you, and I deserved the treatment I got."

"I hold no grudge, Jared. To tell you the truth, I haven't even thought of you since our unfortunate encounter. Today is a new day; relax and tell us what's on your mind."

"I want to sell the plantation and I wondered if you might be interested."

If the Langdons were surprised by Jared's visit, it was nothing compared to their reaction to this last statement. The three men looked at each other in disbelief. They had just been discussing their financial picture and what they needed to do to keep operating. Now the most unlikely person in the state wanted them to buy him out.

"I suppose you know what you're asking, Jared. Under normal circumstances we would most likely jump at the chance to expand. But these are anything but normal circumstances."

"You are quite right, Jim. The economy is spiraling, and it looks like it could be a short drop to the bottom. Anybody who has anything in their pocket is smart to hold on to it. I couldn't be trying to sell at a worse time. But I am going through some life changes of my own, and I am willing to take the circumstances into consideration."

"How so?" John asked.

"Well, you may know that my father died nearly a year ago."

"Yes," said Jim. "We heard about that, and I would like to offer our belated condolences."

"Thanks. Anyway, since then I met a woman; she's from Atlanta. We have been keeping company, and we've decided to get married. She wants me to move to Atlanta; she has a nice home there, and due to her own father's recent death, she is pretty well set financially. I have given it a great deal of thought, and for a number of reasons I believe that I would really enjoy the change."

"You wouldn't miss your home place?" said Jim.

"I guess most people never lose complete sight of their roots, but since my father died it isn't the same for me. I have no brothers, and my only sister has been married and gone for many years now. It's lonely in that big house; I never thought a lot about getting married before. My time is passed for having children; my fiancée was married; her husband was killed in accident almost ten years ago, and she has no children either. But I kind of like the idea of living a quiet life in the city; who knows, I might become a gentleman."

"Well, I'm happy for you, Jared. Sometimes a change can really do a man some good. But what about the sale of your plantation and the circumstances you're willing to take into consideration?"

"Besides the big house there is two large barns, several other out buildings, all sitting on two thousand acres of top quality cotton fields. There is also two hundred acres of pasture and two hundred acres of woods. I want to sell now because I am not planning to put in a crop this year; planting season is just about here. If we can agree on a price, I will make the payments very reasonable, and I will not expect the first one for two years."

"I must say, your terms *are* very agreeable, Jared," said Jim.

"Well, I don't want to give the place away, you understand, but it's not all about money either. I am looking forward to a new lifestyle, and I figure you are doing me a favor if you buy me out. If you buy it you can help out your Negro friends too. There is no one left over there. Many of them left for the North and I gave the last few notice. You can take on a lot more Negroes to help you sharecrop the place."

"I understand about salesmanship, Jared, but it does surprise me to see you come out in favor of the black man."

"I don't think I will ever feel the way you do about them, Jim. But I *was* serious that day outside Greensboro when I said that you did change one man's mind about lynchings. I want no more trouble in my life."

"I'm glad to hear it," said Jim. "If you can give us a chance to talk about this, it just could be that we can work something out. We will discuss an offer for your place, and then we'll contact you. Today is Tuesday; we'll let you know something by Friday."

"That would be perfect. I want to start moving to Atlanta next week."

"I'll show you out, Jared. Be right back, fellows."

When Jim returned he took his seat, looked at John and William, then said, "What do you think of that?"

"I think it could be a great opportunity from a highly improbable source," said John. "I am also amazed by the change in Jared's point of view. Grandfather must be beside himself in heaven. He always believed that for the world to change, it would be necessary for what is in people's hearts to change. It isn't something they can be forced into by war or any other means. It has to come from within. I realize that Jared will never look at a black man and call him his brother. But at least he now understands that the way in which the black man is being treated is wrong."

"It *is* inspiring. If only those who fan the fire of racism could understand or at least lose the ability to influence others."

"You are talking about the Klan," said William.

"I am. A man by the name of David Curtis Stephenson leaps to mind."

"That name is familiar; he was a Klan leader, wasn't he?" John asked.

"One of the biggest. He's a Texan who became a salesman in Indiana. In 1922, he was given control of the

Klan along with the power to organize in twenty states. He made millions selling those evil robes and hoods. In 1923, an estimated crowd of 200,000 attended a rally in Kokomo, Indiana. Publicly he professed to be a protector of womanhood and prohibition. But in reality he drank heavily and abused women. He was sentenced to life in prison in 1925 for abducting and assaulting a twenty-eight-year-old woman named Madge Oberholtzer. After his collapse, many Klan supported politicians were prosecuted on corruption charges, which led to the abandonment of the organization by large numbers of members. A year later, Klan membership had fallen from 350,000 to 15,000 in Indiana."

"It just proves that if those people are held accountable for their actions, they will think twice about taking the law into their own hands," said John.

"We have always known that it would be so. Today there are only about 45,000 Klan members in the whole country. But we must remember that Madge Oberholtzer was a white woman, and that is why the law took charge. It was the same with your grandfather's friend, Chet Rawlins. His murder brought down Harlan Jeffers, the leader of the local Klan back in 1869, because Chet was a white man. We have seen the Klan's ranks diminish before only to rejuvenate at a later time. God only knows if we will ever be rid of them for good."

"While we keep a good thought, Grandfather, let's busy ourselves with the purchase of Jared's plantation," said William.

With the conditions Jared offered, the three of them felt that the risks of buying the plantation were minimal, even in the midst of the Depression. A delay in payments for two years would give them two seasons of production before paying anything out. Cotton prices were down, but they speculated that volume would make the difference between failure and success. An offer was made; Jared accepted, and the deal was finalized in three days.

What they most liked about the acquisition was the immediate need for more sharecropping partners. The only problem was how to find them without being overwhelmed by desperate men. With so many people out of work, the prospect of employment could create a frenzied mob. It was decided that no advertisement would be printed; word of mouth was sure to spread the word fast enough.

Jim put William in charge of the acquisition, giving him the responsibility of hiring men, assigning them to sections of land, and coordinating the housing. Unfortunately, the housing would be a make-do situation at first because the only things available were the old slave cabins, most recently used by Sykes' sharecroppers. Each man would be given the materials necessary for repairs and renovations to make a home for himself and his family.

Next, William set up an office in the main house where he would run the plantation as a separate entity so that profit and loss could be clearly tracked in order to see if the new investment was working.

By the middle of April 1931, the hiring began, and preparation for planting followed immediately. The flood of men looking for work had been diverted by not advertising in the paper, but one or two men at a time trickled in all day long, every day. Within three weeks, the quota was filled, with two additional men hired as foremen—a black man, Henry Monroe, and a white man, Seth Morgan, due to their exceptional experience. After leaving William on his own for nearly a month, Jim paid him a visit to see how he was getting along.

"I'm glad to see you, Grandfather. I was hoping you would come by."

"I just wanted to give you some time, William. I wanted you to adjust to the responsibility. I didn't want you to feel as if someone was looking over your shoulder."

"I appreciate that, Grandfather, and I am pleased that you have so much confidence in me."

"I certainly do that. Do we now have a working plantation?"

"Yes sir, we do. I have hired a large enough work force to cultivate every acre of tillable soil. They have been hired on with the same arrangement as the other men on Langdon Plantation. Everything possible is being done to make the old slave cabins livable, and I never saw a group of men so eager to work or so grateful for the chance to make a living."

"Do most of them have families?"

"All but two, and those men have agreed to share a cabin. One man is black, the other is white. Among the rest, there are three black families to every white family. The planting is well under way and I haven't had a single complaint or problem with anything."

"You've done a great job, William. How many men did you have to turn away once you reached your quota?"

"More than I wanted to. I posted a sign down by the road after hiring the last man, but there were some who came up to the house anyway. It's been quiet the last couple of days though, I'm happy to say. It's been difficult; I feel guilty somehow."

"Why is that, William?"

"I guess because I was really seeing the Depression for the first time. I realized that the Depression has a face, expressions, and feelings. If you could have seen some of these men with their families—ragged clothing, a starved look about them, and a longing in their eyes. Most of them showed up in mule-driven carts. A few have a rattle trap automobile or truck, but all of them carrying everything they own in the world. I was so fortunate to grow up in a house where my family never wanted for anything. I had clothing, food, and a good education. Why do you suppose that's so, Grandfather? Why do some have so much and others, nothing?"

"I wish I could answer that, William, but I can't. Usually I refer all things I don't understand to the Lord. He is the only one who knows everything. The best answer I can give you is that it is His will. Every man has a life designed for him alone, and it is up to him to make the best of it."

"And what about us, Grandfather? What about the people who have it so much better?"

"It is up to us to look to our fellow man and lend a hand in any way we can. Do you feel that we try to do that here?"

William thought about that for a few moments, and then he said, "You know what, Grandfather? I do, yes, I can see that we try to be fair with people and help them all we can. I feel better, thank you."

91

"You are welcome, William. I have to be going. If you need anything, let me or your father know."

"To that end, Grandfather, I do have one request."

"Please make it."

"I think it's time I moved out of Mother and Father's house, and I was wondering if I could live here. I would be so much handier if I'm needed."

"I think that is a wonderful idea. I don't know why I hadn't thought of it. A young man like yourself will most likely be taking a wife sometime soon, and this would make a good home."

"As a matter of fact, I have been corresponding with a young lady I went to school with. She lives in Maryland with her aunt. Her parents divorced about ten years ago; her mother died last year of tuberculosis, and she has not seen her father since the divorce."

"That's a sad story, William. I am sorry to hear it. Please feel free to have her visit anytime."

"I have been considering it," William replied.

"Good for you."

Jim was touched by his grandson's feelings toward people less fortunate than himself. It was a feeling that the entire Langdon family shared. It was in that spirit that Jim prayed that the new plantation prospered so that the partners who sharecropped the land would have a solid future ahead of them.

During President Hoover's fourth year in office, Jim could see that very little had improved in the state of the economy. The masses of poor and destitute people continued to suffer while the president established the Reconstruction Finance Corporation, which eased the credit problems of industrial firms, insurance companies, and large banking. The move was intended to increase consumer spending, create jobs, and stimulate production. But as time went by it was clear that none of the benefits of this program were seeping into the lower levels of society.

By this time, nearly half of all African Americans were unemployed. In some of the cities up north, the whites wanted blacks to be fired until every white man had a job.

And racial violence was on the rise again. The worst of it was still taking place in the South; white workers rallied around slogans such as, "Niggers back to the cotton fields—city jobs are for white folks."

Southern railroads saw the most violent incidents as black firemen were attacked and murdered by unionized white workers, in order to take their jobs. The local paper carried an article in which one contemporary observer said, "The shotgun, the whip, the noose, and the Ku Klux Klan practices resumed in the certainty that dead men tell no tales but create vacancies."

On a Tuesday morning during the last week in July, John walked into his father's office with the morning paper tucked under his arm.

"I hate to bring you bad news first thing in the morning, Father, but I think you should read this," he said as he handed over the paper. The front page headline read, "BLACK MOB ATTACKS WHITES IN ATLANTA!" According to the story, a group of about eight black men on horseback raided the streets of Atlanta around ten o'clock the previous evening, terrorizing white citizens and shooting out windows of white businesses. The mob had struck so suddenly and unexpectedly that the attack had ended and the riders had disappeared by the time the police could come to the rescue.

Eyewitness accounts confirmed that the attackers were black and wore hoods that resembled those of the Ku Klux Klan. At the city line, two of the riders dismounted, grabbed a white man off the sidewalk, put a noose around his neck, and pulled him up against a light post, tying off the rope with the man's feet just inches from the ground. To his coat they pinned a sign that read, "The Black Klan," then they climbed on their horses and led the mob out into the night. The victim, a man by the name of Harmon Russell, was dead by the time two bystanders could get him free. Police pursuit failed to overtake the mob.

"My God," said Jim when he'd finished reading the story. "What sense does this make? How do they think this kind of thing is going to help? The Black Klan indeed."

"I guess that reprisals are inevitable, Father. It's a terrible thing, but after so many of their kind have been murdered, it must be very difficult to keep from striking back."

"I know that, John. I understand how justified they must feel, but they are only going to get the worst of it in the end. They'll all wind up dead, and their people will bear the long-term effects of their actions."

"I disagree with them, Father, but in my heart I can't condemn them. The suffering in this country has reached a very high level. Starvation, privation, and no end in sight is more than human beings should have to endure—but if you have black skin, it does not stop there. Black depression . . . God have mercy."

As the days passed by, Jim read the paper to see if there were further reports of the incident, but it seemed that the authorities had reached a dead end. But he knew that the investigation would continue for as long as it took to find and prosecute those responsible. A white man had been lynched, an innocent victim who left a wife and five children behind. And as Jim predicted, because of the mob's actions, other black families for miles around Atlanta were being rousted, interrogated, and in some cases beaten in an attempt to obtain information that would lead to the mob's capture. Within a week, a company of officers from Atlanta showed up in Macon.

It was a great concern for the Langdons; with so many black families working on their plantations, the officers were bound to pay them a visit. Jim would have felt a little better if Jerome would have been around to give him a firm understanding of how far the authorities could legally go. But he was in Columbus defending a black man against a rape charge, and Jim had no idea when he would be back.

Another week went by quietly, and Jim began to hope that he was wrong. Then one evening after dinner, a knock at the front door put his senses on full alert. When he opened the door, there stood William and another man who Jim did not know.

"I'm sorry to bother you, Grandfather, may we come in?"

"Certainly, William, who is your friend?"

"Grandfather, this is Jake Sheppard. He works with us on the Sykes Plantation."

Jim shook hands with the man and said, "I'm glad to meet you, Jake. I eventually get around to meeting all of our partners; forgive me for not welcoming you sooner."

"I understand, sir," said Jake. "I can imagine you're a real busy man."

"Can we go to your office, Grandfather? I don't want to disturb Grandmother if possible."

"Actually she is over at your parents' house working on a patchwork quilt with your mother, but we can go to the office and talk."

The three men went back the hall and took seats in Jim's office. Jim couldn't help noticing how uneasy Jake and his grandson seemed to be.

"I should have stopped by Father's house and asked him to join us, but when I saw him today he wasn't feeling too well, and I didn't want to interrupt if he was lying down."

"It's all right, William. What's the trouble?"

"Well, Jake here is the single white man I told you about who shares a cabin with our other single man, Sim Jessup, who is black."

"Yes, I remember you mentioned that," said Jim.

"Well . . . I think I'd better let Jake explain the situation."

"Very well. Jake?"

"Yes sir, well, the thing is, sir, uh, Sim and I never laid eyes on one another before we came to work on your plantation. But I'm a pretty easygoing fellow, and so is he, and in the last few months, he and I have become pretty good friends."

"I'm real glad to hear that, Jake. I hope by now you are learning that one of our missions here at Langdon Plantation is to break down racial barriers."

"Yes, sir, I can appreciate that and that's why I'm kind of on edge. Sim is a friend of mine, and I don't want to see him in trouble."

"Has Sim got trouble, Jake?"

Jake let out a long expressive breath and said, "Yes, sir, I'm afraid he does."

"Tell me what it is," said Jim.

"Nobody seems to be talking about anything else except the raid on Atlanta by those black men a couple weeks ago. Sim was one of them."

"Oh my, Jake, are you sure?"

"Yes, sir, I am. He told me himself."

"How did he get involved in it?" Jim asked.

"The leader of the group is a man by the name of Cordell Jackson. Cordell is Sim's cousin. Cordell's father was a conductor on the Southern Pacific Railroad; he lived in Atlanta. He was killed a few months ago by two members of the Ku Klux Klan. The day after his death, a white man named Spencer Doaks had the job. At first, Sim was easily persuaded to join the gang because he was mournful of his uncle's death. Cordell told him that no one would be harmed. Sim was horrified when his cousin and another man Sim didn't know grabbed that man off the street and hanged him. Now Sim is scared to death; he knows that Cordell lied to him about the purpose of the raid."

"What does Sim intend to do now?"

"I'm sure he doesn't know what to do, Mr. Langdon. I guess he's just hoping that the whole thing will blow over, but if he's questioned by the police, he'll break down for sure."

"If he is caught it will go very hard on him. But if he went to the authorities and told them his side of things, he could end up lynched," said Jim.

"I don't believe he would ever go to the police, Mr. Langdon. He's mighty scared of what might happen to him, but I don't think he would ever give up his cousin even if Cordell did lie to him about not hurting anyone. I'm scared too; scared for Sim. It wasn't easy to come to you with this, but I was sure hoping you might be able to help somehow."

Jim looked at William and said, "Telephone service in this area is poor. We have to get a telegram to Jerome in Atlanta right away. If anyone would know the best way to handle this, it would be him."

"I'll go into Macon the first thing in the morning," said William. "I'll send word to Jerome and then wait in Macon until I get an answer."

"Very well. Jake, just try to stay calm and don't say anything to Sim. I don't want him to lose his head and do something to make matters worse. As soon as I talk to Jerome, we'll see what can be done."

"What if the police show up before Jerome can get here?" said Jake.

"We can only hope that they don't," Jim replied. "William and I will do everything we can, but we won't lie to the authorities. We can't criticize those who abuse justice if we do the same thing ourselves."

"I understand," said Jake.

The following day, John came to the house to see Jim. Jim told his son about Jake's story.

"It's a sorry situation," said John. "I don't understand how racial violence from either side can go on and on while the lawmaking arm of this country doesn't lift a finger to put a stop to it. The justice system is so unbalanced that it is in jeopardy of keeling over. I feel like we go on fooling ourselves into believing that we can make a difference when time and time again, we wind up watching the whole thing slip farther over the edge."

"I can't argue with you, John, except to say that nothing on earth is more perfectly stubborn than the human race. I suppose that we are proving to be human too. As stubborn as the people behind the violence can be, we are no less stubborn, going on for as long as it takes to see things change. If we have to be fools, at least let it be for a good cause."

"Somehow, Father, you always manage to say something that makes sense. I don't know how you do it, but you do."

"I learned from a good man," said Jim.

"As have I," said John with a smile.

Shortly after one o'clock in the afternoon, William hurried into the house with Jake Sheppard right behind him. "Father! Grandfather!" he shouted. Jim and John got up quickly and met the two men coming down the hall.

Before they could ask what the trouble was, Jake began to talk so fast he was soon out of breath. "William got an answer from Jerome. He won't be back for two more days, but everything has gone to pieces and Sim is in jail in Macon because—"

"Jake, you have to calm down now," John told him. "Calm down and catch your breath. Everyone come out to the parlor and sit down."

The four of them went to the parlor; Elizabeth came rushing in to see what had happened.

"Please, Elizabeth, could we have some glasses and a pitcher of water?" said Jim.

"Right away," she answered.

When the water came, John poured a glass for Jake and then offered a glass to his father and to William. Elizabeth sat down with the men, and when a sense of calm had been restored, Jake gave them the news.

"Jerome will be back in two days, but Sim and his cousin, Cordell, are in jail in Macon. They will be moved to Atlanta tomorrow morning."

"How did this happen?" Jim asked.

"Cordell led another raid on Atlanta last night," said Jake. "Last evening after dinner, Cordell came over to see Sim. I could hear them talking out behind the cabin. He wanted Sim to go along, but Sim said he wanted no part of killing and refused. Cordell was angry; he cursed Sim and accused him of being a coward. Cordell told him his father had to be avenged, and he wasn't satisfied by what happened on the last raid. Sim said he was real sorry about his uncle being killed, but killing more white people would only make things worse for other black men. Cordell finally left; he was real angry and told Sim they weren't kin anymore."

"I'm glad he stood up to his cousin. It was the right thing to do. How then did they both end up in jail?" said Jim.

"Well," Jake continued, "Cordell and the others rode to Atlanta last night and started shooting up the city as before. It wasn't too smart, going back to Atlanta, because this time the citizens were more prepared. Since the gang had not been caught, they figured the same thing could happen again. The riders had no sooner entered the city limits when white men with guns started coming out from everywhere. Finding themselves in a crossfire, they turned around and tried to get back out, but all of them were shot down except Cordell. He was hit in the shoulder but managed to stay in the saddle and escape. A posse of police and citizens searched most of the night and finally found Cordell in a barn on a deserted farm about ten miles from Macon. They wanted him alive because they are hell bent on hanging him. So they brought him into town, had a doctor patch him up, and then put him in jail for the night."

"What led to Sim's arrest?"

"Sorry to say, when the police asked Cordell who the eighth man was who raided Atlanta the first time, Cordell gave them Sim's name and told them where to find him. They picked him up this morning about eleven o'clock. That's how come I know what happened. One of the officers told me the whole story. I waited for William to get back, then we came here."

"I'd say that Cordell is a poor excuse for a cousin," said John. "Sim would have had to turn himself in to get straightened out, but it will go harder on him now. If only he had that chance back again."

"Is there anything we can do?" Jake asked.

"Not much until Jerome gets home," said Jim. "Jerome will handle Sim's defense, of course. In the meantime, we could all go into Macon to see him. I think he might feel a little better if he knows that we'll be with him in Atlanta."

"That will do him a lot of good," said Jake.

"Elizabeth, would you please fix a little food for us to take along? I'm sure he could use something better to eat than what he'll get in that jail."

"I would be glad to. Should I pack enough for his cousin?"

Reluctantly, Jim answered, "Yes please."

If the four of them were unhappy with the way Cordell threw Sim to the wolves, they were doubly disappointed when they came face to face with Cordell himself. When they had been admitted to the cellblock and told Sim they would be at his trial with a good lawyer, Cordell, who was in the adjacent cell, cursed his cousin and told him he was nothing but an Uncle Tom. When Jake took food from a basket and passed it into Sim, Cordell called him the white

man's dog. Even when Jim promised Cordell the same legal
assistance and tried to hand him the rest of the food they'd
brought, the infuriated man spit at him.

Outside once again after the visit, John said, "You
know, if Cordell is determined to take Sim down with him, I
don't think anybody can help."

"I'm afraid you are absolutely correct," Jim agreed.

The trial began on September 10, and it was clear
almost from the start that Jerome had very little to use in
the defense of his clients. It was a preordained conclusion
inside the courtroom that the defendants were guilty and
the trial itself a mere formality. Jerome argued that there
was no way either Cordell or Sim could have been
positively identified as the men who lynched Harmon
Russell on the night of the first raid.

First of all, and in spite of the street lamp, it was
nighttime, and secondly, all of the raiders were wearing
hoods. But the two citizens who cut the dead man down
that night both swore an oath that they recognized Cordell
and Sim as the men who had done the deed.

Next, Jerome called Jake Sheppard to the stand so
that he could testify to his conversation with Sim and to
what he'd overheard when Cordell came by on the day of
the second raid. Although his testimony technically proved
that Sim was innocent, of murder at least, the prosecution
called it hearsay, and the judge agreed.

On the morning of the third and final day of the trial,
Jerome told Jim that there was nothing more he could do.
"It is difficult enough to defend a black man who is
innocent," said Jerome. "But Cordell was caught in the act
during the second raid, and even if there is no real proof
that he put the rope around Harmon Russell's neck, you
could erase the testimony of those two perjured witnesses,
and still no white jury on earth is going to find those boys
not guilty. On the other hand, we *do* know that Sim was
not the second man who committed the murder. But the
conscience of that jury would have no problem sleeping at
night if they hanged him for it anyway."

"Are you saying that Sim is going to hang for
something he didn't do?" Jim asked.

"I'm saying that his only chance is if Cordell could be persuaded to tell the court that Sim was not the other man who performed that lynching."

The judge had called a recess until one o'clock, at which time he would have the verdict read and then pass the sentence. Jim asked Jerome to use the last opportunity to plead with Cordell to save his cousin. When the court reconvened, Jim, John, William, and Jake took their seats. Jim watched for Jerome to re-enter the courtroom; he looked up to get a sign from the lawyer's expression, but all Jerome could do was shake his head.

No one was surprised when the foreman of the jury read the verdict: guilty of first degree murder. A murmur of satisfaction circulated through the crowd of on lookers.

Cordell was told to stand, and then he was asked if he had anything to say before his sentence was passed. But before he could speak, Jerome stood up, put his hand on Cordell's shoulder, and whispered something in his ear.

Cordell looked at Sim, then back at the judge, and said, "He didn't have nothing to do with it."

Audible under tones of displeasure filled the courtroom until the judge was forced to bang his gavel loudly on the desk. "I'll have quiet in this court," said the judge. "Would you repeat your last statement, Jackson?"

"I said my cousin didn't have nothing to do with the hanging. It was me and another man named Charlie Stewart."

"Why would you wait until now to tell the court your cousin is innocent of murder?" asked the judge.

"I guess I was angry at him before. I thought he was on my side, willing to help me punish the whites for killing my old man. But when I wanted to go back to Atlanta, he wouldn't go along."

"Why wouldn't he go?" asked the judge.

"Because he didn't want to be part of no killing. I lied to him about that when we went to Atlanta the first time. I wanted to see a white man die for no good reason, same as my old man died for no good reason. Now I see there's no good reason for my cousin to die."

Jerome stood up and said, "Your Honor, may I approach the bench please?"

"Granted. The prosecutor may approach as well."

There was a brief, whispered conference among the three men, and when it was over the judge called for a thirty minute recess. The spectators filed out of the courtroom, milling around outside, anxious to find out what would happen next. The Langdons were no less uneasy, nor was Jake Sheppard.

"I wonder what Jerome said to Cordell to make him change his mind," said Jim.

"I don't know, but the important thing is that it worked," John replied. "But I wonder if it will change anything since the jury has already found Sim guilty of murder."

"It has to," said Jake. "It just has to."

When the court was called to order at the end of the recess, Cordell was told to stand as before, and as before, he was asked if he had anything further to say.

This time Cordell just shook his head and remained silent. When the judge sentenced him to hang for the crime of murder, the crowd quietly expressed their approval. Cordell was told to take his seat. Then it was Sim's turn to stand and receive his punishment.

"Have you anything to say before sentence is passed?" asked the judge.

"Yes sir, I would like to say that I have respect for the law even though the law has no respect for me or my kind. If it did, we wouldn't be here today."

"Well that is something we will never know for sure," said the judge. "In any case, in view of your cousin's timely confession and the fact that the prosecution's key witnesses now say you may not have been involved in the hanging of the deceased, Mr. Harmon Russell, I hereby sentence you to serve five years in the state prison at hard labor. Court is adjourned."

Cordell and Sim were immediately led out of the courtroom; the crowd withdrew, moderately satisfied. Many remarks were made in reference to the proceedings; none of them were kind.

"Well, at least one of them is as good as dead and the other one will wish *he* was," Jim heard one man say.

Jim kept his seat along with his son, grandson, and Sim's friend, Jake, to wait for Jerome. When he appeared, the four men rose to speak with him.

"I wish I could have saved Cordell's life," said Jerome, "but no twelve white men in Atlanta would have stood for that. Sim is in for a mighty rough time, but at least he is young enough to endure the punishment and will still be a young man when he is released."

"I think you did fine," said Jim. "It is a sad day when a life is taken due to the taking of a life; no one wins. Violence breeds violence, and unless people decide to make a priority of living in peace with everyone regardless of color, the killing will go on. We must live together, black and white."

"I hope I live to see that day," Jerome replied. "I am going to get my things; I am anxious to get home and see Esther."

"Just one more thing, Jerome. What did you whisper to Cordell before he exonerated Sim?"

"Please don't mention that I told you because, technically, that was lawyer to client and cannot be divulged. I told him if he didn't try to save his cousin then he was no different than the men who killed his father."

"Your secret is safe with us," Jim replied. "Please tell Sim that his job will be waiting for him when he is released."

EIGHT

A New Deal

Although President Hoover's efforts to ease the suffering brought on by the Depression had come to almost nothing, Jim noted that even though African Americans fared even worse, they still rallied to the slogan, "Who but Hoover," in the 1932 presidential race.

However, Jim took it upon himself to speak to all of the black men working on Langdon Plantation, explaining to them why he thought they should vote for Franklin Roosevelt. Although it was not necessary, he made it clear to all of them that how they voted was entirely their own choice. He only advised them that a change from Herbert Hoover seemed logical, and that he intended to support Roosevelt in the upcoming election.

Of course, when all was said and done, he was forced to admit to himself that his speech was a futile gesture because he knew that very few African Americans in the Jim Crow South managed to exercise their right to vote. He simply felt compelled to do or say anything possible to make them feel equal.

Jim remembered the time when his father ran for mayor of Macon. All of the black men from the plantation went to town to cast their vote in support of him. But a group of armed white men refused to let them near the polls. Jim's father had to hurry into town and intervene before any of his friends were injured. The confrontation ended peacefully, but not a single black man voted that day.

Jim was prepared to go against his political affiliation, which was Republican, if he truly believed the Democrats had a better man. In this case, he felt that Hoover was too slow to act in a crisis of great magnitude: an economic downturn that threatened the entire country. But most of his black partners on the plantation believed that the Republican Party was the party of emancipation, partly because the Democratic candidate, Franklin Roosevelt, had embraced the segregationist policies of the Democratic Party.

In any case, Franklin Delano Roosevelt unseated President Hoover and was sworn into office on March 4, 1933. For weeks after the new president's inaugural address, the whole country kept close company with their local papers to see just what the new man had in mind. Every evening, Jim and Elizabeth would go to the parlor and take turns reading to the other any pertinent articles about the Depression.

"I will certainly give the president credit for one thing," said Jim one evening. "He definitely came to work prepared. The day after he was sworn in he declared a four day holiday for the banks in order to stop people from withdrawing their money from those institutions that were already on thin ice."

"Yes," said Elizabeth. "And just four days after that, Congress passed the Banking Act, which closed the banks that were insolvent and reorganized the rest. They say the bank runs are over."

"It was a very wise move," Jim replied. "The Banking Act also established the Federal Deposit Insurance Corporation, which allows the Federal Reserve to guarantee the bank's assets. There is no better way to put people at ease about their money."

"Surely Mr. Roosevelt is heading in the right direction, Jim."

"I just hope he has the good of all Americans in mind."

"Well, for now I'd like to concentrate on something a whole lot more pleasant," said Elizabeth. "Our grandson is finally going to introduce us to his lady friend this weekend."

"That's right, Miss Joanna Sommers from Maryland will be coming for a visit. I am very happy to see him working on that aspect of his life. John and Abbey are happy too. William is a good boy; he works hard, and he needs a good woman such as John and I have."

"I thank you for that, my dear husband. Abbey and I are just as fortunate."

When the weekend came the Langdons had a fine family get together to welcome Joanna. Even Jerome and Esther came down for the occasion. Esther was pregnant with their first child, which was a subject sure to add much conversation to the gathering.

Joanna was a lovely girl with dark brown hair and a smile like sunshine after a storm. She was friendly, cheerful, and very easy to get acquainted with. In no time at all, everyone was laughing and talking as if she were already part of the family. Elizabeth and Abbey set out a delectable dinner of roast beef, potatoes, yams, peas, carrots, and freshly baked bread. Joanna insisted on helping with the dishes, as did Esther, and in no time the task was complete.

As usual, the ladies eventually went off to talk about flowers, fashions, and furniture while the men made themselves comfortable at a huge picnic table under an immense maple tree.

"I'm sure you know that the price of cotton has dropped to less than six cents a pound," said John. "I don't honestly see how it could go down any further. I know that President Roosevelt has begun to pay planters to decrease production to create a shortage and drive the price up, but it will take time to feel the effects of the program."

"You're right, of course," said Jim. "However, I still think that we can outlast the hardest hit of the Depression because of our new land acquisition coupled with the fact that we have two years before our first payment is due."

"I hope it works out that way," John replied. "As long as there are no additional setbacks, we might be all right."

"We'll keep praying and then praying harder if we have to, not just for ourselves but for everyone living with the punishment of these trying times."

"I can't help wondering what my people have to look forward to," said Jerome. "I know that hopes are high with a new president in the White House; change usually spawns new expectations, but they are not always met."

"I can't blame you for being concerned, Jerome," said Jim. "We all worry about the same thing. To this point, there has been little or nothing to support the hopes of African Americans, and it hurts very deeply to admit that it is due to racial discrimination. Most of the jobs that black men hold are very sensitive to economic cycles. They are becoming unemployed in disproportionate numbers because any available openings are reserved for whites. It is the racist attitude that blacks should not be employed while white men are out of work. It is this attitude that is taking jobs that blacks have traditionally held, such as porters, trash collectors, and elevator operators."

"In addition to that, black wages are thirty percent lower than white wages," said William.

"As I participate in this conversation," said Jerome, "I would like to take the opportunity once again to say that I feel very fortunate to have made the acquaintance of the Langdon family. I know that you do everything you can for the black men who work on your plantation and for their families. I see it with my own eyes. You treat them fairly, and you do it because you care about them as people as much as you care for your own. That kind of humanity is exceedingly rare in this country, and it is deserving of recognition."

"We are more than compensated through their friendship, and yours, Jerome," said Jim.

The day had been a very pleasant one; a chance, for a while, to ease the burden brought on by the Depression. Joanna would be staying with John and Abbey for a few days before returning to Maryland, but the consensus seemed to be that the family would be seeing a great deal more of her in the future.

As evening set in, Jim and Elizabeth settled into the parlor and tuned into the radio. It was March 12, and something unprecedented was about to happen; for the first time in history, the president of the United States would be addressing the nation by radio. Roosevelt called it the "Fireside Chat," a new and inspirational way for the American people to get up close and personal with the man who was counted upon to lead them through the dark days of the Great Depression.

Suddenly, President Roosevelt's voice was heard to say, "My friends, I want to talk to you for a few minutes about banking." Then he went on to explain the way the banking system works and why so many of the banks in the country had failed. He explained the reason for the banking holiday and informed his audience as to when the banks would begin to reopen. His speech lasted for a little over thirteen minutes and was delivered in a context that was simple to understand.

"What a remarkable age we live in," said Jim when the program was over. "To be able to sit in our parlor and listen to the president speak to us from the White House in Washington DC is a miracle."

Like most people, Jim and Elizabeth were as pleased as they were impressed with the new president's efforts. They noted that during the first hundred days of his administration, major legislation was initiated as well as a multitude of executive orders, which instituted the New Deal: a plethora of programs to bring relief, recovery, and reform. These initiatives established government jobs for the unemployed, stimulated economic growth, and improved regulation of Wall Street, banks, and transportation.

Unfortunately, it was not long before John and William began to overwhelm Jim with a lot of negative feedback from the black workers who associated with black men working on nearby plantations. "It is sadly apparent that President Roosevelt's segregationist attitude has not changed much since his inauguration," John told him. "Not only does he oppose important civil rights legislation such as anti-lynching laws, but he also does not concern himself with the most obvious exhibitions of racial injustice."

"In addition," said William, "none of the New Deal agencies such as the Civilian Conservation Corp and the Federal Emergency Relief Administration protect blacks against agency officials, discriminating employers, or local whites. In some cases, disastrous consequences have further affected the blacks as a result of some New Deal policies.

"The crop subsidy program established by the Agriculture Assistance Agency has led to the supplanting of thousands of black sharecroppers because they do not receive any part of the federal funds that white planters receive for decreasing their crop production. Many blacks are calling Roosevelt's New Deal a raw deal. Worst of all, racial violence has escalated, and lynchings, which declined to eight last year, have risen to twenty-eight this year."

"I know that black families continue to move out of the South to cities in the North and West," said Jim. "Progress in agriculture, specifically mechanization, is a good thing, but machines take away work that was once done by hand. The black citizens were the first to feel the sting of the Depression, and the way things look, they will be the last to recover from it. I go to bed every night wondering what will happen next."

In the beginning of 1934, most of the American population prayed harder than usual for better times to come. For five years, many people both black and white had endured the hardships of economic attrition to the point of desperation. The cities had their soup kitchens and bread lines; in Chicago, for example, the poor were fed by none other than Al Capone, the notorious gangster. But the rural areas in any state found it much harder to feed their inhabitants.

Small farms shared what vegetables, homemade bread, and meat they could, but even with everything they had it was still difficult to put food on the table. Those not fortunate enough to live on a farm depended on hunting wild game to survive.

However, for Jim and his family, a happy occasion brought a chance to celebrate when in early February, William married his fiancée, Joanna Sommers. Even William's sister, Julia, who had moved to England two years earlier, came all the way back to Georgia for the wedding. But while the joyful couple were on their honeymoon on the beaches of the Florida coast, Jim received word that Aunt Kate had passed away in Columbus.

It was a difficult decision to be sure, but he could not bring himself to interrupt the newlyweds, and so along with Elizabeth, John, and Abbey, Jim left for Columbus after leaving word for William with Henry Monroe.

To add to Jim's sorrow, Uncle Bradford had arranged for Aunt Kate to be buried in his family's cemetery in Columbus. She would be the only member of the Langdon family that would not rest on Langdon Plantation. It was the right thing, and Jim knew it; still, he would always feel a deeper sense of loss not having her next to the rest of the family.

The funeral was a very extravagant affair; Bradford could afford the best of everything and spared no expense in giving his wife everything he could, one last time. Jim, Elizabeth, John, and Abbey spent four days in Columbus, after which time they departed from the grieving widower and headed home. Jim knew that William and Joanna would be about a day ahead of them, and he was anxious to get back and tell them what a nice service it had been.

It was early afternoon when they reached home; Jim dropped John and Abbey at their house and then parked the automobile in his driveway.

"I'll help you get the bags into the house, and then I'm going up the road to see William," he told Elizabeth.

"Would you like me to go along with you?" she asked.

"You must be tired from the trip, dear. I won't be gone too long."

With their hands full, they climbed the steps to the veranda; Elizabeth waited while Jim unlocked the front door. Suddenly he stopped, turned his head to the side, and listened very intently.

"Do you hear that, Elizabeth?"

She listened for a moment and then said, "I don't hear anything, Jim."

"I don't either . . . that is the problem. I don't hear a thing except for an eerie silence. It's as if there is absolutely no one around."

"Now that you mention it, I do sense that something is not quite right," said Elizabeth.

Jim dropped his load on the veranda and said, "Wait here for a minute," then he disappeared into the house. After about five minutes he reappeared and said, "I see nothing amiss in the house. The back door is locked, and nothing has been disturbed. Go on in, Elizabeth; I'm going out back to see who is around at the sharecroppers' quarters."

Jim hurried around the house to the large dormitories and started knocking on doors but could not get anyone to answer his calls. Finally one of the doors opened and an elderly black lady named Mathilda Owens stuck her head out and looked around as if she were expecting to see someone or something she did not wish to see.

"I'm glad it's you, Mr. Langdon," she said in a relieved tone of voice.

"Where are all the women and children, Mathilda?" Jim asked.

"Everyone except for the smallest children are up at the old Sykes place," she said. "And some of them are down the road where the other workers live. The children are here with me."

"Why are the women and the rest of the children away?"

"They had some bad trouble up there last night, Mr. Langdon; up there and down the road. The women and older children are helping to clean up the mess."

"Thank you, Mathilda," said Jim as he turned and ran back to the house.

"Elizabeth!" he shouted as he went through the front door. When his wife appeared he said, "Elizabeth, I have to go see William immediately. Something has happened, and I must find out exactly what it is."

"Oh dear, should I go with you?"

"Yes, but only to John's house. You can stay there with Abbey, and I'll take John with me—hurry now."

Hastily they got back into the automobile and drove back to John and Abbey's house. When they got there, Jim waited while Elizabeth went in to get John. In no time, John came running from the house and got into the automobile beside his father.

"What happened?" he asked with worry covering his face.

"I don't know, son, but Mathilda Owens said there was some bad trouble last night. We have to get up to William's house right away."

The two of them sped off as fast as the Model T would go, up the hill and back the lane that led to the house to look for William. Neither of them was prepared for what they saw when they reached the top of the hill.

The first glance revealed the remnants of the big barn, which was still smoldering, as were several of the smaller buildings. The house appeared to be without damage, but all types of debris was scattered through the yard. The two men got out of the Model T and started walking toward the cabins where the sharecroppers lived. In the distance they could see more smoke rising from some of the cabins and a large number of men and women, both black and white, doing what they were able to restore order and salvage anything they could.

When Jim and John reached the site of the first cabin they found William talking with Henry Monroe and Seth Morgan. As soon as William saw his father he excused himself from the conversation with the two foremen and said, "I am so sorry that I was not here last night."

"I'm glad that you weren't," said Jim. "You were exactly where you were supposed to be; with your wife on your honeymoon."

"I just feel responsible somehow," William replied.

"You know that isn't true," said John. "Those responsible are off somewhere, patting themselves on the back for a job well done. Tell us what you know, son."

"I think I'd rather that you hear it from the men who were here. Henry, Seth," he called to the two men who were left in charge. Henry and Seth joined the conversation and explained what had happened the night before.

"Just after dark last night I heard the sound of a number of automobiles coming toward the house," said Henry. "I started walking down to Seth's cabin, but he met me in between. Others were coming outside when they heard the noise, and we all just kind of stood around wondering who could be coming up the road."

"Pretty soon we could see headlights coming over the hill," said Seth. "Then, faster than we could imagine, there were a whole lot of automobiles and trucks in a double row coming toward us, their headlights near blinding us. Some of the people began to panic, especially women and children, and they ran out into the fields to get away."

"Then," said Henry, "all these men, all white from what we could see, were climbing out of their vehicles, lighting torches, and walking right toward us; there must have been a hundred or more. The rest of us stood our ground; we didn't know what else to do or what they had in mind to do to us. The other thing was that they were all wearing hoods and something like a cape that covered them from the neck to below the waist."

"Klan?" Jim asked.

"Maybe yes, maybe no," said Seth. "It wasn't the robes and pointed hoods like the Klan wears; just some kind of hoods made of cloth to cover their faces and those capes. They certainly meant to disguise their identities. If they weren't Klan, I'm sure that they were certainly Klan sympathizers."

"What happened next?" John asked.

"Well," said Henry, "I guess it was the leader of the gang, a real big man who talked in a rough voice—I think because he was trying to disguise it—walked up close to me and Seth. He said that we were probably too ignorant to know it, but it was against the law for niggers to take jobs that white men needed and that all white men had to go back to work before niggers were allowed to work. He said that if we all packed up and cleared out nothing bad would happen, and if we didn't then we were in for trouble."

"I'm sure I don't have to tell you that he was using a lie to intimidate you, and a very poorly concocted lie at that," said Jim.

"Yes sir," Seth replied. "And Henry told them as much. He told that big man that we knew there was no such law, that we worked here as partners of the Langdon family, and black men worked right alongside white men here. Everything Henry said just made him real mad, and he told us that if the white trash working on the plantation had no better sense than to consort with niggers then they would have to go too. Then Henry told him that he had no right to drive us away from our home and that other men couldn't just walk up and take our jobs."

"What was his reply to that?" asked Jim.

113

"He said if all your help to work this plantation up and left, you wouldn't have any choice except to hire others, and that way respectable, needy white men could take these jobs," Seth replied. "That's when he told his gang that we were going to have to be forced to leave. Then those hooded devils started setting fire to the cabins, the barns, and the outbuildings. They burned everything except the house. We're just glad no one was hurt."

"I want you men to know that you did the right thing," said Jim. "The only way this could be worse is if people had gotten injured. There are other ways to handle something like this, and believe me, it *will* be handled. Henry, you and Seth oversee things here. Continue salvaging as much as you can. Please tell the others that we will pull together, as we always have. Somehow we will double up, make room, and provide shelter for everyone until we can rebuild their homes. John, William, let's get down the road and see how the others are doing."

Jim had just used every bit of self-control he had to assess the situation and remain calm while doing it. In the face of such adversity, which none of his people deserved and no one had the right to inflict, he had to accept the fact that it was an unfortunate sign of the times.

People were getting desperate, willing to do anything to survive. But to exercise those disdainful racist tactics—to walk over top of another race that needed the same vital necessities as themselves—was a bitter upshot in Jim's opinion. However, the perpetrators had made a grave mistake this time. They had set foot on private property in an attempt to force their will, and as he had told his people, it *would* be handled.

John and William headed for the auto at a brisk pace; Jim trailed some fifty yards behind them. As he walked along, ruminating on the possible ways of getting everyone situated temporarily, out of the corner of his eye something caught his attention. He walked a few feet to where a shiny object lay on the ground nearly covered by trampled grass. Jim bent over, picked up the object, used his shirt to wipe it clean, and then put it in his pocket.

When he reached the automobile he climbed into the front seat, and then John sped down the lane and out to the road. Down the road from Jim's house, the same kind of destruction awaited them. The story they heard was an exact account of what had happened at the old Sykes Plantation. Barns, outbuildings, and sharecropper homes were destroyed after an unheeded warning to clear out. The only difference: One of the foremen, a black man named Jonas Spotswood, was badly beaten when he tried to save his home from the torch.

The rest of the day and most of the evening were spent getting the dispossessed taken care of. The sharecroppers' dormitory and William's, John's, and Jim's houses were filled to capacity, as was the house where Jerome and Esther lived. At the end of a very exhausting day, Jim took his son and his grandson aside before parting for the night.

"First thing tomorrow morning we are going into Macon and confronting the sheriff about what happened here. I am going to apply such pressure—I intend to get results and I mean in a hurry."

"I admire your confidence," said John, "and I sure hope you're right, but how much help can we count on from the sheriff, and can we pressure him to act if we can't come up with some idea of who might have done this and some proof behind our allegations?"

Jim reached into his pocket and pulled out the shiny object he had found in the grass at the old Sykes Plantation. He held it out for William and John to see. After a long moment of silent scrutiny the three men looked at each other and simultaneously nodded in agreement.

NINE

Moving Slowly but Moving Forward

The next day, bright and early, Jim walked up the hill to have a talk with Jerome, who had recently gotten home after three weeks in Augusta defending two black men for stealing a hog from a local farmer. Jerome was sitting on the front porch with Esther when Jim arrived. Cradled in Esther's arms was their three-month-old daughter, Mattie.

"Good morning, Jerome, Esther. I'm glad to see you both relaxing for once. I'm sure it isn't easy with your house full of guests."

"We're glad to share," said Esther.

"We certainly are, Jim," Jerome agreed. "Am I right in assuming that you want to talk about what happened the other night?"

"You are indeed, my friend," Jim replied.

Esther got up from her chair and said, "Please excuse me, gentlemen, but it's time for Mattie's nap. Jim, please tell Elizabeth I will be down to see her later."

"I will tell her, Esther," he said.

When she had gone into the house, Jim went up on the porch, took her vacated chair, and then continued explaining the purpose for his visit.

"I intend to hold the sheriff's department accountable for the attack on the sharecroppers, assault on Jonas Spotswood, and compensation for everything that was destroyed."

Jerome moved forward in his chair and said, "You believe that the sheriff is responsible for what happened, Jim?"

"I won't say that he was involved in the attack personally, but I have reason to believe that he was behind it or at least had prior knowledge of it."

"I'm sure I don't have to tell you how serious your charges are," said Jerome. "I can only imagine that you have some pretty positive proof."

Jim reached into his pocket and produced the object he had discovered on the old Sykes Plantation. He handed it to Jerome and said, "What do you think of this?"

Jerome handled the shiny item for a moment and then handed it back to Jim.

"You have my undivided attention. What else do you intend to do?"

"John and I are going in to Macon to see the sheriff shortly. I am going to demand that his office take full responsibility for these crimes and guarantee full compensation or I will bring a lawsuit against the city of Macon."

"I support your ideas, Jim, but not at the risk of being a party to blackmail."

"I think you know me better than that, Jerome. Before I visit the sheriff I will pay a call on the mayor and show him that little piece of incriminating evidence that I showed you. But if the mayor reacts the way I expect him to, I won't even have to visit the sheriff."

"I apologize, Jim, I really didn't mean—"

"I know you didn't, Jerome, and I appreciate that you are only making sure that I haven't lost my senses in a moment of fury. I am hoping that after I visit the mayor he will be making haste to the sheriff's office to take his own bite out of the sheriff's backside. I will be more than happy to let them sweat out the details and then come to me to properly make amends. But if they challenge me and call my bluff, are you familiar with the procedure for a lawsuit?"

"Yes, I am. The process is easy, but getting a city to pay is another matter. First we get a claim form from the city clerk. The attorney for the city will review it and make a recommendation to the city council. Sometimes the recommendation will be to pay, but more often than not, the claim is denied. If that happens we have six months to file a small claims case. We must save a copy of the denial letter for the small claims court; they will want to see it. Then we call the governmental body in question and ask who should be served. Finally, we follow the local rules for service of the process; then comes litigation."

"Well, we won't wait six months," said Jim. "If they deny my claim we'll take them to court much faster than it took to create the havoc that occurred the other night. I have to go now. John will be coming over to pick me up."

The mayor of Macon was the Honorable Edwin F. Blane. Jim had never met the man, nor did he know much about him. By the same token, he was not familiar with Sheriff Frank Pell. But it didn't matter because the Langdon name was known by almost everyone—and disliked by many because of their history of sympathy for the black race. But Jim's family name also carried a reputation for honesty and perseverance, which preceded them wherever they went.

Upon arriving at City Hall, John stopped in front of the building, waited for his father to get out, and then parked the vehicle around back. When he caught up with Jim, a conversation was already in progress between his father and a distinguished looking gentleman in a black suit. Seeing John approaching, Jim turned and said, "John, I'd like to introduce you to Mr. Edwin F. Blane, the mayor of Macon. It seems I've crossed paths with the mayor on his way into work."

John shook hands with the mayor and then Mr. Blane turned his attention back to Jim. "Mr. Langdon, you were about to explain why you wanted to see me."

"I was, Mr. Mayor, but I would like to suggest that we take this meeting inside to your office."

"I don't mean to seem indifferent in any way, Mr. Langdon, but I do have a very busy schedule today."

"I understand perfectly, Mr. Mayor, but I am convinced that you will not want to discuss the reason for my visit in public."

The mayor did very little to hide his irritation but relented nevertheless, leading the way to his private office. He offered chairs to his persistent visitors; Jim and John sat down. Then he called his secretary and told her to rearrange his first appointment.

"Now then, Mr. Langdon, what will I find so interesting about your problem that I was forced to alter my schedule?"

"Just this, Mr. Mayor. You are probably not aware of it, but two days ago, while most of my family and I were away, a large group of men, more than one hundred, wearing disguises, attacked the people living on Langdon Plantation property; burned their homes and most of their possessions, not to mention a number of plantation outbuildings. In addition, one of my friends, Jonas Spotswood, was severely beaten when he tried to defend his home. Apparently it was their intent to drive my sharecroppers away in the hope of forcing me to hire local white men who are in need of jobs."

"Your workers are all black, aren't they?"

"About seventy-five percent of them. I understand that this depression we are mired in has put many people in desperate situations. I also understand that it is the general sentiment in this country, especially the South, that black men should not be employed if there are white men out of work."

"I would have to agree with you on that point, Mr. Langdon, unfortunate though it may be, and I empathize with you concerning the attack. But why are you here? You should be reporting all of this to the sheriff's department."

"You are right of course, Mr. Mayor, however, I have no confidence in a sheriff who may in fact have been one of the perpetrators of this act."

The mayor pushed back into his chair to emphasize the impact of Jim's remark, and his irritation escalated to full-blown anger.

"See here, Mr. Langdon! Up until now I have done you the courtesy of tempering my remarks concerning your family and everything generally known about their history in this region. But it has, for many years, been rather troubling to the natives of Macon and of Bibb County that the Langdons are colorblind in their loyalties—which should be to their own race."

"And it has been equally troubling to my family that the white southern population is sadly misguided in their loyalties to Almighty God," Jim replied in a disrespectful tone.

"Mr. Langdon, I am warning you, one more such remark and you won't have to visit the sheriff because I will see to it that he visits you."

Jim stood up, pulled something from his pocket, and dropped it on the mayor's desk, making sure that the impact would resonate loudly. The mayor picked up the shiny item and said, "This is a deputy sheriff's badge; where did you get it?"

"I picked it up yesterday from where it was dropped on my property during the attack," Jim replied.

Mayor Blane sat very quietly for a moment or two, and when he finally spoke, his tone had mellowed a great deal. "Who else has seen this, Mr. Langdon?"

"Just my son, my grandson, and . . . my attorney."

"I see. Am I to understand that you intend to sue for damages?"

"Isn't that what *you* would do, Mr. Mayor?"

Again, there was a period of silence from the other side of the desk. Then Mayor Blane said, "Isn't it possible that this badge could have found its way to your property in some other way?"

"I will respectfully allow you the opportunity to suggest how that might have happened," said Jim.

The mayor knew that Jim had made a very powerful point. He also knew that the sheriff's office, if not the city itself, was clearly on the hook to provide an explanation.

"I will ask you for some latitude in this matter, Mr. Langdon. I do not want this kind of trouble generated in my city. I would appreciate it if you would allow me to take this badge to the sheriff and see if I can get some answers. I will get to the bottom of this, and then I will contact you immediately afterward—you have my word."

"Very well, Mr. Mayor. I will agree to that, but I will expect to hear from you soon."

"Agreed. Will you be going right home?"

"Right after my son and I visit the *Macon Telegraph*."

The minute they left the mayor's office, the mayor did just as Jim had hoped he would. He left his office and hurried over to see the sheriff.

* * *

Sheriff Pell was sitting at his desk when the mayor, without hesitation, burst into his office. The mayor tossed a deputy badge onto the desk and said, "Do you want to tell me who this belongs to and explain why it is not pinned to his shirt?"

The sheriff picked up the badge and said, "Where did you get this, Mayor?"

"It was delivered to me this morning by none other than Jim Langdon. You know who he is, don't you?"

"I've never met him, but everyone for miles around knows of the Langdons. How did he get this badge?"

"He found it on his property the day after more than a hundred jackasses wearing hoods and capes stormed his plantation and burned a number of sharecropper homes and outbuildings."

"I hadn't heard anything about that," said the sheriff.

"Well you will tomorrow because Langdon is at the office of the *Macon Telegraph* right now. I want you to level with me, Frank. Do you know anything about this, and did you have anything to do with it?"

The mayor wasn't very happy when the sheriff hesitated for a moment before saying, "No, I don't know anything about it."

"I hope you're telling me the truth, Frank, and if you are, then I suggest you find out how many of your men might be involved, and find out quick. I may sympathize with most of the people around here who believe that these damn blacks are second class citizens, and I agree that they should not vote or do anything else except fend for themselves and take up space. But I'll be damned if I will sanction this kind of conduct or defend anyone who takes it upon themselves to perpetrate it."

"What makes you think Langdon can prove his case, Mr. Mayor?"

"This goddamn badge is what makes me think he can prove it! That is unless you can come up with another believable way it could have gotten there. Can you do that?"

"No, I can't," the sheriff admitted. "But what can Langdon do to us? We are the law, aren't we?"

"What can he do? You damn fool! He's threatening to hold the sheriff's department responsible for the damage and sue the city if he isn't compensated. If just one of your men was involved, the city of Macon can be held liable for any injuries or damage. I'm telling you, Frank, find out who was involved in this, and let me know immediately. I have to start somewhere to mollify Jim Langdon, and soon. I have to make him see that the city is cooperating. Of all the places to stir up trouble, those idiots couldn't have picked a worse place than Langdon Plantation. Why would they do that?"

"If I were to guess, Mayor, I would say that most people know that Langdon treats his workers pretty good. I mean, they get good wages besides a share of the crop. A lot of white men are resentful especially because most of his workers are black."

"Yes, so he told me. It makes no difference. This is big trouble."

"But we have the badge back don't we, Mayor? Isn't it his word against ours that he gave you this badge?"

The mayor looked at the sheriff in disbelief. "And just what do you suggest that *I* do as the mayor of this city? Lie under oath when Langdon's lawyer gets me on the witness stand and asks me if Jim Langdon gave me the deputy badge he found on his property? Jim Langdon isn't stupid. Why do you think he brought that badge to *me*? He did it because he knows that I will make his case if he decides to sue. And who knows how many other people he has shown it to."

"It's hard to believe that so much trouble could come from harassing a bunch of nigger sharecroppers, but I guess you're right, Mayor."

"You're damn right I'm right, and by the way, some of those sharecroppers are white, and in case you missed it the first time, it took place on the property of a white man. You get me some answers quick, because if this department has caused the city to be held liable for God knows how many taxpayer dollars, there will be a house cleaning, and you know what I mean."

The mayor stormed out of the office, leaving the sheriff alone to contemplate his future. Sheriff Pell had not actually lied to the mayor, but he had not been altogether truthful either. It was true that the attack on Langdon

Plantation was news to him, but he *did* know who the badge belonged to.

Burly Peters was one of Pell's deputies, a man given the nickname "Burly" because of his large build. Burly had come into work the day before without his badge, and when the sheriff asked him about it he said it was at home; he had forgotten to pin it to the clean shirt he was wearing. Then the sheriff remembered that the badge was still missing when he saw the deputy that morning.

Peters was a useful man because of his size; resistant miscreants were usually helpless against him. But when it came to intelligence or common sense, the deputy left a lot to be desired. It was also true that compassion for the southern way of life was still widely expressed by southern people, including support for organizations such as the Ku Klux Klan, who claimed it was their dutiful intent to preserve it. However, when it came down to white race versus black, Peters was a fanatic.

* * *

The following day, the story of the attack broke in the *Macon Telegraph*. Jim was pleased with the story, especially the mention of the deputy sheriff's badge that was found after the attack. Also, he did not mind that the story alluded to the Depression and the serious effects it was having on people. Jim agreed that in the interest of survival, some people were coerced into doing things that they would not normally do; their actions did not necessarily make them bad people. But he also knew that such a defense would not hold up in court. Of course, there were always those opportunists who would take advantage of any chance to indulge their evil side and justify it by the circumstances. In any event, Jim was confident that it would not require legal channels to settle the matter.

Almost a week passed before Jim heard from Mayor Blane. It was by mail; a request: a date and time to meet in the mayor's office. Jim arrived at City Hall at ten thirty a.m. for an eleven o'clock meeting. Upon entering the

123

building he approached the receptionist and told her he was there for a conference with the mayor.

"You may take a seat until the mayor returns, Mr. Langdon. Mayor Blane was here, but he received a call from the sheriff and then had to go over to his office."

"Thank you, ma'am. I'll take a seat."

Jim was not a clock-watcher by nature, but he was very anxious to find out what the mayor had learned. He was hoping that the situation could be handled without a lot of complications. Jim was more than prepared to carry out his threat and sue the city if necessary, but that would create a huge time delay, and his people needed compensation so that they could rebuild their homes.

At five minutes to eleven, Jim started shifting around in his seat; by ten after eleven he started pacing the floor. Suddenly he heard a commotion just outside; it sounded like a group of very excited people shouting all at once. The door opened, and a deputy sheriff rushed in. He took a quick look around the room, and when he spotted Jim he ran up to him and said, "Are you Jim Langdon?"

"That's right," Jim replied. "What's the trouble, Deputy?"

"I'm Deputy Sheriff Paul Schofield. I need you to come over to the sheriff's office with me right now. Burly Peters has barricaded himself inside the cellblock, and he has the sheriff and the mayor in there with him. He ran the rest of us out at gunpoint. He's threatening to shoot the sheriff and the mayor unless they get you to come over."

Jim was completely overwhelmed, to say the least. At first he didn't know how to respond. He had every reason to believe that those responsible for the attack should be punished and that he should receive compensation for all damages. But he had no idea that the situation would put anyone's life in jeopardy. All Jim could think to say was, "How did this get started, Deputy?"

"Well, I don't have all day, Mr. Langdon, but Burly Peters is another one of the sheriff's deputies. He led the attack on your sharecroppers. The sheriff fired Burly and told him he was responsible for the damage. Burly couldn't believe that the sheriff wouldn't take his side in the matter. Sheriff Pell refused; Burly lost his temper and threatened him with his revolver. Then he forced the sheriff to call the mayor and get him over to the office. Now he's demanding to see you. We tried everything we could think of to reason with him, but he's too far out of his head to reason with. I know Burly pretty well, Mr. Langdon, and I have to tell you that if you go over there I think he'll end up shooting all three of you. I can't force you to go, but if you don't, the sheriff and the mayor are dead for sure."

Without any time to think it over, Jim felt himself letting go of his whole life. He couldn't refuse to make an attempt to get the sheriff and the mayor released, and yet he may end up getting shot without saving anyone. Still, it did not seem to him that he had a choice.

"Let's go, Deputy."

The two of them ran out to the deputy's vehicle, climbed in, and then raced at high speed toward the sheriff's office to the piercing tune of the siren. A crowd of maybe three hundred people were gathered in front of the building. When the deputy skidded the auto to a stop the crowd parted in the middle to open a path to the front door. Someone inside opened the door; Jim followed the deputy through it. Five other deputies were waiting in the outer office, staring toward a heavy wooden door at the end of a hallway.

"The cellblock is through that door, Mr. Langdon. If Burly tries to let you in, don't be in a hurry to go. It makes no sense to send you in there until we believe he is willing to be reasonable. I don't think he has a grudge against anyone else, so as long as you're here we have a bargaining position. If all else fails we may just have to force our way through the barricade, storm the cellblock, and hope for the best. We'll wait and see if you can think of something that we couldn't. Somehow we have to subdue Burly without him hurting anyone. Stand off to the side a bit. I can't guarantee that door will stop a bullet."

Jim said a quick prayer and then walked slowly toward the only thing standing between himself and a madman with a gun. When he got close to the door he could hear the sheriff and the mayor pleading with Peters to give himself up. It was difficult for Jim to listen to two men begging for their lives.

125

"Burly Peters . . . Burly Peters, this is Jim Langdon. I believe you wanted to see me."

"You're damn right I do. I wanna square accounts with everybody who is responsible for me losing my job, but maybe if you wanna see the mayor and the sheriff spared, I'll trade them for you."

"How do you square accounts with yourself, Burly?"

"What the hell are you talking about?"

"You got fired for attacking sharecroppers and burning homes and buildings on private property. As a deputy sheriff, you know that's against the law. Doesn't that mean you caused yourself to get fired?"

"All I did was to put a bunch of niggers in their place—behind white men. Niggers don't have rights, and neither do white men like you who take their side against your own. So I didn't do nothing wrong. *That* is the law, or at least it was before we got a spineless sheriff and a chicken-livered mayor in this city."

"The sheriff and the mayor are good men, Burly. They realize that old beliefs are giving way to a better understanding that God created all people regardless of color, and all people should be treated equally. The sheriff and the mayor are just good men doing what's right."

Jim knew he was distorting the truth concerning the racial attitudes of the mayor and the sheriff, but he figured as long as he was risking his life, he might as well try to get something out of it. He saw no reason to tell Burly that the only concern his hostages had, aside from their hides, was the liability the town was facing due to his actions.

"And you only say that because they're siding with you!" Peters yelled out before proving that Deputy Schofield's warning about the door was well founded. He fired a shot; the bullet passed through the door and lodged in the front wall of the building. But it splintered the wood when it exited the door, embedding several shards into Jim's left shoulder. Jim backed away from the door; Deputy Schofield hurried over.

"You're hit?"

"Not by the bullet; just some wood splinters."

"I'll send a man after a doctor." Schofield motioned to another deputy to get going.

"I'm afraid we need something better to bargain with than me," said Jim. "Does Burly have a wife?"

"Not anymore; she died a couple years ago."

"What about children?"

"We thought about that," said Schofield. "He has a daughter, but she won't have anything to do with him. Burly was pretty hard on her mother; she blames him for her death. That's the reason we didn't ask her to try talking to him."

"How does Burly feel about her?"

"Oh it bothers him a lot that his daughter disowned him. He's mentioned it almost every day for as long as I can remember."

"Then that could be our only chance. She has got to talk to him. Does she live around here?"

"She lives alone in a little house just north of here, but she's probably at work over at Linden's General Store."

"Go and see if she'll help us, Schofield," said Jim.

"I'll bring her even if I have to drag her here," Schofield replied.

"No! For God's sake, don't force her. Do you think it's going to make Burly easier to deal with if his daughter comes here just to chastise him? The only way this might work is if she's willing to help."

"Sorry, I guess I wasn't thinking. I'll do what I can, and I will try to make it quick. We may not have much time left."

"I'll go along with that," said Jim. "In the meantime I will do what I possibly can to stall Burly."

The deputy hurried out to appeal to Burly Peters' daughter, and Jim cautiously went back toward the cellblock door, taking more care to stay as far from the door as possible.

"I wish I could make you understand, Burly, that no one is siding with anyone here. We are only trying to do what's best for everyone concerned."

"Losing my job isn't what's good for me," said Burly.

"I won't argue that point, but we are trying to help you just the same. Think about what you are doing. Think about what the rest of your life will become if you carry out your threats against the sheriff and the mayor. A man can always find another job, but if you push this thing too far, you won't ever be able to repair the damage."

An ominous silence followed, and Jim didn't know if Burly was thinking about what he'd said or if he had made up his mind that negotiations had failed to produce the results he wanted. Then Jim heard the front door open behind him; he looked around desperately hoping to see Deputy Schofield and Burly's daughter, but it was only Dr. Freemont. Jim motioned for him to stay back.

Every minute that ticked by made the situation that much more critical. If the distraught deputy was capable of shooting his hostages, he could decide to do so at any minute. Just when it seemed that time had ceased and eternity had begun, the front door opened again. In walked the deputy and a young woman, maybe early thirties, with long blonde hair and green eyes. She bore an expression of sadness on her pretty face, a look that could only have been put there by years of deep anxiety.

Jim hurried to meet them, fearful that it may be too late.

"This is Sue Ellen Peters," said the deputy.

"I am so glad you're here, Sue Ellen," said Jim. "I'm sure Deputy Schofield has told you why we asked you to come."

"There was no need. The news is all over the city by now. I'm sorry I didn't come sooner, but I didn't want to come at all. I guess that sounds harsh, but I have my reasons. Then I remembered something my mother once said about the need for forgiveness in this world; she was right. Maybe my pa is truly in need of it now. Let me see if I can help."

"We are all very grateful, Sue Ellen. Wait for just a minute; I want to try to ensure your safety."

Once again, Jim went back to the cellblock door. "Burly, there is someone here who wants to speak with you."

"There's nobody else in this whole town that I want to talk to, Langdon. If you wanna come back here with me then I'll let the mayor and the sheriff go. Otherwise this is gonna be over in two minutes."

It was now or never. Jim motioned Sue Ellen forward and then shielded her with his own body. He whispered to her, "Go ahead, Sue Ellen."

"Pa, Pa it's me, Sue Ellen. I want to talk to you, Pa."

"Sue Ellen? I can't believe you're here. Did they make you come?"

"No, Pa, it is my choice to be here. I won't say that it was my idea at first, but I'm here now because I want to be here."

"I got trouble, girl. I guess that's nothing new for me. I always end up hurting somebody . . . sometimes it's somebody I didn't want to hurt at all. You know what I mean?"

"I think I do, Pa. Sometimes we do hurt those we really care about. It's not always easy to fix our mistakes, and we end up making them worse. I'm here because I don't want that to happen to you now. Let me come in, Pa, and we'll talk it out."

"I guess that will be all right. Tell those men out there to stay back, and I'll open the door for you."

"Please go back with the others," she told Jim. "My Pa won't hurt me."

Jim did as requested; Burly opened the door enough for Sue Ellen to slip through, and all that was left to do was wait.

"What do you think?" said Deputy Schofield.

"I think Sue Ellen's presence is the best possible solution to the problem. Nothing else was going to have any success with Burly. A man isn't human if he won't soften under the influence of his daughter, and I think this visit is very important to him."

Jim believed a great deal in his prediction, but even *he* had to admit great surprise when after only thirty minutes the door to the cellblock opened and out walked the mayor and the sheriff. The two men looked a little shaken but completely unscathed. They were quickly surrounded by Jim and the deputies, who expressed much relief at their release. The sheriff handed a revolver to Deputy Schofield and said, "Here, Paul, this is Burly's. He and his daughter asked for a little privacy; Burly even allowed me to lock him in a cell."

"I want to thank you men for all you did," said the mayor. "Especially whoever had the idea to bring Sue Ellen here."

"That would be Mr. Langdon," said one of the deputies.

"Thank you, Jim," said the mayor as he cordially shook Jim's hand. "You may be happy to know that none of the other men in this department had anything to do with the attack at your place. Burly recruited them partly from the local Klan and partly from the unemployment line. I guess old ways go down hard. But maybe some of us learned a few things from this incident. In the interest of being a good mayor, I think I have."

"I am glad to hear that, Mayor, and I want you to know that I am pleased to have a man like you running our city."

"Also, Jim, send your claim through proper channels, and I will see that it is settled in a timely manner."

"Again, thank you," said Jim.

"Now, if you will excuse me, I am going home for the rest of the day."

"Get some rest, Mr. Mayor," Jim replied.

Jim wanted to wait to thank Sue Ellen when she was finished speaking with her father, but the doctor came up to him and said, "Should we take a look at that shoulder now, Mr. Langdon?"

Praise the Lord, Jim thought. His satisfaction with the outcome of the standoff was so great that the pain in his shoulder paled in comparison. "I will accompany you to your office, Doctor," he replied.

Later, as he headed for home with a bandage on his shoulder, Jim could also mentally apply a splint to his recently damaged faith in humanity. Not only would there be no legal pains involved in receiving compensation for losses suffered by himself and his sharecroppers, but he also witnessed a slight turning of attitudes in a few people not easily given to change. The Depression continued to impose its hardships, and the end still seemed somewhere off in the distance, but by the end of the day Jim felt he could see things moving slowly forward.

TEN

Fate Lends a Hand

Mayor Blane was true to his word, and by July of 1934, the buildings and the homes on Langdon Plantation had been rebuilt, permitting the residents to reestablish themselves in a little more comfort than they'd had before.

Burly Peters was the only man to stand trial for the attack, refusing to name any of his accomplices. Jim had to give the man credit for that: bearing the brunt of the punishment because he had devised the plan alone and incited the others to follow. He was sentenced to five years of prison time in Atlanta but accepted it somewhat graciously when Sue Ellen promised to visit at least once a month. Apparently Burly felt that regaining a relationship with his daughter far exceeded any losses he may have suffered; an admirable point of view, Jim thought.

With the general restoration of peace once again, Jim turned his attention to other matters. The incident with the men who had used force in an attempt to get work only served to increase Jim's awareness of the desperation brought on by the Depression. But his main focus was still on the black citizens because they were not protected by the law. It was still his aim to bring about change in the system—to bring about equality for all.

While President Roosevelt was obviously turning the tide of the Depression, he was not including everyone in his visions. If Jim wanted to reach someone who could help, the president would not be the one he would go to.

And as if the country did not have enough problems, since about 1930, the Midwest had been plagued by a number of murderous outlaws whose infamy would be written into the pages of history. Among the better known criminals were Bonnie Parker and her partner Clyde Barrow. Robbing banks was their specialty, which went hand in hand with murder if anyone—police or civilian—should get in their way. Perhaps the most notorious was John Dillinger, who was the first man ever to become public enemy number one, so designated by the Federal Bureau of Investigations.

Their exploits were daring and violent but also very short lived. Bonnie and Clyde were ambushed by police in Louisiana and shot to death on May 23, 1934, after just a two-year crime spree. John Dillinger suffered the same fate on July 22, 1934, in Chicago, after about a year of known criminal activity. How insulting their deeds had been to honest people, stealing their meager savings to live well in the middle of a crippling depression.

As Jim sat in his office deep in thought one Friday afternoon, Elizabeth came in and sat down across the desk from him. When Jim looked up she was smiling a very I-know-something-that-you-don't-know smile. Before she could begin teasing him with a guessing game, however, he said, "I can't guess, dear. What do you know that I don't know?"

"Well, I know that we will be great-grandparents early next year," she said.

"That's wonderful!" he replied. "Now I wish I'd have guessed because I've been hoping to hear news like that; I probably would have gotten this one. I must see William tomorrow and congratulate him."

"Now tell me what's on *your* mind," said Elizabeth.

"I'm not sure I know what you mean."

"Come now, Jim. When I first came in I could see that you were deep in thought about something. Tell your best friend what it is."

Jim couldn't help smiling, and he said, "You most certainly are my best friend, Elizabeth. You are to me the same as Mother was to Father. They were one of the most perfectly matched couples I've ever known. You're right, I was deep in thought when you came in."

"Please tell me more."

"Very well. As usual, I was musing about equality and the movement for civil rights. I'm afraid that our most capable president has not come through quite the way I'd hoped. He's a popular man, I'll give him that. When he ended prohibition last year, I'll bet his chance of reelection went up forty percent—maybe fifty percent. But the consumption of alcohol is hardly the answer to this country's needs, and I still think the black vote is as important as that of the white southerner. Nevertheless, blacks are kept away from the polls in every southern state."

"Have you anything in mind?" she asked.

"Nothing concrete, I'm afraid. I know that I think a lot along the same lines as my father. I always have. He saw the power of politics and what could be accomplished if you can just get the power moving with and not against you. The biggest difference between my father and I is that he had the wherewithal to become a politician, while I prefer to find a politician who shares my ideas and then cajole him into getting the job done."

"But who would that be, Jim? Judging from what you said, I wouldn't think you would be trying to cajole President Roosevelt."

"No, I wouldn't, and there is the rub. Who might fit the profile is the answer that I haven't come up with yet."

"Try not to push too hard, Jim. Just allow the thought to rest in your mind, and the solution will come when you least expect it. Perhaps fate will lend a hand."

"I will take your advice, dear," said Jim. "I'm hungry; let's have dinner."

Two weeks later, Jim and Elizabeth traveled to Atlanta to spend a weekend away from routine matters, minor distractions, and preoccupation with an inability to change the world. They checked into a very nice hotel, intending to spend a couple days doing nothing but enjoying each other's company. The July weather was hot, but low humidity and a pleasant breeze made the out of doors perfect for walking around the city and peeking into storefronts.

On Saturday afternoon, as the couple was passing by a soda fountain on Peachtree Street, out of the corner of her eye, Elizabeth noticed two women sitting at a table inside the establishment enjoying a cold refreshment. Something about one of the women caught and held her attention. Jim was talking and did not realize that she had stopped. When he looked to his right and did not see her, he turned just as Elizabeth was hurrying to catch up.

"Jim," she said in an innocent voice. "I think I would like some ice cream, how about you?"

"You know, dear, that sounds like a wonderful idea."

"Good," she replied as she took hold of his hand.

They retraced their steps to the soda fountain, went inside, and took a table of Elizabeth's choosing near the back wall. As they waited for someone to take their order, Elizabeth alternated her attention from Jim to the table where the two women were sitting and then back again. Jim did not notice her behavior until he had to tap her arm after the waiter asked for her order a second time. When the waiter walked away Jim smiled and said, "It breaks my heart to think there is something more worthy of your attention than I."

The remark brought her out of the trance she had slipped into, and she said, "Oh, dear, I am sorry. I didn't realize I was acting so strangely. As discreetly as possible, peek at the two women sitting at the table behind us near the counter."

Jim did as she requested; after a casual look he turned back and said, "The woman who is facing toward us does look familiar, but I can't quite put a name to the face."

"My dear husband," she whispered emphatically. "*That* is Eleanor Roosevelt."

Jim looked at her in disbelief. "Are you sure, Elizabeth?"

"I would bet the chocolate sundae that I ordered, and you know how I love my chocolate sundaes."

Jim *did* know exactly how much his wife enjoyed a chocolate sundae. Trying to be inconspicuous, he turned and looked again at the two women. This time, the one facing toward them caught his curious glance, and she smiled quite pleasantly. Jim smiled in return, hoping his face did not reveal the embarrassment he felt at being spotted.

"I can't believe it," said Jim. "That *is* Eleanor Roosevelt. I have heard that she is a very independent woman; I mean she takes a lot of road trips, usually with one of her close friends. I wonder if they have been or are heading to Warm Springs."

"I don't know," said Elizabeth. "But do you remember that *someone* you were talking about who might listen to your grievances concerning black citizens?"

Jim thought about her comment for a minute and said, "By golly, you're right. The president resists the pleas from the black population, but the first lady, on the other hand, seems to take quite an interest in their welfare. This could be the chance of a lifetime. You said that fate might lend a hand, but I never expected an opportunity like this. What should I do? I can't just walk up there and bother her, can I?"

"Leave this to me, dear," said Elizabeth.

She got up from the table and approached the two women as Jim looked on. In about a minute, Elizabeth was engaged in conversation with Eleanor Roosevelt and her companion. In another minute, Elizabeth was heading back toward Jim with the two women right behind her. He was so unnerved that he stood up quickly, knocking his chair over, causing a loud noise and drawing the attention of everyone in the place.

"Jim," said Elizabeth. "I would like you to meet Eleanor Roosevelt and her friend, Lorena Hickok."

"I'm sorry," Jim replied. "I mean, I am most honored to meet you, ladies. I'm sorry for the noise and everything, I mean, I guess I got nervous because you're the first lady, and your husband is the president, and I think I should stop talking before I make a complete fool of myself."

The women enjoyed a hearty laugh, and then Eleanor said, "Would you mind if Lorena and I joined you and your wife?"

"We would be most flattered, Mrs. Roosevelt," Jim replied.

"Oh please, Eleanor will do just fine."

"Yes, Eleanor, Lorena. Please sit down."

"Thank you, kindly. Elizabeth tells me that you are looking for someone who can help with a very big problem. I don't know that I am the one who can solve it, but I do enjoy talking with local folks wherever I go. It helps me to understand what is going on in the country."

"You are most gracious, Eleanor," said Jim. "I would be only too happy to speak my mind, but sometimes, in so doing, some comments could be construed as offensive."

"Jim, please don't worry about hurting my feelings," Eleanor replied. "When one finds herself in a position such as mine, one has to be prepared to hear comments both agreeable and disagreeable. I think I can handle anything you wish to say."

"I understand your meaning, and again, you are very gracious. I can only imagine the weight Mr. Roosevelt must be carrying on his shoulders, leading this entire country in the midst of a terrible depression. And I must say that he has already made great strides toward getting America back on its feet. However, my concern is that not all of our citizens are being given the same consideration, nor are they all receiving whatever aid the country can provide. But worse than that, not everyone enjoys the accounting of their worth as citizens or as human beings."

"You are speaking of the African Americans, Jim?"

"Yes, Eleanor, I am. I am sickened by the indiscriminate murdering of black people and the unwillingness of the law to raise a finger against it. I am appalled at the practice of pushing blacks out of their jobs by whatever means necessary even though it is painfully obvious that they, along with their families, need to eat, the same as white people do. As a devout servant of God Almighty, it is simply beyond my ability to comprehend the thinking of those who do not believe that people are all the same. I am sorry if I am emotionally offensive."

"On the contrary, Jim. I admire your stand against a racially unjust world," said Eleanor. "The fact is that I agree with you, but sadly I have to admit that I did not always see it that way. I don't mean to say that I once believed that black people were inferior. I only mean that I just didn't recognize racial discrimination until last year when I moved into the White House. Looking back now I wonder about it myself, especially since my social activism days actually started in 1903 when I worked with the immigrant communities of the Rivington Street Settlement House."

"What turned things around for you?" Jim asked.

"I think I can answer that for you, Jim," said Lorena. "In her capacity as first lady, Eleanor has traveled the United States extensively and has witnessed the hardships created by the Depression."

"Lorena is quite right," said Eleanor. "Aside from being my devoted friend and mentor, she is also a journalist whom I met in 1932 during Mr. Roosevelt's election campaign. Her reports from the field detailed the shortcomings of the Federal Emergency Relief programs and brought stories of personal hardship to my attention. Even after visiting poverty-stricken areas inhabited by black people, I did not comprehend the depth of institutional racism until I pushed the Subsistence Homestead Administration to allow African Americans to live in Arthurdale."

"What is Arthurdale?" asked Elizabeth.

"It was one of several resettlement towns under the New Deal designed to take needy laborers to newly constructed communities and give them the opportunity to become economically self-sufficient," Lorena explained.

"Unfortunately I failed," said Eleanor. "So I invited Walter White, president of the NAACP, and many of the presidents of African American universities to the White House to discuss the situation. I asked Donald Richberg of the National Recovery Administration for an investigation into the race-based wage differences by southern industries, and I have pressured the secretary of the navy to explain why blacks were confined to assignments in the mess hall."

"I had no idea, Eleanor," said Jim. "Of course I read all the papers, but they do not even explain a fraction of what goes on behind closed doors. Results are more important than knowing what led up to them, and the people are only concerned with results. But it is a very great comfort to me to hear that someone is doing so much to help our black citizens."

"Well," said Eleanor. "I wouldn't explain as much to everyone I meet, and I'm sure I haven't said anything that would threaten national security, but I believe you to be very sincere in your concern for black Americans so I did. I'm glad it makes you feel better."

"It does. It most certainly does. I would also like to say that if there is ever anything that my wife and I can personally do to help, I beg you to call on us."

"You know something, Jim, I will keep that in mind, and I just might hold you to that sometime," said Eleanor.

"It would be an honor," said Elizabeth.

"You folks live near Macon, don't you?" asked Lorena.

"We do," Jim replied. "About twenty miles south."

"We must be going," said Eleanor. "It was a genuine pleasure meeting you both."

"The pleasure was all ours," Jim replied.

Jim watched, still finding the meeting hard to believe, as the two women left the soda fountain and disappeared out of sight.

"What do you think of that, Elizabeth?"

"I think this has been a great day."

"I couldn't agree more. Yes, a great day."

"Do you think there is really a chance we may hear from her sometime?" asked Elizabeth.

"Honestly? I doubt it. I think she is a wonderful person, but I think she may have said that to humor us. After all, she is a very busy lady with no time to spare, and anyway, what could we do?"

"I don't know, Jim. But if she ever does call upon us, we will be ready."

"That we will, dear, that we will. But I must say, she really did put things into perspective for me."

"What do you mean?"

"I mean that the problem is so huge, even the president's wife is doing all she can, and still it sometimes seems that little progress is being made. And she *is* doing all she can."

"I suppose you're right about that," said Elizabeth. "We can't even imagine how busy the president must be, and it is understandable for a number of reasons why he can't give Eleanor much help with her own agenda."

"I agree with that too," Jim replied. "I don't expect him to ignore everything else on his plate for one cause. However, I do think that when it comes to things like anti-lynching bills he should be giving her his full cooperation. I can think of no acceptable reason for him to skirt such issues, and you can be sure that it has something to do with the fear of losing the support of white southern voters."

When they returned home, Jim immediately told Elizabeth to invite John and Abbey to supper. He couldn't wait to tell them about the chance meeting with the first lady. When he'd finished the story, both John and Abbey were quite impressed with what they'd heard.

"You must have been overwhelmed just being in the presence of Eleanor Roosevelt," said John.

Elizabeth laughed and said, "You should have seen your father, John. When I brought Eleanor and Lorena over to the table he stood up, knocking his chair over, and for a moment he couldn't speak a coherent sentence."

"Your mother is right. I did not handle things too smoothly. But when we started talking, the two of them were so open and friendly that conversation came easily. We had a wonderful discussion; Eleanor even said she might find a way that we can help."

"I hope she meant it," said John. Everyone nodded in agreement.

As 1934 wore on and then came to an end, the meeting with Eleanor and Lorena faded a bit as other things diverted everyone's interest.

The following February, William and Joanna welcomed into the family a son. They called him Martin J. Langdon and explained to the family that the middle initial stood for both Jim and John; thus no middle name appeared on the birth certificate.

A fine celebration followed after Joanna had time to get back on her feet; William's sister, Julia, made the long journey from England to be there. The Depression was beginning to weaken; even the black population was faring a little better. Three hundred and fifty thousand African Americans were being employed by the Works Progress Administration annually making up about fifteen percent of the work force of the Civilian Conservation Corps. A quota had been established for black laborers per a clause the Public Works Administration added to all government construction contracts.

Over one million illiterate blacks learned to read and write under the New Deal's educational programs, increasing the number of black children attending primary school. But, basic rights had not been bestowed upon the African American people, which placed these benefits on a tenuous footing. They still had no vote; the Fifteenth Amendment, which was added to the US Constitution in 1791, was still not being upheld. Consequently, they had no voice.

It was a beautiful spring day in early June when Elizabeth asked Jim to take her into Macon to buy material for some new curtains she planned to make. When they returned to the house there was an automobile in the driveway that neither of them recognized.

Retrieving their packages from the back seat they walked toward the house, but upon approaching the veranda they could hear laughter and conversation coming from the direction of the sharecroppers' quarters. After putting the packages on the steps of the veranda, Jim led the way around the house.

Sitting at the outdoor tables beneath the giant maple tree were three of the older black women and two white women, sipping lemonade, heavily engaged in friendly socializing. Jim took one look at Elizabeth, and her expression showed the same surprise he knew his own must be exposing. They walked over to the little gathering; the women acknowledged their presence, and Jim said, "Hello, Eleanor, Lorena, we are so happy to see you both."

"Welcome to Langdon Plantation, ladies," said Elizabeth. "I hope you haven't been waiting long."

"Well if we were, we'd never have noticed," said Lorena. "We have been having the most wonderful conversation with Martha, Thelma, and Miranda."

"Indeed," said Eleanor. "We have been given a detailed story of the Langdon family history, and I must say that it is as interesting as it is impressive."

Under mild protest from Jim, the three black women excused themselves; Eleanor and Lorena thanked them for their hospitality.

When they'd gone, Eleanor said, "Jim, when I met you in Atlanta I thought I'd gotten a very good understanding of how concerned you are about the black Americans, but I had no idea just how committed the Langdon family is and has been to their cause. Those three ladies we were talking to have spent their whole lives here, and their knowledge and their memories go back to the days of your grandfather, when the African Americans living here were slaves."

"I suppose our concern just comes naturally, at least it did for my father. I can only imagine how difficult it must have been for him being so torn between his loyalty to my grandfather and his loyalty to what he knew in his heart was right. But I have never doubted that he made the right choice, and from what he told me, my grandfather realized it too, in the end."

"But it must be something that you feel in your heart too, Jim," said Lorena. "Your father could teach you the difference between right and wrong but it was still up to you to make up your own mind."

"You're right about that of course," Jim replied. "It was no struggle for me. I understand as he did that God made us all, and therefore, we are all equal."

"It is a lovely sentiment," said Eleanor. "That is why I want to see to it that you receive recognition. I want to nominate you for the Nobel Peace Prize."

Jim was shocked, stunned, and speechless all at once. When he regained his composure he said, "Eleanor, I cannot begin to tell you how flattered, not to mention how grateful I am, but I could not accept such an honor."

"Why not?" she asked.

"It just wouldn't be right. It would be like helping someone less fortunate than I and then running into the local paper to have a story printed. No, I want no recognition; if anyone deserves such a thing it would be my father. He risked his life, time and again, for what he believed."

"Then what if I nominated the Langdon family, past and present, and you could accept it for your father as well?"

"No, thank you very kindly. I know my father would feel as I do."

Eleanor's face broke into a broad smile and she said, "God bless you, Jim. I knew before I mentioned it just what your reaction would be. I just wanted to hear it. Very well, I won't bring it up again. But in Atlanta you offered your help, and that I could use."

"You have but to tell us what we can do," said Jim.

"Include me too," said Elizabeth.

"Indeed. I would like you to assist Lorena in keeping me up to date on the conditions and the needs of the African American population in Georgia, or at least as much of it as you can cover. She will leave you with all of the contact information you need to stay in touch with her and to send your reports directly to her."

"I will also drop by from time to time," said Lorena. "The more information Eleanor has, the better she can outline her own agenda. Send me reports on everything from employment to housing, education, civil rights issues—anything that affects a person's way of life. Even if you don't think it is worth mentioning, include it in the report. I will sort it out as we go along. How does that sound?"

"We will devote ourselves to this," said Jim.

"Splendid."

Jim and Elizabeth took their distinguished guests on a walking tour of Langdon Plantation; Jim asked the ladies if they might consider staying for a couple days. Of course their busy schedules did not allow much leisure time, but they did agree to spend the night before moving on.

That evening, Elizabeth, Abbey, and Joanna provided a meal that almost made everyone feel guilty to partake of considering the Depression. In addition to the entire Langdon family, Jerome and Esther were invited, and of course, their daughter Mattie, who was a lively little lady at eighteen months of age.

After the supper dishes were finished, the group moved out to the veranda, where they indulged in stimulating conversation until Mattie let them know that it was time to call it a night. William and Joanna headed for home with little Martin; Jerome and Esther walked up the hill to get

Mattie ready for bed. John and Abbey were the last to leave, and then Elizabeth took Eleanor and Lorena upstairs to show them the accommodations.

The following morning they were all assembled again to say thank you and goodbye to their distinguished guests.

ELEVEN

A Challenge Not a Triumph

As Jim and Elizabeth prepared to fulfill their promise to Eleanor and Lorena, they both realized that a few life-changing alterations were in order. At the age of 73, and taking into consideration the time involved in the new undertaking, Jim decided that he was ready to turn over complete control of the plantation to John and William. He accepted the fact that the last stage of his life was staring him in the face, and it was his wish to spend it, as always, doing whatever he could to make a positive difference. He knew that Elizabeth felt the same way.

Included in the preparation for their travels, Jim purchased a brand new Chevrolet Master Deluxe with an improved master blue flame engine, pressure steam oiling, cable brakes, and shock-proof steering. It would serve them well in their travels. Of course they would not travel continuously like nomads; a few weeks at a time on the road would be followed by a few weeks at home to rest and write reports for Lorena.

One other change occurred before the couple began their assignment: Jerome told Jim that he wished to open a law office in Macon. But he assured Jim that he would always be available to the Langdon family if they ever needed him. The two men shared a bond of trust and friendship that would never be forsaken by either of them. They both had new worlds to conquer; Jim would continue his fight for human equality, and Jerome would expand on his quest for racial justice.

Jim did not feel it was necessary to make out an itinerary or even follow a map. They would just chose a direction and stop at small towns, larger cities, and isolated farm houses; in short, anywhere they found people. The reports would be random samples from all over the state, describing living conditions, needs, problems, and suggestions on the best way the government might lend assistance.

On the first of July in 1935, Jim and Elizabeth were packed and ready to test their abilities to gather useful information. From home they headed northeast and made their first stop in the little town of Dry Branch. Although he'd never been there before, the town held great significance for Jim, owing to the fact that his mother had come from Dry Branch. It was also the place where his father had lived between trips north in the company of runaway slaves. Jim's parents met in Dry Branch and later married and established a residence in Mapletown, Pennsylvania, where they lived until after the war.

Jim became very nostalgic as he and Elizabeth walked around the town talking about the past and wondering what remained unchanged since the days when his parents resided there. It was a temptation to do some research to see what he could find out, but then he remembered the purpose of the trip, and they left Dry Branch having talked to no one.

They moved on to Milledgeville, the former capital of Georgia until 1868 when it was moved to Atlanta. After a noon meal they walked the streets and engaged some of the locals, both black and white, in conversation.

It was not at all difficult to find individuals or families who were poverty stricken, but it was still an immediate conclusion that conditions were worse for African Americans. In addition to the unemployment problem, lack of proper education kept many blacks from ever possessing the skills that would promise them a future. Twenty-five percent of the African Americans were on welfare as opposed to fifteen percent of the white inhabitants.

As Jim and Elizabeth moved around the state, they did find evidence that the New Deal programs were finally beginning to affect the black population in a very general way, meaning that sometimes the feedback they received was positive—other times it reeked of despair. In the same fashion, some of the people they met were friendly, open, and eager to talk. Others became angry as soon as the name Roosevelt was mentioned. More than once they were threatened with violence if they didn't mind their own business and move on.

President Roosevelt continued the onslaught of government programs to help pull the country out of the Depression; still, little was trickling down to the average black citizen at that point.

In August, the Social Security Act, which provided monthly checks to senior citizens, was signed into law. In November, Jim read an article in a Gainesville newspaper concerning the Maryland Supreme Court ruling, which stated that the University of Maryland had to either admit black students to their law school or institute a separate school for blacks. The university relented and admitted the first black pupils.

The National Labor Relations Act gave labor the right to organize, which led to the establishment of many labor unions. Their mission was to gain better wages, working conditions, and benefits for workers. However, as from the inception of the Great Depression, time was a very large component of the healing process, and it would take plenty of it before results would be realized.

Still, it was not only a matter of survival in reference to food, shelter, and clothing that confronted the blacks; the vote was still denied to many, the monster referred to as discrimination flourished, and the threat of death by lynching remained a part of everyday life.

Early in 1934, the Costigan–Wagner Anti-Lynching Bill was introduced; FDR did nothing to encourage its passage even though he agreed with its ideas. The president would not support the bill because he continued to fear the loss of southern votes in the next election. Although Jim and his wife now worked unofficially for Eleanor Roosevelt, their opinion of her husband was by no means flattering. It was impossible for them to understand how the president could so blatantly turn his back on his fellow man for what he believed was vital to his own benefit.

And so, equal justice was on the minds of most of the blacks Jim and Elizabeth met. Until equality was won, life would go on pretty much as usual.

Part of their routine was to read the newspapers daily; it was an effective way to monitor conditions in Georgia as well as the rest of the southern states. All too often, the stories were tragically unjust.

On October 27, 1934, in Marianna, Florida, a black farmhand named Claude Neal was lynched after being accused of the rape and murder of Lola Cannady, a nineteen-year-old white girl. Even though there was insufficient evidence to convict Neal, after moving him from jail to jail to avoid lynch mobs, he was discovered in Marianna, removed from jail while the sheriff's attention was diverted, and was tortured and hanged.

When another crowd of about two thousand reached the town and found that Neal's body had already been buried, they tried to force Sheriff Chambliss to dig up the corpse and hang it outside the courthouse. When he refused, a riot broke out causing injuries to about two hundred black citizens. Finally, the National Guard was called to end the riot.

Maybe it was because of the dreadful toll taken by the Depression, or maybe more and more people simply grew sick and tired of so much violence, but the only thing that concerned Jim was the huge impact on the American people brought about by the Neal lynching—and their reaction, which he hoped signaled the beginning of the end of the dreaded practice. The extensive national media coverage of the lynching created strong opposition to the practice nationwide. Many southerners began to see lynchings as evil, which served to deter some would-be perpetrators. Due to the horrific nature of the Neal incident, they became convinced that a federal law against the practice was crucial. It made clear the fact that the current federal and local policies preventing lynchings in the United States were useless. Angry Americans throughout the country were determined to rid the nation of lynchings and similar practices.

However, one of the many characteristics Jim inherited from his father was intuition, and he did not believe that Claude Neal would be the last man, black or white, who would fall victim to murder in the name of justice at the hands of self-righteous madmen.

Still, Jim did his best to reassure the people he met that changes were coming, and for the better; Elizabeth did the same. But it preyed on their minds and consciences because they realized that those who had endured for so long could not stand one more letdown.

In 1935, Eleanor Roosevelt began writing a nationally syndicated column called, "My Day." She faithfully wrote six days a week and addressed such issues as anti-lynching, fair housing for minorities, and the right to organize. Jim and Elizabeth knew that their reports were represented in part in that column. It made them feel that what they were doing was worthwhile.

Then one afternoon, as they were driving on a dry, dusty road about twenty miles from Dalton, they came upon a rundown farm out in the middle of nowhere. The roof of the house sagged in many places, and the house itself had lost its support on the right side, making it appear as though a giant hand had twisted the entire structure. The barn and two more tiny buildings looked as though a gentle breeze would blow them over, and there was not a shred of evidence that anything had ever worn a coat of paint.

Several black children wearing ill-fitting rags played in front of the house; a mangy, mixed-breed dog frolicked with them. An elderly man sat in a rocking chair on the crooked porch, swatting flies; to the left of the house was a large cotton field where a younger man worked beside an old wagon hitched to a mule.

Jim pulled the car just off the road in front of the house; the children swarmed around the car in awe. By the time Jim and Elizabeth got out of their vehicle, the younger man was in his wagon heading toward them. Elizabeth offered the children, three girls and two boys, some taffy that she had picked up in town. But a shout from the man in the wagon scattered the children before they could accept. As the man in the wagon drew near, Jim noted that the wheels on the dilapidated vehicle did not spin true, and the mule was in no better condition than anything else on the property. The farmer's overalls were covered with patches, and the brim of his straw hat could not possibly keep the sun out of his face.

When he pulled the mule to a stop, the farmer jumped down quickly and wasted no time confronting Jim and Elizabeth.

"What's yo business here?" he demanded.

"My name is Jim Langdon, and this is my wife, Elizabeth," Jim replied.

"What's that to me?" asked the farmer.

"We are here on behalf of Eleanor Roosevelt," said Jim.

"Who's Eleanor Roosevelt?" asked the farmer without easing his tone.

"She is President Roosevelt's wife," Jim answered.

"The president? You mean the man who tries to help the white folks while the niggers gets lynched?"

"I cannot argue with you, mister . . ."

"Charles Jess is my name."

"Mr. Jess. I cannot argue with you about the interests of the president. I watch what he does pretty closely, and while I can see that he is working hard to pull the country out of this depression, I can also see, as you do, that he sidesteps issues that are desperately in need of attention."

The farmer relaxed his posture a bit and said, "So what is you doin' for the president's wife?"

"Eleanor Roosevelt is a good woman who cares about all the people in this country. Understanding the plight of the African Americans, she badgers the government, including her husband, day and night to support anti-lynching laws, back new legislation for civil rights, and see that fair wages and proper education are available to all Americans. She has asked my wife and me to travel all around Georgia to check on the state of affairs, talk to as many people as we can, and then send her reports so that she knows which issues need attention the most."

"That's why you stopped to talk to me?"

"Yes, sir, it is."

"Well," said Charles Jess. "I reckon I'm sorry for actin' the way I did. I thought with your fancy new car and all that you were here from the bank to say that I have to leave this here farm. I ain't made a payment in six months, and I got a letter some time back that said I had to come up with some money or git. I can't read, but the preacher down to the black folk's church read it for me."

"I see," said Jim. "If you don't mind my asking, how much do you owe the bank?"

"I owes eighty dollars. It was three hundred when I came here, and I'd give the bank more if I could, but hard times got harder and I got seven mouths here to feed."

"Seven?" asked Elizabeth.

149

"Yesum. My five young'uns, my old pappy sittin' over there, and me."

"You have no wife, Mr. Jess?"

"No ma'am, she died of the small pox a year ago. The white doctor down the road wouldn't come lest I could pay him, and so my wife died."

"I am very sorry," said Elizabeth. "That doctor should be punished for neglecting his duty."

"I reckon if we was white folks he might a helped. It don't matter none now. Her body is in the ground, and her soul is in heaven. She is better off."

"What about your children?" Jim asked. "Do they attend school?"

"No, sir, they don't because the close by schoolhouse is for white children only. But the black preacher's wife comes by once a week and helps them with some readin' and writin'. Them young'uns is smarter than me," he said smiling, which showed that several teeth were missing.

"How is your pappy's health?" Elizabeth asked as she glanced at the old man in the rocking chair.

"He is ninety years old, almost deaf, and can't rightly do more than sit in that chair and swat flies. He never hits none, but it helps pass the time. But his memory is near perfect, and he can tell you all you need to know about being black and living in this here country."

"I assume that he was born a slave," said Jim.

"That he was. Many times he told me about the Jubilee, as they called it back then. The time when they knew they was free. The people thought they was about to live in a new world until they found out that life was worse than it was in the old world. By law they was free, but it didn't come to much."

"Yes, my father fought for the Union during the War Between the States, and he made that very prediction even before the fighting ended," said Jim.

With Mr. Jess' anxiety completely gone, his true nature was revealed. He was a friendly man who only wanted what any normal human being wanted: a life of peace and a chance to take care of his family.

"It was a great pleasure to meet you, Charles," said Jim. "And we will include your remarks and your needs in our next report to Mrs. Roosevelt."

"I hope the president's missus can change his way of thinkin', and I am glad that you stopped here today. It would be my pleasure if you and your wife would take supper with us before you go."

"Your hospitality is very neighborly, Charles, but we really must go. But first I want to give you something. Mrs. Roosevelt gave us a small pool of financial resources to distribute as we see fit."

"What does that mean?" Charles asked.

"It means that she gave us some money to help people in need. I want to give you a hundred dollars so that you can pay off your farm. The rest you can use for whatever you need. You won't have to worry about the bank anymore."

"Lordy Lord, I heard a miracles but never did one of them happen to me. I don't rightly know what to say 'cept that I won't never forget this day or you and your wife stoppin' here. I won't never forget the president's missus neither."

"It was our pleasure, Charles, and we wish you and your family the best."

The two men shook hands, Elizabeth gave Charles a handful of taffy for the children, and then they got into that new car and drove away.

"That was the most beautiful lie I ever heard, Jim," said Elizabeth.

"I believe it was the only way he'd have taken the money," Jim replied. "Charles is a good man, and I wouldn't insult him by offering a handout. Instead I simply gave him help from a friend."

"It was a wonderful thing to witness."

"He struck a nerve, you know," said Jim.

"What do you mean?"

"I mean I felt a twinge of shame when he mentioned the new car. When I bought it I was only thinking of reliable transportation."

"Well of course you were. Why should you be ashamed?"

"I guess people are born into different circumstances, which were set in motion without their knowledge or contribution. We all take our places accordingly and accept where we are put and what we are given. Sometimes we make changes, sometimes not."

"I guess that's true, Jim."

"I never cared enough about worldly possessions or social classes to look at my life and decide whether or not I had enough to suit me. I always had a good life, and I've always been more than satisfied."

"What is your point?"

"My point is that when Charles mentioned the new car I became keenly aware of how much better I have it than he does. I did not realize that visiting people who don't know where their next meal is coming from, driving up in a brand new car, which is an expensive item, made me look like the banker—the well-to-do citizen who wants his money even if he has to foreclose on people who have nothing."

"I see. I think, my dear husband, that you are in need of an objective assessment. You are so very much your father's son. Your father, like you, was filled to the brim with goodness. When your grandfather tried to convince him that slavery was simply a way of life for black people, he would have none of it. Even his fierce loyalty to your grandfather did not cloud his judgment."

"That's true," Jim said with a smile.

"Your father loved all people, and he saw them as equal in every way. He fought a war to prove it. He was a champion of the oppressed; he took up their fight for freedom, for equality, and he made it his own. He lived for many years as an outcast in his own environment because of what he'd done for others. Do you think he ever felt that he was better than anyone else because he owned a successful plantation?"

"I know that he did not," Jim replied.

"Of course he didn't. If anything, having more than others only enabled him to *do* more for others. It is all right to have resources if it is in your heart to share with those who have less. Did you not just do that a short time ago for Charles Jess? Helping that man came as naturally to you as breathing. Your father was a good man. You are a good man. You inherited a Christian's mission, and I have watched you fulfill that mission since the day I met you. It is the reason why I love you so much, and it was the reason why your mother loved your father."

Jim smiled; it was a smile that only pure happiness can produce. He looked over at his wonderful wife and said, "I have a girl just like the girl who married my father."

After spending the night in a hotel in Dalton, Jim bought a copy of the *Dalton Daily Citizen* outside the café where he and Elizabeth had taken their breakfast. He tossed the paper on the back seat of the car, intending to read it later in the day.

The couple headed north toward Ringgold, a small town near the Tennessee state line.

"I am feeling good today," said Jim. "Sometimes a feeling can predict the future. If the feeling is good the future is promising, and that's how I feel today. I think it's possible that the worst might be behind us; the worst of the Depression, and the worst of the racial tension."

"I will share your good feeling," said Elizabeth. "The newspapers are full of articles that talk about the need for more responsibility from lawmakers and less violence of every kind. Perhaps some of the old hatred is dying out."

"Speaking of newspaper articles, there is that copy of the *Dalton Daily Citizen* on the back seat. Why don't you find a good story and read it to me."

"Very well."

Elizabeth reached for the paper, turned back around, and spread the paper out on her lap. For several moments she stared at the front page without a word. Quietly she opened to the second page, and a near silent gasp escaped her mouth.

"Is anything wrong, Elizabeth?"

She looked over at him, still without a word. By that time, Jim didn't need an explanation to tell him that something had definitely upset her.

"Pull over, Jim," she said.

"He pulled the car off the road near a small grocery store and shut off the motor. Elizabeth handed him the paper; he took it and scanned the front page. The headline at the top right side of the page read, "NEGRO FARMER LYNCHED IN FT. LAUDERDALE." A homeless tenant farmer named Ruby Stacy was lynched in Ft. Lauderdale, Florida on July 19, without a trial of any kind. Stacy had gone to the house of a woman named Marion Jones to ask for food. When Jones saw Stacy's black face, she became frightened and screamed.

The police were called, and Stacy was arrested on no particular charge. While being escorted to the Dade County Jail by six deputies, Stacy was taken by a white mob and hanged next to the house of Marion Jones, the woman who had made the original complaint.

The second page of the paper carried a picture of Stacy's body hanging from a tree; several children appeared in the picture. Jim looked over at Elizabeth; she was crying. Jim started the engine, turned the car around, and headed south. "It's time to go home for a while," he said.

TWELVE

A World on the Edge

Among other things, the repeal of prohibition, as Jim had noted, made Franklin Roosevelt a very popular man, which led to his landslide victory for president over Democratic candidate Alf Landon in 1936.

Jim and Elizabeth continued to gather information for their reports to Eleanor, but due to consideration for their age, the trips became shorter, and the time spent at home became longer. The world was rapidly changing; tension between some countries and alliances between others made the future seem precariously unpredictable.

Jim constantly followed all news media sources believing that it was important for every American to be as informed as possible concerning world issues. Most troubling was the news in Europe: Adolf Hitler, chancellor of Germany, and his Nazi party had gained absolute power under the guise of restoring the economy and getting Germany back on its feet after the devastation of the Great War. But his motives were suspect in the opinion of much of the world—perhaps to all but the German people. It was obvious that much like President Roosevelt's progress in the United States, Hitler was rebuilding Germany and putting its destitute citizens back to work. It was understandable that he would have the support of the people, but at what cost?

At the end of the Great War, the Treaty of Versailles had placed a series of very harsh punishments on Germany. Much of their territory was taken away and their military power was severely limited. The Nazi party promised to restore Germany's territories, and on March 7, 1936, Hitler ordered troops into the Rhineland, breaking the treaty as well as the Locarno Pact.

In addition, Hitler's anti-Semitism and his treatment of the Jewish people had also come to light. Nazi officials claimed that their treatment of the Jews was no business of the League of Nations. The German press stated that Jews who voted in future elections would be arrested.

"Reading the newspaper has become a gloomy pastime, Elizabeth," said Jim one evening after supper. "There is so much going on around the world that suggests trouble ahead."

"Do you really think so, Jim?"

"I'm afraid I do. It seems as though there is extreme unrest in the world; lines are being drawn, and various countries with similar interests are bonding. Great Britain, France, and the United States have signed a naval accord in London. Fascist Italy under Benito Mussolini, Nazi Germany, and Japan appear to be establishing friendships. There is civil war in Spain; Japanese military troops staged a coup in Tokyo to assassinate political leaders. Great Britain is testing new fighter planes and building war ships—all of this is merely the tip of the iceberg."

"I was not aware that so much was going on," said Elizabeth. "I guess I don't read the paper as closely as you do, although I daresay that I am better off for it."

"For the sake of peace of mind I suppose you're right. But, unfortunately, ignoring it won't make it go away. I only wish it did."

"I prefer to read Eleanor's column."

"I read that too, Elizabeth. It keeps me up on what she is doing. I sometimes wonder where she gets her strength, tireless worker that she is."

"I suppose she gets it from the Lord, just as you and I do, Jim."

"Touché," Jim replied.

By the spring of 1937, Jim was beginning to notice a slight decline in his normal level of energy. He reasoned that it was merely seventy-five years of living creeping up on him ever so slowly. A heart attack had claimed his father's life at the age of seventy-six, but Jim knew that some restrictions on longevity were hereditary; age itself was not. Still, he decided that a little more rest and no mention of how he felt to his wife was the proper prescription.

"I would like to gather the family for a reunion of sorts," he said to Elizabeth one morning at breakfast. "It has been far too long since we've been together."

"That's a wonderful idea, Jim. It will take time to arrange though."

"I certainly agree, because I want to reach Julia in England; Madeline and Andrew in California; all of Aunt Kate's sons; even Willis and Emma in Canada."

Elizabeth put down her coffee cup, eyed Jim wistfully, and said, "Are you feeling quite all right?"

"I feel fine," he answered a little too quickly. "Why do you ask?"

"Call it a woman's intuition. I can think of no better way to lift the gloom you spoke of than to see family that we haven't seen in years, but your sudden notion joined with your recent signs of fatigue does worry me a little."

Jim was no less than astonished. A man's most foolish endeavor, he thought, is trying to deceive a caring wife because it simply cannot be done.

"I didn't know you were aware of it."

"I did not want to raise an alarm unnecessarily. I decided I would try to slow you down a little and see if that helps."

"I appreciate your concern, and especially the way in which you chose to handle the situation, but I am sure that it is just age making its presence known."

"I hope you're right, Jim. But I *was* thinking that maybe we should curtail our trips for a while. I know that Eleanor will understand. I am sure she worries about her own husband's health and well-being."

"I am sure she does, Elizabeth, but I don't think we need to be that concerned. I promise to try to get more rest."

She stared hard for a moment, trying to read his thoughts, and then said, "Well, if you promise."

"I do. Now, will you write some letters and we'll see who can make it to the reunion?"

"Of course I will."

"Good, and I think we should leave next week for the southern part of the state."

"Very well," she said reluctantly.

The morning before their trip to Albany and eventually to the town of Bainbridge in southern Georgia, John, William, and two-year-old Martin stopped by for a brief visit. Martin took his usual seat on his great-grandfather's lap; Jim was overjoyed by the boy's attention.

"Have you seen this morning's paper, Father?" John asked.

"No, I haven't. I don't think it has arrived yet."

"The news is not good. The front page is nothing but stories about the recession."

"Recession? I thought we were recovering from a depression."

"Apparently the state of the economy is spiraling again," said William. "The unemployment rate, which had gone down considerably after 1933, has hit twenty percent. Industrial production has fallen thirty-two percent."

"Indeed?" said Jim. "I thought we were heading out of this thing. What on earth has brought about a recession?"

"The payroll tax for Social Security started this year on top of the tax increase mandated by the Revenue Act of 1935," said John. "The paper says that the Federal Reserve and Treasury Department policies have caused a contraction in the money supply. It will take time to straighten it all out."

"I'm sure it will. In the meantime, a population on the brink of disaster takes another demoralizing setback. Your mother and I are leaving for Albany this morning. I'm sure we'll get a firsthand look at the effect this recession is having on the average citizen."

"I hope that you and Mother will be very careful on your trip. And don't overexert yourself, Father."

"I gather your mother has mentioned that I've been a little fatigued lately."

"I'm sorry, Jim," said Elizabeth. "I only wanted a second opinion."

"It's all right," Jim said with a smile. "I know you are all concerned. I guess I wouldn't have it any other way."

At ten a.m. they were on the road; Jim was careful not to comment on the brief dizzy spell he had experienced while loading the car.

The trip to Albany only took about three hours, but by the time they arrived, Jim was suffering from an acute headache. It was not his first in recent months, but it *was* the first that Elizabeth was aware of. At her insistence, they located a hotel room, got their bags inside, and then Jim was put to bed. By six p.m. he had awakened from a deep sleep, still a bit tired, but the headache had subsided.

"What time is it?" he asked.

"Just past six," Elizabeth replied. "Are you hungry?"

"As a matter of fact, I am. Should we find a little home-style diner somewhere?"

"I think a home-style hotel would be better, Jim."

"Excuse me?"

"I will go out and get something for the two of us. How does some soup and a sandwich sound?"

"It sounds very inviting, Elizabeth, but I don't like the idea of you going out alone."

"I will be just fine. There is an accommodating little place just two blocks up the street. I will be there and back in no time. You rest, and I will take care of everything."

To say that Jim counted the minutes until his wife returned would be a slight exaggeration, but he felt a sense of relief when he heard her at the door. The soup she fetched was hot and nourishing; the sandwich stuffed with country ham was delicious.

"I feel ready to take on the world again, thank you," he said.

"I'm happy to hear it, but the world can wait until tomorrow." Then she hesitated a moment before she said, "Jim, would you be upset with me if I suggested that we go home in the morning?"

"Never upset, Elizabeth, but I don't think there is any reason for it. My headache is gone, and I think after a night's rest I will be back to my old self again. We've come all this way; I'd hate to think it was for nothing."

"I understand. Would you be inclined to a compromise?"

"How so?"

"We won't go home, but we won't go any farther south. We'll head north but veer off to the east a bit. You have mentioned going through Mount Vernon a couple of times.

That's a little over a hundred miles northeast of here, but when we get there we'll only be about eighty miles from home. That will give us a chance to see if you are really your old self."

Jim could not bring himself to tell her he thought she was being overly cautious. He knew that if it were Elizabeth who had been feeling a little weary, he would be just as cautious.

"You're right about Mount Vernon. We'll set a course for that destination in the morning."

"Thank you, Jim. I feel like my old self now too," she said with a smile.

On the way to Mount Vernon the following day, the couple left the road every two hours for a break, and still, Jim was suffering from another headache by the time they arrived. Though he felt guilty, he did not mention it to Elizabeth. When they reached a hotel, he told her that he felt a nap would do him good—a decision with which she did not argue.

When Jim awoke, the headache had eased up to some degree, and he suggested that they take a walk around the town. They were just beyond the public square when they saw a black woman kneeling down on the sidewalk and crying as if her heart would break. They drew angry stares when they stopped beside the crying woman and bent down to place a comforting hand on her shoulder. Elizabeth said to her, "Is there something we can do to help?"

The woman looked up, tears streaming down her face. She replied, "The police, they done shot my son, and I don't think there was no reason for them to do that."

"How do you know this?" Jim asked.

"A man come to my house from the sheriff's office and he say that my son done murdered a man in Albany two days ago. Then he say my son skedaddled up to South Carolina to hide out. The man say my boy was catched up in South Carolina last night, and when they was bringin him back to Albany he tried to run away so they shot him dead."

"When did you see your son last?" Jim asked.

"I seen him yesterday mornin'. He was gonna go up to Atlanta and see his Uncle Obediah 'bout a job on the railroad. Til that time he was home wit me."

"Then he couldn't have been in Albany two days ago," said Elizabeth.

"No, ma'am, he couldn't," she replied.

"What is your name?" Jim asked her.

"My name is Sadie Reed. My boy was named Arthur."

"Where is your boy now, Ms. Reed?"

The morose woman pointed across the street. Jim followed her direction; she was pointing to an undertaker's parlor.

"That there is a black people's undertaker," said Sadie.

Elizabeth looked at Jim; she could plainly see the anger in his eyes.

"I guess this is another story, the truth of which will never be told," he said.

At that moment, several automobiles came down the street at a reckless speed. Two blocks beyond the undertaker, the vehicles slowed; one by one they made a U-turn in the street and came back, the lead auto stopping the motorcade in front of the parlor.

A mob composed of white men and women got out of the vehicles, rudely kicked in the front door of the establishment, and rushed inside. To the horror of Jim, Elizabeth, and Sadie Reed, the mob came out to the street carrying the body of a young black man. Someone produced a length of rope, tying one end around the rear bumper of the first automobile and the other end around the neck of the corpse.

Before the three terrified onlookers could object, the mob got back into their vehicles and headed toward the square, dragging the dead man up the street.

"My God!" Jim screamed. "I can't believe what I'm seeing!"

Elizabeth was crying and praying out loud; Sadie was screaming and rending her garments. Jim was trying to calm them but failed due to his own loss of self-control.

The gruesome procession was making circles through the square; men and women were poking their heads out of the windows and howling as if they were celebrating the Fourth of July.

"Take care of Ms. Reed!" Jim yelled and then he headed up the street as fast as he could.

"Jim, please don't go!" Elizabeth screamed, but his anger drove him on toward the square. By the time Jim reached the scene the automobiles were turning up a side street; he followed after them.

Through the black district they went, shocking the residents who were lining the street. When the caravan reached a black baseball park, the vehicles came to a halt; the mob got out, untied the corpse and dragged it to the middle of the field. Men began to knock boards from the fence that closed in the field on three sides.

After making a pile of boards, they threw the body on top of the pile, doused everything in gasoline, and then set it on fire. The body was fully engulfed in flames by the time Jim got to the field. The mob formed a circle around the pyre, chanting the words to the song, "Jump Jim Crow."

Short of breath from all the exertion, Jim pushed between two men, nearly knocking them to the ground. He stood inside the circle, sickened from the odor of the burning body. With his remaining strength he called out to the mob, "What in God's name is wrong with you people? You would rejoice in the murder of this man who was not even justly tried and convicted, then desecrate his remains in front of his own mother. You are not humans, but animals!"

A tall man in overalls and a flannel shirt came up behind Jim, grabbed him, and shoved him to the outside of the circle. "Get outta here, old man, before you get hurt!" he yelled.

Jim fell flat on his face, but he got up and managed to get inside the circle once again.

"You must stop this inhuman behavior! You must have respect for this man who was unjustly murdered! I beg you, stop . . ." Without seeing who was wielding it, Jim was smashed in the back of the head by a piece of the board fence, and everything went dark.

When he regained consciousness he had no idea where he was. He did not know how much time had passed since he blacked out. His vision was blurry, and it took several minutes to realize that he was lying in bed in a room with dark green wallpaper and a snow white ceiling. Then he could hear quiet voices, and he could feel someone holding his hand; a cool, damp cloth was laid on his forehead.

"Jim," a soft voice whispered. "Jim, can you hear me?"

"I hear you," Jim replied.

A few minutes more and he began to make out the faces of perhaps four people standing over him. He recognized Elizabeth; then his son, John; his good friend, Jerome; and another man he did not know.

Slowly, the pieces in his mind began to come together, and he remembered some of what had taken place.

"Elizabeth," he said. "How did John and Jerome get here?"

Elizabeth began to cry in response, clearly relieved that her husband was showing signs of recovery but worried about his disoriented state of mind. Then she said, "You are home, my dear husband. Don't you recognize your surroundings?"

Somewhat disconcerted, Jim scrutinized the room again and realized that he *was* at home, lying in his own bed.

"I've lost some time, Elizabeth. How long have I been unconscious?"

"Almost two days now."

"Mother called me right away from Mount Vernon," said John. "She told me what happened; I couldn't reach William, but Jerome was able to drive down with me. You were transported here by ambulance. We drove Mother home."

"I am glad I was able to help out," said Jerome. "But I'm not finished yet. I intend to find the man who hit you and see that he is tried and punished."

"Jerome, you are a wonderful friend, and I understand your feelings as well as your thirst for justice. But I will ask you *as* my good friend to let it pass. I don't want you to get involved. What I saw in Mount Vernon was a tragedy perpetrated by inexplicable hatred. I realize that to some extent I have been all too naïve. I wait and I hope and I pray for the world to turn around; to break this evil bond of racism; to see the evildoers asking God for forgiveness. But when I looked upon a gleeful crowd of men and women abusing the corpse of a man who was murdered because of the color of his skin, I understood just how far away dreams can be from reality."

"Father, I know you will be comforted to hear that we took care of Sadie Reed," said John. "By the time Jerome and I got there the mob had vanished. We did the best we could to give her son a decent burial. Then we gave her some money and put her on a train to Atlanta so that she could get to her brother Obediah's house."

"God bless you, son. We must all pray for that good woman and her son."

"Jim, I want you to meet Dr. Simon Rogers, a newcomer to Macon," said Elizabeth. "He was waiting here at the house when we arrived; he has been treating you."

"I appreciate your help, Doctor," said Jim.

"I am truly glad to be of service to you, Jim. As your wife mentioned, I am new to the town of Macon, but I have already heard quite a lot about you and your family—admittedly from many who oppose your efforts. Nevertheless, I admire your work and your dedication to a just cause."

"I thank you, Doctor, but I hardly deserve admiration for doing only what the Lord expects from all of us."

"I couldn't agree more, Jim, but when you consider the state of humanity in this world, you and your family try harder than most to combat this injustice."

"Again, I thank you, Doctor."

"Now, Jim, as for your condition. You have suffered a severe concussion. I am very concerned about the length of time that you were unconscious. I have taken care of the wound to your head; aside from the swelling, it should heal just fine. I am far more interested in any damage that might have occurred on the inside."

"I understand," said Jim.

"I want you to rest, and I mean right here in your bed, for at least a week. I will be back to check on you once a day until I'm sure that you are out of danger."

"I will keep a close watch, Doctor," said Elizabeth.

"Good. Now I will take my leave and ask that the rest of you, save for Elizabeth, do the same. Quiet and rest is my prescription for the moment."

After expressing their good wishes, John and Jerome walked out with Dr. Rogers. Elizabeth stayed behind to sit with Jim until he closed his eyes to sleep.

THIRTEEN

The Road Gets Rougher

The following week, Dr. Rogers stopped by to see Jim each day, as he had promised. While Jim's condition seemed to be improving, the doctor did not appear as satisfied with the examinations as Elizabeth would have liked. Dr. Rogers always requested that she leave the room before the examination—a request that became increasingly difficult for her to grant.

Finally, at the end of the week, Elizabeth could not keep her patience in check any longer.

"My husband and I have faced much adversity in our lives, Doctor, and we have always managed to get through it because we have each other. If Jim is facing something of that nature now, I must know all there is to know."

"You are absolutely right about that, Elizabeth, and I apologize for my delay in giving you a full appraisal of the situation. It is just that I wanted to be positive of any conclusions before I did so. But I believe that I can tell you with certainty now that Jim's injury was not limited to a severe concussion."

"What are you trying to tell me?"

"I believe that the blow to his head has left him with sensory problems."

"I see. How will that alter the rest of his life?"

"It may be a bit premature to determine what might pass and what might become permanent, but I can tell you what his symptoms are now. Some of them you may have already seen for yourself. Jim has a persistent ringing in his ears—has he mentioned that to you?"

"No, he hasn't."

"He has difficulty recognizing objects, his hand to eye coordination has been impaired. Jim also suffers from double vision, and after seeing him today I can verify that he has trouble with dizziness; he cannot maintain his balance."

"I was not aware of all of this. He has not complained of anything, and I have cared for him as if he were a child—including hand feeding. Maybe that's why I haven't noticed any of his disabilities."

Dr. Rogers' prognosis took a toll on Elizabeth. Her eyes were wet with tears; she sat down in the closest chair and bowed her head.

"Please understand, Elizabeth, that the news is at its worst right now. It is still just over a week since the injury. If Jim were younger there would be more cause to worry. But he is an older man and will need more time before the status of a full recovery can be determined. In addition, when the time is right, there will be a period of therapy that may reverse some of these symptoms."

Elizabeth looked up at the doctor and said, "I thank you for everything you've done and everything you've told me. I will adjust to this, and I will help Jim get through his recovery, keeping a positive outlook at all times."

"I know you will, Elizabeth. I will be checking back next week. In the meantime, call me if you need me or if you have questions."

When Dr. Rogers had gone, she went upstairs to sit with Jim. He was sleeping, but her presence in the room soon caused him to stir.

"I didn't mean to wake you," she said.

"I'm glad you did. I was dreaming about you, but seeing you beside me is much better," he said with a smile. "I can see concern in your face, dear. What did Dr. Rogers tell you?"

"Everything," she replied. "It is not easy to control my anger toward the mob in Mount Vernon for what they did to Sadie Reed's son and for what they did to you. I have always shared your opinions about the violence and the failure of the law to bring violators to justice—now I feel it like never before."

"I will pray that you do not become bitter, Elizabeth. We are unpopular ambassadors, and we represent unpopular ideas. But I have no regrets for anything I've done to help our black brothers and sisters."

"I know that, Jim, and I love you for it. I will not give way to bitterness. I will stay by your side, and if it is God's will, you will recover and go on serving Him as you always have."

"We will do it together," he replied.

A month passed before Jim was able to get out of bed, but when he did, a wheelchair became his next challenge. Elizabeth busied herself with moving their bedroom to the first floor; John and William carried him down the stairs; a ramp was built outside the kitchen door in the back of the house for access.

When the arrangements were complete, John stayed for a while to visit with his father.

"Abbey and I have been talking, Father, and we would like to take the place of you and Mother. We will continue with your work for Eleanor Roosevelt."

"I think that is a wonderful idea, son. I must admit that I sometimes wonder how much good we were really doing, but what might seem small to us might be much larger to Eleanor. I suppose that every little effort made could add up to something helpful."

"I believe that too, Father. What you and Mother accomplished was to be the voice of the people, giving them a chance to be heard by someone who could really be a champion of their cause."

"I never thought of it in quite that way, but you're right. We were able to lay their troubles on the doorstep of the highest office in the land. By all means, you and Abbey must take our places."

Elizabeth wrote to Eleanor, informing her of the situation. The first lady sent her condolences and promised to visit when she was in the area. She was, in fact, very grateful to learn that the reports on conditions in Georgia would continue to reach her.

Under the guidance of Dr. Rogers, Jim did what he could to bounce back from the blow to the head he'd suffered in Mount Vernon, but progress was very slow in coming.

Most of his days were spent sitting in the parlor listening to the radio or resting in bed. Most of his evenings were spent listening to Elizabeth as she read the newspaper to him. His faculties had been compromised, but his mind continued to process every scrap of information he could get concerning the world and what was going on in it.

As often as possible, John, Abbey, William, and Joanna would visit, which always led to deep conversations about current events. Their company was good therapy for Jim, especially when his great-grandson, Martin, was there to sit attentively by his side.

Once again, in 1938, the attempt was made to push the Costigan–Wagner Anti-Lynching Bill through Congress, and once again it was defeated by southern opposition. Jim was listening to the news on the radio and heard the announcement just as John and Abbey were arriving from their latest trip. Elizabeth greeted them when they knocked on the front door. When they came into the parlor, Jim turned the radio off.

"It was defeated again," said Jim.

"The Costigan–Wagner bill?" John asked.

"Yes, for the fourth time now."

"I guess that is FDR's definition of gratitude. Mary McLeod Bethume and Walter Francis White of the NAACP were actively involved in getting Roosevelt elected. They thought he would get anti-lynching legislation passed. But he was too afraid he'd anger the South and wouldn't get reelected," said John.

"Yes, I realize that nothing is perfect, and if the president delivers on most of his promises, a person might be inclined to cut his losses. But to decide that he will not directly oppose lynching is totally unacceptable. Some of his policies *have* helped the African Americans, but if he employs you or feeds you or gives you shelter but says he will not oppose those who might lynch you . . . what *kind* of a new deal is that?" Jim asked.

"Seventy-three years since the end of the Civil War, and what has really changed? I think of Grandfather's words every day. How he predicted a very long time before the ex-slave would enjoy the same rights as other Americans."

"I think about that too, John. And you are right. The vote is still denied, protection under the law, equal wages, and so much more. The only thing that has eased a bit is trouble from the Klan. Their numbers are nothing compared to what they used to be. I have not seen a burning cross in quite some time. Let us hope that there will never be another resurgence."

"Amen to that, Father. In the meantime, southern blacks are still dirt poor, and help from the government is little or nothing. The only blacks in the South who are living a better life are those lucky few who managed somehow to get an education and have a business or a profession. But the black majority is still living hand to mouth," John explained.

"We've seen some very dire situations in the places we've visited. It breaks your heart to see human beings with so little of what it takes to sustain life," said Abbey.

"It makes you feel guilty to be white," said Elizabeth. "And yet we've met black people who spoke with us and treated us as if they didn't notice the color of our skin. So understanding are those people in whom the Lord dwells."

"Poor people both black and white have been doing whatever they can since the beginning of the Depression. Backyard gardens are still shared with neighbors and famished passersby. Some people are even doubling up in their own living areas to make room for relatives who have no income, and barns have become homeless shelters," said John.

"In the South, Georgia is one of the states that has been hit the hardest by the Depression. With African Americans condemned and crushed under the Jim Crow laws, it is certainly expected that they would be relegated to the most menial, low-paying jobs," said Jim.

"In addition, the federal government bows to the state of Georgia's wishes to curtail benefits for blacks because of its congressional delegation to Roosevelt's programs and because of its white supremacy politics. The National Youth Administration, which brings employment relief to poor rural blacks, is the only exception," John remarked.

"It seems that some of the progress the country had made has now languished with the outset of this downward spiral into a recession," said Elizabeth.

"It is still a curse to be black in this country. If our entire landmass was suddenly covered with water, the blacks would be the last to be provided with life preservers," said John in a cynical tone of voice.

"The troubles of the world are great," said Jim. "Like the African Americans here at home, many people in other countries are being persecuted for reasons of religion, ethnic background, and yes, in some cases, skin color. It is my firm belief that war, perhaps another world war, is not more than a couple of years away."

"Do you really think so, Father?"

"Yes, John, I do. With so much time to do nothing, I listen and absorb more news than I ever have before, and my advice to the world would be to watch out for Germany and Japan. There may be others planning some kind of conquest, but I think that the Japanese and the Nazis in Germany will be some of the principal players."

"A reprisal by the Germans, Father?"

"Yes. Germany was totally and utterly defeated in the Great War. They were defeated and punished by the severe conditions of the Treaty of Versailles, which imposed reparations to certain countries that formed the Entente Powers. They were ordered to disarm, and substantial territory concessions were exacted. In a word, Germany had been destroyed."

"I guess they feel it is time to wreak a little vengeance for all of their suffering," John replied.

"That would be my guess too," Jim agreed. "This new leader, Adolf Hitler, and his Nazi party have already violated the treaty by moving an army into the Rhineland, and they are building their war machine—also a violation of the treaty. His army has taken over Austria, and I doubt that his territorial interests will stop there. Back in 1933, Herbert Hoover told Hitler that his doctrine would not be tolerated in the United States, and the United States then asked all powers to help refugees who are fleeing the Nazis. President Roosevelt must deal with Hitler now. As for the Japanese . . . they have just declared war on China."

FOURTEEN

The Consequence of Prediction

By the end of 1938, the recession was over, and conditions continued their slow ascent out of the economic collapse of 1929.

By the beginning of 1939, Dr. Rogers told Jim that any improvement he'd made since his injury was now most likely a permanent condition; it was doubtful that he would progress further. The ringing in his ears had diminished, and his eyesight allowed him to read for short periods of time. He was able to walk a little with the help of a cane; anything more would require the use of his wheelchair.

"I would do anything to soften the blow of this final evaluation," said Elizabeth after Dr. Rogers had gone.

"Please don't let it trouble you, my dear. All things considered, I feel that I am very lucky to be no worse off than I am. There are others who have much more room to complain. Even our president uses a wheelchair much of the time. I am happy that I can read again."

"Your strong constitution is to be admired, Jim, and your gracious acceptance of the situation deserves a reward. I think good news would be appropriate, and I have some for you."

"A rare and cherished event these days. Please share it with me."

"William and Joanna are going to have another child; it should come late in the summer."

"You tricked me, Elizabeth. Here I was expecting good news, and you gave me heartwarming, absolutely wonderful news. Wouldn't it be nice for Martin to have a baby sister?"

"You're hoping for a granddaughter?"

"I am indeed. I haven't seen a darling little girl in a lovely flowered dress since Julia was a child. I really miss her."

"I do too," said Elizabeth. "I hope she is home for Christmas again this year. England is so far away."

"Not only that, but it is much too close to Germany."

"You're still worried that trouble is brewing over there, aren't you?"

"Yes, I am. Germany is occupying Czechoslovakia now. I fear that it is just the beginning of Hitler's territorial interests. There are more and more inferences concerning the treatment of the Jews as well. I am not ashamed to say that that man frightens me."

"I have more news, Jim."

"As pleasant as the first?"

"I would say more good than pleasant."

"I will settle for that," Jim replied.

"I received a telephone call from Eleanor this morning, and I want to tell you what she said."

"That was so good of her; I don't know where she finds the time."

"She asked me how you were doing. I brought her up to date—she wishes you well. She told me that she has decided to attack the hypocritical way that the country deals with racial injustice. She wants her fellow Americans to see how their guilt in speaking and writing about democracy with no consideration of the limitations within our system with regard to African Americans encourages racism. She said that the white people of America want only to speak of the good features of American life while hiding the problems like skeletons in a closet. Terrorism and intimidation promote racism, and Americans must take action against such ridiculous behavior."

"I'd say that she gets right to the point, as always," said Jim. "I remember she once told me that she agitates J. Edgar Hoover so much that he very nearly accused her of having black blood. She is an angel on the shoulder of the African Americans, and I hope someday she is rewarded in heaven. Did she say anything else?"

"Just that she still means to stop and see you if she gets the chance."

"I would enjoy seeing her, but I would hope that she puts seeing me on the bottom of her list of things to do. I spend a lot of time trying to think of something more I can do to help her."

"I understand your feelings, Jim, but I think that your health is most important right now. You know what Dr. Rogers said, and I think he is a pretty good doctor."

"I quite agree, Elizabeth, but it can't hurt to think positive, and if I try hard enough I think I can get a little more out of this old body."

"Please promise me that you won't push too hard," said Elizabeth in a worried tone.

"I promise that I won't put myself in harm's way again—not like I did in Mount Vernon."

"That makes me very happy. I will hold you to your promise."

That night, as Jim lay in bed trying to fall asleep while battling another terrible headache, he thought about the discussion he'd had with Elizabeth about his health. He could sense the weaknesses that had set in, and he knew that his limitations were very definite. He couldn't help wondering how much more time God would give him.

On August 15, William's wife, Joanna, gave birth to a seven-pound baby girl, whom they named Maryann. Her arrival brought such joy, lifting everyone's spirits like a tonic. In thanking God for a gift as special as a great-granddaughter, Jim also prayed that the Almighty would protect her and the whole family as they moved forward into a very uncertain time.

As the days went by, it seemed to Jim that the condition of things in the world was changing rapidly. He could only imagine that world leaders were contemplating the future with much consternation. Nations were choosing sides, and the stage was being set for what was sure to be a war of epic proportions.

By the latter part of August, the Nazis had demanded Danzig from Poland. Great Britain and France had agreed to support Poland if invaded by Germany; Italy had invaded Albania. Russia signed an anti-Nazi pact with Great Britain and France; Germany and Italy had announced an alliance called the Rome-Berlin Axis; Dutch border guards took up positions for a German invasion; Belgium and the Netherlands mobilized.

World War II began on September 1, 1939, with Germany's invasion of Poland. On the third of September, a German U boat sunk the *Athenia*, a British passenger ship, killing 117 people. In the wake of this unprovoked tragedy, Great Britain declared war on Nazi Germany, and they were followed into battle by France, Australia, New Zealand, South Africa, and Canada.

On the last day of September, Jim was sitting in the parlor at six a.m. with his first cup of coffee; Elizabeth was in the kitchen. Jim rolled his wheelchair to the front door when the first knock sounded.

He could not imagine who might be at the door at such an early hour, and his surprise only increased when he saw John and Abbey standing on the veranda.

"Good morning, you two," he said. "Why do you feel the need to knock on the door? The door is always open, you know."

At first, neither John nor Abbey answered, and after a closer look at their stoic expressions, fear gripped Jim as it rarely ever had before. Finally, they stepped inside. John said, "We have news, Father."

Jim was afraid to ask what the nature of the news might be, so he ushered them into the parlor at the same moment that Elizabeth entered the room.

"Good morning, children," she said. "Would anyone like some coffee?"

"No, Mother," said John. "We have to talk to you and Father."

"Oh, won't you make yourselves comfortable?" Worry quickly appeared in Elizabeth's face as she sat down and braced herself for bad news.

"There is something that we have been saving . . . something intended to be a wonderful surprise," said John. "We received a letter from Julia a little over a month ago. She told us that she did not feel secure in England anymore—not since the Nazis came to power, creating what she described as a sense of foreboding hanging heavily in the air. She told us she had decided to move back to

Georgia, possibly for good, or at least until everything was peaceful again. She expected to be home by early October."

John stopped and looked at Abbey; tears were streaming down her face; she put her head on John's shoulder. Jim and Elizabeth held their breath, waiting for their son to continue.

John pulled a piece of paper from his shirt pocket and unfolded it. He tried to read what was written but could not get the words out. He folded the paper, put it back in his pocket, and said, "This telegram from London confirms that Julia was on board the *Athenia* when it was torpedoed by the German U boat and sunk."

Jim felt his heart skip a beat; Elizabeth went over to John and Abbey; the three of them began to weep uncontrollably. Jim wheeled his chair over to them and broke completely down. It could have lasted for a full ten minutes or it could have lasted for over an hour. None of them would ever know. Time seemed to stop when John finished the announcement. No one could stop crying; no one wanted to.

They could picture Julia in their minds and wished with all their hearts that the news was somehow a mistake. They prayed that she was with God, waiting for a reunion with them that would someday take place in heaven.

But when the bereaved parents and grandparents could look each other in the eye, the horribly visible pain of their loss confirmed that the grief they felt would be a long time fading away. Eventually, there was a cold empty silence, and then Abbey said, "I cannot even bury my child. She will never be recovered from a cold watery grave. A place I can never visit to place flowers in her memory." And she started to cry again.

Elizabeth did what she could to comfort Abbey, a near impossible task, mired as she was in her own anguish. Jim rested his hand on his son's knee and said, "You've told William?"

"I have, Father," he replied. "That poor boy is in pieces. Thank God he has Joanna, Martin, and Maryann. We will have a service for Julia, Father. We'll have it here, and we'll place a stone in our family cemetery; a place where we can go to be with her. I know her spirit will come home to stay."

"I know she will, son," said Jim through another deluge of tears. "I know she will."

The following Sunday, a service was held for Julia. Distant family members were notified but asked not to make the trip because their beloved Julia was not really there. Prayers could be sent from anywhere *to* anywhere, and that was the request made by John and Abbey.

Everyone on Langdon Plantation was in attendance; Jerome, Esther, and Mattie were there too. It was good to have so many friends, Jim thought. They helped to shoulder the burden that God had placed upon them.

After Julia's death, nothing was the same for the Langdons. Eventually the family was able to let her go, but the pall that hovered over them would not quite disappear. Maybe it was because Jim's prediction about an impending war had come true, and the consequences of that prediction's materialization were already beginning to ensue in a way no one would have dreamed possible.

A cherished member of the family had been lost because of it—one who hadn't even been involved. Now the question on everyone's mind was: When will the United States get involved? But the war had dramatically increased the country's industrial production, and it seemed that the Great Depression was over; life was good. Vivid memories of the First World War still haunted the American people; they did not wish to get involved in another war in Europe. Most people felt that the war was Europe's problem.

But Jim knew that it would only be a matter of time. Great Britain, an old and trusted ally, had locked horns with the Nazis. German bombs were falling on London like raindrops, and it was no secret that Winston Churchill was pleading with President Roosevelt for help.

The president declared a limited national emergency due to the war but nothing more until March of 1941. It was then that Jim read about the Lend-Lease Act, which provided military aid to foreign nations.

This act authorized the president to allocate military arms and other equipment, for which Congress appropriated money, to the government of any country whose defense was deemed vital to the defense of the United States.

Thus it was decided by the Langdon family to become more aware of their opportunity to keep their loved ones safe by supporting the government and its allies in defeating those who would seek to destroy the peace and tranquility of the world.

They would do everything possible to increase their production of cotton. The demand for cotton goods had been heavily boosted by the National Defense Act of 1940. The federal government had been given the power to establish a peacetime draft due to this legislation.

It was the mere possibly of conscription that had enticed the textile industry leaders and War Department Officials to the conference table, where a coordinated effort was planned to supply the Quartermaster Corps with the huge amount of cotton material it would need to supply an army.

The summer of 1941 seemed like a true revitalization to many Americans. In spite of the headlines in the papers, the war in Europe seemed far away, while everything at home was getting better and better.

Jim, however, was falling back away from the final condition in which the injury in Mount Vernon had left him. Scarcely a day went by without suffering from an excruciating headache, an occurrence that he did his absolute best to hide from Elizabeth. By day he tried to appear normal, but at night before going to sleep he prayed to the Almighty that he be taken quickly if he was of no further use.

Of course he could not know what the Lord had in mind for him until the day in December when he last remembered sitting on the veranda in his wheelchair and then awoke in his bed not knowing how he got there. Elizabeth was sitting by his side, and Dr. Rogers was standing near the head of the bed.

"How are you feeling?" asked the doctor.

Straining just to speak Jim replied, "Strange as it may sound, Doctor, I think that you are in a better position to answer that question than I am."

"I know that you and Elizabeth both want the absolute truth, and I would not disrespect either of you by giving you anything other than that."

"You have gotten to know us well," Jim replied.

"I do not believe that you will ever leave your bed," said Dr. Rogers in a sad tone of voice.

"We thank you for your honesty, Doctor," said Elizabeth. "Do you know how long it will be?"

"Soon," he answered. "I will leave you now. I am sorry I couldn't do more."

Dr. Rogers took hold of Jim's hand and squeezed gently. He noticed the weakness in Jim's grip and he knew the time would arrive within a matter of hours. Then he picked up his bag and left the room.

Much to Jim's surprise and comfort, Elizabeth did not break into tears. He knew she understood that she had to be strong for him, and it made the moment so much easier. She was matter of fact; as if they were discussing the weather or something in the daily newspaper.

"Well," she began. "I guess the time has come for us to be separated for a little while. Find a beautiful place beneath a huge tree next to a clear running stream, and wait for me there. I know after you leave I will be ready to follow soon."

"My darling Elizabeth. I will be fine until we meet again. Stay with the children for as long as you can. We will go back to the beginning, and there will never be another parting. I am sorry that we never had the family reunion. It would have been nice."

"I am sorry that I never wrote the letters you asked me to write," she answered.

"It's all right, dear. I understand why you didn't. I couldn't fool you about my condition, could I?"

"I know you too well, my dear husband."

"I need to rest now, Elizabeth."

"I will have the children here tonight to see you."

"I would like that very much," Jim replied.

Elizabeth got up, went out into the hallway, and closed the door. Jim heard her painful cries as she made her way downstairs. He stared at the ceiling and spoke to his Creator, praising His holy name and expressing his gratitude for having been given so much. Then he closed his eyes and thought of the children; he couldn't wait to see them.

As the sun was going down, Jim fell into a very deep sleep, and before the children could arrive, the Lord called him home. It was December 6, 1941.

FIFTEEN

Jim Crow Goes to War

On Sunday morning, December seventh, Elizabeth sat in the parlor with the rest of the family seated around her. So recently she had contacted distant family to relay the sad news of Julia's death. Now she had faced the grim task again; this time to let them know that her beloved Jim had passed away. She even called Washington and left a message for Eleanor—not really expecting her to attend the funeral but thinking that she might like to know. Jim's body had been transported to Macon; all the arrangements had been made. The service would be held in three days.

Grief had once again created a very quiet, subdued atmosphere. The bereaved family sipped coffee and spoke very little. Everyone was resigned to allowing their pain to dissipate; they prayed and looked for strength from within because they all knew that the loved and lost would want it that way.

It was nearly four o'clock p.m. when a knock came at the front door. John got up and left the parlor to see who was calling. When he opened the door, there stood one of the Langdon family's dearest friends; it was Jerome Tomkins. The sadness was etched into his face, and it was clear that he had been crying.

"Welcome, Jerome," said John. "I am very glad you are here. I know I don't have to tell you how much my father valued your friendship; that goes for the rest of the family as well."

"I certainly *do* know, John," he replied, his voice shaking from unrestrained emotion. "I want to extend my most profound sympathies to you and your family. There is not another man on this earth I respected more than your father, and not another man who was as great a friend to me as he was."

"Won't you come in and have some coffee, Jerome?"

"Certainly, John."

When Jerome walked into the parlor, everyone extended and affectionate welcome. Elizabeth rose and held out her hand to him. John brought a hot cup of coffee; Jerome sat down beside Elizabeth.

"Thank you for coming, Jerome," she said. "You were a great friend to Jim, and he would be happy to know you're here."

"It is very hard to acknowledge his death, Elizabeth. I find it difficult to deal with a loss so great; Esther has had an even harder time. She could not bear coming along this morning, but she and Mattie will be with me at the funeral."

"I understand," said Elizabeth. "God bless her compassionate heart."

"Forgive me for asking at a time like this, Elizabeth, but have you listened to your radio yet this morning?"

"Why, no. Is there something we should know?"

"I'm afraid so. About an hour and a half ago newsman John Daly of WCBS radio in New York broadcast the report of an air attack on Pearl Harbor, Hawaii by the Empire of Japan. Our Pacific Fleet was almost completely destroyed; numerous planes were also destroyed, and over twenty-four hundred servicemen were killed."

A collective gasp came from everyone in the room; tears came to every eye immediately, and it felt as though a shroud had completely covered the earth.

"What will come of this?" said Elizabeth to the gathering.

"War will come of this," said John. "The American people wanted so badly to stay out of the conflict, but this appalling act will reverse that desire and turn it into a thirst for vengeance."

"I'm afraid he is exactly right," said Jerome. "President Roosevelt will not sit still for this. I am sure a declaration of war is imminent."

"Would you like me to turn the radio on, Mother?" John asked.

"No, son. This attack is news of epic proportion; something that will affect every man, woman, and child in America, and we will seriously consider the matter and what our part might be. But first we will allow ourselves a period of mourning and the opportunity to say goodbye to your father."

"Of course we will, Mother," said John. "Of course we will."

In spite of their grieving, the entire family listened to the radio the following day, and at 12:32 p.m. they heard President Roosevelt speak for six minutes and thirty seconds as he addressed a joint session of Congress to ask for a declaration of war against Japan.

Within an hour, Congress voted almost unanimously to acquiesce to the president's request, and the United States was plunged headlong into World War II.

On Tuesday, December ninth, Jim was laid to rest in the family cemetery near his mother and father. Although the Langdons had long been outcasts in their native land near Macon—labeled as lovers of the black-skinned race; hated especially by the Klan ever since Jim's father had returned home from fighting for the Union—Elizabeth could remember a large turnout when Jim's father died. She was pleased to see that there were many people who had a great deal of respect for her husband as well.

Much to her surprise, Eleanor Roosevelt and Lorena Hicks *did* in fact make an appearance at the service. Elizabeth, knowing how terribly busy they were, thanked them over and over for their time.

"There are some things too important to let pass by," Eleanor told Elizabeth. "Your husband and his whole family are very special people, and I had to come and pay my respects. I want to thank you for all the work that you and Jim did for me, not to mention your son and his wife. We really must be going, but I would like to meet the rest of your family first."

"And you shall," Elizabeth replied.

The three ladies made a brief pass through the crowd; Elizabeth made the introductions as they went. Everyone was pleased and quite impressed by the presence of the first lady. As Elizabeth walked them to their car, William came up behind them and said, "Mrs. Roosevelt I know you must leave—I thank you again for coming—but could I please have a quick word with you before you go? It is a matter of utmost importance."

"I would be happy to spare you a few minutes, William," she replied.

Elizabeth bade the ladies goodbye and turned to go back to her guests. She briefly wondered what it was that William wanted to speak to Eleanor about, but it passed out of her mind when she rejoined the gathering.

That evening, John and Abbey went over to sit with Elizabeth for a while. They thought she might like some company as a comfort after the hustle and bustle of the day.

"I like to think that Father is enjoying a reunion with our family in heaven," said John. "It makes his passing so much easier to picture it that way."

"I envision the same thing," Elizabeth replied. "It most certainly helps to heal the pain of separation, knowing that your loved one is with God. After all, death is part of life. We all know that we are just passing through to another place—a far better place. I will surely miss your father and look forward to our reunion; I know that I am bound for the same destination, and that is a great comfort."

"We will keep his memory alive forever," said Abbey. "He will always be with us in spirit; he will be close by."

John got up to fetch more coffee from the kitchen, but a knock at the door changed his direction. Elizabeth and Abbey could hear him identify William as the visitor. The two of them entered the parlor, and William said, "Good evening, Mother, Grandmother. I would like to talk to all of you, if I'm not interrupting anything."

"Gracious me, not at all," said Elizabeth. "Your mother and father and I were just sharing some consoling thoughts about your grandfather. Please sit with us a while. Would you like some coffee?"

"No, thank you, Grandmother. I have something I'd like to get off mind."

"Sit yourself down, William," said John.

William took a seat next to Elizabeth, and then he began to explain the reason for his visit.

"I have made a decision and it will have a direct effect on the whole family but especially Joanna, Martin, and Maryann."

"Please tell us," said Abbey.

"Well, you know, Grandmother, that I spoke to Mrs. Roosevelt before she left."

"Yes, I remember."

"In light of the Japanese attack on Pearl Harbor and the subsequent declaration of war by the president, I have decided to enlist in the army."

The announcement came as a bit of a surprise to William's family. At first, no one quite knew how to react. After a few minutes of digesting the news, John said, "From what I understand, the young men of this country are heading in increasing numbers to the recruiting stations to sign up in the aftermath of this appalling act. I think that I can speak for your mother when I say that this is a decision that would make any parent proud. But I *would* like to know how Joanna took the news."

"Well, Father, I didn't make this decision alone. I did not simply tell Joanna that I was going to join the army. I engaged her in conversation, and being the intuitive wife that she is, after a few minutes she knew what I was leading up to. She said that she was proud of such an unselfish sacrifice and proud of me for the inclination. Of course the separation will be difficult for us as well as for the children, but it wouldn't be a sacrifice if it didn't hurt a little. But, Mother, Father, I want to know what you think—you too, Grandmother."

"I could not speak against this," said Elizabeth. "As you know, your great-grandfather fought for the Union during the Civil War. He was recovering from battle wounds far from home when your grandfather was born. He was fighting to free the slaves, and he stayed the course until the end came. The separation *will* be difficult, William, for all of us. But the only thing necessary for evil to flourish is for good men to do nothing."

"Your grandmother is right, son," said John. "We do what we must do under the Lord's supervision. He is guiding you, He will watch over you, and He will bring you home again."

"There is nothing I can say that could improve on what has already been said," Abbey answered. "I am honored that you are my son and gratified that you wish to serve your country."

"A blessing from all of you is what I needed. I know I don't have to worry about Joanna and the children while I'm gone. I know that you will be looking out for them."

"Of course we will," John replied. "I was wondering, William. You could have gone into Macon to enlist—what did you need from Eleanor?"

"Well, there is a little more to this besides serving my country. I know that, just like in all previous wars, many black men will answer the call to arms. I know also that they will not receive the appreciation and respect the white soldiers will receive. I want to be there with them, even if I am the only one treating them as an equal. I asked Mrs. Roosevelt to help me secure an assignment with a black division."

"This is a special moment for us and for the entire Langdon family, past and present," said John. "With the slightest concentration I can actually hear exactly how your grandfather and great-grandfather would reply to that. It's wonderful, William."

"I have you and my ancestors to thank for the wisdom and the ability to see that all men are equal under God. Some of my best friends are African American; I may never have enjoyed that part of my life if not for you."

"When will you be leaving, son?" asked Abbey.

"In a few months, Mother. I am waiting to hear from Mrs. Roosevelt. She intends to have me placed in officer training then assigned to a black division after that. She said that there may be some junior officers who are black, but senior officers and the commanding officer will all be white. Not much has changed since the Civil War, has it?"

"No, not much," John replied.

"Mrs. Roosevelt said that if I am an officer I will have more authority and may be in a better position to look out for the men."

"She is very wise. What a help it will be to have someone like Eleanor on your side."

"Indeed it will, Father. I must be getting home to Joanna and the children. We can talk about this again when I know more."

When William had gone, Elizabeth cried for a minute or two, partly, she said, because Jim was not alive to bear witness to his grandson's bravery; partly because she was worried about William; and partly because she was so proud of him.

It was not long before William heard from Mrs. Roosevelt, and in April 1942, he boarded the train in Macon, bound for training at Fort Benning, Georgia. After seventeen weeks, he graduated as a second lieutenant. He was granted leave for two weeks, which was a most precious period of time for William and his family.

Everyone knew that when he left home again, it would likely be a very long time before they saw him. Two days before it was time to leave, the family had a gathering that included most of the sharecroppers and their families. One young black man by the name of Howard Clay, who was born on Langdon Plantation, enlisted in the army and would accompany William to Camp Claiborne in Louisiana. In fact, they would be serving together in the 761st Tank Battalion.

The last day of William's leave was spent with Joanna and the children. The following day, a small crowd of family and friends were at the station to say goodbye to the two men, black and white; many tears were shed, many silent prayers were sent.

When the train finally left the station, John stared after it, wondering how much different the experience in the army would be for a white officer and a black enlisted man. However, he was very proud of his son for requesting an assignment with a black unit because John knew that as soon as William's peers realized that he did not have a natural hatred for the black man he would in all likelihood be ostracized by them. It would be a rough road to travel, but other members of the Langdon family had navigated that road before.

Camp Claiborne, which was near the town of Alexandria, Louisiana, was situated in the snake-infested swamplands inside the Evangeline section of the Kisatchie National Forest. The camp consisted of a few permanent buildings, some dilapidated barracks; the rest was made up of tents and hutments.

When William and Howard reached the camp, the reception they received was about what they both expected. William was greeted with respect and hospitality; Howard was quickly marched away by a black sergeant who was clearly driven by anger and hostility.

William was taken to the office of Major Raymond E. Cruise, the commander of the 761st. Major Cruise was not large in stature, but his appearance was as intimidating as William had ever laid eyes on before. He was in his fifties with coarse black hair, deep-cut lines in his face, and a large nose that resembled a buzzard's beak. Although he seemed friendly enough when he shook hands with William, he resonated an aura—a warning that his mood could become ugly at any time.

After taking the chair offered to him by the major, it only took about two or three minutes before William had to actually remind himself why he had been so dedicated to the mission he had undertaken.

Although he had been raised in close proximity to racial prejudice and violence aimed not only at African Americans but toward his own family for their belief in equality, Langdon Plantation was like a world unto itself. Because of his great-grandfather there were twenty-five hundred acres in central Georgia where racial discrimination did not exist. William could see for himself what it was like for the black and white races to live in harmony and friendship. It was something that he held very dear.

But when Major Cruise began to speak, William felt that he was being subjected to the hatred of the African Americans for the first time.

"Boy, I'm gonna teach you about Nigras," the major began. "You're down here with Eleanor Roosevelt's niggers, boy, and I'm gonna tell you that these monkeys have got to be handled differently. The fact that we have to put up with them at all just goes to show you how gone to hell this world is. It was those damn uppity niggers, the NAACP, and the Congress of Racial Equality putting pressure on the War Department and President Roosevelt to let nigger soldiers serve on the same level as white soldiers."

The major seemed to have an inexhaustible supply of racial wrath, not to mention the huge waste of breath he spent on expressing it. It was hard to believe that a man of his ilk would be put in charge of a black battalion, but then William remembered that in the southern United States it would take a very long time to find a man who was any different from this insufferable bigot. He was in fact probably chosen for his overseer's mentality. The worst part was that, given the situation, there was no way William could simply tell the commanding officer to keep his foul remarks to himself.

"But these niggers will never be put into combat," the major continued. "You're in a safe place; we're just marking time down here."

Just then a black first sergeant, a man by the name of Sam Turley, came into the office.

"I want you to meet our new second lieutenant, Turley."

Then William made an instinctive but terrible mistake; he shook hands with the first sergeant.

"Get outta here, Turley!" the major shouted. Then he stuck a finger out at William and said, "Boy, don't you ever put yourself on the same level with a Nigra!"

But it wasn't until the commander finally picked up William's personnel folder and started to scan it that the situation really got rough. After a minute or two he looked up from the folder with an expression of total disbelief on his unpleasant face.

"It says here that you're from Georgia."

"Yes sir, about twenty miles south of Macon."

"I thought I heard a southern accent in your voice, but when you shook hands with that Nigra sergeant I figured I musta been wrong. Were you born in Georgia?"

"Yes sir. My family owns a large cotton plantation that goes back five generations."

"Then it musta been worked by slaves."

"My great-great-grandfather owned slaves, sir."

"Then why in hell did you offer your hand to that shuffle butt coon a couple minutes ago?"

In his mind's eye, William saw that he was closed in by four walls; no doors and no windows; there was no way out.

With no time to think, he had to make a monumental decision. Should he paint over the major's objection to his shaking the black sergeant's hand and turn himself into the commander's puppet? Or should he take the major head on and let him know that he was *not* a southern racist?

William was not concerned about his own hide. He was not afraid of the treatment he would face if the other white soldiers found out about his beliefs. His great-grandfather did not let the Ku Klux Klan drive him out of Georgia. But it was a transfer that William feared. He wanted to fight with a black unit. What could he do if the major decided he didn't want William in the outfit?

William stiffened his backbone and said, "All people were created equal by God no matter what their race, creed, or religion might be. The African Americans who joined this army are willing to lay down their lives for their country just as they did in all previous wars. They have suffered long and hard and deserve respect as people and especially as soldiers, sir."

Major Cruise stood up, placed his hands down flat on his desk, and leaned towards William. Then in a steady, chilling voice he said, "Off the record, boy, if we were in a combat zone right now I would see to it that you meet with a bad accident and the report would read, 'killed in action with the enemy.' I would expect this kind of bullshit from a Yankee, but from a man born in Georgia with your background it makes me wanna puke. You can't begin to understand the deep resentment and contempt I have for you!"

"I beg your pardon, Major," William interrupted. "But I understand all too well, sir. Ever since my great-grandfather stood up against his father and disagreed with him over the issue of slavery, my family have been outsiders in our home state. But we would not let ourselves be driven out; we stood by our beliefs, and I have no intention of doing any different, sir. Regardless of how you feel about me, I will always respect you as my commanding officer and accept the fact that we have different points of view."

For a few moments Major Cruise said nothing. It was as if William's bold admission, complete with a brief history, caught him by surprise, and he didn't quite know how to respond. It seemed like he had expected William to cower before him, deny his true feelings, and beg for forgiveness for crimes against the South. When the major spoke again, William's heart sank.

"Keep your shit packed and be ready to leave here just as soon as I can find a place to dump you," he said.

William had only one hole card, but it was one that he had never intended to reveal. Now he had no choice.

"I think you should know, Major, that Mrs. Eleanor Roosevelt is a personal friend of my family. Not only that, but it was she who helped me get into officer training and had me assigned to a black outfit at my request."

The major looked as if he might explode. Buried in a pitiless vendetta as he was with no recourse for his subjugated black soldiers and no one to challenge his abusive conduct, William possessed the one bit of leverage he could not deal with. It was certain that if the 761st ever got into the war, William would have more to fear than just the enemy. But his only concern was remaining with the battalion; he would worry about the future when it caught up with him.

"Eleanor's niggers," said the major. "And now they've got you to look after them. You'll stay here all right, but I promise you that Hell itself will seem like paradise compared to what you're in for. You'll rot here in this snake pit because you'll never get a furlough or even a weekend pass. I will personally read every letter you write or receive to make sure you don't bellyache to the outside world. And if at any time you think that I'm breakin' the rules concerning your treatment you'll be right. You'll find that, in this camp, the *white* men stick together. You may know the president's wife, but this is my battalion, and as long as you don't mysteriously end up dead, I got nothing to fear."

"You *have* nothing to fear, Major. You'll hear no complaining from me, sir."

"Get your ass the hell out of my sight!"

As William walked out of the office, Major Cruise yelled, "First Sergeant Turley, get your black ass in here!"

William was relieved to get outside and take a deep breath. The only problem was that he didn't know where he should go. He was given no direction to his quarters, and no one he saw, white or black, offered any assistance. Just when he decided to look for an empty tent or an open spot in one of the barracks, a voice behind him said, "I'll show you where to bed down, Lieutenant."

William turned around, and there stood First Sergeant Turley. The expression on his face was one of confusion and uneasiness. He was a muscular man about thirty years old with several scars on his face; probably reminders of life in a world in which his self-appointed white superiors felt he didn't belong.

"I appreciate your help, First Sergeant," said William.

"No need to thank me, sir. I just follow orders. Climb into this jeep over here. Your barracks is about a half a mile from here; other side of the camp."

William put his belongings into the jeep and got into the front seat. The first sergeant sped off down a long, dusty road that led to a small group of broken down buildings on the outskirts of the camp. There was no conversation on the way; the sergeant looked straight ahead, and William wondered if he had heard any of what had been said in Major Cruise's office.

When the jeep stopped in front of one of the barracks, the sergeant started to get out, but William put a hand on his arm and said, "If you don't mind, First Sergeant Turley, I would like to talk to you for a minute."

"I don't have too much time, sir. If the major needs me for something and I ain't there, I may not get no supper tonight."

"Very well, First Sergeant. I wouldn't want to be the cause of your getting into trouble."

Turley looked thoughtful for a moment and then said, "It's all right, Lieutenant. The major was leaving to go into town when I left. What do you want to know?"

"I'd like to know a little bit about the battalion."

"Well, the 761st just became a battalion about two weeks ago. Right now we got three hundred and thirteen black enlisted men and twenty-seven white officers. We call ourselves the Black Panthers, and our motto is *Come out Fighting*. That's kinda funny when you think about it because we're told all the time that we ain't never gonna be put into combat. We are only here because a few black organizations raised enough hell about letting us serve. We are here for appearances you might say, just to make our people in Washington think we are getting somewhere."

"But if pressure got you and your comrades here on a military base and into training, maybe the same tactic will get you into the war someday," said William.

"Well, all we know is that the white soldiers are sent overseas after a few months' training, but we'll probably still be here two years from now. We are all mighty anxious; we want to fight for our homes and our country just like the white soldier. We are hoping that if we can prove ourselves, maybe we will be treated like everyone else when it's over. But I guess we're all dreamers."

"I think you have the right idea, First Sergeant. Maybe you won't convince everybody, but maybe you can convince enough of them to bring about changes."

"My great-grandfather was a soldier in the 54th Massachusetts during the Civil War. I've heard that he felt then the way I feel now. What he did made no difference. What hope do I have?"

"I guess I can't argue with that, First Sergeant. What are you training on?"

"We have the M5 Stuart light tank. The men already handle them pretty well. We'll know them better than we know ourselves before we're through. Do you mind if I ask *you* something, Lieutenant?"

"Not at all," William replied.

"What are you doing here?"

"I don't follow."

"The walls are thin as paper around here, and I work in the room next to the major. I heard him talkin' to you. You sound like a rich white man from Georgia who came here to hang around a bunch of niggers and get kicked around by Major Cruise. He's a mean man, and the only thing he probably hates more than a nigger is a white man who would take a nigger's side. Why would you do that?"

"I guess the only way I can answer that is to say that every man stands up for what he believes in. The consequences are part of the price he pays for the privilege. You men are doing the same thing. It is more difficult for you because of racial discrimination, but you still have the freedom to stand up for yourselves, and that's more than your ancestors had."

"I guess you're right. I never looked at it that way before. It took a couple hundred years to get our freedom, and it might take a couple hundred more before we are treated equally, but we are farther down the road than we were. I'm glad you're here, Lieutenant, and I wish you a lot of luck. Try not to take it hard when you find that the black soldiers don't welcome you right off. You are a man without a race. Watch your back—the other whites stick together like pine sap. It's gonna be mighty rough for you."

"Thank you, First Sergeant. I'll keep my eyes open. This is my barracks here?"

"Yes sir, you and eleven black enlisted men. Ordinarily you'd be bunkin' with the other white officers, but putting you in a barracks with niggers is the major's way of humiliating you in front of the other officers."

"Too bad he's wasting his time," said William. "I think I will be happier living with the enlisted men. By the way, First Sergeant, I don't like that racial slur you use."

"You mean niggers, sir?"

"Yes, that's what I mean. I would think you'd have had enough of that vile insult by now. You should be proud of your heritage; please try to show it."

"You mean my heritage of slavery, sir?"

"You are not a slave, and God willing you never will be."

"We'll see," said Turley. "I gotta get back."

William took his gear out of the jeep; the sergeant headed back down the dusty road toward headquarters.

The barracks was as shabby on the inside as it was on the outside. It was a miserable one-story building with a coal-burning heating stove at each end. The bunks were old, made of wood, and appeared to be very uncomfortable.

With the men out of the barracks, William made up the only vacant bunk and unpacked his things in the afternoon solitude. When he was finished, he stretched out on the bed and allowed his mind to wander, but he was not contemplating what his life would be like in camp. He thought of home, his family, and when he might see them again.

It was nothing short of wonderful, the loving support that he could count on from all of them. Without it he knew the separation and the loneliness would destroy his will and make it impossible to endure what was sure to be one of the most unpleasant experiences of his life. He did not doubt the major's warning for a second; letters from home and the letters he would write were to be his only line of communication.

But no matter how tough his life promised to be, he was resolved to rob the major of a triumph over him. His letters would be pleasant and without elaboration; he would give the commanding officer no reason to keep them from being sent. At length he dozed off, looking forward to his first day of training, and he did not awaken until the men came back to the barracks.

SIXTEEN

War on the Homefront

It was nearly dark when the deafening sound of a large truck intruded on William's peaceful slumber. The truck stopped out front of the barracks; the diesel engine whined at a high pitch. He sat up, rubbing the sleep from his eyes, and waited for the men to enter. He heard someone jump to the ground from the back of the large vehicle, then footsteps echoed across the old wooden porch.

One man came through the door and walked down to the end of the building where William was sitting. To his delight and surprise, it was Howard Clay. Howard came to attention, saluted him, and said, "We are going to the mess hall, Lieutenant, and we stopped to pick you up. Sergeant Hicks said it's a long walk to the mess hall so they always ride down in the truck."

"I appreciate that, Private Clay. I'm happy to see you. How was your first day?"

"Beggin' your pardon, sir, but the men are hungry and in a hurry to go to chow. Maybe we can talk a little later on."

"Of course," said William as he got to his feet. "Lead the way."

When they got outside, Howard climbed into the back of the truck; Sergeant Jeremiah Hicks was standing near the front at attention. He saluted William, who returned the gesture, and then the sergeant said, "You can ride up front with me, Lieutenant."

"Very well, Sergeant."

They rode in silence to the mess hall, and when they stopped in front of the building, the men got out and formed a line. The sergeant told William to go to the front of it and lead them into the mess hall.

A simple thing like walking through a door became one of the first experiences at Camp Claiborne that William would remember for the rest of his life. To his left were rows of plain wooden tables and chairs; most of them taken up by black soldiers as they ate their evening meal. A plywood partition, eight feet high, ran the entire width of the building, creating a separate room. The black soldiers called it the segregation wall because it was intended to keep the whites from having to share dining space with the Negroes.

Straight ahead were several tables covered by white tablecloths; pitchers of cold water were spaced out over the length of them along with salt and pepper shakers and other assorted condiments. Those tables were for the white officers. To his right was a long row of tables lined with huge metal pots, pans, utensils, and trays behind which stood the black servers who spooned and ladled out the food. Large bowls of steaming fare were served to the officers by the blacks on mess duty—undoubtedly to preserve the memories of slavery.

For just a foolish moment, William was unsure as to whether or not he was supposed to sit with the officers. But one glance toward the master's table, as he quickly christened it, and he knew where his place was. As if by order, every white man stopped eating, put down his cutlery, and stared at William. The hatred in their expressions was so unmistakable that William completely lost his appetite.

He remembered the story his father told him about the first time the Ku Klux Klan came to Langdon Plantation after finding out that William's great-grandfather was with the Union during the Civil War. How frightening it must have been, facing the Klansmen dressed in heinous disguises, lighting the night sky with fiery torches. The leader threatened his great-grandfather with violence if he did not take his family and leave Georgia; a rope with a noose on the end was thrown onto the veranda to punctuate the warning.

As William read the meaning in the faces of those racist officers, for good measure, Major Cruise stood up, pointed a hostile finger at him, and then pointed to the Negro side of the mess hall. William walked to the chow line, waited for a server to put stew and bread on his tray, and then went to the other side of the partition and found a seat.

The odds against him were that of a sailboat opposite a fifty foot wave, but William's family had a history of using adversity to make them stronger. He held a great deal of admiration for all that the Langdons had withstood and for all that they had accomplished, and he was determined to deny Major Cruise and his minions the pleasure of seeing him collapse.

That night, the barracks was very quiet. William figured that the men, seeing the drama unfolding in the mess hall, were not quite sure what to make of the situation. Hopefully they would not decide that the wisest thing they could do would be to keep their distance from him. Maybe when he had the chance to talk to Howard Clay, he could decide how best to approach the men and gain their trust. William was weary from the events of the day and fell asleep before he could finish his prayers.

The following morning, First Sergeant Turley was at the barracks at five thirty a.m.

"Good morning, Lieutenant. Here is a copy of the training schedule for today. Actually, the training schedule is pretty much the same every day, so it won't take long for you to understand what goes on. Sergeant Hicks can get you started, and then you take charge of Company A. You are supposed to have an executive officer, but so far, none of the other officers will work with you. I say that you're better off. In a way, you've been cut off from the rest of the battalion. Run your company and don't concern yourself with the rest, Lieutenant. For now, Sergeant Hicks can be your exec. You'll be in charge of fifteen tanks and sixty men, four to a tank."

"I appreciate your help, First Sergeant Turley."

"I've already heard a whole lot of stories about you from Howard Clay. I don't quite know what to make of it all. Neither does the rest of the black soldiers. But you sure as hell are not what we are all used to. I'll try to help you as much as I can to adjust to this place, but I can only do so much. I have to watch my ass—all of us do."

"Believe me, First Sergeant, I understand. Again, I appreciate your help, and I wouldn't want you to do anything that might bring trouble for you or any of the men. We'll have the best company of tanks in the army, and that's what counts. Maybe someday men like Major Cruise will see that they've been wrong."

"I wouldn't count on it, sir. You keep looking over your shoulder too, Lieutenant. I think these crackers are out to get you." First Sergeant Turley saluted and left the barracks.

William certainly didn't believe what he'd said to the sergeant about Major Cruise changing his mind. But somehow he wanted to project a positive attitude, hoping to encourage the men. They had to have someone who believed in them, and William very much wanted that responsibility.

After breakfast, he got together with Sergeant Hicks, and the day got underway. Along with Howard Clay, whom William requested, and a corporal by the name of Judah Spears, the four men simulated a tank crew in action, practicing deployment, controls, and operation of the tank, maintenance and repair, and target practice. The rest of the company followed their lead.

William found that training in a tank was fascinating. Everything he'd learned up to that point had been in the classroom. He had never seen a real tank before, and he was impressed by the size and capabilities of the formidable machine. The M5 Stuart was powered by twin 220hp Cadillac V8 engines. Its maximum speed was 40 miles per hour and had an open road cruising range of 172 miles. The tank boasted a 37 millimeter cannon and a .30 caliber machine gun mounted to fire along the same axis as the cannon. When the tracers were on target, the cannon was zeroed in for a direct hit. The M5 also had a . 30 caliber machine gun on the turret and one on the bow.

He was also impressed by what the men had learned so far and at how well they handled their jobs. What a genuine pity it would be if they never got the chance to prove themselves.

At noon, the company stopped for an hour to rest and partake of some field rations. William sat down with Sergeant Hicks, Corporal Spears, and Private Clay, and a very informative conversation ensued.

"I wonder, Sergeant Hicks, if you and Corporal Spears would mind talking to me about your duty here at Camp

Claiborne. You may know that Private Clay and I both come from Georgia; we both live on a plantation not too far from Macon."

"We know that, Lieutenant," said Sergeant Hicks. "It's kinda good to hear you back up Clay's story, not that we don't trust him, but it ain't easy to believe there's a place where white folks treat black folks with respect. I come from Mississippi, and there ain't no place like that over there."

"Clay said you came here because you wanted to serve with a black unit, Lieutenant," said Corporal Spears. "Mind telling us why?"

"I don't mind," said William. "I believe that all men are created equal. Not like the Constitution says, but like Almighty God says. My father believes that, my grandfather believed it, and so did my great-grandfather. I know it must be difficult for you when you've been kicked around your whole life by white men, but not everyone sees things the same way."

"Most white men sure as hell see things the same," said Sergeant Hicks.

"I guess it seems that way in the South," said William. "But think back in history. Think about the time before the Civil War. In the North there were many white people who believed that slavery was wrong. They called themselves abolitionists, and they worked tirelessly to see that slavery was outlawed forever."

"I guess you're right about that," said Hicks. "But what good is freedom if it's the same as being a slave?"

"That's true," William replied. "That is why there is another movement in this country—the crusade for equal rights. There are many white people involved in that struggle too."

"And you are one of those people?" asked Spears.

"My family and I have been involved for years," said William.

"Then I guess you figure we owe you something," said Sergeant Hicks.

"Knock off that kinda talk, Sarge!" said Howard. "You're way off your course saying something like that to the lieutenant. I was raised on Langdon Plantation just like

I told you. My parents lived there, and so did my grandparents. You got no idea how much the lieutenant's family sacrificed and suffered because they stood up for us. They looked to gain nothing while having everything to lose. Look how his own kind treats him only because he doesn't hate us like they do. So don't you ever doubt the lieutenant's reason for being here."

"I'm sorry, sir," said Sergeant Hicks. "I didn't mean no disrespect."

"Don't be sorry, Sergeant. Your suspicions are certainly justified. Besides total segregation, how bad *is* life for the men here?"

"It stinks," said Corporal Spears. "Any black man who leaves this camp is taking his life into his own hands. Most of the 761st don't take any chances of putting themselves in a situation where they might get into trouble. The boys that come from the North ain't used to the Jim Crow way of life, and they learn the hard way that a black man can be beaten or even tortured to death. A black woman can be raped by a white man with no fear from the law."

"They find dead black soldiers all the time in these little towns right outside the camp," said Sergeant Hicks. "All the bus drivers around here carry pistols, and if they tell you to sit in the back of the bus and you don't do it, they stop at the nearest MP station or sheriff's office. We all just go along with the rules; we don't try them."

"All the clubs, movie theaters, and post exchanges are strictly segregated," said Spears. "Even the church is segregated. The white officers sit on the ground level; we have to sit in the loft. We aren't really free here in this camp. Most of the time we are confined to the barracks so there isn't any trouble even though it's mostly the whites that start it. We just try to stay clear of trouble and concentrate on mastering the tanks."

"We have no rights here of any kind, Lieutenant," said Howard. "Things are so tight, it's hard to find free space in your own uniform. You just yield the sidewalk and every other right of way to the white man and hope he doesn't decide to beat on you anyway."

"Maybe you didn't hear," said Hicks, "but back on January 10, there was a bloody riot in Alexandria. A few of them northern blacks I was talkin' about got pissed off at the violent arrest of a black soldier by some white MPs. A fight broke out and soon the MPs were joined by some local police and a mob of white civilians. A bunch of people, most of them black soldiers, got themselves killed."

"It was real bad," said Corporal Spears. "But the worst of it is that it brought Hell's fire down on everybody. The blacks that started the fight may have had good reason; I don't doubt that the black man the MPs arrested would have wound up dead. But having no rights or protection under the law, it made us look like troublemakers. We are supposed to take whatever the white man hands us without objection, without fighting back. So, the black soldiers who tried to defend the man being arrested just gave these local sons a bitches an excuse to bust a nigger's head, and in the eyes of the law, they would be doing the right thing."

"The only choice we have," said Sergeant Hicks, "is to learn our jobs and hope that we get the chance to show that we can do them better than anyone else. We have to get to Europe somehow; we have to get the chance to help defeat Hitler, and maybe in the doing, defeat racism."

"You just put into words my reason for being here," said William. "If there is anything in this world that I can do to help give you the chance to accomplish your goals I will do it. I am proud to know men of your caliber, and I would be even prouder to go into battle with you. Let's get back to our business. Our time will come."

For the next four months, William trained the men from dawn to dusk, sometimes six days a week. By August, the ranks of the 761st had swelled to 545 enlisted men and 34 officers. Except for meals at the mess tent, church on Sunday, and an occasional trip to the post exchange, he spent all of his time at Company A's end of the camp, avoiding Major Cruise and all the other white officers. He may have alienated all the white men, but he soon had the friendship of the black soldiers and he believed that he was associating with a better class of people.

When he did come in close proximity with any of the whites he was treated the same as the men in his company. He was no longer a white man in their eyes nor was he a true southerner, but none of it bothered William. The only difficult part was that the only links to his family were the letters he sent and the ones he received. And even his mail was tampered with, sometimes in a very ugly way.

Occasionally his letters were deliberately dropped in a mud puddle before he received them; the dirt and the blurred ink made them challenging to read. Other times his name and address was scribbled out and readdressed to the White Nigger of Company A.

Of course William knew that so many of his punishments were illegal, and if he had wanted, he could have made life very rough for Major Cruise. But he would not give the major the satisfaction of any kind of victory over him; he would never accept being treated better than his men.

On a Sunday morning on the fifth of November 1942, William was lying on his bunk thinking about home; his parents, and his beloved Joanna, and their children. Martin had turned eight in February; fortunately William had been home for his birthday. But Maryann had her fourth birthday on August 15, and it hurt him very deeply to miss it.

There was no doubt that his imprisonment, as it were, gripped his heart like an icy fist at times and threatened to force him into submission. If only he could see his family for a few hours.

Much to William's surprise, as he lay there trying to pull himself together, Sergeant Hicks came into the barracks to find him.

"First Sergeant Turley told me to come and get you, Lieutenant. You have visitors. They are waiting at the front gate."

"Visitors? I am not allowed to have visitors."

"I don't really know anything more, sir. I was told to find you and have you go to the front gate. There's a jeep outside you can use."

Without hesitation, William sprang up from his bunk, ran outside, and got into the jeep. As he hastily made his way down the road toward the gate his mind was reaching far and wide for an explanation. Was it possible that Major

Cruise was easing up a bit or might he have decided that
he may be taking William's restrictions a bit too far? It was
difficult to say. No one had tried to visit him during the
seven months he had been at the camp. William had
discreetly explained in his letters that his training schedule
didn't allow time or opportunity for it. He did not want his
family mixed up in his problems with the commanding
officer.

When he reached the front gate, he stopped the jeep
and hurried over to the guard shack to see if he was indeed
free to have visitors. Inside he found two black enlisted
men who had the duty. First Sergeant Turley was there as
well.

"Your wife, your children, and your parents are here,
Lieutenant. You have an eight-hour pass. Enjoy it—might
be awhile before you get another."

William didn't know what to say. Under the
circumstances, he wanted to know how this miracle had
come about. On the other hand, he was so desperate to see
his family that he decided it best to go and ask no
questions. Still, there was something in the first sergeant's
manner and a look on his face that bothered William a
great deal.

He took the pass handed to him by First Sergeant
Turley and then waited for one of the sentries to open the
gate. There, on the other side, was a sight that filled him
with joy. Martin and Maryann ran to him; he scooped them
up in his arms and carried the children over to Joanna and
his parents.

He put them down, took Joanna in his arms, and
kissed her for the space of thirty seconds. Never in his life
had he felt so good. He could feel the misery of the past
seven months fade away. Then he hugged his mother; then
his father.

"I am so happy to see all of you!" he said in a shaky
voice.

"We are happy to see you too," his family said in
unison.

They laughed and cried at the same time, and when
they had gathered themselves once again, William said, "I
can't believe you are here. I had no idea you were coming."

"It was First Sergeant Turley," said Joanna.

"First Sergeant Turley?"

"Yes," said his father. "Joanna received a letter from a First Sergeant Sam Turley. The letter explained that the training is so intensive here that the men of the battalion are rarely given time off. The training is such because of the demand for trained outfits in Europe. He further explained that today would be the day for a visit if we could make it. Naturally we were not going to miss this opportunity. We were so grateful for his letter. He must be a fine man to take the time to let us know."

The strange feeling that came over William when he accepted the pass was intensified immediately. He didn't know what was going on, but nothing Turley wrote in the letter was true. And where was the major? He was certain that his pass did not have the commanding officer's blessing. William was so happy his family had come and so in need of being in their company, but something wasn't right and he knew it.

"William? Are you all right?" asked his mother.

He hadn't realized that he had frozen in his tracks.

"Yes, yes, Mother. I am just fine."

At that they all got into John's car and headed for Alexandria to enjoy the eight-hour pass. It was difficult for William to carry his burden and forget about what he was feeling inside, but he made a conscious effort to keep it from spilling over into the visit with his family.

At one point that afternoon, Joanna, the children, and his mother wanted ice cream. William and his father declined but took an outside table to wait while the women went into the shop to get their frozen treats.

"I was hoping we might get a few minutes alone," said his father. "I will keep this conversation between us, but I have to ask you how you've really been getting along."

"I appreciate the confidentiality, Father. I do have a great need to unburden myself to someone, and I would choose no one but you. It is as bad as you can imagine and worse. I understand the reason these black soldiers joined the army, but I don't understand where they get the heart to stay the course. Camp Claiborne and all the southern army camps, from what I understand, operate under the

Jim Crow laws of separate but equal. The camp's leadership condones the hostile treatment the men receive from the white officers."

"I suspected as much," said his father. "I have heard that the War Department believes that because of their life experiences, white southerners know best how to handle Negro troops." John paused for effect and then continued. "They handle them the same way they handled their slaves. In the Old South, the overseer would chose the biggest, loudest, nastiest, and most brutal black man to instill fear in the other slaves. They have been doing it for generations. The only difference in the army is that they make them sergeants."

"Yes, the army's official policy is non-discriminatory, but it is a farce," said William, with a scowl on his face. "The beautiful thing, Father, is that, in spite of limited recreation, mistreatment of the worse kind, and substandard living conditions, the battalion's morale remains high. They have more guts than those white officers at the camp will ever have; it is truly amazing. They are not ignorant as the white racists would lead the world to believe either. I wish you could see them in training; they are superb. They also know what they are up against, and they go out of their way to deny the leadership the chance to do them any harm."

"But it isn't enough, is it, son?"

"No, Father, it isn't. The blacks who venture off camp are in constant danger. For centuries, these local communities have harbored an unyielding tradition of intolerance, segregation, and a belief in black inferiority and white supremacy. And they defend those traditions through intimidation and Ku Klux Klan-inspired violence. Many black soldiers have been killed in this area. It is worse than the lynching issues in the civilian world."

"And what about you, son? How do they treat you?"

"Can you cover me, Father? Can you support me in spirit and leave the rest to me?"

John took a very deep breath. "I know what you're asking, son, and it is completely against my nature to be accepting of it. But my respect and admiration for you knows no bounds and so, I promise, William."

"I might just as well paint myself black and be done with it," William replied.

"I have been afraid of that all along, son."

"Please don't worry about me, Father. I am handling it just fine. The restrictions the commanding officer has put on me are difficult, but there is a lot of camaraderie between me and my men, and I know that I'll get through it. I realize of course that in the army there are rules against fraternizing with subordinates, but it evens things a bit for the way the other white officers regard me."

"You know of course that Eleanor Roosevelt could help."

"No, Father. That would only make things worse for the men, if that is possible."

"You're right, son. Forgive me for saying that. It's just that I love you, and it's hard because I can imagine what you must be going through. All I can do is pray for you and ask you to be careful."

"There is one more thing, Father. This pass I have today. It bears the major's signature, but there is no way that Major Cruise would have authorized this for me. I fear that First Sergeant Turley went out on a limb for me—too far out. The letter he wrote . . . there was no truth in it. We do train long and hard, but there are weekend passes, furloughs, and the like. The part about trained outfits in Europe is untrue also, at least it is in the case of the black units. It is like all previous wars. No one who matters thinks that the black soldiers should fight. My men know that after a few months of training, the white soldiers go to Europe. At this point, they have no hope of getting into the war. Instead, they are fighting their own war on the home front."

"Then what is it all about, son?"

"As I said, I have made a lot of friends among the black soldiers. I think the first sergeant must have seen an opportunity to get us together today. He knows how much I miss all of you, and so he did this behind the major's back. If I'm right and he is discovered it could mean his life."

"Good Lord. I feel that this situation is going too far. What's to keep you safe, William?"

"Don't worry, Father. When the major found out my point of view about the black soldiers he was going to have me transferred. I let him know then that I got here with help from Mrs. Roosevelt. I don't think he will risk his own neck."

"I *do* hope you're right, son."

"Please trust me, Father."

"I do, son. And I will not volunteer any of this information to your mother or Joanna; I think it best. I know that God is on your side. I will also pray for the good sergeant."

When the visit was over, William went to First Sergeant Turley's quarters to learn the truth about the pass he'd been given. He was relieved to find Turley reading a book; all seemed well.

"I apologize for the interruption, First Sergeant, and I can't thank you enough for your resourcefulness in getting me a pass, but I have to know how you managed it. I don't believe the whole thing was Major Cruise's idea."

"No sir, it wasn't. He doesn't know anything about it."

"That's what I was afraid of," said William. "What happened to watching your ass? You know better than anyone what the major will do to you if he finds out. Why would you put yourself in such danger?"

"I guess I just figured I owed you, Lieutenant."

"Owed me for what?"

"Every black man in this camp knows about your differences with the major, and they all know the price you are paying for it. We all feel that we are partly to blame."

"That is ridiculous, First Sergeant. You and the rest of the men are not to blame, nor are any of you responsible for how the major treats me. It is the major who is at fault, along with all the other ignorant, narrow-minded, and dishonorable white supremacists in this world. I do not expect you or the men to make matters worse for yourselves by getting between me and the poor excuse we have for a commanding officer."

"It seems like you stuck your neck out for us, Lieutenant."

"That's different," William replied. "Because of the warped sense of justice in the South I don't have as much to fear."

"Then why do you let the major get away with keeping you chained to this lousy camp with no leave or furlough, not even a weekend pass?"

"Because he threatened to transfer me, and I don't want to leave. In return I tolerate his abuse and keep my mouth shut about it. It won't last forever; one day the major will be nothing more than an unpleasant memory."

"I never knew anyone like you, Lieutenant. I see it but I don't believe it. I keep telling myself that you *must* be like all the other whites, and you keep proving me wrong. On top of that, we are in the South and you are from the South. It just don't figure."

"It doesn't have to, First Sergeant. How did you arrange the pass?"

"It wasn't hard. The major's home is in Baton Rouge. He left on Friday night to spend the weekend there, and he invited all the white officers, all except you, to join him there for a party he was having today. He told me to keep an eye on things. All of the officers but three were planning to go to Baton Rouge; the other three went home for the weekend. Sometimes the major signs some passes and lets me fill them out if one of the enlisted men requests one. I knew about the officers' plans far enough ahead to write your wife and tell her it would be a good time to visit. I only gave you an eight hour pass so you'd be back in plenty of time; I figured it was better than nothing. I hope you don't mind my taking that liberty."

"I understand, and I don't mind. What happened to my pass when I turned it in?"

"I burned it, Lieutenant."

"All right, for now," said William. "I really appreciate what you did, but I will accept your word that it won't happen again."

"All right, Lieutenant. You have it."

When William got back to his barracks he felt a lot better and reasonably satisfied that the first sergeant had pulled it off. No one who knew about the pass would ever say anything, and William enjoyed a badly needed visit with his family. He slept better that night than he had since he arrived at Camp Claiborne and was looking forward to training the following day.

It was customary on Monday mornings at about five thirty a.m. for First Sergeant Turley to come by William's barracks to let him know if it was a routine day or to inform him of any deviations from the usual schedule. After that, Company A would head for the mess hall for breakfast.

But at the usual time, when the battalion jeep pulled up in front of the barracks, someone else was driving it. A black soldier wearing first sergeant stripes walked into the barracks, saluted William, and then said, "Good morning, sir. This is your training schedule for the day; only one or two minor changes."

The soldier saluted and turned for the door, but William stopped him, saying, "Hold up there, First Sergeant. Where is First Sergeant Turley?"

Without hesitation the soldier said, "He's in the guard house, sir."

"For what?" William asked.

"For disobeying orders and insubordination, sir."

William was outraged. No one had to tell him what the disobedience of orders charge meant. Somehow Major Cruise found out about the unauthorized pass. The man and his followers were like bloodhounds, never missing an opportunity to track down and destroy their victim. William knew he had to act, and quickly. No matter what it took, he had to get First Sergeant Turley out of the guard house and out of the major's line of fire.

The day's work dragged by; he couldn't concentrate on anything except the problem created out of nothing more than an excuse for the major to wield his authority and satisfy his racial hatred toward the blacks.

At the end of the day, William stayed in the barracks when the rest of the company went to chow. He was trying to decide how best to handle the situation before confronting Major Cruise when a young private from Company B entered the barracks.

"Lieutenant, my name is Private Willie Brown. I have to talk to you. It's about the first sergeant."

"Yes, Private, what's on your mind?"

"I just got out of the guard house; I've been there since yesterday. I was in town on a pass, and I came back to camp after a little too much to drink. The duty officer put me in the guard house to sober up. Early this morning two officers brought First Sergeant Turley in. They thought I was out like a light, but I wasn't. I woke up when they came in." The private hesitated for a moment.

"Go on," said William.

"Well, sir, the first sergeant was beat up pretty bad; he could hardly stand up. I heard one of the officers, Lieutenant Thomas, say that he had seen you in town with your family yesterday. The major had four of his officers beat on First Sergeant Turley until he admitted to giving you a pass. Lieutenant Thomas said the major wants to make an example of the first sergeant to show you and Turley what happens when the superiority of the white man is challenged."

"That despicable son of a . . . What else did they say, Private?"

"Usually the guards on duty are enlisted men. Tonight it will be three of the major's most trusted lieutenants, Thomas being one of them. After 'Taps' they plan on taking Turley way out into the forest, and they ain't figurin' on bringin' him back."

"It can't be!" William exclaimed. "How do they plan to get away with this?"

"They plan to report that the first sergeant tried to escape. That they tracked him to the forest and they fired shots but never found Turley or his body."

"And that's all there is to it?"

"You just have to understand, Lieutenant Langdon. There won't be any fuss made about another dead black man."

"I have understood it all too well my whole life, but it's not going to happen this time. Thank you for the information, Private Brown, and thank God that you were in the guard house last night."

William ran to the barracks next door to find Sergeant Hicks. When he located the sergeant he repeated every detail that Private Brown had divulged.

"What are we going to do, Lieutenant?" Sergeant Hicks asked.

"We are going to stop it," William replied. "I want you to get the men together; both companies, and get them into formation out in front of the barracks. I'll be out in a minute to march them over to the guard house."

"Right away, sir," said Sergeant Hicks.

When William went outside, Company A and Company B were in formation, standing at attention. From the barracks porch, he addressed them.

"Good men of the 761st. I have asked you to assemble in haste this evening for the purpose of coming to the aid of another good man. Some of you may already know, and I have just been informed that First Sergeant Sam Turley was put into the guard house, charged with disobeying orders and insubordination after issuing a pass to me on Sunday so that I could visit with my family. I have also learned that because of his kindness to me, he has seriously put himself in harm's way. But I do not intend to let harm come to him. We are going to march to the guard house in a show of solidarity with First Sergeant Turley, but as a nonviolent demonstration. I will handle these proceedings asking only that you men bear witness to what occurs. Any man who does not wish to be part of this may stay behind without fear of chastisement. Above all, remember, there will be no display of violence by this battalion. Do I make myself understood?"

"Yes sir," came the reply from five hundred and forty-five throats.

William walked to the head of the formation and said, "Forward, march!"

It was already dark when the battalion stepped off and headed down the road toward the guard house, which was located adjacent to the mess hall. "Taps" was played promptly at ten o'clock p.m. every night. It would take about twenty-five minutes to march the distance, and as the battalion moved, William's mind was racing far ahead.

In his heart he believed that he was doing the right thing, but he also knew the kind of resistance he was up against. His intentions were purely passive, however, he could only control one side of the action that might take

212

place. What if the officers who intended to dispose of First Sergeant Turley saw the battalion's presence as an attack, a riot, or a mob that threatened violence? What if they used deadly force against his men? Is it possible that he could be doing something that he would regret for the rest of his life?

Suddenly, the sound of "Taps" could be heard through the still night air. Another hundred yards and they would reach their objective. William summoned the only protection he and his men had on their side, the only power that could save everyone involved; he began to pray to God.

He prayed for the salvation of First Sergeant Turley, and he prayed for a peaceful outcome to their attempt to free him; he promised that no matter what happened, no aggression would be shown by him or by his men.

When they reached a spot about thirty yards from the guard house, William hollered, "Halt! At ease."

A jeep was parked just outside the guard house, but no one was in sight; all was quiet. Five minutes passed, then ten, and then twenty. William began to wonder if they might be too early or worse, too late.

Suddenly the front door to the guard house opened. In the glow of the pole lights that illuminated the area, he could clearly see four men exit the building: three white officers including Lieutenant Thomas, and First Sergeant Turley. Turley was cuffed at the wrists and gagged to suppress any attempt to cry out for help. As the 761st battalion was standing within the lighted area, they were immediately spotted by the prisoner and his escort.

"What in the hell is going on out here?" shouted Lieutenant Thomas. "If you don't disperse these niggers in about ten seconds I'll order my men to open fire, Langdon!"

William turned to his men and said, "Stand fast." Then he approached the four men standing near the jeep.

"Lieutenant Thomas, we are not here for the purpose of creating an incident or initiating trouble of any kind. We come in peace and hope that you and your men are of the same mind."

"If that's true then get them out of here!"

"I think that you should let me speak," said William.

213

"We aren't interested in one damn thing you have to say," said one of the other officers, whose name was Andrew Rutledge. "You're interfering with officers in the performance of their duty."

It was all that William could do to maintain his composure. Three men taking a helpless victim out to the forest at night to murder him and they described it as performing their duty? And for what? For an infraction that wouldn't normally warrant anything more than a reprimand.

"If you mean to do harm to this man then you must take me with you and do the same to me," said William.

"Are you crazy?" said Rutledge. "Don't you understand the difference between black and white?"

"There *is* no difference, unless you count the mere color of his skin. Other than that, he is a man the same as you, and if you kill this man it will simply be murder. I knew that the pass First Sergeant Turley gave me was not authorized by Major Cruise, but I was so desperate to see my family that I took it anyway. I am just as guilty as he is. You despise me as much as you despise him. Why would you hesitate to punish me the same as him?"

The third officer, a lieutenant named Russel Brisbane, said, "This son of a bitch *is* crazy but I'm not gonna have anything to do with killing a white man, even if he is a nigger lover. The major told me Langdon is a friend of the president's wife."

"The major is correct," said William.

"How about it, Thomas?" Brisbane asked. "Are you willing to risk your own neck?"

"I ain't riskin' a damn thing. We put this coon in the jeep and do what we set out to do, and if Langdon gets in the way we'll lay him out cold. By the time he wakes up this nigger will be the buzzard's responsibility."

"You can overpower me and execute this crime if you wish," said William. "But I promise you that it will not end tonight. I will spend my last breath to see that the three of you along with Major Cruise are brought up on charges. I have over five hundred witnesses with me, and all of them will know what happens here. And even if a black man cannot testify against a white man in a court of law, I can testify, and I assure you that my testimony will be heard all the way to Washington."

The upper hand was beginning to shift a bit. William had given the three officers a lot to think about. It was clear that they had never experienced a protest of any kind for ridding the world of a black man. But now, with so many eyes on them—even if they *were* black—and a white man leading them—even if he *was* a nigger lover—made the three racists uneasy.

"Make up your minds," said William. "You have the law on your side, as shameful and inhumane as it is. None of you were raised to think for yourselves. You were taught to hate anything with black skin, and so you harass, terrorize, brutalize, and kill with no more thought or reason than a predatory animal. These men standing behind me are human beings; so is First Sergeant Turley, and yes, so are you three. But you have been brainwashed and convinced that you are superior to them when the only one superior to any man is Almighty God."

"What are we gonna do, Thomas?" asked Brisbane.

"I say kill them both," Lieutenant Thomas retorted.

"Not me," said Rutledge. "I feel the same way as you, Thomas, but I'm not doing anything that's gonna cause *me* trouble."

"Do you want to be the one to tell the major we chickened out?"

"I don't look at it that way," said Brisbane. "I think Rutledge is making sense. Do you see the major out here anywhere? Don't you think there is a reason for that? I'll bet he's not looking to lose his pension after spending twenty-five years in the army, not to mention maybe winding up in Leavenworth."

Lieutenant Thomas, with his support collapsing, was finished. He hadn't the nerve to carry out the deed on his own, and it was obvious that he couldn't convince his comrades to follow through.

"You may think you've won, Langdon, but don't fool yourself. If this battalion ever gets into the war, you be real careful about watching your back. The next time, I *will* settle with you."

"I'm sure I will remember," said William. "I have become quite accustomed to being threatened."

With that, the irate lieutenant removed the handcuffs from First Sergeant Turley's wrists and then put his foot against the former prisoner's back and shoved as hard as he could. The beaten and bloody man was flung forward and landed hard facedown in the gravel road.

"There's your nigger sergeant," said Thomas. "Take care of the son of a bitch. Let's get out of here," he said to Brisbane and Rutledge.

"Give me a hand," said William over his shoulder. Several of the men rushed forward to help Turley to his feet.

"It looks like they worked you over pretty good," said William.

"I'm alive, thanks to you all," Turley replied.

"Sergeant Hicks," said William. "Do you think you can carry the first sergeant on your back?"

"All the way," Hicks replied.

"If he can't make it we'll take turns," said Howard Clay.

"Very well. Let's get the first sergeant to his quarters and see what we can do to clean up some of these cuts."

So, thought William, with the help of the Lord and a first-rate bluff, the 761st won their first battle: a battle against racism. The following day, the first sergeant was getting around pretty well despite the beating he had taken the night before, but even more surprising was the fact that William didn't hear a word from Major Cruise.

Maybe Lieutenant Brisbane had it pegged when he said the major didn't want to run the slightest risk of buying himself any trouble, or maybe he let the incident drop because he knew he was transferring out and the battalion would soon be getting a new commanding officer.

A week later, Major Cruise turned the responsibility of the battalion over to Major John R. Wright Jr., but it was an interim position. Nothing whatsoever changed under Major Wright; the training went on nonstop as usual, as did the treatment of William and the black soldiers. The battalion waited with great anticipation for their new leader.

SEVENTEEN

The New Commander

On the morning of July 3, 1943, William learned that the new commanding officer was Colonel Paul L. Bates. The air was full of rumors flying here and there, but the only thing he was able to find out for sure was that Colonel Bates hailed from California.

Anticipation was rampant, affecting not only William but all the enlisted men as well. What kind of man the colonel might be remained to be seen, but the battalion *knew* what Major Cruise was like, and they were willing to bet that the new man had to be more agreeable than him.

The following day the colonel arrived at ten o'clock a.m., and at one o'clock in the afternoon the new commanding officer sent for Lieutenant William Langdon. Upon arriving at battalion headquarters, he was greeted by First Sergeant Turley, whose mood was unlike anything William had ever seen. His jovial demeanor could only mean that the new commander had made quite an impression; William's expectations were high.

Turley knocked on the office door, and when the reply came to enter, the first sergeant opened the door and led the way inside.

"Lieutenant Langdon to see you, sir."

"Thank you, First Sergeant, that will be all."

Turley left the room; William stood before the commander's desk at attention. He saluted and said, "Lieutenant Langdon reporting as ordered."

Colonel Bates returned the gesture and said, "Please sit down, Lieutenant." He waited for William to make himself comfortable and then he said, "I have heard quite a lot about you, Lieutenant, and frankly, I've heard a lot about what has been happening since you arrived here. I don't propose to dwell on it. I feel that it is better to close the book and begin a new chapter."

"I am in full agreement with you, sir," William replied.

217

"Good. I am somewhat influenced by what I've heard, but much to the resignation of setting a few things right and shaping this battalion into something we can all be proud of. I believe that we have the men to do it, we just need to give them the proper direction and a sense of self-respect. I believe that any prejudice against one of my black tankers is a prejudice against me. We'll still have to deal with the naysayers and the racial discrimination, but we will make a point of keeping that kind of negativity from destroying morale."

"I too believe in closing the door on what is in the past, Colonel," said William. "I will only say that, in my opinion, our previous commander, Major Cruise, and his subordinates were a disgrace to the United States Army. I now believe that these men have a commander whom they can respect and look up to."

"Thank you, Lieutenant. I believe in these men without the privilege of actually knowing them as yet. I think that each one of them will to be as good a soldier and as good a tanker as any white man in the army, and my intention is to prove it."

"You can absolutely count on my full and unwavering support, sir."

"Now then, Lieutenant, as I said earlier, I've heard a lot about what's happened to you under Major Cruise's command. That being said, I want you to pack your bags because you are going home for a month of leave. In addition, you will trade in your gold insignia for silver because I am promoting you to First Lieutenant. Get plenty of rest because when you get back you'll be helping me polish this battalion until it shines like a new dime. That's all, Lieutenant Langdon."

William stood, came to attention, and saluted Colonel Bates. "I can't thank you enough, sir."

"Sure you can, son," he replied. "Give my regards to your family."

William's spirit was soaring when the train pulled into the station at Macon. It had been fifteen months since he'd seen home, and only once had he seen his family in that same period of time. Before leaving Alexandria he sent a telegram to Joanna, informing her about his homecoming.

Only his father was at the station to meet him; the rest of the family, John explained, was at home preparing for his arrival.

"It's so good to see you, William," said John as he embraced his son. "There is so much I want to ask you."

"It is wonderful to be here, Father. We can catch up on the way home."

The conversation was nonstop as William explained everything that had happened since their visit a few weeks earlier. John was most impressed when his son told him about the new commanding officer of the 761st.

"It is truly a blessing that the Lord should provide a man like Colonel Bates, son. What has become of Major Cruise?"

"He transferred out along with several of his officers including Thomas, Rutledge, and Brisbane."

"Oh yes, the three men who attempted to execute First Sergeant Turley."

"That's right. Unfortunately, the racial tension will still be a big problem, but having an impartial commander will help to strengthen the resolve of most of the men."

When John and William reached the plantation, the festivities began in earnest. How good it was to have the family together again. William's grandmother, Elizabeth, had been unable to visit her grandson with the rest of the family because the trip to Louisiana would have been too taxing. But with everyone now gathered in the parlor of her house, the same house once occupied by each generation of Langdons since they came to Georgia, William sat next to her as the conversation went on for hours.

Every day was spent with family, and they enjoyed their time as never before. It even became difficult to believe that a war was raging on the other side of the world.

However, as usual in such circumstances, William's leave passed by before he was ready to see it end. But he knew that the war would not wait, and it was essential to return to duty. If the 761st went to Europe, he wanted to be with them.

For the most part, nothing had changed in his absence except that the battalion operated far more efficiently under Colonel Bates. William's quarters had been moved to the barracks that housed the other white officers, but it was not due to any racial inference. It was a matter of army protocol; William was an officer, and his men were enlisted.

His new bunk mates were not overly friendly toward him but they were not terribly abusive to the black soldiers, which more than made up for it as far as William was concerned. Most of them intended to make the army their vocation and would do anything to further their careers. It became clear in the early going that Colonel Bates did not share their prejudice, and so if promotion meant placating the commanding officer by easing up on the blacks, so be it.

On September 15, 1943, the 761st moved to Camp Hood, Texas for advanced training, and after a month they were upgraded from the M5 Stuart light tank to the M4 Sherman medium tank. The battalion was glad to leave Camp Claiborne, where they obviously were not wanted. Claiborne was swampy, flat, and densely vegetated. In contrast, Hood was hills, valleys, woods, and open ground.

But Camp Hood like all the rest was a segregated post, and the men of the 761st soon accepted the fact that there were two Camp Hoods, one white and one black. As before, William was amazed at how well his men handled the situation. Several black junior officers had joined the battalion; their officer's club was separate, and all special services clubs were separate from the whites. When the men needed supplies from the Post Exchange, they would take their merchandise to the cashier, but if a white man approached they were pushed aside. So they learned to stuff it; it was required; they had no choice.

Still, the men were determined to fight back the only way they knew how, which was to train hard until they were the best; they would make a name for themselves. The one and only time the abuse got the better of them and they wanted to retaliate, Colonel Bates talked them out of it. He also wanted them to be the best, especially at proving themselves as men.

William was on maneuvers with his men constantly; against everybody they tested their skills. Army Ground Forces Tests were being conducted to see if the tank destroyers were ready for combat. The 761st thoroughly enjoyed beating them, and they did so many times.

The men learned not to rely on anyone else during those maneuvers. Their own abilities would be relative to anything they were going to accomplish. Most importantly, the men learned to respect their comrades and themselves; supporting each other was the only way they could exist. If a tank was not properly maintained and had to fall out on a maneuver against a tank destroyer, the ruling went against the crew and they received a demerit. William would say to them, "If this was real combat, you would be dead. So do it properly."

After awhile, the men developed a real sense of pride within themselves, William wrote to his father in a letter. Having their own tailor shops enabled them to be the best looking outfit on the post. Their boots were shined, their uniforms were pressed, and when they encountered white officers they would salute and think to themselves, you're going to have to return my salute because I am a man.

Still, the weeks and months passed by without a word about going to Europe. The battalion had been in training for over two years. But just when it seemed that all their work had been for nothing, the word came down that the 761st was finally heading to England to await deployment.

About the middle of August 1944, they left Camp Hood with no other thought than to distinguish themselves against the Nazi war machine. Along with the 784th and the 785th, the 761st was part of the 5th Tank Group, the first American Armored Tank Group. All of the senior officers were white with a few black junior officers overseeing 675 African American soldiers per battalion.

The night before leaving, William wrote his last letters home from the United States. He asked Joanna to pray for him as he vowed to pray for her and the children. He asked his wife not to worry and reminded her that God would be shipping out with him.

In a letter to his parents, he told them that he had been promoted to the rank of captain; he knew they would be proud of him. To his grandmother, Elizabeth, he wrote that he would carry the memory of his great-grandfather into battle with him because he knew it would give him great courage.

It was a long trip across the "big pond," as it was referred to, longer than anything William had ever experienced. With every nautical mile, he could feel the distance as it grew between him and his family. He believed that he would see them again but realized more certainly than ever before that the decision was in the hands of his Creator.

After final preparation, the 761st was attached to the XII Corps, 26th Infantry Division assigned to General George Patton's Third Army, an army already racing eastward across France. They were deployed October 10, 1944, on Omaha Beach.

On November eighth, the battalion was ready for combat; the order to move was imminent. Suddenly a jeep pulled up to the head of the column and stopped. Although none of the men had ever seen General George S. Patton Jr. before, they did not need anyone to tell them that the general himself was sitting in the front seat of that jeep. Colonel Bates gave an order for everyone to dismount and gather round the general.

When he began to speak, the authority in his voice was enough to stiffen the weakest backbone and enable it to challenge hell's fury without any hesitation.

"Men, you're the first Negro tankers to ever fight in the American Army. I would never have asked for you if you weren't good. I have nothing but the best in my army. I don't care what color you are as long as you go up there and kill those Kraut sons of bitches. Everyone has their eyes on you and is expecting great things from you. Most of all, your race is looking forward to your success. Don't let them down, and damn you, don't let me down! They say it is patriotic to die for your country. Well, let's see how many patriots we can make out of those German sons of bitches."

"Move them out, Colonel!" he said to Colonel Bates and then turned to his driver and motioned him forward. The battalion was ordered to take their objectives while supporting the 26th infantry.

William appreciated the fact that General Patton tried to build the men's confidence, but he knew that Patton, like almost everyone else in high command, did not think the black man could think quick enough to be a good tanker. Once again, they would have to be shown, he thought.

As the tank column moved out, Colonel Bates paralleled them from a distance in a jeep so that he could direct the action. William could only think of how much was riding on their success. Primarily, the goal was to defeat the Germans and win the war.

Behind that was the goal to help their commander, Colonel Bates, achieve success. The whole battalion knew how hard the colonel had worked to gain command of the tankers. He was always fair and square with the men, and he stood by them against the oppression of discrimination and racism. The colonel trained them over and over again so that when they met the enemy they could achieve success for themselves.

William was in command of Charlie Company, riding in the lead tank ahead of the column. His four-man crew was comprised of Sergeant Walt Jones, the main gunner; Corporal Randal Riley, who loaded the .75 MM gun; Corporal Ron Dixon, machine gunner; and Corporal Norman Smith, who was the driver. There wasn't a man involved who wasn't wondering what it would be like when they finally met the Germans; it did not take them long to find out.

After traveling for about two hours, Staff Sergeant Ruben Rivers, who was riding in the lead tank of Able Company and leading the entire column, radioed to the battalion that they were coming to a town. Every tank in the column buttoned up its hatches and followed Rivers' tank into the narrow streets of Moyenvic.

About a second after William wondered where the enemy could be, the air was instantly full of projectiles from small arms, bazookas, and mortar rounds. The Germans were concealed in every building on both sides of the street. The noise was ear splitting as hundreds of chunks of metal struck William's tank from all sides. Screaming out orders, he directed fire on the buildings

223

closest to him as the other tanks in the battalion did the same.

"There's a roadblock up ahead!" Rivers shouted over the radio. "I got to move it outta the way or we're stuck here like sitting ducks!"

Looking out through his periscope, William could see the lead tank. What he witnessed next was a sequence he wished he could film and personally show to General Patton. Without a thought for his own safety and under direct enemy fire Rivers boldly climbed out of his tank, hooked a cable to the roadblock and moved it out of the way. Due to his perilous but rapid solution, a serious delay was averted allowing the tanks to continue moving and enabling them to fight their way through the town.

The remaining enemy soldiers withdrew, and the column continued on toward Vic-sur-Seille, where the opposition was more intense than before. The ground was boggy, but it was open and pretty well suited for armor. All over the valley were little farms with their boundaries clearly marked by hedgerows and stone walls. Reports of casualties and tank losses were coming across the radio after Able Company ran into a minefield. William's Company C was to the right of Able.

Armor and combat commanders had set up their command posts along the tree lined main road that led to Vic-sur-Seille. Colonel Bates was on the high ground overlooking the battle.

Like the men of the 761st, the colonel was green to combat, but he was a complete professional, always in control of the situation. He radiated an air of confidence that passed to his subordinate commanders, junior officers, down to the non-coms and enlisted men. His code name was "Hard Tack," and he was on the radio often to offer encouragement, advice, orders, or to change a movement. As long as he was in command, the Panthers believed that there was nothing they couldn't do.

The German resistance was unwavering, but the 761st answered them blow for blow. The valley was becoming littered with burning tanks and dead infantrymen. Then came news over the radio that stunned the battalion worse than the fiercest German onslaught.

Colonel Bates had been hit. His driver, sounding like a madman over the radio, was shouting and crying at the same time.

"Oh God, oh God! The colonel's hit, the colonel's hit! A German recon/combat patrol came out of the wooded thickets behind us and opened up at close range. The colonel was standing on the hood of the jeep! He tried to jump for the back seat, but he was hit and knocked to the ground! I don't know if he's—"

The driver's voice was cut off. William tried to reach him, but there was no reply. Word of the colonel going down spread through the battalion like wildfire. William's crewmen were more upset about losing their commander than they were about the predicament they were in.

"Keep your mind in the battle, men," said William. "We don't even know how bad he was hit. All we know is that he was evacuated. I think as much of the colonel as you men, but you know what he'd say if he were here."

"Yes, sir," said his driver, Corporal Smith. "You men heard the captain. Keep your mind in the battle."

When darkness fell, the fighting ended, and the 761st gathered themselves physically and emotionally. Although shaken by the loss of their beloved commander on the very first day, their determination to overcome all odds remained intact.

The following morning before moving on, William's company received a visit from Colonel Hollis E. Hunt from Yuma, Arizona.

"I am assuming command of the 761st. I have news about Colonel Bates. His leg was shattered, but he will live. Whether or not he returns to combat is uncertain. I wish I could tell you more. I understand that you men were especially fond of the colonel. I'm sorry."

"If you don't mind, Colonel," said William. "What happened to the executive officer, Major Wingo?"

"He went nuts."

"I beg your pardon, sir?"

"He should have taken over when Colonel Bates got hit, but he fell apart like a homesick six-year-old on the first day of school. When he was told to take over he started crying that he would be killed; he said he couldn't take command. The last anybody saw of him he was in a jeep heading to the rear."

"He always said niggers won't fight, and then he turns yellow and runs off," said one of the enlisted men.

"Well he was wrong about that, soldier," said Colonel Hollis. "Get your men ready, Captain. We move out in one hour."

As the battalion was moving toward Moreville, Charlie Company ran into an anti-tank ditch. Once again they were immobile targets. German Panzers moving toward them began to knock out their tanks one by one.

"Get out of the tank!" William shouted. "Get out of the tank now!"

Out through the hatch at the bottom of the tank went William's crewmen; he was right behind them. They dropped into the icy ditch and crawled through the freezing muddy waters. Falling all around them were hot shell fragments. At that moment, German artillery opened up; each shell hit closer and closer to the ditch. William and his men returned fire on the Germans, but machine guns against artillery was hopeless.

Thirty feet away, another tank was on fire; it was First Sergeant Turley's. Turley and his crew had also evacuated their tank and were pinned down by the enemy. Suddenly William heard Turley order his men to retreat. Then he jumped out of the ditch, stood up straight, and laid down covering fire so his men could get to safety.

For only a moment that seemed like forever, William watched in awe as Turley stood there firing his machine gun, an ammo belt around his neck. He was scattering bullets back and forth across the line, keeping the Germans' heads down.

"You men get the hell out of here under Turley's cover!" William shouted to his crew.

When the men were out of harm's way, William got up and ran toward Turley while spraying the enemy with his Thompson Sub-Machine gun. But just before he could reach the first sergeant, that daring, selfless man was cut through the middle by German bullets. In spite of the enemy's fierce firepower, William dragged Turley to cover behind his tank. He could easily see that the first sergeant's wounds were fatal.

"You saved our lives, Sam," said William.

"It's all right, sir. You all saved mine at Camp Claiborne." His eyes closed, and he was gone. William knew immediately that he would see this hero's broken body in his dreams for the rest of his life.

EIGHTEEN

The Wolf Defends His Lair

William had once heard that nothing makes people colorblind like combat; nothing will evanesce faster than bigotry when opposites find a common enemy. Never in his life had he expected to experience combat; consequently, he never thought he would have the opportunity to find out if what he'd heard was true. But in that bloody November of 1944, his opportunity came.

Sergeant Warren G. H. Crecy was a mild-mannered, baby-faced youth from Corpus Christi, Texas. He was quiet, polite, and very well-liked. But when he was on the field of battle, a fire deep inside him would erupt into a conflagration that turned him into the baddest man in the 761st.

The battalion was moving on after the devastating engagement at Moreville when they were attacked from a German stronghold on the side of a steep hill overlooking a small village. The infantry division they were supporting, part of Patton's Third Army, had made it inside the village and were now cut off from the tanks. German artillery was bombarding the village and the American tanks simultaneously. In addition, enemy infantry was making its way down the hill toward the village.

Able Company and Charlie Company spread their tanks out across the open fields to make things more difficult for the German guns. Up ahead of William's tank was Sergeant Crecy, who fought through the deadly shell fire until his tank was destroyed.

"Move on up and cover Crecy and his crew," William told his driver.

But the sergeant had no idea of quitting the battle. While his crewmen got to the ground and moved behind William's tank for cover, Crecy manned the .50 caliber machine gun on his disabled tank and took out the enemy forward observers directing the artillery fire pinning down the infantry in the village. Then he turned his attention to the German riflemen who were moving down the hill.

All the while, William and the other tank commanders were working their vehicles closer and closer to the village while they poured barrage after barrage into the German defenses on the hillside. As they moved past Crecy's burning tank, William unwisely stuck his head out of the turret and screamed, "Get your ass down from there, Crecy, and find some cover! Are you begging to get your head shot off?"

A bullet ricocheted off the side of the turret and cut a gash in William's right hand. He dropped below the hatch and pulled the cover into place. He could not worry about Sergeant Crecy any longer. It seemed that the more fire Crecy drew, the harder he fought. All William could do was to pray that he survived, somehow.

Able Company had lost two tanks, and Charlie Company lost one, but they finally made it to the village and sealed off both ends of it. The infantry was now enclosed by their friends in armor. The Germans launched a frontal assault on the village, but with the protection of the tanks, not to mention the heavy firepower they provided, the assault was thwarted three times before the enemy withdrew.

They spent that night in the little village. Campfires were burning everywhere in the main street; the soldiers huddled around them doing their best to prepare a hot meal. But what amazed William was that there was no segregation that night.

Each group of soldiers around every one of those campfires was an equal mixture of black and white. They were eating together, talking together, and laughing together. It was exactly the way it should be, and the way it should have always been. That day, they had fought together, supported each other, and even saved each other's lives. Now they were indebted to one another because the fear, the sacrifice, and the bravery had been shared equally.

The next morning, the Black Panthers moved on. Fighting an enemy who desperately contested every foot of ground was made much more difficult in the cold, mud, and freezing rain. The battalion fought their way through the

French towns of Obreck and Dedeline. This time Sergeant Ruben Rivers of Able Company was leading the way.

William, having recently been attached to Charlie Company, was now back with Able, as he had been at Camp Claiborne and Camp Hood. Rivers, from Oklahoma, was an excellent soldier who was fast becoming a legend in the battalion. Once, as the 761st was approaching the heavily defended town of Chateau Voue, William told Rivers via the radio, "Stay out of that town, Sergeant, it's too hot in there."

"I'm sorry, sir, I'm already through that town," he respectfully replied.

On November 16, the battalion was on the way to Guebling, France when a Teller anti-tank mine exploded under Rivers' tank, knocking off the right track, the volute spring, and the undercarriage, hurling it sideways. When William got to him he was behind his tank with one leg shredded to the bone. The leg bone was sticking through his trousers. William got on his radio and called for the nearest medical team to get there in a hurry.

"Sergeant Rivers is hurt badly," he told the medic when he arrived. Then he watched as the medic cleaned and dressed the wound, but when he tried to give Rivers a shot of morphine, the sergeant refused.

"I want to keep my mind clear," said Rivers.

"You know, Captain," the medic told William. "This man should be evacuated immediately."

"I'm not going anywhere," said Rivers. Then pulling himself to his feet, he limped passed William toward another tank.

"What do you think you're doing, Rivers?" said William.

"I'm taking over Corporal Miller's tank; I outrank him."

At that instant, mortar rounds started dropping all around. "Take cover!" William shouted. "Rivers, get in Miller's tank. Move, move, move!"

"Get your tanks rolling!" William shouted over the radio. "We're headed for Guebling. We got to get to the river and see if the engineers have got that Bailey bridge finished yet."

When the battalion reached the river, the bridge was not yet finished, but even worse was the fact that the engineers were under fire. "Take up positions along the riverbank, and start backing off those Krauts," William ordered. "Give the engineers some cover—let them have it!"

The Germans tried hard to halt construction, but by afternoon of the next day, Sergeant Rivers led the way across; the 761st moved into and around the town. William was right behind Rivers' tank as he headed into Guebling. Together, they engaged two German tanks and disabled both of them. Two more Panzers came into view, but a half dozen well placed shots forced them to withdraw. The fighting at Guebling lasted all night in one continuous battle.

The following morning, William, along with a medical team, visited each tank. When they got to Sergeant Rivers, it was not difficult to see that he was in excruciating pain.

"If you don't evacuate now, that leg's gonna have to come off," the medic told Rivers.

"I appreciate your advice, Doc, but I ain't leavin' my men."

"Listen, Sergeant, nobody appreciates your dedication more than I do, but sometimes you have to think of yourself. Even the colonel had to come out of the fight when his leg was shattered," William told him.

"You're a good man, Captain, and I know you're just looking out for me, but I ain't leavin' my men."

William had no more time to argue because artillery fire forced the battalion into defensive positions again. All day long each side held their ground. The ongoing conflict was enough to incite madness. Weary from lack of sleep and starving from so little opportunity to eat, the battalion began an assault on the village of Bougaltroff on the morning of November 19, as one day rolled into another.

Outside Guebling, the air was full of tracers from German guns the minute the 761st emerged from cover.

"Captain Langdon!" came Sergeant Rivers' voice over the radio.

"Go ahead, Rivers."

"I can see the anti-tank guns from here. All tanks concentrate your fire on my order."

"Give us the coordinates, Rivers," said William.

At the sergeant's direction, the battalion smashed the enemy almost out of existence; the 761st moved out toward

Bougaltroff. Spinning the turret around, William could see Rivers' tank still firing at the enemy's position. Suddenly he saw several tracers go into the sergeant's turret. The Germans threw in two high explosive rounds, one of which scored from a distance of two hundred yards.

The shot hit the front of the tank, penetrating the steel walls and undoubtedly ricocheting around inside. William knew that Sergeant Rivers would no longer need the medics; they could not help him now.

"He didn't have to die on this cold, miserable November morning in France," said William.

"A few days ago he got the million dollar wound, didn't he, sir?" said Sergeant Dixon.

"He certainly did," William replied. "He could have gone home a hero with his Silver Star and his Purple Heart, knowing how much the battalion respected him as a first-rate soldier and friend. But he wouldn't abandon his men; he stayed, and he died."

By the end of November, the Allied commanders thought they had formed an impenetrable line with Germany on one side, France and Belgium on the other. The objective was to cross into Germany and end the war. But in late December 1944, Colonel Hollis informed William and his other subordinates that Adolf Hitler had launched a surprise offensive in the Ardennes Forest, pushing a bulge in the line that extended for fifty miles.

Still a part of Patton's Third Army, the 761st, along with the infantry, pulled out of a battle in France and marched through the ice and snow for three days to reach Belgium; the objective was to rescue the paratroopers surrounded in the town of Bastogne.

But the town of Tillet, a major supply artery for the Germans, stood in the way of the Third Army's advance. The 87th Infantry and the 761st were ordered to take the town.

"If you think this war has been rough to this point, brace yourselves for something even worse," William told his crew.

"How can it get worse, sir?" asked Sergeant Jones.

"The wolf is now defending his lair," William replied. "The Germans had quite a buffer between us and them when we landed in France. But now we are knocking on the door of their home country, and they'll try anything to keep us out of Germany. This offensive is intended to push us back, to give the damn Nazis more breathing room."

"I guess that does make sense, sir," the sergeant replied.

"We kicked their asses out of Italy and Africa too," said Corporal Dixon.

"Indeed we did, men. Hitler's hold on Europe is slipping away fast," said William.

Upon reaching the town of Tillet, every man in the 87th Infantry and the 761st Tank Battalion could see that Hell still stood in the way of victory. The defense that the enemy had put together breathed fire on the Americans on that icy winter day.

For five days, the tanks laid down a continuous barrage covering the infantry, but they could not break the line and force the Germans back. Finally, on January 8, they were able to fight their way into the town. The streets of Tillet were just barely wide enough for the tanks, which made it difficult to spin their turrets and use their main guns efficiently. Fierce house-to-house fighting ensued, leaving many casualties on both sides in the wake of the battle. After two days, all of the Germans were either killed, captured, or had fled.

The 761st immediately headed for Bastogne to assist in rescuing the 17th Airborne Division before they were overrun by German armored units.

"From battle to battle nonstop," William told his crew. "Take a breather on the way because you'll not get one in Bastogne. We've been on the front line so long we've lost the mental picture of what the rear looks like."

"Are you all right, Captain?" asked Corporal Riley.

"Why do you ask?" said William.

"You just seem a little bug house is all."

William knew the corporal meant that he was acting a little strange the way some men do when exposed to death and destruction for too long. After what he'd seen of the war, the carnage, the blood and guts of friends lying on the ground, William guessed maybe he was a bit tetched, as they say. Before the war, in his wildest imagination, he could never have conjured up images such as those he'd seen. But with each passing day he wondered if the end of the war would come in time to spare his sanity.

"I'm all right, Corporal," he said. "Let's lend a helping hand to our comrades in Bastogne."

When the 761st reached the outskirts of town, they were fired on from several German positions. One by one the tankers destroyed those positions until they could enter the town itself. As they rolled down the main street, the grateful paratroopers shouted and waved as if they'd just been told that the war was over. The poor bastards had been hanging on by their fingernails. They were short on ammo, food, winter clothing—everything but morale and determination. The Battle of the Bulge ended on January 28, 1945.

Hitler's last ditch effort to drive the Allies back failed; German soldiers surrendered by the thousands. The war was winding down; William and his comrades actually began to think that they might survive to see home again. The 761st, now the spearhead for the 103rd Infantry Division, took part in a number of assaults that resulted in the breach of the Siegfried Line. The Allies had placed their footprints on the Fatherland.

In mid-February, the battalion was elated by the return of Colonel Bates. The end was in sight, and it was only fitting that the man who cared about the men most should be with them for the conclusion. In William's opinion, Colonel Bates was a man who was out to make right an unspeakable wrong. But William knew that only the future could reveal the answer to whether the colonel failed or succeeded.

The 761st moved through Germany into Austria, and it was there that William and the men of the battalion encountered something worse than the carnage of combat. They had reached the Hausruckviertel, which was a region belonging to the state of Upper Austria. They were supporting the 71st Infantry Division when they came upon a camp with guard towers and high fences around the perimeter topped with barbed wire. The huge front gates stood open; the tanks stopped outside the fence, the men wondering what the camp might be.

By the time William and the 761st arrived, the infantry had already gone inside. Not knowing what to expect, the tankers walked cautiously through the gates looking for the foot soldiers. Before they'd gone a dozen paces, soldiers from the 71st came out to meet them leading a large group of the feeblest, most emaciated and hollow-eyed human beings they'd ever seen. The prisoners were all dressed in filthy rags; something that resembled stripped pajamas. About where the left breast pocket would be there was a cloth star, yellow in color, sewn to the shirt.

Some of the people were crying, others were moaning; all of them were slowly starving to death. In their criminal state of abuse, having lost all rationality, they were like little children, whimpering, trying to hug and kiss the soldiers. The smell of the place was the most terrible odor William had ever experienced—like the smell of decomposition, like the smell of death. A lieutenant of the 71st was leading the way, but William stopped him.

"Who are these people, Lieutenant? What is this place?" he asked.

"This is Gunskirchen, a sub camp of the Manthausen-Gusen concentration camp. Most of these people are Hungarian Jews."

William was about to ask the lieutenant to repeat himself, but before he could speak, a connection in his mind made very clear what he'd just heard. For the past two years, rumors, stories, and eyewitness accounts propagated the belief that the Nazis were exterminating the Jews of Europe. But it seemed an impossible idea, so huge, and so inconceivable that it was often dismissed as just that.

Years earlier, before the war in Europe began, William heard his father speak of Hitler's treatment of the Jews. Could this be proof that such a heinous crime could be possible after all?

"Good heavens," said William. "What are you doing for these people?"

"Everything we can, Captain. We have a medical team on the way, and we are already sharing what food we have. Through an interpreter we've been talking with one of the prisoners here . . . this is just the very tip of the iceberg.

There are thousands of these camps. Most of them are in Poland because they have the largest Jewish population."

"You said most of these people are Jews—what about the rest?"

"There are about four hundred political prisoners here also. The Nazis built different camps for different reasons: forced labor, detaining people thought to be enemies of the state, and death camps."

"Death camps?"

"Yes, Captain, death camps. They were built for the systematic extermination of the Jews. The Nazis referred to it as the final solution to the Jewish problem. Hitler's SS bastards apparently hauled ass a couple days ago. They knew we were coming. Hitler's SS guarded all of the camps; it was their assignment under that son of a bitch Heinrich Himmler."

"Why the Jews?" William asked.

"Can't say for sure, but Hitler hates them, and he convinced the German people that they were responsible for Germany's problems. There were many others murdered—Gypsies, homosexuals, Jehovah's Witnesses—anybody who was either nonessential to the Nazis' needs like the infirm, the elderly, and children, or anybody who was not an acceptable example of a true Aryan."

"These poor souls look like walking corpses," said William.

"There are piles of the real thing over behind those buildings," said the lieutenant as he pointed a finger. "Some of these people are alive, but they won't make it. Typhus and dysentery are rampant in the camp. I have things to do, Captain, excuse me."

William was shocked by what he heard and saw. Judging by the expressions on the faces of his men, so were they. His first inclination was to walk out of the gate and cower in his tank. But something drew him in, something he could not explain. Maybe he felt an obligation to those people to bear witness, to be one more voice to testify to this horrific crime against humanity.

He walked deeper into the camp, oblivious to everything except for the sights around him. When he walked around to the back of the building the lieutenant had pointed out, he saw them. A huge pile of bodies numbering in the hundreds; lifeless skin and bones, discarded like so much garbage. William stood and stared so intently that he broke into tears as he wondered who they were, where they came from, and what sin they could have possibly committed to end up this way.

He thought of what life means to every human and what it must have meant to them; he wondered how long it had been since they laughed or sang or hugged their families the way he wished he could be hugging his own at that moment. And he wondered about how they had suffered from cruelty and starvation because of a man so evil, who was not only capable of such brutality but so accomplished at influencing others to follow his example.

Suddenly he was victimized by his own senses; the sight of the decomposing bodies, the stench of rotting flesh, and he collapsed to his knees and dumped his guts into the snow. William heard footsteps coming from behind and then someone knelt down next to him. He looked around and saw Howard Clay.

"Are you OK, Captain?"

"I'm glad it's you, Howard. I'm glad to see a face that reminds me of home. That's where I want to be right now. I pray this horror is soon over."

"It will be, sir. The wolf has no place else to run. The battalion is getting ready to move out."

As Corporal Dixon moved the tank into line and the 761st headed out, William prayed for all the victims of the Holocaust and for the survivors. He also beseeched Almighty God to not allow him to become vengeful.

It would now be so easy to see the enemy not as men but as savages and to enjoy putting them to the slaughter. He must continue to do what he had to do, but in the interest of ending the war, not for the purpose of punishing the Germans—that was strictly the Lord's domain.

Against vicious German resistance and far in advance of friendly artillery, the 761st attacked and destroyed many defensive positions along the Siegfried Line from March twentieth to the twenty-third. The Axis forces were being pushed back on all fronts; the Allied armies were finally closing in.

Among the first American units to link up with Soviet forces were the Black Panthers. On the fifth of May 1945, the 761st reached Steyr, Austria on the Enns River, where they joined the Russians. The official surrender of Germany was signed on May 8, 1945.

Unlike the front line units made up of white soldiers, who seldom remained on the front line for more than a few weeks at a time, for one hundred and eighty-three straight days, the 761st was on the front line without any relief.

In William's mind, the African American soldiers performed above and beyond the call of duty, proving once again that they were not only up to the task but also deserving of their country's gratitude and respect.

He had seen for himself the trials and tribulations they endured both from their fellow countrymen and from the enemies of the world without allowing themselves to abandon what they believed to be their patriotic duty.

With the war in Europe at an end, William resigned his commission and prepared for the long journey home. In spite of his overwhelming desire to be back with his family, he also found it very difficult to leave the men with whom he had been through so much.

For William it was much like leaving one family for another because the men of the 761st were truly his brothers. Now his only hope was that the country who owed them so much would be ready to admit their terrible misjudgment and bestow upon them the equality they so rightfully deserved.

NINETEEN

The Absence of Gratitude

For William, surviving the war to see home again was perhaps the most wonderful experience of his entire life. Not one to take things for granted, he felt as though he needed to be especially thankful to be with his family again.

Although the war in the Pacific theater was still raging, the newspapers were full of stories about the defeat of Germany and a grateful nation that welcomed their victorious soldiers back with open arms. But what of the 761st and the thousands of other African American men who risked their lives, some of them never to return? What would their homecoming be like?

Like spending time outside on a frigid winter day and then going into a warm house, the extreme difference in temperature required a period of adjustment. On a much larger scale, spending a long period of time in constant danger also required a period of adjustment upon reaching the safety and security of home. For William, the horrors of war, he soon realized, made a change in him that he would not easily overcome.

It was a very great help to him that no one, not even his ten-year-old son, asked questions about the war in the interest of making it easier for William to put the past behind him. He did not speak of the friends he lost in combat or of the terrible things he'd seen at the concentration camp. At times, he would walk out to the open fields of the plantation alone; there he would battle his memories, defeating them little by little with rationalization and a lot of prayer.

Joanna understood, as did William's parents, and they gave him all the space he needed to work through the trauma. They would always be there if he wanted to talk; William knew that too.

It took about six months before he felt the war was fading a bit and he had finally come to terms with all that had happened. On September 2, 1945, the Japanese finally surrendered after the late president Roosevelt's successor, President Harry S. Truman, ordered two atomic bombs dropped on Hiroshima and Nagasaki. World War II was over; peace had finally come.

John and Abbey were having coffee in the kitchen on a chilly November morning when William stopped by for a visit. His expression was that of a man who had something very troubling on his mind. Without asking, Abbey poured her son a hot cup of coffee and put it on the table in front of him; they waited for William to speak first.

"Owing to the grace of God, I believe that I am able to make sense of the war and why it had to happen. The facts behind the reasons and the events leading up to it are the best explanation. But then there is the other side of reason; what makes people do the things they do and how so much hatred can be the motivation for premeditated killing on such a huge scale. I don't know how sin is committed so boldly by the human race, who is so powerless against God's will and punishment."

"I suppose that all we can do is to accept what we don't understand and rely on our faith," said John. "We only know a small part of what the Lord has in mind for us; the rest is dependent on trust that right will prevail and justice will win out in the end."

"Your father is right, William. Our faith is what has sustained us over the years; faith is what gave us the gift of contentment when your sister, Julia, was called home. We lamented her loss because we loved her then as we do now. But we can go on because we know that she has completed her journey and has reached her final destination in heaven."

"Of course, Mother. I know what you're saying, and I agree. I guess it just helps to hear it said out loud from time to time. It's just that in the wake of this terrible conflict, I want to see a change in people. I want them to fall in love with peace, love, kindness, and brotherhood. I want them to stop the hatred; end the false pretense and become hopelessly susceptible to the perfect example of Jesus Christ."

"We don't have to tell you how proud we are of you, William," said John. "We cannot imagine what you've been through because of your dedication and selflessness."

"I literally have not the strength of mind to tell you what I've seen, Father. I have to repress as much as possible to maintain my sanity. I haven't the stomach to explain in detail what the black men in my unit suffered while attempting to gain acknowledgment as human beings, nor do I have the stomach to explain what I saw when we reached that dreadful concentration camp in Austria. Most of the soldiers did not see that horror until the end, but generally speaking, the world knew what was going on years ago when the Nazis first came to power. They knew and they turned a blind eye."

"Sadly, that is true, son," said John. "It took twelve years for the world to liberate those camps. Sometimes I wonder if the Lord will ever forgive us for what we've done to each other."

"I hope the Jews can find a way to forgive, Father, for the sake of their own souls, I hope they can find it in their hearts to forgive. They must let the other man be the one who makes the mistakes if that man is truly willful, but they must be forgiving and let the Lord allot His punishment."

"Prayer is what we have to combat the forces of evil," said Abbey. "Pray every day, William, and God *will* take care of the rest."

For all their good wishes, it soon became clear to the Langdons that the African American soldiers had done nothing to change the feelings of white Americans towards them. Their attempt to help defeat the Germans and racism in a single stroke had failed. They had referred to it as the "Double V," victory in Europe and victory over racism. William could still see evidence of Jim Crow wherever he went, but it could not have confronted him more personally than it did in May of 1946, when he attended a reunion of the 761st in Corpus Christi, Texas.

Sergeant Warren G.H. Crecy, a soldier whose bravery William would never forget, organized the reunion in his hometown. Of course, the whole battalion was not there, but there were one hundred or so; a good turnout, William thought.

He was greeted by Warren Crecy, who shook his hand cordially.

"I'm glad you could come, Lieutenant," he said.

"Oh please, Warren. I'm trying to put that military rank business behind me. I'm just plain William now."

"Yes, I guess it doesn't mean much anymore. I don't know that it meant that much during the war. A black man didn't get much respect with or without stripes, except from you and the colonel."

"Is the colonel here?" William asked.

"No, he couldn't make it. He sent his regrets, I know he really wanted to come, but I think his leg is still giving him trouble."

"Speaking of legs, how is your wound coming along?"

"It's all healed," said Warren. "At least as healed as it's going to get. I applied for some help from the VA hospital, but my application got turned down. They said I make too much money to get any aid."

"That is sad," said William.

"Not as sad as my income. If they won't help people that make no more money than me then nobody will get help. Of course, there is more to it than that, you know."

"Yes, I know, Warren. But I meant that it's sad because I know what you did for this country. I saw it firsthand."

"No matter, William. We all knew that it was a long shot that things would change here. But you know something? I think most of us would have gone anyway. I know you remember how bad we all wanted to go."

"I certainly do. If it's any consolation to you, Warren, I think they kept the best troops for last."

"Well it *does* seem like that's when they needed us most. But when we all got back, the white man was ready to put us back in our place; no offense intended."

"None taken, Warren. None at all."

It was good to see some of his old friends again, but the more William talked to them, the more depressed he got.

Henry Murphy told him that when he got back to the states he called his father in Mississippi. His father told him not to come home wearing his uniform. His father said that the police were beating and searching black men in uniform, and if they had a picture of a white woman in their wallet the police would kill them. Henry went home dressed like a sharecropper.

Joe Carney went back to Alabama wearing his war medals and when confronted by a white man he was told, "You got some nice shiny medals there, boy, but remember, you're still a nigger."

Later that afternoon William was talking with Ron Dixon, his former machine gunner who said, "I'm quitting this country, William. I'm glad I was here to see some of my buddies again, but I've already had enough of this *United States*," he said with disdain in his voice. "I'm going back to France. I'm gonna find myself a nice French lady and have myself a happy life. Over there they don't seem to care about what color a man is. It was hard to believe how good they treated us. There were times when I forgot that I was black."

"I cannot fault you one bit, Ron. If I were in your place, I'd probably do the same thing."

"It wasn't just France, William. There were a lot of countries in Europe that treated us like everyone else. You know, a lot of the boys came home spoiling for a fight. After seeing the differences in other parts of the world, they figure the South doesn't have to be the way it is."

"I don't figure that it has to be either," said William. "For many years my family has stood against bigotry in the South while bearing the shame of our slave-holding past. We've been pulling away ever since my great-grandfather fought for the Union to help put an end to slavery. But sometimes I think it will never end."

"Well it's sure gonna take longer than *I* can wait," said Ron. "I'll drop you a line on my wedding day."

"I wish you all the best in the world, Ron. God bless you, my friend."

Eventually, William had heard enough about the treatment his comrades were receiving since they came home. The racism was still there, the criminal refusal of their rights was still there, and the benefits that the white soldiers were entitled to were not for 'niggers.'

William made a polite exit and left for home in a state of utter disgust.

TWENTY

What about Truman

Harry S. Truman had become the thirty-third president of the United States when Franklin D. Roosevelt died in office on April 12, 1945, at Warm Springs, Georgia. For as long as William could remember, his family had always followed the political process and the man elected to the highest office in the land—an interest that captivated most Americans.

His father, John, was very pleased to learn that his old friend, Eleanor Roosevelt, was still bending rules and breaking her back to support the African American cause. In May of 1945, she joined the board of directors of the NAACP and that fall she became a member of the Congress of Racial Equality Board.

But for the Langdons, the nation's president held another key to *their* intense concentration: the man's point of view on equal rights. President Roosevelt had not been the man they had hoped for, even allowing him a great deal of latitude; after all, he had a lot on his plate with the Great Depression and a world war to fight.

Still, they knew FDR's feelings concerning African Americans, and it was doubtful he would have stuck his neck out far for them regardless. But a new man was in office now, and there was always hope that he would be more inclined to take on the white supremacists of the country and bring about reform.

At sixty-five years of age, William's father was still the leader of the family's activism in the civil rights movement. At least one evening each week they would get together, usually at the old homestead, to discuss new ways of serving the cause. William's grandmother, Elizabeth, always joined them. He understood how much it pleased her to know that her family was so dedicated to the ongoing struggle that her late husband had continued after the death of his own father. Generation after generation had kept the promise: to carry on the work begun by

James Langdon in 1863, when he joined Mr. Lincoln's Army. And she knew that one day her grandson, Martin, would take his turn.

By May of 1946, the family was still undecided as to how effective President Truman might be as a supporter of the civil rights movement.

"It has been a little more than a year now since President Truman took office," said John. "We have all been following his moves pretty closely, but I can only conclude that it will take more time before we will know how far he is willing to go on the issue of civil rights."

"I believe, Father," said William, "that Mr. Truman does genuinely care about our black citizens, but as you said, we don't know how far he will push his executive power to advance the movement. I also believe that he cares even more about the black men who served in the recent war."

"I can attest to that," said Elizabeth.

"Please do, Mother," said John.

"I recently read a story in *Life Magazine* about a black soldier by the name of Isaac Woodard. In February of this year, Isaac was on his way home by bus to South Carolina, just having been discharged from the army. On the way, he was involved in a verbal altercation with the driver about using the restroom. After Isaac used the restroom he quietly returned to his seat. However, when the bus made a stop in Batesburg, the driver contacted Sheriff Linwood Shull, who removed Isaac from the bus by force. The sheriff demanded to see his discharge papers and then a group of deputies took him into an alley and beat him with their nightsticks. Then they arrested Isaac and jailed him for disorderly conduct.

That night, the beating and the jabbing with nightsticks continued until both of Isaac's eyes were ruptured. The next day he was taken to a local judge who found him guilty and fined him fifty dollars. Isaac ended up in a hospital where he received substandard care. It took his family ten days to find him. When President Truman learned of the incident he demanded action from the attorney general. The sheriff was taken to court, where he admitted that he had blinded the soldier. But after only thirty minutes of deliberation, the sheriff was acquitted, walking out of the courthouse under a hail of applause."

"I see your point, Mother," said John. "Perhaps Mr. Truman has a soft spot for the black American, especially a soldier, but if the story ends there, his concern was no more than a placebo prescribed for a serious illness."

"I'm afraid that's true," Elizabeth replied. "I still think, as you said, it is too early to make judgments on his ability or willingness to help the civil rights movement, but that story does not end on an optimistic note."

"So we give him time and hope for good things, but there may be something we can do to produce faster and more tangible results," said William.

"Have you an idea, son?" John asked.

"I do, Father. Looking at the big picture, we see that the problems facing the African Americans have not diminished much since the end of slavery. Until federal laws are put into place and enforced to protect the rights of these people, they will go on without hope forever. Many black citizens are still unable to vote. They are discriminated against in every segment of society including jobs, housing, schools—the list goes on and on. Policies that reinforce patterns of segregation issued by the Federal Housing Administration deny low-interest loans to non-whites on a regular basis. Here in the South, exploitative tenant sharecropping systems keep blacks in perpetual debt."

"So what's the answer, Father?" asked eleven-year-old Martin.

"You're right, son, I should get to the point. I propose that, for the time being, we do something that will actually help these deserving people—to start with, the black men who have families, and the men who served their country during the war. I want our family to establish a small lending institution and help as many people as we can to get the low-interest loans they need."

"I think that's an excellent idea, William," said John. "And low-interest loans they will be. In actuality, it would be a non-profit organization because the interest we charge should only be enough to cover operating costs. How does it strike you, Mother?"

"I wish I'd had the idea myself," Elizabeth replied. "But the loans should be for a wide variety of purposes. A home mortgage, business loan, debt consolidation, and so on."

"We can use Jerome's help in this, Father," said William. "We'll need an attorney. It may not be Jerome's specialty, but I'm sure he can handle it."

"We will need a name for the institution," said John.

"I've thought about that too, Father. How about the African American Relief Bureau? I think it might be best if the name doesn't exactly spell out the nature of the business. I am sure that information will circulate easily enough. We should try to begin slowly. Given the extent of the need, we could be overrun."

"I agree, William. If we can make our plan work, I would not be averse to expanding when the time is right. I will pay a call to Jerome tomorrow, and then I will report what I've learned."

"Some of the men I served with live in the South," said William. "I will contact as many as I can. I would like to offer help to them. I would like to end on an optimistic note by saying that, although the black servicemen came home to a country that still doesn't give them full rights, a movement to expand their rights has been born. We need to embrace this birth and nurture it as much as possible."

Two days later, John visited William and Joanna with news.

"Our idea is already taking shape. Jerome tells me that it could take at least six months for all of the legal red tape. In the meantime, he will try to find a location in Macon that is suitable for a business of this kind. He will be in touch with us if he needs anything."

"It is really something to look forward to," said William.

"Who will run the business, and what about a qualified staff?" Joanna asked.

"Jerome has volunteered to find the people we need when the time comes. I tried to get him to include everything he handles in an invoice to me every month, but he refused. He wishes to contribute to this undertaking; he won't take a penny."

On November 10, 1946, the African American Relief Bureau opened in downtown Macon, Georgia. At John's request, Jerome hired six African Americans—four men and two women—from the newly graduated class of Washington University in New York to fill the positions of loan officer. But the surprise came when Jerome told John that his wife, Esther, would accept the managerial duties.

"She is more than qualified, John. As you know, she began her education in Pittsburgh, Pennsylvania, but when she met this enchanting young law student she dropped out and got her degree at a Negro college for women in Little Rock, Arkansas."

"Your word is more than good enough for me, Jerome. In any case, I would never argue with a former enchanting young law student," John said with a laugh. "But what about Mattie?"

"Mattie *is* only twelve years old, but she will be in school while Esther is at work."

"Then it's settled. Esther will be the manager."

There was a lot of satisfaction in seeing their fledgling idea come into being; watching it take shape and then enjoying satisfactory results. For the first few months, William's idea proved to be the answer to a prayer for many black families in and around the city of Macon. Because of the African American Relief Bureau, homes were being built, small business were getting under way, and for the first time in the lives of a group of people who had known only degradation, the American dream actually seemed within reach.

But from some unknown source, from some unknown time and place, perhaps from an individual whose life on earth was a never ending struggle, came the phrase, "No good deed ever went unpunished."

One evening in March, Jerome, Esther, and Mattie drove out to John's house for a friendly visit and to talk about how well things were going at the bureau. They knew of course that they were quite over matched as far as the numbers in need and the numbers they were able to help. But they *were* helping, and that was enough for the time being. When the telephone rang, John got up to answer it.

The others never heard him say a single word, but when he came back to the parlor, the grimace on his face was frightening.

"It's gone, it's been burned to the ground," he said.

There was nothing more that he needed to say. Jerome, Esther, Abbey, and even young Mattie, understood that the African American Relief Bureau had gone up in flames.

"We're going home," said Jerome. "I guess you know how we feel . . ."

"Yes, Jerome, I know. Please drive carefully. Good night."

When their guests had gone, John and Abbey went up to bed without a word. They were both too mired in despondency to be able to discuss the situation or even comfort each other.

The following morning John broke the news to William and Joanna. Joanna cried, and William's temper showed signs of becoming unleashed. After an hour of coming to terms with the full meaning of what had happened, John and William drove into Macon to confront the sheriff.

The sheriff in Macon was Harman Shafter, a man they were not acquainted with in spite of the fact that they had both voted for him two years earlier. In the past, the Langdon family knew some of the town's sheriffs very well; some of those relationships were good, some were not. John's grandfather, James, was once the mayor of Macon; during his tenure he became close friends with Sheriff Jude Renner, who was killed by James' Uncle Stanley—a member of the Ku Klux Klan.

The sheriff was alone in his office when John and William walked in. Shafter was a dark-haired man with a full beard, neatly trimmed. He appeared to be mid-forties, and it was easy to see, even as he sat in his chair, that he would stand over six feet tall. The expression on his face was quite pleasant as he acknowledged John and William's presence.

"What can I do for you, gentlemen?" he asked.

"My name is John Langdon, and this is my son, William."

"Oh," he said. "Won't you sit down?"

"Thank you, Sheriff," John replied.

"I think I know why you're here. I understand that you gentlemen are the founders of the loan company that burned down last night."

"That's correct," said John. "We've come in to find out exactly what happened."

"Unfortunately I haven't gotten all the facts of the incident from the chief of the fire department yet, but when I am able to shed some light on it I would be happy to—"

"Please don't patronize us, Sheriff," said William. "We know you've been sheriff here for over two years now, and if you've spent any time around Macon, especially in some official capacity, you are familiar with the name Langdon. We did not come to town looking for trouble. We only want to know the truth. We want to know if our suspicions are correct."

Shafter looked pensive for a moment, adjusted his posture a little, and said, "I respect your forthright approach, gentlemen, and I am going to honor your request. First let me say that, like you, I am a native of Georgia. I am from Albany, and my wife was born here. We decided to live here after we got married. I was in law enforcement in Albany, and I managed to get this position in the last election. I'm telling you this so you'll know that I *could* be sympathetic toward those who do not approve of what you were trying to do with the loan company, but I'm not."

"I get your point, Sheriff, but I'm not sure I completely understand what you're trying to tell us," said John.

"Just this. You *are* a very well-known local family with quite a history of being at odds with nearly everyone in Bibb County. Please understand that I am not judging you or finding fault. In some ways I admire your courage, and I'm sure you have your reasons for inviting so much opposition from the locals by siding with the blacks. Just between us, I have grown tired of the constant racial trouble in the South. I sometimes think that the people down here should accept the fact that times have changed and that they should change with them."

"But?" said John.

"But I live here, I like it here, and I am not going to muddy the water for my family. I admit that I may be derelict in my duties by upholding the law the way I do. But I satisfy my conscience by telling myself that in this country the majority rules, and the majority around here is not willing to accept the blacks as equals. It has always been this way, and I am not able to change it no matter how I really feel."

"You're forgetting one thing, Sheriff," said William. "This discriminatory bureaucracy in the South refuses to treat the African Americans fairly when it to comes to jobs, housing, schools, etc. I just helped to fight a war, and I fought it alongside African American men who sacrificed every bit as much as any white man alive. Still, the ungrateful white population in America will not treat them as they deserve. What we tried to do with our lending establishment, we did on our own. We didn't ask anything from the government or anyone else. Are you telling me that it was not our choice, our decision, and our right to do what we did?"

"I can't dispute that, Mr. Langdon, and I know it doesn't help much, but all I can do is point out that the situation could have been worse."

"And how could it have been worse?" asked William.

"There could have been people hurt. If there had been, even *I* would be taking a different position. The fire was set after the business was closed for the day. No one got hurt, and the insurance company will cover the damages to the property, which will compensate the man you rented the building from."

"Unbelievable!" said John. "You know who set the fire, don't you, Sheriff?"

"I do not. I know it was arson, but I have no information concerning identities."

"So that's it then," said William. "You and your good friends and neighbors squashed the futures of several hundred *niggers* to show them once again where their place is. You tied it up all nice and tidy, and you can sleep at night because the majority got its way. Of course your position would be different if someone *had* gotten hurt."

"If you're expecting us to give you credit and say that we appreciate the thoughtful way you handled this situation, you are sorely mistaken," said John. "You are a disgrace to your profession, and you would do well to reexamine your assessment of upholding the law the way you do. All that you have to worry about now is that we might decide to take this matter to a higher level of the law."

"I don't have to worry about that, Mr. Langdon, and I implore you to reconsider any such measure. This incident is buried and sealed within the city of Macon from my office on up. I will have to live with myself, and you will have to live with the fact that nothing can be done about that fire. I'm sorry, but it is the world we live in."

"It sure as hell is," John replied in an insolent tone.

"The lady who managed that business is a very good friend of ours and so is the attorney she is married to," said William. "You just may find that this incident is not as tightly sealed as you . . ."

"Mr. Langdon!" said the sheriff, showing obvious irritation, "If necessary, the owner of that building will swear that the fire was caused by an electrical malfunction."

"I imagine his compensation went beyond the amount of the damage," said John.

"Buried and sealed," the sheriff replied.

Without additional comment, John and William left the sheriff's office and headed for home.

"Is there nothing we can do, Father?"

"Not unless we owned that building, William."

"Then maybe we should buy one and start over."

"Too risky, I'm afraid. If we up the ante, the opposition might also. Maybe the next time, someone would get hurt."

"You never get used to it, do you, Father?" said William.

"No, son, you never do. When a representative of the law won't uphold the law, there is nowhere else to go. It's no longer enough to look to the future and to hope that some legislator will push some bill through the House and the Senate that will force all levels of the law to protect every citizen of this country."

"I agree, Father. But I'm beginning to wonder if we'd really have anything worthwhile if someone did. I remember the story you told me about my great-grandfather, James. How he understood that the Confederacy could be defeated, but he knew that it wouldn't change the way those soldiers felt in their hearts, and he sure was right. The end of racism will only come if people have a change of heart."

"Yes, William, and I'm not sure they ever will. I believe that the two races may get to some level of tolerance of one another, and I think that legislation may help achieve that goal. But people will never learn to love one another the way that God wants them to unless they truly change."

"But our family will never quit trying, Father. It is our discipleship and our life, and we will never quit trying."

"No, son, we will never quit trying."

The Langdons continued to follow President Truman's political agenda to see where it would lead.

On December 5, 1946, the president established the Committee on Civil Rights. He instructed the committee to take a hard look at the status of civil rights in the US and to suggest ways that the rights of American citizens could be protected.

After reading the paper, John said to Abbey, "These words serve to give me hope, but it must always be remembered that the president cannot do everything on his own authority. Getting the support of Congress is the key."

On July 29, 1947, Truman became the first president to address the NAACP; Eleanor Roosevelt joined him on the steps of the Lincoln Memorial. In December of the same year, the president's committee produced a 178 page report. Included in the recommendations were improving the existing civil rights laws and establishing a permanent Civil Rights Commission, a Joint Congressional Committee on Civil Rights, and a Civil Rights Division in the Justice Department. In addition, the report suggested the development of federal protection from lynching and the creation of a Fair Employment Practices Commission.

On February 2, 1948, Truman became the first president to send a Special Message to Congress on civil rights, requesting that Congress implement the committee's recommendations.

Once again, the words describing such measures by the president were encouraging in the minds of John and William, and they could not help waiting in anticipation to see if the storm produced a rainbow. It seemed a victory in itself, especially to William, when on July 26, 1948, Truman issued his executive order 9981, banning segregation in the armed forces.

At the age of thirty-nine, and in spite of his prior military service, William chose not to rejoin the army when the fighting broke out in Korea in 1950. If not for his family, who he promised never to leave again, he would have returned. The urge was that strong within him to see what conditions desegregation might have brought about. After another three years of war at a high cost in human life, a ceasefire brought the soldiers home again, but still nothing had weakened the racial barriers.

Though the steps taken by President Truman were important, without congressional legislative action they were largely symbolic and failed to have any bearing on the day-to-day lives of black Americans. Unfortunately, the president did not use the power at his disposal through the Fourteenth and Fifteenth Amendments, which would have given him the power to combat discrimination. In the critical area of voting, by the time Truman left the White House in early 1954, black Americans in the South continued to be denied.

TWENTY-ONE

Martin Gets Involved

When William and Joanna's son Martin turned eighteen, it was simply taken for granted that he would enter the world of higher education. The subject had been discussed many times; Martin's enthusiasm was proof enough that college was part of his future plans. However, two years later, at twenty, he was not yet in school; it seemed he had something more important on his mind.

On a rainy day in April 1954, Martin drove in to Macon to run a few errands for his father, and as usual, his sixteen-year-old sister Maryann had to tag along. Martin was very fond of his little sister and thoroughly enjoyed her company in spite of the difference in their ages and the fact that she was a girl.

Martin had male friends his own age; all of them were black, and all of them had grown up with him on the plantation. But there was one fellow in particular who he was very close to. His name was Manny Coulter, a mentally challenged young man who was born three days before Martin. He lived with his parents and worked on the plantation alongside his father. Manny was an exceptionally hard worker, and he knew just about everything there was to know about growing cotton. But he was socially awkward and was never able to understand when he was being made the butt of a joke.

He was well liked by everyone on the plantation, only suffering from ridicule when he encountered a troublemaker in town. But Manny never went into Macon alone, so there was always someone to look out for him.

Martin spent most of his childhood running over the fields and woodlands with Manny, in search of adventure—sometimes finding a little too much adventure, such as the time they tried to adopt a black bear cub only to be treed for several hours by the cub's irate mother.

Once, Manny saved Martin's life after Martin swam out too far in the big pond in the pasture. Manny was strong as a bull but as gentle as a kitten and he *was* the brother that Martin never had.

When Martin and Maryann reached Macon, the rain was slacking off, but the areas along the street that had no sidewalk were extremely muddy. The town was busy; Martin did the best he could to find a suitable place to park.

"Watch your step, little lady," said Martin. "If you're not careful you'll be up to your ankles in mud."

"I'll make do," Maryann replied.

"I'll go with you if you want."

"No need, and anyway I know you have some things to do for Father."

"Yes, we better split up. How long will you be?"

"About an hour. I have to go to Saunders' Dress Shop and try on the new dress Mother ordered for me. It's for the Spring Dance at school. Wait till you see it."

"Then I'll meet you here in an hour."

Martin parked along the street; there was a five foot embankment with steps cut into it, which led up to the sidewalk. The steps were ten feet from the car; Maryann made use of them rather than trying to scale the muddy bank. Martin had business on the other side of the street.

When he had taken care of everything on his list, Martin left his last stop, the hardware store, and stood beneath the awning over the door. The rain had picked up again; a heavy stream was gushing down the gutter along the sidewalk. From his vantage point he could see that Maryann was not yet back to the car.

Deciding to wait until she came into sight before crossing—hoping the rain would slow up again—Martin watched a scene unfold before his eyes.

A short distance down the street from where the car was parked, a black man was approaching, walking slowly along the storefronts. Martin was sure that it was his friend, Manny, except for the fact that he was alone. In his mind, he was going to run across the street to talk to him, but since it couldn't be Manny walking alone and the rain hadn't let up yet, he stayed put and kept watching.

Suddenly, he noticed Maryann heading for the car from the other direction. It was raining harder now, and she was in a great hurry to reach the car before the packages she was carrying got soaked. But this time, instead of going the extra distance to the steps, she decided she would take her chances and go down the embankment directly to the car.

Halfway down the hill, she slipped on the wet grass, slid down the embankment, and ended up on her backside in the muddy water, packages and all. Immediately she began screaming and crying at the top of her lungs. Then Martin heard the young man holler, "I'm comin', Miss Maryann, jus' you hold on. I'm comin'!"

Martin, now sure it was Manny, watched as his friend quickly slid down the embankment, helped Maryann to her feet, and then began retrieving her packages before the muddy water could carry them away. Maryann, still shouting, slammed her back to the car, pounding on the door with her fists.

At that point, Martin started across the street, taking his time to avoid the larger puddles and trying to suppress the laughter that he knew his sister would be in no mood to hear.

Seemingly from nowhere, a sheriff's deputy appeared on the sidewalk above, gun drawn, and yelling at Manny to get away from the white girl. After that it became the classic dream when you try to run from disaster, but your efforts are futile.

Martin raised his arms in the air, shouted at the officer, and tried his best to cross the endless expanse of street. But before he could reach the car the deputy fired his revolver, and Manny fell against the embankment and then rolled into the gutter.

Martin stopped in his tracks as if he had been struck by the bullet. Maryann became completely silent, and seconds passed before the siblings regained their mobility. Together they approached Manny's motionless body, knelt down beside him in the muddy, bloody water, and unleashed their pain with a torrent of tears.

At length, when Martin stood up, he saw that a crowd had appeared above them on the sidewalk; then he saw Manny's parents rushing down the steps to their son. Martin stepped aside, helped Maryann to her feet, and then moved outside of himself and briefly became someone who no one acquainted with Martin Langdon would recognize. He pointed a finger at the deputy and said, "You son of a bitch! You murdering son of a bitch! You murdered our friend, and all he was trying to do was to help my sister because she had fallen. I hope one day you suffer greatly for your wickedness, you racist bastard! And that goes for everyone in this whites-only town who feels just like you do."

With that, the crowd started to move away. Maybe they felt a twinge of guilt, or maybe they just became indignant as they listened to Martin's remarks. The deputy was the last to leave; he wore a contrite expression on his face but he never said a word.

Martin did his best to console Maryann and Manny's bereaved parents and to convince the Coulters that they were not to blame for Manny's straying from them. Then he told them, "Let us get Manny to a proper place and prepare him for his journey to the house of the Lord."

They took Manny's body to a Negro mortician and then Martin and Maryann went home to break the news to their parents and to the other inhabitants of Langdon Plantation.

However, when they reached home, Maryann took the sad tidings to their parents alone. Martin could not bring himself to speak of what he'd witnessed; he needed time out in the fields and the woodlands to seek solace for his spirit.

For two days he stayed away, taking shelter in a lean-to like the kind he and Manny had many times built together. When he finally went home, John and Abbey could easily see that their son had lost part of himself, and they prayed that his spirit would be restored. The following day they all attended what was quite possibly the most heartrending funeral of their lives.

For weeks it was difficult for the rest of the family to get close to Martin, to converse with him, or to hear him speak at all. They speculated about his future and wondered if he would ever heal; if he would move on with his life by furthering his education. It became reason for great concern, but when the young man was finally ready to talk, it was his great-grandmother, Elizabeth, to whom he chose to unburden himself.

"I don't know how to overcome this terrible pain inside of me, Great-Grandmother. Certainly it is due to the death of my friend, Manny, but it is more than that. It is because if he were white he would still be alive today. There is no reason that I can think of that justifies the killing of a human being. But to kill someone just because he is of a different race is inexplicable; and for the law to condone it is utter madness."

"I have lived a long life, Martin, and for most of that time I have pondered the very same questions that are facing you right now. The sad truth is that there isn't a justification for killing, and even less for killing in the name of racial differences. It is the brainwashing of generations that has kept this particular hatred alive."

"But when will it end?" he asked.

"It may never end, Martin, not until the end of the earth. The best we can ever hope for is to accomplish what the good people of the world, people like your ancestors, have been trying to accomplish for nearly a hundred years. That is, to bring about changes through peaceful effort—changes in the laws, changes in the Constitution."

"In other words, forcing people to do what is right by making laws against discrimination."

"It may seem that way, Martin, but those who God has ordained to lead do so by example, and laws can be examples of how people should live. If laws are made and enforced, eventually most people will accept them and— even if they don't say it out loud—admit that it *is* the right thing."

"I think I understand, Great-Grandmother, but it still leaves me with one problem."

"What is that, Martin?"

"What can *I* do? I feel it inside like a volcano in my stomach, this compulsive need to lend myself to the movement. You spoke of my ancestors and of course my own father and grandfather. Look at all they have done. But what can I do?"

"My dear great-grandson, you are so very much like all the men of the Langdon family: honest, compassionate, and you are wise beyond your years. I cannot tell you what you must do, but there is no need. It is something that you will discover on your own. It will come to you when you least expect it, and its arrival will be unmistakable."

Martin left her bedside still somewhat confused but strangely comforted by his great-grandmother's words.

That night, an angel slipped into her bedroom and took Elizabeth home.

As he stood near the graveside in the Langdon family cemetery, a feeling came over him, and the meaning of it was unmistakable. Martin was the last person his great-grandmother had spoken to on earth; it was as if when their conversation was over, the Lord decided that her work was done. At that moment he knew what he must do, and with the Lord at his side, nothing would stand in the way.

During the week that followed Elizabeth's funeral, Martin's parents noticed an encouraging change in his demeanor. Although he still did not speak of such things as plans for further education, he seemed at peace with recent events, which caused William and Joanna to wonder what he had on his mind.

The only information anyone was able to gather was when he told his sister, Maryann, that he knew what he must do and he would explain when he was ready. The only thing Maryann noticed was that her brother was spending more time than usual at the homes of the black sharecroppers.

Finally one evening at the dinner table, Martin made an announcement that made his family proud and nervous at the same time.

"Mother, Father, Maryann," he said. "I am going to lead a march through the streets of Macon on Sunday afternoon."

At first the members of his family looked at each other not quite sure of what to say or which one of them should say it. When all three started to speak at once, William raised his hand for silence.

"A march, you say, son? Could you give us a few more details?"

"Of course, Father. I intend to hold a peaceful demonstration in Macon. We will begin on the edge of town, march through the downtown section of Macon, and end up at the site of Manny's death. There, I will speak to whomever will listen."

"Of whom are you speaking when you say 'we,' and what will your speech be about?"

"When I say 'we,' I am talking about many of our black and white friends who work here. Jerome and his family will meet up with us in Macon. They have all agreed to walk with me through town, some holding signs if they choose. When we get to the place where Manny was killed I intend to appeal to the white population of Macon to recognize that, white or black, we are all the same."

"What will be written on the signs, Martin?"

"I told the people to write what they feel as long as it is in no way provocative."

"What will you do when you are confronted by the law, which will surely happen?" asked Maryann.

"I will convince them that we come in peace, wishing only for the opportunity to be heard as human beings, by human beings. If the slightest threat is made by the law or anyone else, we will leave immediately."

"I must admit that I like your idea very much," said William. "But I cannot help being fearful of what might go wrong."

"I remember a story about Great-Great-Grandfather James at the time he was running for mayor of Macon. Some of the black sharecroppers went into town with the intention of voting for him. Of course a group of armed white men stood in front of the courthouse where the voting took place and threatened violence if the black men tried to force their way in. Great-Great-Grandfather received word of what was going on, and so he hurried into town to get between his black friends and the armed townsmen. Suffice to say, his friends did not vote that day, but a confrontation that could have ended in bloodshed ended peacefully."

"Yes," said William. "I know that story, and you're right. Peace did prevail."

"I think I can handle any such situation just as Great-Great-Grandfather did."

"You know something, son? I think you can too. This is your march—you shall lead the way, and we will all be there to support you."

At ten o'clock on Sunday morning, everyone wishing to participate in the march was assembled. Some would go by automobile; several large trucks were provided for those without transportation. Altogether, two hundred and twenty-two people were prepared to attempt a peaceful march through Macon. Most were adults, some small children, and some were young women with babies.

Martin drove his car, which led the way, with his parents and sister riding with him. Due to a severe cold that John had contracted, he and Abbey reluctantly stayed behind but supported the march through the power of prayer. No one in Martin's car said a word during the twenty-mile trip to Macon; they were much too preoccupied with their thoughts.

William thought back to the night at Camp Claiborne when he led two companies of his battalion to rescue First Sergeant Turley from the hands of three white lieutenants. He wondered then if he was doing the right thing. Now he was wondering if his son was feeling the same way.

On the south side of Macon was a large open area used for community picnics, summer carnivals, and the like. It was the perfect spot to park the vehicles, assemble in a column of twos, and begin the march through town. Martin was not concerned about the signs the people would carry because he trusted them to use their words appropriately. As they lined up in the open field he could see many of them, and he was pleased by what he saw.

Some of them read, "We Feel Love," "We Feel Pain," "All People Can Live Together," and things of that nature. Clearly they did not project threats, violence, or antagonism in any way.

When the moment had come, Martin turned to the people and said, "My dear family and friends, I cannot thank you enough for the courage you've shown by walking with me today through this town where so recently we lost our dear departed brother, Manny. But we are not here with vengeful hearts. Rather, we are here to show that we believe in forgiveness, and we believe that we can live together in peace and harmony as the good Lord intended."

With that, Martin took his first step toward what he hoped would somehow bring some semblance of unity between the races to Macon, Georgia.

As they entered the town limits, they immediately drew attention from everyone along the street; people in their automobiles began to pull over to make way for the strange looking procession heading toward them. Fingers were pointed, heads were shaking, and comments such as, "What is this?" and "Do you see what I see?" could be heard. But not one profane word or gesture had as yet been issued.

Martin's first thought was that the march had taken the town by such surprise that no one, white or black, knew quite what to think. As they moved along, word was spreading far ahead of them. More people came from homes and businesses up and down the street until their path became lined with onlookers.

As anticipated, after traversing a few blocks, the inevitable occurred. Sheriff Shafter came running out to the middle of the street waving his arms and yelling, "Stop!"

Martin turned around, raised his right hand, and then turned back to face the sheriff. But, noticing William, Shafter walked up to him and said, "What's going on here, Mr. Langdon?"

"I beg your pardon, Sheriff, but my son, Martin, is leading this march, and you will have to speak to him."

"I'll do that," the sheriff replied. He then turned his attention to Martin and said, "What's going on here, young man?"

"This is a peaceful demonstration, Sheriff. We are here to state very simply that all people are alike, and we are like all people. We want nothing more than to be accepted as citizens of this town and to have a chance to prove that we can be good friends and neighbors. It is our intention to continue up Ash Street to 2nd Street, turn right, and then right again onto Felton Avenue. From there we will march to the location where our friend, Manny Coulter, was killed. We will spend a few minutes of prayer and remembrance; then we will go home."

"I can't let you do that. Do you know how many city ordinances you are violating?"

"I was not aware of it, Sheriff," Martin replied.

"Well I am not going to stand here blocking traffic while I explain them to you. I want you to get these people out of the street, head them down a pedestrian thoroughfare, back to their cars, and take them home. If you don't want any trouble then that is what you will do."

"We did not mean to disrespect the law, Sheriff, or create trouble of any kind. Manny Coulter meant a great deal to us; we are seeking closure so that we might heal our torn hearts."

"I understand that, but this is not the way to go about it."

At that moment, a man dressed in the uniform of a sheriff's deputy came over to Sheriff Shafter and said, "Can I talk to you for a minute, Harman?"

Martin recognized the deputy as the man who had killed Manny. The name plate on his shirt said Cpl. Dawkins.

"I know this demonstration is out of line, but couldn't we let them finish what they came for? What would be the harm?"

"Have you lost your mind, Dawkins? You're supposed to be arresting law breakers, not aiding and abetting them."

"I know that, Harman, but this is different."

"How in the hell is it different?"

"Maybe because I shot a man who didn't have it coming. Can you tell me you wouldn't feel the same if it was you? Maybe I just don't have the stomach for hatred like some people do. I wish just this once we could show that we are better people."

"What about the way they're disrupting traffic? You want to be responsible for any accidents they cause?"

"There won't be any accidents, Harman. I'll get my patrol car and lead them to their destination on Felton Avenue. How about if I do that?"

With an audible sigh the sheriff said, "I can't believe this is happening. I'll probably lose my job over this, and if I do, so will you. Get your damn car and get this over with." Then the sheriff walked over to Martin and said, "Corporal Dawkins is going to get his car and lead you down Felton Avenue. I want you to know that if you ever pull a stunt like this again I'll jail you and everybody with you even if I have to build a new jail big enough to hold them all—if I'm still the sheriff, that is."

Martin thanked the sheriff for his courtesy, but the lawman stomped off without another word. Looking around at his father, Martin was given a wink and a nod. Several minutes later, Corporal Dawkins was back with his patrol car, lights flashing, and led the procession down Felton Avenue to the place where Manny had fallen.

If the sudden turn of events wasn't difficult enough for the marchers to believe, when Martin took his place atop the little embankment they saw that a crowd of some two hundred people had followed the procession to its destination; about half of them were white.

As he spoke to the crowd about Manny Coulter, about God's creation of all people, and about the choices people have concerning what kind of world they want to live in, he became acutely aware that his prayer for a peaceful demonstration had been answered.

He could not be sure whether or not the day would have any lasting effect on the town of Macon, but he knew that every inch of progress brings you closer to a mile, and eventually the world would be on the road to lasting peace.

When Martin had finished speaking, Corporal Dawkins led the procession back to their vehicles, and everyone went home. The ride back was much like the one into town—not many words were spoken—only this time it was because everyone was lost in pleasant thought about the day. But when Martin turned into the driveway and brought the car to a stop he turned to his parents and said, "Tomorrow let's have a talk about Washington University."

It had been a great day and a proud day for the Langdons—for all people who believe in racial equality—and it was a stride in the journey toward that long-awaited climax. The direction was forward, perhaps with some difficulty, as usual, but forward.

As if God had smiled upon the peaceful gesture executed by the marchers that day in Macon, something wonderful was bestowed upon them; something that would help to offset whatever difficulties they might face in the future. On May 17, the United States Supreme Court declared public school segregation unconstitutional in *Brown v. Board of Education.* It was now only a matter of time before school districts throughout the United States would be forced to desegregate their public schools.

TWENTY-TWO

The Emergence of a Leader

In the fall of 1954, Martin left for New York to begin earning his degree in business at Washington University. William and Joanna were so relieved that their son had recovered from the loss of his good friend, Manny, and the passing of his beloved great-grandmother. They were also very pleased and proud of the courage it took to organize the Macon March, as it came to be known.

According to their friends, both black and white, who lived on the plantation, some of their experiences in town since the march attested to the fact that a few of the white citizens in Macon had considered the demonstration quite inspirational. It almost made one think that the old racial issues were ever so slowly dying.

In late November, William and Joanna received a visit from a very good family friend who was also deeply moved by Martin's effort to bring the civil rights movement directly to Macon. William's parents were over; they had just finished dinner when they heard a car pull into the driveway and then someone knocked at the front door.

When Joanna answered, she was happy to see Jerome and Esther Tompkins standing on the porch.

"Good evening, Joanna," said Esther. "I hope we haven't come at a bad time, but we have something we'd like to ask you and William."

"It's never a bad time, Esther, please come in. Hello, Jerome. William's parents are here. Everyone is in the living room."

"Thank you, Joanna," said Jerome.

Everyone was made comfortable; Joanna brought their guests some tea, and then Jerome explained the reason for the visit.

"My conscience is bothering me, my friends, and I have decided that it is time to do something about it."

"What is the problem, Jerome?" John asked.

"I have known all of you for many years now, and I have witnessed all that you have done for the sake of my race. More than that, I am aware of the trouble and hardships you have all endured because you would not conform to the notion that African Americans are second-class citizens. I am ashamed that I have not been more active in the civil rights movement myself. But when I saw the willingness of your twenty-year-old son to strike a blow, my shame reached its zenith."

"What can we do to help?" asked William.

"I want to join the ranks of the movement. I want to get involved in a big way, in a small way, in any way I can. I have been reading about a man from Atlanta by the name of Dr. Martin Luther King Jr. He recently became pastor of the Dexter Baptist Church in Montgomery, Alabama. He got his BA degree in 1948 from Morehouse College in Atlanta, and then he studied for three years at Crozer Theological Seminary in Pennsylvania, and he was awarded the BD in 1951. After that he enrolled in graduate studies at Boston University and completed his residence for the doctorate in 1953."

"Those are some very impressive credentials," said John. "Is there a specific reason for telling us about Dr. King?"

"Yes, John, there is. I believe that he will emerge as the foremost leader of the civil rights movement. He has been in the background for some time now, but I think he will soon step forward and take charge. It is my intention to go to Montgomery, seek out Dr. King, and offer my services to him. In a situation of this nature, there is always a need for an attorney—maybe more than one. I am going to find out, and that's why I'm here. I want to ask a favor of William and Joanna."

"What can we do for you, Jerome?" William asked.

"I was wondering if Esther could stay with you and Joanna while I'm gone. Esther and I talked about it; I know that she can take care of herself while Mattie is away at school. I would just feel better if she was with friends while I'm away."

"I think it's a perfectly wonderful idea," said Joanna. "Esther, we would be only too happy to have you staying with us for a while."

"You know, Jerome, I have an even better idea," said William. "How about if Esther stays with Joanna and Maryann, and I go with you to Montgomery?"

"Do you mean it, William?" Jerome asked. "I would be happy to have your company, and one more soldier in Dr. King's army would be welcome I'm sure."

"I certainly do mean it, Jerome. It is a very exciting prospect, meeting Dr. King and joining the movement in a utilitarian way. How long do you expect to be gone?"

"I'm afraid that is a bit of a gray area, William. It could be weeks or months, but if that ends up being the case I will be traveling back and forth quite a bit. I won't stay away for a continuous indefinite period."

"Then I'm your man," said William.

"This is wonderful," said Jerome. "I can't believe my request for a favor has expanded into such a magnificent idea."

"What do you think, Father?" William said to John.

"I think I am wishing I were younger. I would give anything to be going to Montgomery with you and Jerome."

"Fear not, Father," said William. "I will be keeping you posted."

"Please do, son," said Abbey."

"So when shall we leave, Jerome?" William asked.

"I will need a little time to tend to a few things; how about November thirtieth?"

"That sounds fine," William replied. "I will be ready."

At noon on their chosen day, William put his bags on the back seat of Jerome's car, and the two of them left for Montgomery. They expected to reach their destination no later than four o'clock p.m., but some seventy-five miles outside of Montgomery Jerome's car began to overheat. Four times they had to stop for water and to let the engine cool for a while before moving on. Consequently, it was nearly seven before they reached the Montgomery city line.

As if things weren't difficult enough, Jerome was fighting a cold and was in need of aspirin and some rest.

"Keep an eye open for a garage, William. We'll stop at the first one we come to."

Not too far inside the city they saw a sign that read: Mo's Garage Just Ahead on Left.

When they pulled into the garage, William discovered that they had two problems. The first was that Jerome had a splitting headache, and the second was that the proprietor was just about to close for the night. A burly, middle-aged black man was just locking the front door when Jerome approached him.

"Are you the owner, sir?" Jerome asked.

"Yep, I'm Mo. Looks like you got a hot one."

"Indeed we do," said Jerome as William got out of the car and joined them. "We've been stopping to add water for the last few hours."

Mo gave William a curious glance and then he said, "Well, I'd like to help you out, but I gotta get home for dinner. My wife gets mighty upset if I ain't home when she puts it on the table."

"I can understand that," Jerome replied.

"But if you can leave it here I'll get right on it in the morning. An overheating problem is usually pretty easy to fix if you haven't let it get hot enough to damage the motor."

"Well, I guess we don't have a choice," said Jerome. "Unfortunately we're from out of town. We haven't even secured a place to stay yet."

"There's a bus stop about three blocks down the street. You shouldn't have a problem getting dropped off at a hotel, but you might have a problem riding the bus together."

"Why is that?" asked William.

"You ain't the same color. In this town, if you ain't the same color, well, it can be a problem if you're traveling together."

"We'll have to risk it," said Jerome.

"Suit yourself. Write your name, home address, and phone number on this," Mo said as he handed Jerome a note pad and a pencil he'd pulled from his pocket. "Come on back tomorrow around noon. I should have you fixed up by then."

"We appreciate your help. We'll be back tomorrow," Jerome told him.

"Careful on the bus," Mo said again.

William and Jerome retrieved their bags from the car and headed up the street to the bus stop.

"Are you worried about riding the bus, William?"

"I'm not sure. Mo certainly seemed to be trying to warn us about something. We never use a bus where we come from so it will be a new experience. I guess we'll have to wait and see what happens."

Not five minutes after reaching the stop, a city bus pulled over to the curb. The door opened and Jerome stepped into the bus.

"Wait up there, boy," said the driver. "Let that white man on first."

Jerome looked back at William, who in turn looked at the driver and said, "It's all right, sir, I don't mind."

"You don't mind? Well I don't give a damn if you mind or not, mister. We have laws in this city, and that Negro better get behind you in line or he'll find himself in the city jail."

Jerome stepped off the bus and said, "It's fine, William, you go ahead."

Extremely perturbed but understanding the need to keep the peace, William stepped onto the bus, put his money in the fare box, and started down the aisle toward the only available seat. When Jerome had caught up to him William said, "You sit down, Jerome. You're not feeling well."

Exhausted by this time and simply not realizing what a mistake he was making, Jerome took the seat; William reached over his head for some support to hold on to. At that point the driver came up out of his seat and said, "What do you two jackasses think you're doing? Tell that black son of a bitch to get his black ass out of that seat, and you sit your ignorant ass down right now!"

William felt his self-control disappear and shouted back at the driver, "My friend isn't feeling well, and it is my right, if I choose, to let *him* have the seat!"

Two very rough and rowdy white men near the back stood up, and one of them said, "Let's throw these two troublemakers off this bus."

"I'll handle them," said the driver.

Then he got off the bus, pulled a whistle from his shirt pocket, and started blowing it until a policeman came running down the street.

"What's the trouble here?" the policeman asked the driver.

"I got a nigger who won't get out of his seat and a nigger lover who's arguing with me to let him keep it. They're about to cause a riot on my bus."

The officer got on the bus, pulled his revolver, and pointed it at William.

"Move slowly toward me and bring your nigger friend with you, now."

William helped Jerome to his feet and then walked toward the policeman with his friend right behind him. The policeman kept backing up, gun in hand, until he had backed out of the bus and onto the sidewalk.

"Go ahead on," he said to the driver, who muttered a few dirty remarks before getting back on the bus. Then the policeman used his radio to call for a patrol car.

"We didn't mean to start trouble, Officer," said William.

"Maybe you didn't mean to, but that's exactly what you did. What do you want to get arrested over this Negro for?"

"He's my friend, but I guess you can't comprehend that, can you?"

"No I can't, but I can comprehend when I've been insulted. You just stand there real still, the both of you. There will be a car here in a minute."

Winding up in the last place they ever expected, William and Jerome were taken to City Hall, where they were fingerprinted, photographed, and then taken to jail to adjacent cells until they could arrange bail.

"Quite an inauspicious beginning to our stay in Montgomery," said Jerome.

"It certainly is. How is your headache?"

"To tell you the truth, this sudden turn of events seems to have taken it away. Either that or it pales in comparison with this new circumstance," Jerome said with a smile.

"Well as soon as they prepare the paperwork we'll get ourselves out of here and find a hotel."

"I guess we'll need to find two," said Jerome.

"I never thought of that," William replied. "I hate the idea more than bigotry itself, but I suppose we'll have to do things a little differently while we're down here."

"I suppose so," said Jerome. " I guess we are used to the way things are at home, and now that I think about it, we've never traveled together before."

"No we haven't, but none of that should make a difference, and it wouldn't if the world wasn't so populated with narrow-minded people. I think Mo could have been a little more informative too. He knew we didn't understand the problem with riding the bus together."

"Some people don't want to get involved in other people's problems for the slightest risk that it might come back to them," said Jerome.

"Well then Mo is as cautious as they come," William replied.

Two hours later, a sour-looking officer opened the cell doors and said, "Follow me."

The two men paid their bail, signed some papers, and were told not to leave the city. They were also told to appear at the Montgomery County Courthouse on December 5 for trial.

As they were being given their belongings, a sedate-looking black woman, early forties, wearing dark-rimmed glasses was brought from the women's cellblock to the sergeant's desk. A well-dressed black man carrying a briefcase walked over to her and said, "Are you all right, Rosa?"

"I'm fine, Edgar. Thank you so much for coming."

"You're more than welcome. I'll have you out of here and home in no time."

The desk sergeant handed William and Jerome copies of the papers they had signed and told them to be more aware of the laws in the city of Montgomery unless they wanted to end up in jail again.

The black couple turned their attention to the two men as William and Jerome picked up their bags and left the police station. Out on the street again, they stopped, set down their bags, and tried to decide exactly what to do next.

"Should we hail separate cabs and find rooms for the night?" asked Jerome.

"I suppose we should start there. What we need right now is something to eat and a good night's sleep. In the morning after breakfast we can meet at the Dexter Baptist Church and see if we can locate Dr. King. Let's agree to be there by ten a.m."

"That's an excellent idea, William. You try to get the first cab that comes along, and I'll get the second."

As William picked up his bags and started toward the street he heard a voice say, "Just a minute, gentlemen, please."

They turned to see the black couple coming down the steps of the police station. When they reached the sidewalk the black gentleman held out his hand and said, "My name is Edgar Nixon, but everyone calls me E. D."

Jerome and William shook his hand and introduced themselves in turn.

"And this young lady is Rosa Parks."

"Hello, Ms. Parks," they replied. Rosa nodded politely.

"We don't wish to pry, but we couldn't help overhearing what the sergeant said to you. It sounds as though you had some trouble with the bus line here in Montgomery."

"Yes, E. D., we certainly did," said Jerome.

"Would you mind telling me what happened?"

Jerome explained everything that had happened from the time his car began to overheat. He also explained why he and William had come to Montgomery in search of Dr. King. Mr. Nixon seemed very impressed.

"I came down here to bail Rosa out of jail for pretty much the same reason that you gentlemen were arrested. She refused to give her seat to a white woman; she is tired of being considered a second-class citizen. The African Americans here in Montgomery are preparing to do something about segregation in our city, and we thought we would start with the bus line."

"Then you can probably help us find Dr. King," said William.

With a twinkle in his eye, Mr. Nixon said, "Yes, I believe that I can help you find the good reverend. I want you gentlemen to come along with us. I would like to offer you the hospitality of my home for as long as you wish to stay. I have a surprise for you, which I will reveal when we get there. First we'll take Rosa home. She's had a trying day."

After seeing Rosa Parks safely home, they drove to Mr. Nixon's residence. When they entered, it appeared as though there was a meeting in progress in the living room. There were several well-dressed black men and a well-dressed black woman, some of them sitting, some of them standing, and all of them sipping coffee as they discussed the arrest of Rosa Parks.

The arrival of William, Jerome, and E. D. Nixon interrupted the meeting; everyone turned their attention to Mr. Nixon and his guests. A very distinguished-looking man with a pleasant smile on his face got up from the sofa and said, "Who are your friends, E. D.?"

"I would like to present Mr. Jerome Tompkins and Mr. William Langdon from Macon, Georgia. Mr. Tompkins, Mr. Langdon, I would like you to meet Dr. Martin Luther King Jr."

William and Jerome looked at each other in disbelief. The distress of their earlier arrest immediately vanished as they bumped into each other in their haste to shake hands with the very man they'd come to Montgomery to see.

"These gentlemen have come a long way and have suffered through quite an ordeal just to see you, Martin," said E. D.

"Indeed," said Dr. King with raised eyebrows. "Tell me about it."

Again, Jerome explained why the two of them had come to Montgomery and what had happened after they arrived. Dr. King was no less impressed than Mr. Nixon had been when he heard the story.

"I am very pleased that you men have come to offer your services to us. We need every good man and woman that we can get. There is much to be done. The fact that you are an attorney will be invaluable, Jerome, and it will not be difficult to find tasks for you either, William. We were discussing a boycott of the bus line when you gentlemen arrived—would you like to join us?"

"Yes!" they decreed in unison.

"Would you mind getting some coffee for our friends, Jo Ann?"

Jo Ann Robinson was the president of the Women's Political Council; the rest of the men were ministers and local leaders of the black community, including Ralph Abernathy, who was Dr. King's closest friend. During the meeting, Jo Ann called for a one-day protest of city buses to take place on December fifth.

At midnight, the group, exhausted but still enthusiastic, decided to get some badly needed rest. As an executive member of the NAACP, Dr. King set a planning meeting for the following day at the church on Dexter Avenue.

When the meeting broke up, E. D. prepared accommodations for Jerome and William; they fell asleep as their heads touched the pillows. The next morning, after calling Joanna and Esther to bring them up to date, they attended the meeting in the church on Dexter Avenue, at which time the leaders agreed to publicize the December 5 boycott.

After the meeting, Dr. King asked Jerome if he had time for a conversation concerning the legal aspects of the boycott that was about to be initiated.

"Absolutely, Dr. King."

"Martin, please, Jerome, call me Martin—you too, William"

"We'd be honored, Martin," William replied.

"Oh, wait," said Jerome. "I nearly forgot. I have to get down to Mo's Garage to pick up my car."

"I'll pick it up for you, Jerome. You stay here with Martin."

"I appreciate that, William. Let me give you some money."

"No need. We can settle up when I get back."

When William returned, Jerome was brimming with excitement.

"Martin wants me to team up with another attorney, a Mr. Fred Gray. The leaders want to file a lawsuit against the bus line, and they want you, me, and Rosa Parks to be the plaintiffs. Fred Gray and I will prepare the papers and file the suit. Martin also wanted me to ask if you would be interested in going along with a young man named George Brent. Jo Ann Robinson is preparing leaflets at Alabama

State College to be distributed throughout the black community. You can pair up with George to cover part of it."

"I would be happy to," said William. "I find this all very exhilarating, Jerome. I can't believe that we are actually a part of this. We are helping in the fight against segregation, and it feels wonderful; we are making history, my friend."

"That we are."

"When will the leaflets be ready?"

"It should be any time. George will come by and pick you up when he receives them."

Two hours later, young George Brent stopped at Mr. Nixon's home to meet William. When Jerome made the introduction, George appeared to be more than a little surprised.

"I'm sorry if I seem a little confused, Mr. Langdon. It's just that no one told me you were a white man."

"Maybe no one noticed," William replied with a laugh. William's remark caused George to chuckle as well; the tension of the moment immediately disappeared.

All afternoon and into the evening, they traversed the black community, handing leaflets to residents or leaving them in their mailboxes. William enjoyed the experience and never minded the strange looks or the direct questions from the people who asked him why he was supporting the boycott.

At about eight o'clock, George took William back to Mr. Nixon's house.

"I want to thank you for your help, William, and I don't just mean passing out leaflets. I never met a white man who made me feel like I was with someone who was black. I mean I never felt comfortable around them the way I feel around you."

"I take that as a very great compliment, George. I enjoyed your company too. I was raised to believe that people are all the same, and you know what? They are. I only wish the whole world felt the same way."

"So do I, William, so do I. I'll say good night now."

"Good night, George. Get home safely, son."

When William entered the house, he was surprised to find Dr. King there alone. Jerome was still out with Fred Gray, and E. D. was visiting with Rosa Parks.

"I was waiting to speak to you, William. Jerome told me quite a lot about you and your family and all that you've done for my people over the years. I understand that you fought with the 761st Tank Battalion during the Second World War."

"Yes I did. That was a great group of men. I am very proud to have served with them."

"I understand it was rough for you when your fellow white men found out you didn't hate Negroes."

"I suppose so, but I just considered the source and figured that ignorance is as ignorance does. But it was still rougher for the black men I served with, and I took my strength from that. I knew that if they could endure the abuse *they* were subjected to then I should certainly be able to endure mine. I guess we helped each other through it."

"Jerome also told me that your twenty-year-old son organized a peaceful march through your hometown of Macon."

"Yes he did. The march was in honor of his black friend, Manny, who was shot down in Macon by a white officer. My son wanted to show that people are all alike and that they can live together in peace and harmony; there is no need or purpose for violence. His name is Martin too."

"I find that very flattering. His method was very sound. I believe in the same principle: a non-violent approach is the only way. Your family is astonishing, William. I would very much like to meet the rest of them someday."

"You would be most welcome anytime, Martin."

On the morning of December 5, William, Jerome, and Rosa were all at the Montgomery County Courthouse to stand trial for refusing to obey orders from a bus driver. The trial lasted for no more than thirty minutes, at which time they were all found guilty and each fined ten dollars plus four dollars for court costs.

As they left the courthouse, they found out that ninety percent of Montgomery's black citizens had stayed off the buses. Unexpected publicity had appeared in the weekend newspapers, on the radio, and television news reports. That afternoon, William and Jerome joined the black ministers and local leaders directed by Dr. King at a meeting to discuss extending the boycott into a long-term campaign. At the meeting, the Montgomery Improvement Association was formed, and Dr. King was elected president. That evening at the Holt Street Baptist Church, Dr. King addressed nearly five thousand people, and at that time he announced that a vote had been taken that had decided the extension of the boycott.

Meetings were set for Dr. King, Fred Gray, and Jerome Tompkins to negotiate with city commissioners and the bus line, but the talks were unsuccessful. On December 8, Fred and Jerome, representing the Montgomery Improvement Association, presented the commissioners with a list of demands including courteous treatment by bus operators; first come first served seating for all with blacks seating from the rear and whites seating from the front; and black bus drivers on predominantly black routes.

Despite the efforts of city officials and white citizens to defeat the boycott, when the demands were not met, the black residents stayed off the buses. Two weeks later, William and Jerome attended a meeting of the MIA to find a solution to the black citizens' need for alternative transportation.

"The city has begun penalizing black taxi drivers for supporting the boycott," said Dr. King. "I have decided that we have need of a carpool to counter this measure. I have been in touch with a friend, Mr. T. J. Jemison, who organized such a carpool in 1953 in Baton Rouge. Under his guidance we will develop the same thing here in Montgomery. If anyone can help or knows someone who can, please let me know as soon as possible."

After the meeting, William and Jerome spoke to Dr. King.

"Jerome and I must go back to Georgia for a week or so to see our families," said William. "But when we come back, Jerome will bring his car, and I will drive mine. We would be happy to add our cars to the pool."

"That would be greatly appreciated, gentlemen. I won't try to thank you because anything I could do or say would just be too inadequate. God bless you both, and I'll see you on your return."

Then one evening at home in Georgia, William and Joanna were visiting with William's parents, discussing the boycott and the significance it carried should it be successful. John decided to turn the television set on so they could all watch the news. William left the room to get something in the kitchen when suddenly he heard exclamations and loud protests. He rushed back to the living room in time to hear a reporter say that Dr. King's and E. D. Nixon's homes had been bombed.

"Oh my God! Are they all right? Have they said whether or not they are all right?"

"Yes, no one was hurt," said John.

A moment later they saw Dr. King speaking to the reporter and assuring the viewers that he and his family were fine.

"We know that the opposition in Montgomery is trying anything they can think of to stop the boycott. I was afraid that something like this would happen," William said. "We have also heard talk in Montgomery that the Ku Klux Klan is building their ranks again."

"It has always been the same," said John. "Even when violence is not instigated, the anti-African American supporters have always been happy to make use of it. They are cowards. They terrorize non-aggressors without their own lives, homes, or livelihoods ever being threatened. They skulk around in the dark or beneath hoods and robes and consider themselves men of honor, but they are cowards."

"I am leaving for Montgomery in the morning," said William. "I will call Jerome—he will probably be ready to return as well."

"Be careful, son," said John.

"We'll keep you in our prayers," said Abbey.

That night, as William prepared to head back to Montgomery, Joanna waited until Maryann had gone to bed before speaking her mind.

"I pray for you constantly too, William. I am so weary of the violence not only surrounding the struggle for equal rights for our black friends but throughout the world. It just goes on and on."

"Never wishing to be pessimistic, I would still have to say that wishing for peace sometimes seems like a fool's errand. But we both know that there is good and evil in the world and there always will be. One by one the sources of evil have to be conquered. That's what we were doing in Europe, and that's what we are doing now."

"I understand that, and I would never hinder your efforts in any way, but I can't help worrying. When you and Jerome were in Montgomery you were staying at Mr. Nixon's home. What if you had been there when it was bombed?"

"In God we trust, Joanna, and right will prevail in the end."

"Yes, William, it will. But it means sacrifices, as always, and I hope that I won't have to see you become one."

"I will be careful."

"That is all I can ask," Joanna replied.

William and Jerome were in Montgomery in February 1956 providing black citizens with transportation to and from work when city officials obtained injunctions against the boycott and indicted over eighty boycott leaders. The charges stemmed from a 1921 law that prohibited conspiracies that impeded lawful business. Tried and convicted, Dr. King was ordered to pay a fine of five hundred dollars or serve 386 days in prison. Despite the attempt to disrupt the MIA's plans, the boycott continued.

Finally, on June 5, 1956, the Federal District Court ruled in *Browder v. Gayle* that segregation of the city bus line was unconstitutional, and in November 1956, the United States Supreme Court affirmed *Browder v. Gayle* and banned laws regarding segregated seating on public buses.

"It's over, William, and our efforts were not in vain," said Jerome.

"It is a great day, my friend," William replied. "It has been over a year since the boycott began, and this morning Dr. King called for it to end. Tomorrow, officially, the buses will no longer be segregated."

"This is certainly an inspiration to the good reverend and all of us who follow him. This was a great test of his theory that a mass, non-violent action can win the day."

"Well, Jerome, I remember over a year ago when you first spoke of coming to Montgomery you told us about Dr. King. You said that he may become the foremost leader of the civil rights movement, and by golly you were right. Now, it's time to go home."

TWENTY-THREE

The Shifting of Momentum

For many years and over many hurdles, the Langdon family stayed the course of the struggle for equal rights. Like a path laid out with stepping stones, they had either witnessed or taken an active part in every advance along the path, whether it was large or small, in the constant hope of traversing the distance to the achievement of equality.

Considering the victories and defeats, there were times when it seemed that the goal was moving away rather than coming closer. It appeared as though the hardened hearts, especially those of people in the South, would never soften and the racist grip that constantly hindered the federal government would never break.

But as the oldest surviving member of the Langdon family and a seasoned activist, John began to feel the momentum shifting in favor of the African Americans. He knew that time and pressure would eventually weaken the opposition just as a concrete wall will crumble under the same circumstances. He also knew that the fight was not yet over; there was still ground that needed to be gained. However, it had come to the point that he allowed himself to believe that he may actually live long enough to see the dream of racial equality come true.

Then at the end of August 1957, John was further enlightened when two old friends made a surprise visit. He had just settled himself on the front porch, waiting for Abbey to bring glasses of iced tea, when a car bearing two ladies pulled into the driveway. When the occupants got out of the car he saw that it was none other than Eleanor Roosevelt and her friend, Lorena Hickok. John got up and called to Abbey to bring two extra glasses and the pitcher of tea.

"This is indeed a most pleasant surprise," said John when Eleanor and Lorena reached the porch.

"I hope we are not interrupting anything," said Eleanor. "We were passing so close by that we just had to stop and say hello."

"Well we are certainly happy that you did," John replied as Abbey came through the front door with the tea.

"Please sit with us and have a cold drink. The weather sure warrants it."

"That it does," said Lorena as the ladies seated themselves.

"I wanted to speak with you, John and Abbey, because as fellow activists for civil rights, I know that you will understand my frustration."

"Abbey and I are more than willing to lend an ear, Eleanor."

"I have become quite impatient with the Democratic Party's commitment to civil rights, and I am working more with activists who want to change the system rather than political officials who are only interested in their own causes. I don't know if you've heard about President Eisenhower's Civil Rights Act."

"We have not. Please tell us about it."

"It is the first civil rights legislation since Reconstruction, and it could have been a landmark piece of work, but unfortunately a vital part of it has become a victim of politics. This law was designed to protect the voting rights of black Americans. Eisenhower and Attorney General Herbert Brownell Jr. proposed the legislation, but Lyndon Johnson and his southern comrades deteriorated it beyond recognition."

"Johnson is the Senate's democratic majority leader, isn't he?" asked Abbey.

"Yes, he is," Eleanor replied. "He wanted a superficial bill that would augment his presidential ambitions, but not at the price of distancing his white southern base. But Eisenhower's proposal had four parts: Creation of a civil rights commission to investigate voting irregularities, and a civil rights division in the Justice Department. Part three of the proposal was to grant to the attorney general unprecedented authority to file law suits to protect constitutional rights, such as school desegregation. Part four provided for federal civil suits to prosecute voting rights violators."

"I think I can guess what most rubbed the Democrats the wrong way," said John. "They want jury trials for voting rights violators instead of going before a federal judge because the all-white juries in the South would make it impossible to get a conviction."

"You are absolutely correct," said Eleanor. "That is why Eisenhower and Brownell wanted to open the cases to civil suits without juries because it could result in a court order, and if ignored, a contempt citation."

"But the southern Democrats argued that the civil suits would be criminal trials in disguise," said Lorena. "They insisted that the defendants would be denied their constitutional rights to trial by jury."

"On the first of this month, Johnson and his southern brethren managed to pass an amendment to the bill requiring juries in such trials," Eleanor explained.

"Couldn't Eisenhower veto the amended bill?" John asked.

"He was very angry and threatened to do just that. The pressure he applied caused a democratic retreat and a compromise based on a Justice Department proposal that would allow civil suits before a judge without a jury as long as the predictable punishment was not more than a three hundred dollar fine or forty-five days in prison. The compromise bill passed the Senate two days ago."

"I see," said John as he took a gulp of his iced tea. "I suppose that the congressional deadlock has at least been broken."

"Yes, and it should open the door for bigger things in the future," said Eleanor. "I suppose we should be going, Lorena. We still have a long drive ahead."

"That we do, but as always it was a pleasure seeing the two of you, John, Abbey."

"You know that you're more than welcome to stay the night," said Abbey.

"We thank you, Abbey," said Eleanor. "You are a most gracious host, but we are heading back to Washington and we must put some miles behind us yet today. Perhaps we can stay another time, and if that should never happen we will not forget the two of you or your wonderful family."

"We are not likely to forget you either," said John. "History will celebrate your hard work and your achievements, without which the possibility of equality for the African Americans would never be as close to reality as it is."

"Let us hope that *close* is the right word to describe it. Farewell to you both."

As the two ladies were backing out of the driveway, William was making his way across the road to see his parents. He spoke to Eleanor and Lorena for just a minute, and then they were on their way.

"That was a nice surprise, wasn't it?" said William when he reached the porch.

"It certainly was," said John. "It was good to see the ladies again. Eleanor explained the circumstances surrounding President Eisenhower's Civil Rights Act. It seems that the Democrats, led by Lyndon Johnson, would not allow the bill to pass the way Eisenhower intended. Johnson made sure there was a loophole that voting rights violators could exploit."

"White southern Democrats," said William. "Will they ever give in?"

"Not even if they're holding on by their fingernails to the last possible way of keeping the South segregated. Did Martin get settled back in at the university?"

"Yes, he did. We probably won't see him again until Christmas. This is his final year. He is looking forward to graduation next spring."

"I assume he will take an active part in running the operations here," said John.

"Among other things, Father. He will also be looking for ways he can stay involved in the movement. I know that he wishes to meet Dr. King someday."

"I too would enjoy meeting him," said John.

"Maybe that could be arranged."

"Will you and Jerome be going back to Montgomery?"

"We hope to go eventually, Father. Dr. King knows he can call on us at any time, but for now, Jerome will resume his law practice. One of the reasons I stopped by was to tell you that Jerome and I are going to Arkansas for a week or so. As you know, Jerome is from Arkansas. He is going to Little Rock to settle an estate that was owned by his grandmother, Ida Tompkins. She passed away a few weeks ago at the age of ninety-four."

"I'm sorry to hear that. I must send him my condolences."

"I am just going along to keep him company. Esther and Mattie have been in Florida for the last month. Esther's sister is ill, and they went down to take care of her. I must get home and pack a bag. We are leaving in the morning."

William had never been to Arkansas and was looking forward to the trip. It was actually more of a vacation because while Jerome was busy during the day, William planned to walk around Little Rock and take in the historical sights.

Jerome arranged for them to stay at his grandmother's house—a lovely Victorian brick home built in 1842. It was rumored that several Confederate generals spent time there as guests of a white family by the name of Sheffield, who lived there during the war. Jerome's grandmother was born into slavery in a cottage behind that house; near the end of the war the Sheffields moved farther south, ahead of the Union army, leaving the home to Ida's family.

On September 2, William took breakfast at a little café on Monroe Street. On his way out he purchased a copy of the *Arkansas Gazette*. There was no television or radio at the house, and William was hungry for news. But he tucked the paper under his arm without even glancing at the front page and continued his morning walk.

When he reached the house in the middle of the afternoon, he sat on the screened-in porch and opened the paper. A headline on the front page grabbed his attention immediately.

"Desegregation of Central High School."

With great enthusiasm he read the story of the Supreme Court ruling and how the school officials of Little Rock had agreed to comply. Nine students chosen from a group of eighty, as the result of a series of arduous interviews, were to be enrolled on September third. "That's tomorrow," William said out loud.

When Jerome returned to the house for the day, William was waiting on the porch with the paper in his hand.

"Have you seen this?" William asked as he showed Jerome the paper.

"Yes I have. Everybody downtown is talking about it," said Jerome in a guarded tone.

"You seem subdued, Jerome. Is something wrong?"

"No, it's just that as much as I want to be excited, I can't help wondering if it will happen."

"I suppose you're right. I guess I was too caught up in the significance of it."

"It would be a wonderful beginning, I don't deny it," Jerome replied. "If one school integrates it could have a domino effect. If buses and schools and other public places do away with the color barrier the existence of segregation could collapse."

"Well, I must be there to bear witness. I will be at Central High School in the morning," said William.

"I will be there too," his friend replied.

The next morning they took Jerome's car and parked a few blocks from the school. The minute they got out of the car they could hear loud voices coming from that direction.

Jerome looked at William and said, "Are you sure you want to go up there?"

"I do, but if you'd rather not, I understand. I know we've seen so much of this kind of thing in Montgomery. I doubt that those voices belong to the welcoming committee."

"I'm here now, William. I'll lend my support to those nine young people."

When the school came into view, so did the crowd of about three to four hundred people. As they got closer they could see that many were holding signs; none of them bore a word of friendly greeting. Ugly comments and curse words emanated from the crowd; William took Jerome by the arm and said, "Maybe we should go back to the house."

But Jerome was angered by what he heard and what he saw; he pulled away from William and kept going. As they reached the outer rim of the mob, a convoy of military vehicles filled with soldiers converged on the site. A moment later, an army of men in uniform, brandishing weapons, climbed out of the trucks and formed a human barricade at the entrance to the school.

"This doesn't look good," said William. "It's the Arkansas National Guard. This has all the signs of danger, Jerome. Let's go back."

But Jerome refused to leave. At nine o'clock, a bus came up the street and stopped almost bumper to bumper with a National Guard truck. The door opened, and the nine students, notebooks and lunch pails in hand, filed cautiously out of the bus. Immediately the crowd of white students, parents, and citizens, erupted with a barrage of racial slurs and threats of violence.

A handful of black onlookers shouted back at the whites and at the guardsmen to obey the court ruling and let the nine students enter the school. It did not take long before rocks, bottles, and fists were flying. In the midst of the melee, Jerome pushed his way through the other black men and women, stood in the open, raised his fists in the air, and began yelling at the racist crowd.

"I am an attorney! I know the law and you people have no right to do this! These students are people just like you! All they want is a chance for an education! Please let them enter your school!"

A musclebound white man half Jerome's age came out of the crowd yelling, "Damn you and your nigger law!" Grabbing him by the throat, the man smashed his fist into Jerome's face. Jerome fell to the pavement; the bully pulled him up and was about to administer another blow when William took hold of the muscular man's arm and threw him into the mob of whites. William glanced up at the closest soldier with an appeal for help in his eyes. The little grin on the man's face told him he was on his own.

Jerome, his face covered with blood, tried to get to his feet. William put his arm around his friend's waist to help him. The bully came at them again, but William placed a well-aimed kick into the attacker's crotch.

An older black man dressed in a moth-eaten suit took Jerome by the right arm.

"Let's get him out of here," said the samaritan.

The small group of blacks opened a path to let them through, and the helpful stranger assisted William in getting Jerome back to the car. William thanked the old man for his help and then got in behind the wheel.

"I'll take you to the hospital, Jerome, you need medical attention."

"No, William, I'll be all right. Any pain I feel is not of the physical kind. I just need a warm, wet compress."

As William started the engine and prepared to drive away, the bus bearing the nine students was coming back down the street. When the bus passed them, William looked up and saw the faces of two of the young ladies; tears were streaming down their faces. When he looked over at Jerome, he saw the same thing.

Back at the house, William ministered to his friend with a wet towel and a couple of aspirin. Jerome was bruised and badly shaken by the ordeal but otherwise uninjured. The evening was passed in silence. The following day, Jerome concluded his business, and they left Little Rock.

It was a relief to William to reach home again, but his friend had remained sullen and restless throughout the trip. Joanna was saddened when she heard the story, as was the rest of the family. They sympathized with Jerome, and they prayed that his spirit would not suffer any permanent damage.

On September 20, the local paper carried the story of the court order issued by Federal Judge Ronald Davies demanding that Arkansas governor Orval Faubus remove the National Guard from Central High School and allow the school to be integrated.

The following day the paper reported that Faubus defied the order resulting in the dispatching of one thousand paratroopers by President Eisenhower. The president also federalized the ten thousand National Guard troops to ensure the school would be open to the nine black students. On September 23, the students returned to the school, where they were enrolled.

William spoke to Jerome that night on the telephone, hoping to find that his friend was pleased with the news and fully recovered from the attack in Little Rock. Despite Jerome's insistence that his well-being had been restored with the end result at Central High School, William still worried that such a close encounter might have caused him to become bitter. Only time would tell.

TWENTY-FOUR

Evil Dies Hard

Martin's graduation in the spring of 1958 was a pleasant distraction for everyone. The whole family made the trip to New York, including Jerome, Esther, and Mattie—who was now working in her father's law office. For three days they enjoyed the sights of New York City, despite the fact that they had to separate by race when it came to restaurants and hotel accommodations.

However, there was something new that caught Maryann's attention, and when she mentioned it to everyone at a moment when Martin and Mattie were beyond hearing distance, they all acknowledged the same circumstance. "Is it my imagination or does it seem like Martin and Mattie always end up side-by-side and acting like they've forgotten the rest of us are here?"

"You know, I thought it was just me, but now that you say it out loud, Maryann, I do believe that you are right," said Esther. "Of course we could be jumping to conclusions. They *are* the same age, both educated now. They've known each other all their lives; they have things in common."

Just then Martin and Mattie turned and started back toward their families.

"What do you think now?" asked Maryann as she nodded in the direction of the young couple.

Mattie had taken Martin's hand, and when they reached the others, Martin said, "Would anyone mind if Mattie and I went off on our own for a while? We can meet up later."

Not a single face was lacking a smile, which caused Martin and Mattie to lose their composure just a bit. When everyone told them to have fun and be careful, Martin put his arm around Mattie's shoulder and off they went.

The families were in complete agreement that the two of them made a handsome couple. Martin, like all the Langdon men, was six feet tall with brown eyes and dark wavy hair. His smile displayed perfect teeth and was so welcoming that people he met usually liked him immediately.

Mattie stood five foot six with a beautiful light brown complexion that was flawless. Her eyes were warm and friendly; her hair was coal black, reaching to the middle of her back. Like Martin, her teeth were perfect and her smile was infectious.

Maryann's keen observance proved to be quite accurate; when the families returned home, Martin and Mattie began spending a great deal of time together.

When a relationship begins there is no telling where it might lead. It may languish and fizzle out or it may eventually produce grandchildren. Martin and Mattie's parents were very pleased that their children were so taken with one another, but as time went by, secretly, each of them began to have certain reservations.

No one pried and no one thought to try discouraging the young couple, but two years later when Martin announced that he was going to propose to Mattie, William and Joanna went to see Jerome and Esther.

After telling Mattie's parents about Martin's pronouncement, William said, "I know that I don't have to tell you how happy we would be to see the children get married. We would be very proud to have Mattie as our daughter-in-law. Furthermore, after all these years of being friends, what a joy it would be to have our families united in such a way. It just worries Joanna and me that their happiness might be marred by the evil in this world that we call racism."

"You needn't feel uneasy about broaching the subject," said Jerome. "Esther and I have the same concern, and I could not improve on the way you put things. The problem is real, and I'm sure that Mattie and Martin would understand our anxiety with no offense taken. In fact, if they intend to marry, they could not do so in Georgia, nor could they live here."

"Then what should we do?" Esther asked.

"Maybe we should wait to see if Mattie accepts," said Joanna.

"Oh I think I can answer that question," said Esther. "Martin is all that she talks about. She is in love—that is certain."

"Martin feels the same way," said William. "And I will not interfere in any way."

"Neither will I," said Jerome.

"Then there is only one thing left," William interjected. "We wait until they are engaged, and then we'll sit down with them and make sure they understand the challenges with which they might have to contend, including the very difficult point that you just made, Jerome. I read about a white man who married a black woman in Washington DC in June of 1958. How ironic it is that their last name is Loving. After the wedding they went to their home state of Virginia, but they were arrested for living together as husband and wife. The judge in the case released them with the understanding that they would leave Virginia for twenty-five years."

"I read that story too," said Joanna. "But they say that love conquers all, and I think our children have what it takes to make it work. Someday the world will be full of interracial couples, but it must have a beginning. Let's be proud that our children are pioneering this expression of love among all people, by all people."

After William proposed—and Mattie accepted—their parents held the discussion concerning interracial marriage. It was a foregone conclusion that their words would not deter the young couple, and in the end they were overjoyed to discover that they were right. It was decided that the couple would be married in Washington DC, and there they would live until the day the laws against interracial marriage were abolished and they could return to Georgia.

Esther, Joanna, Abbey, Maryann, and Mattie set to work on plans for the wedding, and on May 15, 1960, Martin and Mattie became husband and wife. The ceremony took place at a Baptist church in Washington; a black preacher, Desmond Lowery, officiated.

How amazing was life, and how far the black man and white man had come through life together, thought William as he sat in the church's social hall sipping champagne during the reception. If only they had come through it as friends instead of enemies.

William felt wonderful and proud that his family worked, fought, and struggled so hard to make a difference in the world—a difference that they hoped would benefit all mankind. Still he knew it was not over yet, but he also knew that as long as his family lived on, they would continue as allies to work, fight, and struggle for racial equality.

That night, as he was about to go to bed, William passed by the window and noticed a flickering light off in the distance. He stopped, stared for a moment, and then called to Joanna.

"Come here and have a look at this."

She joined him, looked through the glass, and said, "What is that, William? It looks like a cross burning."

"That's exactly what it is. I remember Grandfather Jim telling me that the local Klan members would burn a cross out in the field every so often as a reminder that they knew where the Langdon family stood on the issue of segregation. It started shortly after his parents passed away. Years ago, when the Klan died out around here, so did this petty form of intimidation, as he called it. The Klan has come to life again in Georgia, and the way word gets around, I would be willing to bet that they heard about Martin marrying an African American girl."

"I hope our concerns about their marriage are not coming to life as well," said Joanna.

"Don't worry, dear. They will get through it together. They are legally married and living on legal ground. They will be fine."

But evil dies hard, William thought to himself; evil dies hard.

TWENTY-FIVE

Ride to Freedom

A year after they were married, Martin and Mattie were living the dream of love and happiness, and it tempered the difficulties to some degree. Still, Washington DC was more than six hundred miles from home in Georgia, and Martin's work was at Langdon Plantation. Traveling back and forth was tedious, and sometimes he stayed at the plantation for days at a time. Martin tried not to worry when he was away for so long; he put it in God's hands to watch over Mattie.

At a time when the happy couple should have been concerning themselves with starting a family, it seemed far more important to concern themselves with the kind of world their children would live in.

There was a new man in the White House—John F. Kennedy—a man who seemed to take a proper interest in the civil rights movement. But until positive results materialized, no one could be sure exactly what that meant. It was for that reason that Martin invited his parents, grandparents, and Mattie's parents to dinner on Sunday, May 7, 1961. At the conclusion of dinner, everyone gathered in the living room; Mattie served coffee and tea.

"Mattie and I have invited you here today because we are intending to get involved in something that we think you have the right to know about. We have learned of a new strategy proposed and sponsored by the Congress of Racial Equality and the Student Nonviolent Coordinating Committee to challenge the segregation laws of interstate buses in the South. It is called the Freedom Riders. Mattie, if you please."

"As we all know, the United States Supreme Court decision in *Boynton v. Virginia* says that it is unconstitutional to segregate public buses. The southern states have ignored this decision, and as usual, the federal government has done nothing to implement the law.

296

Boynton also forbids racial segregation in the terminal waiting rooms and restaurants where state lines are crossed."

"In the *Boynton* ruling," said Martin, "the Interstate Commerce Commission delivered a ruling in *Sarah Keys v. Carolina Coach Company* that specifically condemned the *Plessy v. Ferguson* policy of separate but equal concerning interstate bus travel. However, Jim Crow laws remain in place throughout the South because the ICC has not enforced its ruling."

"We intend to contest the existing conditions by riding interstate buses in the South in groups of mixed race to defy local laws and customs that demand segregation in seating," said Mattie.

Jerome stood up suddenly and said, "No! I absolutely forbid it. I will not sacrifice my daughter, my one and only child for the cause. I am as devoted as any of you, but there are some things you just can't ask."

"I completely understand how you feel, Father," said Mattie. "But what of all the blood that has been shed in the last three hundred years and the sacrifices that have gotten us this far? Should we just quit now and allow it to come to nothing? Our people have made great strides because they refused to give up. If we stop now, Jim Crow, which has barely loosened its grip, will gain so much strength from our submission that it will never be broken."

"It's true, Mattie," said Jerome with tears streaming down his face. "But the method you propose will provoke such violence, and the people in the South who call themselves the law will just stand by and let it happen."

"But, Father, the reaction from those people will reinforce the creditability of the civil rights movement. We will bring national attention to the contempt for the federal laws and the violence used to forever ensure segregation in the southern United States."

"How can I give my blessing when I know that you could be seriously injured or killed?" said Jerome. "Martin, I love you, son, but I love my daughter more than anything in this world. How can I agree?"

"We are talking about rights, Father," said Mattie. "Would you deny mine? Do you think that it was easy for

me when I found out about what happened to you in
Montgomery and in Little Rock? We must continue the
effort. The Freedom Riders will accept the torch passed
along by those who took part in the sit-ins all over the
South to desegregate the lunch counters."

"As painful as it is, I have to agree with Mattie," said
William. "Jerome, my very good friend, I know the measure
of your resolve. I was with you in Montgomery, and I was
with you in Little Rock when your tolerance became paper
thin and you risked your person by stepping in front of a
hostile crowd of racists, demanding that they allow nine
deserving students to enter Central High School. I am also
a loving father, a man who would do anything to protect
his family. And like you, I say 'Lord God Almighty, take me.
Spare my son and take me.'"

"My dear husband," said Esther. "I knew Mattie before
you because I carried her. I nursed her and saw her come
into this uncertain world. She is the definition of happiness
to me, but I know that *she* can never be truly happy until
the curse of segregation is lifted. I am powerless to deny
her the right to seek her freedom."

"With great difficulty, I must also agree," said Joanna.
"I waited and worried for three years while my husband
went to war in the hope of ending tyranny abroad and at
home. If we stop now, the brave and patriotic black
soldiers who gave their lives so that their families might be
accepted as equal citizens will have truly died in vain. I
cannot deny the debt we owe them."

"We would like to hear what you have to say,
Grandfather, Grandmother," said Martin.

"I believe that I can sum it up for you by saying that
for fifty-one years I have been haunted by the memory of
Regis Poe," said John.

"Who was Regis Poe, Grandfather?" asked Martin.

"He was an orphan black boy who your great-
grandfather Jim and I met in Charleston back in 1910. We
saved him from two white men who were bent on hanging
him for taking scraps from a barrel of garbage that was
sitting in front of one of the men's homes. We sneaked him
into our hotel room that night with a makeshift rope. The
next day we bathed him, fed him, and bought him some

new clothes. If only you could have seen how happy he was just to receive the treatment that any young boy should receive. We had a plan to get him on the train—we were going to bring him home to live on the plantation.

"The following morning we lowered him out the window to the alley below. The men who were chasing him must have still been in the area searching because by the time your great-grandfather and I got out to the street, Regis was nowhere to be found. After a search of the area we finally located him—hanging in an old shed along the alley."

By the time John finished his story there was not a dry eye in the room.

"That is why the struggle must continue," said Abbey. "History is full of stories like your grandfather's, and it must stop. But we have the strength to win this fight because the Lord is on our side. Someday the Lord's army will defeat Satan and his minions, but the war we wage on segregation will be won before that time. Let us pray for Martin and Mattie. Let us pray for all who do the Lord's work."

Abbey led the family in prayer; the spiritual uplifting put everyone more at ease. They believed that the young couple now wore God's impenetrable shield. As they prepared to leave the company of the children Jerome said, "I would like to apologize for my outburst earlier. I know these two young soldiers have a destiny, and it is no one's place to stand in their way. May they go forth with God's protection, their family's love, and their good sense to guide them."

The following Friday evening the family gathered again in Washington to see the young couple off and wish them well. Martin and Mattie would catch the Trailways bus the following morning, May thirteenth.

An hour before the bus was scheduled to leave, Martin and Mattie met up with the other riders at the terminal. A black man in his forties by the name of James Farmer was in charge of the ride. After introductions had been made, James laid out the plan for the group.

"The plan is to ride through Virginia, the Carolinas, Georgia, Alabama, and Mississippi, and end in New

Orleans, Louisiana, where a civil rights rally will be held.
There will be at least one interracial couple sitting in
adjoining seats and at least one black rider up front in a
seat, which, anywhere in the South, would be reserved for
white passengers. The rest of us will be seated randomly
throughout the bus. One rider will sit according to
segregation law so as to avoid arrest. That rider will also be
our lifeline. That person will contact CORE to arrange bail
for those who are arrested. I would like that person to be
you, Mattie."

"No, James. I will sit with my husband and go where
he goes."

"My apologies. I missed the fact that you two were
married. Very well. Steven, you will ride safe," said James
to a fellow CORE member. "Now I want you all to
remember that we are a nonviolent group. What we are
doing will serve to anger many people. Do not make things
worse with offensive language or actions of any kind. If you
are arrested, our people will get to you and bail you out. I
also have some cards here with the telephone number of
CORE's main office written on them. It might come in
handy. Take one and pass them around. That's about
it . . . good luck and God bless."

As the bus made its way south, only minor trouble was
encountered in Virginia. But when the riders reached Rock
Hill, South Carolina, a member of the group, John Lewis,
was attacked by three white men and beaten. As the bus
left the station, Martin saw John being dragged to a police
car in the terminal parking lot. The incident was a bit
unnerving to the rest of the riders, especially because they
knew that their own arrests would come sooner or later.

"Are you all right, Mattie?" asked Martin.

"I'm fine, Martin, but I'm awfully hungry."

"So am I. I will try to do something about that when we
get to the next stop."

After four hundred sixty-five miles and seven and a
half hours of riding, the bus pulled into the Trailways
terminal in Winnsboro, South Carolina. Martin told Mattie
to stay aboard while he went inside to get food, but Mattie
was desperate to use the restroom. She located the facility

that was intended for black women; Martin went to the lunch counter and ordered hamburgers and french fries.

Martin waited near the door with the food until his wife came out of the restroom. When Mattie saw the hamburgers she reached for one immediately and began to eat. From behind them a man behind the lunch counter yelled, "Hey, you! You didn't say them burgers were for no nigger!"

The loud-mouthed man in a stained apron ran out from behind the counter, hurried over to the couple, and slapped the food out of Martin's hand. Then he grabbed Mattie by the wrist and wrested the hamburger from her fingers.

"We don't serve niggers or anybody who buys food for niggers," said the unpleasant man.

Ignoring James Farmer's warning and incensed at the way his wife was being treated, Martin shoved the bigot up against the wall so hard that pictures of menu items fell to the floor. The man yelled at a woman behind the counter to call the police. The couple made a dash for the door, but the woman dropped the phone and came running to the aid of her coworker with a small revolver in her hand.

"Hold them here while I get the police," she said.

Fifteen minutes later, Martin and Mattie were in the back seat of a patrol car on their way to the police station in Winnsboro. It was nearly nine o'clock at night before they were taken before a magistrate, who set their fine at fifty dollars cash or three days in jail. Martin produced the fifty dollars and then the magistrate told the arresting officer to drive them to the North Carolina state line and dump them out.

"Let North Carolina deal with this trash," he said.

The officer did as he was told; ninety minutes and seventy-five miles later, the couple was standing along a desolate stretch of road inside the border of North Carolina.

"Despite our dire straits, I feel we are pretty lucky," said Mattie.

"I don't wish to squelch your optimism, my dear, but an interracial couple on a deserted road in the middle of the night in this part of the country could be in dire straits indeed."

"I guess I didn't think about that," she replied.

"And I am a darn fool for mentioning it, Mattie. I'm sorry."

"It's all right, Martin. Our relationship is based on love and truth. I wouldn't want you to sugarcoat anything. I'd rather you tell me exactly how you feel about everything."

"Then I always shall."

Martin was tired, but Mattie was exhausted. They had no idea how far it might be to the next town; even the card with CORE's number did no good without a telephone. If no other alternative presented itself soon, they would have to get away from the road and find a hidden spot where they could rest until morning.

At almost midnight, the sound of an automobile could be heard approaching from behind them. As they looked back, illumination from the auto's headlights came into view.

"What should we do, Martin?"

"I hate to take the risk but we need help. Not too many saints or churchgoers are on the road at this time of night. Get over there behind that big tree," he said pointing to a large oak. "I'll see if I can get this traveler to stop. If I can and it appears safe, I'll call to you. If not I will try to get them to move on and we'll stay here a while and rest."

Mattie hid herself behind the tree and Martin started waving his arms when the auto was just fifty yards away. The vehicle slowed, then passed him, then stopped and backed up to where he stood. Inside the vehicle was a black couple probably in their late sixties. The woman rolled down the window slowly as if she didn't know whether or not she should. Martin tried to be as cordial as possible in spite of his fatigue.

"Good evening, folks. I can't tell you how much I appreciate you stopping."

"What's the trouble, young man? What are you doing out here alone?"

"I do not wish to alarm you, folks," said William. "But I'm not alone. My wife is with me."

"Where is she?" the man asked.

"Mattie," Martin called out. "It's all right, Mattie."

The young woman appeared from behind the tree and walked over to the automobile.

"This is my wife, Mattie."

When the couple got a good look at Mattie the old man said, "Lordy, Lordy, are you young people looking to get shot? It ain't safe for a white man and a black woman to be walking the roads."

"That is one of our concerns, sir," said William. "The others are that we are hungry, exhausted, and we have no idea where we are."

"Well, we live just a few miles up the road. We aren't usually out this time of night, but we were visiting my wife's sister, Lucy, in South Carolina and we left kinda late. I guess we could take you to our house, give you something to eat, and try to help get you to where you're going."

"We would be very grateful, sir."

"That's enough of that sir stuff. My name is Otis Brown, and this here is my wife, Opal."

"We're pleased to meet you. My name is Martin Langdon and as I said, this is my wife, Mattie."

"Well," said Otis. "Open up the door, Opal, and move forward. Let these youngsters in the back."

On the way to the Browns' home, Martin told them the story of how they came to be on the road in the middle of the night.

"So you two are civil rights workers?"

"That's correct, Mr. Brown. We need to get in touch with the Congress of Racial Equality in Washington DC to find out where we can catch up with the bus of Freedom Riders."

"We'll do what we can to help, won't we, Opal?"

"Yes, Otis, we will help all we can."

When they reached the Browns' modest home, Mattie sat at the kitchen table and talked to Opal while the older woman heated some ham and green beans. Martin used the telephone to call CORE. When he was finished, he paid Otis for the long-distance call in spite of his protests.

"If we can get to Monroe in the morning we can catch the second bus—the Greyhound—at the terminal there."

"Monroe ain't too far from here," said Otis. "I can take you there in the morning."

Martin and Mattie slept very well that night owing to the Browns' hospitality. When morning came, Opal put together a very hearty breakfast; Martin called CORE again, but this time Otis would take no money.

"When they got to Monroe, Otis profusely thanked the couple for what they were doing. He told them to be careful and that he would never forget them.

"Goodbye, Otis. We'll never forget you and Opal, or your generosity."

"Goodbye, Martin. Take good care of your Mattie."

At eight a.m., a bus pulled into the terminal. Martin asked a passenger if he happened to know if a Joe Perkins was on board.

"I am Joe Perkins," was the reply.

"I'm happy to meet you. My name is Martin Langdon, and this is my wife, Mattie. I guess this comes as a surprise, but we are here to travel with the rest of the Freedom Riders. We were on a Trailways bus out of Washington yesterday morning but were arrested in South Carolina late last night, paid a fine, and were dumped just over the North Carolina line by the police. A nice local couple picked us up—we spent the night at their home, where I was able to get a call into CORE. They told us to be here this morning, wait for the bus bearing Joe Perkins, and continue on with your group."

"That's quite a story, but not a very unusual one, I'm sorry to say. Welcome. We pull out in just a few minutes, so I'll introduce you to the others when we get on the road. Find a spot on the bus, and sit in adjoining seats."

The bus pulled out heading south for a stop in Atlanta. Joe introduced Martin and Mattie to the rest of the riders. The four and a half hours to Atlanta went by quickly—perhaps it was because it was not a pleasure trip. It was, in fact, a journey overshadowed by the possibility of injury or even death. The Freedom Riders meant business, but they were no more serious than the white southerners and their Klan supporters.

It was a ninety-minute trip to Tallapoosa, the riders' last stop in Georgia on Highway 78. Conversation among the passengers was limited to a few nervous words. The bus crossed the Alabama line at about one o'clock following a southeasterly direction to a small country town called Heflin on the edge of the Talladega National Forest. In Heflin, the bus made a brief stop then continued west through DeArmanville and Oxford then north toward Anniston, the largest city in Calhoun County on Highway 21.

"Some of the most violent Klansmen in Alabama are known to live in Anniston," Joe said to Hank Thomas.

"I could have gone all day without hearing that," Hank replied.

"Sorry," said Joe. "That was a stupid thing to say."

As the bus was traveling just south of Anniston, the driver of a Greyhound heading in the opposite direction motioned for O. T. Jones, the driver of the Freedom Bus, to pull over. A white man came running across the highway and yelled at Jones through the window. "There's an angry, unruly mob assembled at Anniston. There's a rumor that a sit-in is going to be staged by some of the people on this bus. The terminal is shut down. Watch yourself."

"I don't like the sound of this," Martin told Joe.

"It could just be an exaggeration or even a bluff," Joe replied. "Keep going, driver."

Just after the bus passed the city limits, Martin and Mattie noticed that the streets were lined with people. The scene was mighty suspicious for a Sunday afternoon in a Deep South town. Everyone felt something very strange as the bus pulled into the station parking lot just after one o'clock p.m. The station was indeed shut down, and there was an eerie silence that made all the passengers uncomfortable.

Without warning and seemingly out of nowhere, a screaming mob ran toward the bus. A young man about eighteen years old laid down in front of the bus to keep it from leaving while a crowd of about fifty, some carrying pipes, clubs, and chains, surrounded it.

They milled around the vehicle of frightened passengers screaming, "Dirty niggers!" and "Sieg heil!"

After the driver opened the door, two white men, Ell Cowling and Harry Sims, who had been sitting in the back of the bus, hurried to the front to prevent anyone from entering. They leaned on the door lever, closed the door, and sealed the bus, but nothing could be done to stop some of the more enraged assailants from slashing tires and smashing windows.

The siege, which seemed to go on forever, lasted about twenty minutes before the Anniston police arrived. By that time the bus looked as though it had been in a bad accident.

"The police are here," shouted Jimmy McDonald. "Maybe we'll be safe now."

"Don't count on it," Martin retorted.

The terrified riders watched as the police strutted through the mob with billy clubs, examining the smashed windows and slashed tires but making no move to arrest anyone. Members of the mob chatted with police as if they were taking part in a picnic rather than an assault. After a few minutes, the police cleared a path and waved the bus out of the parking lot.

With a police escort, the bus was led to the city limits, where the squad car turned back, leaving the passengers to the mercy of the mob. It was plain to see that the people following the escort in a long line of cars and trucks were just waiting for the chance to renew the attack. On an isolated stretch of Highway 202, east of Brynum, two cars got in front of the bus and then slowed to a walk, forcing the bus to do the same. Thirty or forty cars filled with incensed white people, some with their children, trailed behind.

Finally, with two flat tires, the bus pulled to the side of the road in front of the Forsyth & Son grocery store. Like a swarm of maddened demons, the mob rushed toward the bus as the driver flung open the door and ran into the grocery store. A man brandishing a steel pipe tried to enter through the front door while another group of boys and men rocked the bus in an attempt to roll it over. Martin rushed up the aisle and quickly locked the door.

"What'll we do?" the riders were shouting.

"Stay in your seats!" Joe shouted back.

"If they get hold of us we're dead," said Hank Thomas.

"I'm afraid, Martin," said Mattie.

"I know you are, sweetheart, and I am afraid for you. Try not to worry. I won't let them harm you, I promise."

For the next half hour, the mob—which the riders knew included Alabama Klansmen even though they wore no robes—pounded on the bus, screaming for the riders to come out and take what they deserved. Even when two highway patrolmen arrived, the riders kept their seats; the patrolmen did nothing to break up the mob.

Finally, two members of the mob grew tired of waiting; they set fire to a bundle of rags and tossed it through a broken window. Dark gray smoke filled the bus as the bundle exploded.

The women on the bus broke into a screaming panic. Several of the upholstered seats burst into flames, and the smoke got blacker and blacker.

"We are in serious trouble!" Martin yelled at Joe. "If we don't get out of here we're going to burn to death!"

"Do what you have to do!" Joe yelled back. "All of you do whatever you can to save yourselves!"

Several of the attackers pressed against the door of the bus and screamed, "Burn them alive! Fry the niggers!"

Suddenly, a fuel tank exploded and the mob backed off. Martin opened the window by their seat as far as he could then told Mattie to squeeze through the opening.

"I'll be right behind you, now go!"

Out the window she went; Martin heard her scream when she hit the ground. He crawled through the window, fell into the grass, and then helped Mattie to her feet. A second fuel tank exploded, convincing the mob that the whole bus was about to go up. More passengers were coming out through the windows, choking and gasping for air. As they staggered across the street, some of the Klansmen attacked with baseball bats. Hank Thomas was hit in the head as he lay on the ground hardly breathing.

A large white man still dressed in a Sunday suit, his face contorted in anger, rushed toward Martin and Mattie with a bat in his hand. Martin reached for the bat, but the man swung the weapon under Martin's arm and hit him square in the chest, cracking his ribs. "Take one from the Klan!" he shouted.

Mattie screamed; Jimmy McDonald grabbed Martin around the waist, and the three of them finally got out of range of the attack. Eventually, a few shots in the air from the revolvers of the highway patrolmen signaled that the fun was over.

No one in a position of authority tried to identify or arrest anyone responsible; the disappointed mob slipped away. The officers did not take down any license plate numbers, nor did they seem in any hurry to call an ambulance.

Some of the riders were in dire need of medical attention. Martin was hurt badly, and Mattie sustained a broken right arm when she fell from the bus; all were suffering from smoke inhalation. When an ambulance finally arrived, the driver refused to transport any of the injured black riders.

Martin, who had already been loaded, crawled out of the ambulance and told the driver that he would not leave Mattie. His determination and a few stern words from one of the patrolmen finally convinced the driver to relent. Soon they arrived at Anniston Hospital.

When they reached the hospital, the situation did not look much better for the riders. The Klan made an unsuccessful attempt at blocking the emergency room door. Inside, there was no doctor, only a nurse. Finally, a female doctor came in, but she had to look up smoke poisoning in a book before she could treat them.

The Klansmen lurking just outside became more restless and menacing by the minute. When several members of the mob threatened to burn down the hospital, the superintendent told Joe Perkins that the riders would have to leave; several of them, including Martin and Mattie, were in no condition to go. One of the riders, Bert Bigelow, called friends in Washington in a futile effort to get help from the federal government. Joe Perkins called Fred Shuttlesworth, a civil rights activist and minister in Birmingham.

When Joe told the riders that a rescue mission was under way and that they would be taken to Birmingham and cared for there, Martin called his father.

"Martin, is that you? You sound as if you're in trouble—are you hurt, son?"

Struggling to speak, Martin told his father what had happened and where he and Mattie were. Having little time to use the phone, he gave his father the phone number for Fred Shuttlesworth in Birmingham.

"Call him when you get to Birmingham, Father. He'll know where we are."

"I'll see you in Birmingham, son."

Just as time had run out on the riders, eight cars sent by the Reverend Shuttlesworth arrived at the hospital in Anniston. The police held back the jeering mob of Klansmen, and the grateful riders walked through them to the waiting vehicles. On the way to the hospital in Birmingham, they learned that the Trailways bus had also run into trouble, but details were few.

By five o'clock on Sunday, May 14, Mother's Day, Martin and Mattie's parents arrived at the hospital in Birmingham. After confirming that the couple had been properly treated and were able to be moved, William and Joanna hired a private ambulance to transport Martin and Mattie to a hospital in Washington DC.

TWENTY-SIX

The Hardest Mile to Travel

A few weeks prior to the election of John F. Kennedy, William had read in the paper that his friend, Dr. Martin Luther King, had been arrested yet again for leading a protest in Atlanta. After Attorney General Robert Kennedy put in a call to the judge, Dr. King was released.

Among the number of African Americans who managed to cast a ballot in the election of 1960, seventy percent voted for John Kennedy; once again, they looked to the new administration with eager anticipation. But since his election, they discovered that Kennedy, like a number of his predecessors, was reluctant to jeopardize southern support and push too hard for civil rights legislation.

Martin and Mattie had fully recovered from the injuries they had suffered in Alabama. Joanna and Esther had stayed in Washington for two months caring for them. But for the young people, the active war was over, and it was time to start a family. For the rest of the summer, they followed the ongoing efforts of the riders and stood with them in spirit as the arrests, the beatings, and the fight to destroy segregation continued.

Early in September 1961, Martin called the family to announce that Mattie was with child. It was a most happy occasion, a celebration of their union, and for their parents, the answer to a prayer. All of the family in Georgia drove to Washington to visit.

"We look to the arrival of the seventh generation of the Langdon family with great joy and anticipation," said John. "May your son or daughter and the brothers or sisters who follow inherit a better world, a free and equal world where no one is denied the right to life, liberty, and the pursuit of happiness."

Nearly a custom of the Langdons at a family gathering, the ladies eventually moved to the living room to discuss Mattie's pregnancy, preparations for a nursery, and all things concerning children, while the men went out to the front porch to talk about what might be ahead in reference to civil rights.

"If the struggle is nearly over, and I somehow believe that it is, you know that the last mile to travel is always the hardest," said John.

"That's very true, Father," said William. "The winter of 1944 to the spring of 1945, was without a doubt the most difficult period of World War II. Hitler knew that Germany was nearly defeated, and he threw everything he had militarily into the Battle of the Bulge. When that failed, he declared total warfare—meaning that he expected every man, woman, and child to enter the fray to bring about a German victory or cease to exist."

"That is why I believe that the end is near, but the suffering will be greater now than ever before. The evil that manifests itself in the form of hatred and bigotry will do as Hitler did and make one last all-out effort to turn the tide of the battle and bring back the power of the Old South," said John.

"By the same token, the side of righteousness has come so far and gained so much that it will not regress now that full legal equality is finally in sight," said Jerome.

"The question now is, will President Kennedy be the man to go down in history as the champion of civil rights?" asked Martin.

"I think Kennedy is a good man, but have the influence and the power of the white southerners weakened enough to allow the legislation we need to pass through their fingers?" said William.

"That is my concern," said Martin. "I have to tell you that the Klan did not seem weakened in Anniston that day when Mattie and I were trapped on the bus with the other Freedom Riders."

"Perhaps I should also mention that the Battle of the Bulge, Hitler's mass offensive, came as a complete surprise to the Allies. I remember that we all thought we'd be home by Christmas in 1944. We didn't think the Germans had that much life left in them," said William.

"I prefer to believe that the movement is a juggernaut that can no longer be derailed or immobilized," said Jerome. "I keep telling myself that the building blocks put

311

into place by the last few presidents will not topple but will become the foundation upon which equality will soon rest."

"We all want to believe that, Jerome, but there is evidence that Kennedy's plan is to placate the African Americans while he maintains his presidential footing. He has appointed an unprecedented number of black men to high-level positions in his administration."

"But won't that give the black man more power from within? Won't that give him the opportunity to be more persuasive in government?"

"Yes, Jerome, but if that is the extent of his efforts, it will also slow up the progress and take longer to accomplish what he might very well be able to finish right now."

"But he speaks out in favor of desegregating schools. He has put Lyndon Johnson in charge of the President's Committee on Equal Employment Opportunity and Robert Kennedy, the attorney general, has turned his attention to voting rights."

"All of this is true—maybe the man we've needed for so many years *is* sitting in the White House this very minute," said John. "We've had so many previous reasons to believe that we were on the brink of success, only to be disappointed. This time let us wait until we are sure before we celebrate."

When Martin and Mattie's son was born, the struggle for equal rights took on a whole new meaning for the Langdon family. If the two races could not coexist in harmony, and on equal terms, what chance would a child from a mixed race couple have? Would this boy be torn for a lifetime between the two sides, most likely discriminated against by both?

But no one, most of all the young parents, would ever accept failure as an option; their son would grow up with every opportunity life could offer no matter what kind of sacrifices they might have to make.

He was baptized Michael Jerome Langdon—Michael after the archangel who leads God's armies against the forces of evil.

"Let us pray that he is the first generation untouched by discrimination, free to go where he pleases and do as he chooses without concern or consternation," said Martin after the ceremony.

"Amen," the family responded in unison.

That night, while waiting for sleep to arrive, William thought of his grandfather's cousin, Emma, her husband, Willis, and their son, Nicolas. Emma and Willis were married in 1922 and moved to Canada just before Nicolas was born because it wouldn't have been safe for them to live in the United States.

For forty years, only letters bridged the gap between Georgia and part of William's family living in Canada. Now Emma and Willis were close to eighty years of age; Nicolas was age forty with a family of his own.

Consequently, Canada had become their home and always would be, as stated by Emma in her most recent letter. Even if they wanted to return, they still could not legally live as husband and wife in Georgia.

Now, William's son, Martin, his wife, Mattie, and their son, Michael, could not live closer to home than Washington DC. While he was praying that the sacrifice made by Emma and Willis would not come to nothing, William fell asleep.

In the spring of 1963, Jerome went to see William with a letter he received from Ralph Abernathy.

"I wanted to share this with you, William. I received this yesterday from the Reverend Abernathy. Dr. King and the Reverend Fred Shuttlesworth are about to launch a campaign of mass protests in Birmingham. He asks that we support the campaign in prayer and be ready to be called upon if need be. I will let you know if I receive further word."

But on Good Friday, William found out from a television broadcast that Dr. King was arrested and confined in the Birmingham jail. For days following the event, the Langdon family gathered at John and Abbey's house along with Jerome and Esther to watch the daily news.

With Dr. King in jail, one of his young lieutenants, James Bevel, led the black youth of Birmingham in a march through the streets of the city. The civil rights movement was striking while the iron was hot. As the Langdon family had surmised, the movement had reached a fever pitch. There was no turning back; it was freedom or failure forever.

But as they watched the horror unfold on the news broadcast, they witnessed the brutality unleashed by the Birmingham city commissioner, Eugene "Bull" Connor. Police dogs and high-pressure water hoses decimated the ranks of the demonstrators, and in the end nearly a thousand people had been arrested.

"Now Kennedy will be forced to act," said John one evening after the news ended. "The entire nation has had the violence of segregation thrust directly into their homes. The situation can no longer be pacified or side stepped. He must act for the good of his administration."

John's prediction proved to be correct because the president invoked federal authority by sending several thousand troops to an air base in Alabama, and his staff expedited the process of drafting a comprehensive civil rights bill.

At his inauguration, the governor of Alabama, George Wallace, vowed that he would protect segregation, and then upheld his word by standing in the door of the schoolhouse to prevent two black students from entering the University of Alabama. The president responded much like his predecessor, Dwight Eisenhower, by federalizing the Alabama National Guard, clearing the way for the students to enter and enroll in the school.

But the most exciting moment for the family and the country came on June 11, 1963, when they gathered in front of the television and watched with bated breath as President Kennedy addressed the nation. The president defined the civil rights movement as moral, constitutional, and legal. He announced that major civil rights legislation would be submitted to Congress to guarantee equal access to public facilities, to end segregation in education, and to provide federal protection of the right to vote.

When Abbey turned off the television, the members of the family cheered, hugged each other, and felt in their hearts that they were on the threshold of something never before experienced by the African American citizens: full legal equality.

On August 8, 1963, everyone traveled to Washington DC to see Martin, Mattie, and Michael, to join with Americans of all races in a celebration of the centennial of the Emancipation Proclamation, and to participate in the March for Jobs and Freedom. The march was led by some of the most prominent leaders of the civil rights movement such as A. Phillip Randolph, Roy Wilkins, Bayard Rustin, and Whitney Young.

As the crowd of more than two hundred thousand stood quietly watching and listening, one of the most eloquent speakers of his time, Dr. Martin Luther King Jr., capped the historic event by delivering a speech titled, "I Have a Dream," from the steps of the Lincoln Memorial.

Afterward the Langdons and the Tompkins toured the city and then put together a picnic lunch on the lawn near the Lincoln Memorial Reflecting Pool.

"As the oldest member of this group," said John, "I wish that I had the ability to express what's in my heart as movingly as our dear Dr. King, but I thank God that I am able to be here today with my family and my extended family, Jerome and Esther. We have come a long way to experience such a gratifying moment, and it is worth every sacrifice and every heartache we've endured because we endured them together."

"I think your ability to express what's in your heart is *very* moving, John," said Jerome. "Our association with you and your family has made Esther and me better people, and we are proud that our daughter is your grandson's wife."

The family returned home to revel in the aftermath of the day in Washington, looking forward to the realization of President Kennedy's promises. But pride cometh before a fall, according to the Bible, and like the former slaves who cried out in anguish when their beloved emancipator was murdered, the world was shocked on November 22, 1963, when President Kennedy was gunned down in Dallas, felled by an assassin's bullet.

TWENTY-SEVEN

An Unexpected Ally

Before the death of President Kennedy, the comprehensive civil rights bill had passed several obstacles and had garnered the endorsement of House and Senate Republican leaders. Now, the bill was in the hands of Lyndon B. Johnson. Southern blacks were terrified when they learned that a southerner was in the White House.

"What do you suppose will become of the dream now?" Martin asked his father a week after President Kennedy's death.

"I can't answer that, son. The black sharecroppers have been asking me the same question all day. But somehow I don't think it will be too long before we find out. President Kennedy had made some very bold moves before that fateful day in Dallas. The passing of the civil rights bill was nearly imminent. The issue is too hot for President Johnson to hold onto for very long."

William's prediction proved to be correct, and though Johnson hailed from Texas, he followed through with Kennedy's promise to end segregation.

Using his influence with southern white congressional leaders, assistance from Robert Kennedy's Justice Department, and the overwhelming emotion after the president's death, the Civil Rights Act was passed on July 2, 1964, as a way to honor President Kennedy.

"You know," John told his son and grandson when they heard the bill had passed, "I believe that President Johnson did something that the late President Kennedy would not have been able to do: put together a coalition of northern Democrats and liberal Republicans to push through landmark legislation."

"I think you're right about that, Father," said William. "I think we underestimated Mr. Johnson. Apparently he cares a great deal about social justice. But when will the violence end? What about the three young civil rights workers who have been missing since June 22 down in Neshoba County, Mississippi?"

"I shudder to think of what might have happened to them," said John. "Missing in Mississippi while attempting to prepare and register African Americans to vote does not bode well for their safety."

"Their car was found three days after they turned up missing," said Martin. "I hold out little hope that they are found alive."

The passing of the Civil Rights Act was a huge step for black Americans, but the inhabitants of Langdon Plantation were not yet ready to claim a complete victory. The guaranteed right to vote had not yet come, and how much further President Johnson's administration was willing to go remained to be seen.

On August 5, the bodies of the three civil rights workers were found buried in an earthen damn, sparking a full-scale investigation by the FBI.

At the end of February the following year, Jerome once again received word from Dr. King. A peaceful demonstration was planned for March 7 in Selma, Alabama, for the purpose of bringing attention to the struggle for voting rights.

"Dr. King feels he may need my help again as a legal representative, and he told me to invite you to come along," he told William.

"I have been following the campaign in Selma. It began on January second," said William.

"The Southern Christian Leadership Conference chose to focus on Selma because the local sheriff is the notorious Jim Clark. They anticipate violence on his part, which they hope will gain national attention and put pressure on the president and Congress to produce new national voting rights legislation," said Jerome.

"Yes," said William. "The campaign in Selma and nearby Marion began with lots of arrests but little violence, but that all changed on February 18 when Jimmie Lee Jackson was shot by that Alabama state trooper."

"The demonstration is in response to Jimmie's death. It will be led by Dr. King's Southern Christian Leadership Conference colleague Hosea Williams and Student

Nonviolent Coordinating Committee leader John Lewis. We
will march from Selma to Montgomery."

"I will go with you, Jerome."

"I'm sure I don't have to tell you that it could be
dangerous."

"No more than it was for our children in Anniston,"
William replied.

"Right," said Jerome.

On Saturday afternoon, March 6, 1964, the family got
together to spend a little time with William and Jerome
before they left for Selma. Everyone knew that the civil
rights movement was reaching its climactic juncture, and
the slightest involvement meant the expectation of violence.
They held their own version of a prayer service, appealing
to Almighty God for the safety of the marchers.

"We all know that Governor George Wallace has put a
ban on protest marches in Alabama," said John.
"Unequivocally, that means that if this march takes place,
there *will* be bloodshed. I know I speak for everyone when I
say that while we are not recruiting martyrs, we must have
an unprecedented respect for those who are willing to face
the teeth of the tiger for a cause so precious that it sits on
a higher pedestal than life itself. Without those people who
are willing to make the ultimate sacrifice, tyranny would
rule the world; because of such people, freedom is able to
spread. The struggle for freedom must go on."

Owing to the perpetual motion of time, Sunday
morning arrived in Selma, Alabama. When William and
Jerome reached the Brown Chapel AME Church, a large
number of people, both black and white, were already
there. When the crowd of about six hundred was
assembled, one of the leaders of the group, Mr. John Lewis,
stood before his followers and imparted a few remarks.

"My friends, we are here today gathered in peaceful
demonstration against the refusal of our constitutional
right to vote. We are also here to remember our faithful
comrade, Jimmie Lee Jackson, who was killed for nothing
more than protecting his mother from a violent attack in
Marion, Alabama on February eighteenth. I have asked the
Heavenly Father to march with us today, to guide us,

protect us, and help us show the nation that our cause is just. I will see all of you in Montgomery."

With that, the leaders took their places on the street, and the crowd fell in behind them four abreast. As they made their way through the town, some of the people sang hymns; others carried signs that said, "Black lives matter, all lives matter."

"Are you ready, Jerome?" William asked.

"I am ready, my friend," he replied.

When they were about a hundred yards from the Edmund Pettus Bridge, the protestors could see a frightening sight up ahead. An assembly of about one hundred and fifty Alabama State Troopers stood menacingly at the foot of the bridge. When they advanced another forty yards, they could also see a posse of local police and sheriff's deputies led by none other than Sheriff Jim Clark.

The marchers stopped singing, stiffened their resolve, and continued forward. Just short of the bridge, the marching came to a halt when Sheriff Clark, with the use of a bull horn, ordered the protestors to disperse. Everyone stopped and stood like statues.

One minute and five seconds after the warning, the state troopers charged at them like an army on a battlefield. The local police and sheriff's deputies followed right behind them, swinging bullwhips and rubber tubing wrapped in barbed wire.

In an instant, the protestors felt the effects of the charging mob, which tore through their numbers with the fury of a tornado. The first ten to twenty people were knocked to the ground in a tangle of arms and legs; the sound of their screams filled the air.

While the lawmen did their best to inflict injury on the nonviolent marchers, a crowd of whites cheered as if they were at a sporting event. William saw John Lewis hit the ground hard while a state trooper smashed him in the head with a nightstick. Most of the protestors still on their feet began retreating back through the town, but the police chased after them on foot and on horseback. William looked around and realized that he had lost sight of Jerome. He called out his name, but the pandemonium was reminiscent of so many days he'd spent on the battlefields of Europe and he knew his friend could not hear his shouts.

Then several loud popping sounds could be heard above the din; William feared the police had opened fire. He soon discovered that they had done exactly that but with tear gas canisters instead of bullets.

Clearly the protestors had abandoned the march, desperately trying to escape the violence, but the beating and the whipping continued. People were lying on the ground, trying to crawl away, or staggering around aimlessly, half blinded by the tear gas. The sights, the sounds, and the terror of the moment had William nearly in panic. Worst of all, he still had not located Jerome.

A young woman right in front of him was knocked to the ground by a trooper on horseback. Blood covered her face, pouring from a deep gash above her right eye. William gathered her in his arms and started back into Selma. He had taken just a few steps when he heard an angry voice behind him say, "You shoulda stayed home today, nigger lover." Then a staggering blow came down on his head. He fell to the ground, the young woman landed on top of him, and then everything went black.

When William regained consciousness he was dizzy and disoriented. He wasn't sure where he was, but he could hear a mixture of moaning and voices all around him. When he opened his eyes his vision was not clear, and the pain in his head was severe.

At length, a middle-aged black man wearing the garb of a clergyman came over to lay a cold compress on his forehead and ask how he was feeling.

"I am the Reverend Paul Blankenship. What is your name, sir?"

"William . . . William Langdon."

"Could you sit up, William? Or would you rather lie still a while longer?"

"I can try to sit, Reverend. My head hurts. Feels like I was kicked in the head by a mule."

"I am sorry for your injury, William. There is a doctor here. He is looking at the injured and sending them to the hospital if need be. I will have him look at you shortly. Nearly fifty people have been sent to the hospital already. A terrible day, and a poor commentary on those who represent the law in this state."

"I have to agree with you, Reverend, but I have a bigger worry than that right now. Before I was knocked unconscious I was trying to find my friend, Jerome. Jerome Tompkins. Have you seen him?"

"Yes, I do remember Mr. Tompkins. He was directly exposed to tear gas and is suffering from temporary blindness. He has been sent to the hospital, but the doctor said that he should recover completely. All things considered, you were both pretty lucky. We've had people with fractured legs, arms, and ribs, not to mention numerous cuts and bruises. Mr. Lewis has suffered a fracture to the skull."

William felt a little better knowing that Jerome was not seriously injured.

"Help me sit up, Reverend."

When he was able to get a better look at his surroundings he realized that he had been lying in one of the pews at Brown Chapel. His vision was clearing, but his head still hurt a great deal. Amazingly enough, his scalp had not been opened, but he had a large bump on the back of his head.

When the doctor examined him it was decided that a visit to the hospital would be the wise thing to do. It was possible that William had suffered a concussion; a night of observation was warranted.

When he reached the hospital he was examined further. The prescribed treatment was rest and an ice pack to help reduce the swelling. Before he was satisfied to lie down, William insisted on making two phone calls and a visit to Jerome's room.

Jerome was in bed at a forty-five degree angle; a wide gauze bandage wrapped around his head completely covered his eyes.

"It's me, Jerome. How are you feeling?"

"My eyes burn a bit. How are you?"

"Aside from a lump on my head the size of a golf ball and a miserable headache, I think I am all right."

"I'm glad of that. They tore us up pretty good. A large number of our people are here."

"I know. I wonder how Mr. Lewis is doing. A skull fracture is very serious."

"God will look out for John," said Jerome. "He always has. John is a good man and a real fighter for our cause. He has been arrested many times. He spent forty-four days imprisoned in Mississippi during the Freedom Rides in 1961—he spent his birthday there. He organized sit-ins at lunch counters in Nashville, Tennessee, while he was a student at Fisk University. John will survive. He is an indomitable spirit."

"That describes quite a few of your people, Jerome. They've come a long way, and most of the credit goes to them. They never quit no matter what."

"A lot of credit goes to people like you and your family," said Jerome. "We never quit, but we still wouldn't have gotten this far without at least some of the white population siding with us."

"We are all brothers, Jerome. What else could we do?"

"I'm proud to know you, William Langdon. Very proud."

"You rest now," said William. "I have already called home, and then I called Martin and Mattie. They know we are all right. I told them we'll be home in a day or two. Martin said they watched the whole thing on television. They were very glad to hear from me."

"Thank you, William. I'm glad the nation bore witness to the violence. It's what we bled for today. I can rest a little easier now. Let's talk later."

"I'll be right across the hall, my friend."

That evening, television news broadcasts were inundated with information concerning the attack at the bridge. Dr. King sent numerous telegrams and issued public statements, prevailing on religious leaders from around the country to join the nonviolent march, which he planned to retry on March ninth.

However, the movement attorney, Fred Gray, circulated a message to Jerome and the other protestors that he had been notified by Federal District Court Judge Frank M. Johnson Jr. that a restraining order would be issued, prohibiting the march until March eleventh. They also learned that President Johnson was pressuring Dr. King to wait until protection for the marchers could be provided by the federal court.

Two days later, William and Jerome were released from the hospital. Although Jerome's eyesight had been restored, he wore dark glasses in bright sunlight, which still caused his eyes to tear easily. They found lodging with a local black couple, David and Loretta Green, who were very happy to have the company of two men involved in the march to Montgomery.

After dinner on March 9, the two men were walking through Selma on their way to a meeting led by Dr. King when they heard the sounds of an altercation in a dark alley between two warehouses. It was impossible to see what was happening, but the sounds of someone being beaten were unmistakable.

"What's going on there?" William yelled into the darkness.

In an instant, five white men came running out of the alley nearly knocking the two of them over. The ruffians turned the corner at the next street and were gone. The sound of moaning issued from the alley; William and Jerome moved cautiously into the darkness. Fifty feet from the street, dim light shone through a warehouse window on the right.

Much to their surprise, they came upon three white men, battered and bloody, their clothes muddy and torn. Two of them were conscious, but the third lay on the ground unmoving.

"Take it easy," said William. "What happened here?"

"We were attacked," said one of the men. "We need help. Our friend was hit hard on the head. We need assistance."

"Stay with them, Jerome. I'll call for help."

William ran out to the street, looked left and right, and located a pharmacy a block away. He ran to the pharmacy, thanking God that it was open, made an emergency call for help, and then ran back to the alley.

"Help is on the way. Do you know who attacked you?"

"No idea. We just came from dinner. We were on our way to a meeting when those men dragged us into this alley and started beating us. My name is Orloff Miller, this is Clark Olsen, and our friend here is James Reeb. We are Unitarian Universalist Ministers. We are in Selma to support Dr. Martin Luther King."

"Oh my," said William. "We were on our way to the same meeting as you, with Dr. King. I am William Langdon, and my friend is Jerome Tompkins."

The sound of sirens could be heard coming down the street.

"We thank you for your kindness," said Orloff.

Suddenly, headlights from an ambulance illuminated the alley. Two men jumped out, retrieved a stretcher from the back, and hurried toward them. William and Jerome helped Orloff and Clark to the ambulance while the two attendants put Reverend Reeb on the stretcher.

When the victims were loaded, the ambulance backed out of the alley and raced up the street. A police officer questioned William and Jerome. After telling the officer what little they knew, he got into his car and followed after the ambulance.

Upon reaching the meeting place, Jerome told Dr. King what had happened. Everyone bowed their heads in prayer for the three ministers. Two days later they learned that the Reverend James Reeb died of his injuries.

The death of James Reeb further fueled the fire and the outrage of the nation over the issue of civil rights, demanding that action be taken. As the president addressed Congress on March 15, he identified himself with the demonstrators in Selma.

"This cause is our cause too. Because it is not just Negroes, but really it is all of us, who must overcome the crippling legacy of bigotry and injustice. We shall overcome."

On March 17, the president submitted voting rights legislation to Congress.

Four days later, William and Jerome left Selma with the federally-sanctioned march under the protection of hundreds of federalized Alabama National Guardsmen and agents of the FBI. Their progress was seven to seventeen miles a day, camping on the properties of loyal supporters along the way.

"What a difference it is marching under the protection of the law rather than being attacked by it," Jerome told William.

"This time we will make it to Montgomery," William replied.

At the end of the journey, Dr. King made a speech on the steps of the capitol in Montgomery. A delegation of the leaders then attempted to deliver a petition to Governor Wallace but were rejected. But the back of segregation had been broken, and the tide had turned forever.

On August 6, in the presence of Dr. King and other civil rights leaders, President Johnson signed the Voting Rights Act of 1965.

TWENTY-EIGHT

A Second Revolution

After the passing of the Voting Rights Act, there was still work to be done concerning issues such as economic change, but after a struggle that began for the African Americans in the seventeenth century, full legal equality had finally been won.

It was no less joyful for the Langdon family, who for five generations had come to the aid of their fellow man in the unified hope of seeing the promises of the United States Constitution upheld for all men regardless of race.

A massive celebration was initiated by John Langdon; the peace and joy of brotherhood was like nothing ever seen in the state of Georgia.

"It is with indescribable pleasure that I stand before you on the veranda where my grandfather, James, stood many years ago, dreaming of this day. His spirit, the spirit of my grandmother, Polly, and the spirits of my parents, Jim and Elizabeth, celebrate with us.

"On July 4, 1776, the adoption of the Declaration of Independence by the Continental Congress decreed that the thirteen colonies were a new nation: the United States of America, no longer part of the British Empire. The fledgling nation went to war, and after seven years of bloodshed, privation, and sacrifice, independence was won. The Constitution was signed on September 17, 1787.

"But there was a flaw in the new nation's Constitution, written by our third president, Thomas Jefferson. In that document he wrote that 'all men are created equal,' a very misleading statement to be sure. It is difficult to understand how a man as eloquent and refined as Thomas Jefferson could have composed those words and at the same time overlooked an entire race of people. To have denied freedom to the African Americans was a sin of the highest commission, but then to have subjugated them for over one hundred years in spite of emancipation was an abomination before Almighty God.

326

"And so, from April 1866 until August 1965, a span that should be known as a Second Revolution, the African Americans fought against the toughest foe since Lucifer was thrown from God's Heavenly Kingdom to reign over the darkness of Hell: his name was Jim Crow.

"My friends, not one of us will ever forget this gathering today, or more importantly, the meaning of it. The war is won, the day is ours—all of ours—and we must now busy ourselves with the healing of our hearts as we remember the sacrifices made by ourselves and our fallen compatriots. For we have buried Jim Crow in an unmarked grave without hope of resurrection; I thank God that I lived to see it."

Early in 1967, John was sitting in his favorite living room chair when William tapped on the storm door and then entered the house.

"Am I disturbing you, Father?" he asked.

"When you're eighty-five, you need someone to disturb you now and then. It lets you know you're still alive."

"I was just reading the paper. Since Mississippi officials wouldn't prosecute for murder those men who killed the three civil rights workers, the federal government, led by a prosecutor by the name of John Doar, has charged eighteen Ku Klux Klan members with conspiring to deprive those young men of their civil rights. It's amazing how difficult it is to prosecute someone for such a capital crime."

"It certainly is," John replied. "But some people will always be the last to let go of the past. Sooner or later they will realize that times have changed and that they must comply, like it or not. But I'm glad the federal government has taken the matter into their own hands."

"I have to run, Father. I just wanted to let you know. I'll keep you up to date as the trial gets under way."

On February 28, 1967, William read that after the indictments brought by the federal government had been thwarted on three different occasions, re-indictments had finally been won.

But his beloved father had passed away on February first.

William knew that his father died peacefully and happy to have seen so much good come about in his lifetime.

However, his father knew that there are beginnings and endings and that God is in charge of choosing the time and the place for both.

On June 12, 1967, William and Joanna received a call from Martin—a call that would forever mark the date as another personal victory for the Langdons and for all of humanity.

"Have you heard the news, Father?" said Martin in an excited tone of voice.

"I'm not sure that I have, son. Judging from your enthusiasm I would say it is possible that I missed something."

"I know you're familiar with Richard and Mildred Loving from Virginia and their struggle to change the law concerning interracial marriage."

"Oh yes. I know they have been challenging the law in the courts," William replied.

"Yes, Father, and they have succeeded. Today the US Supreme Court ruled that Virginia's law prohibiting such unions is a violation of the Fourteenth Amendment. The court unanimously struck down the law, and any state with such a law will have to amend their state constitutions."

As William listened to his son's words, he slowly grasped the full impact of their meaning. As his face broke into a broad smile and he took a deep breath to express his joy, Martin said, "We can come home! Mattie, Michael, and I can come back to Georgia!"

"This is wonderful, Martin. I can't wait to tell your mother. You'll live in the main house on the plantation, the house that your great-great-great grandfather, John, built in 1840. It will be the perfect place for you and your family. After one hundred and twenty-seven years it will evolve from the home once occupied by a slave owner to the home of a mixed race couple with a man who only sees the woman he loves and a woman who sees only her cherished husband."

"Mattie is waiting to call her parents. We will begin planning the move right away. I love you, Father."

"I love you too, son."

On October 20, 1967, seven Ku Klux Klan members, including Samuel Bowers, the Imperial Wizard, were found guilty of civil rights violations against the three murdered young men in Mississippi. Unfortunately, their sentences were not appropriate for the crime of murder.

But with the accomplishments of the civil rights movement came a special sense of peace and satisfaction for William. It struck him as odd that for the first time in years, his primary focus was directed to the plantation: simply growing cotton, in addition, of course, to his growing family.

His grandson Michael was five years old, and Martin had recently announced that Mattie was pregnant again. After a four year engagement, Maryann would soon marry her fiancée, Mark Walton, the president of the First National Bank in Macon. Jerome had gone into semi-retirement; he and Esther planned to do some traveling in Europe.

The growing concern over the war in Vietnam had taken the place of the war over segregation, and President Johnson's administration continued to face difficult times. But as a nation, the equality of America's citizens was the first step for a more promising future.

William knew that a period of adjustment was in order, a time for learning to live together on the same level. But he also realized that the law could not force and could not expect racism to end overnight; it would take time—lots of time.

For a true leader like Dr. Martin Luther King Jr., the desire to see his people live a better life would lead him down new roads, seeking progress wherever it was needed. In the spring of 1968, his destiny took him to Memphis, Tennessee, to support a strike initiated by the local sanitation workers.

It was merely coincidence that Jerome and Esther stopped by William's house before leaving for a trip to England on the fourth of April. They were to be gone for a month and wanted to know if William might look after Esther's prize azaleas. It was just after eight p.m., and the lure of a good cup of coffee was enough to ensure a brief visit before they left for a flight out of Washington Dulles International Airport.

As they sipped their coffee and chatted pleasantly, William decided to turn on the television to see if there was any word concerning the sanitation strike in Memphis. When the picture came into focus, in bold letters across the bottom of the screen were the words, "Special Bulletin." The reporter on the scene was, in fact, broadcasting from Memphis, but as William, Joanna, Jerome, and Esther listened to the commentary, they were immediately plunged into disbelief by what they heard.

"Dr. Martin Luther King Jr. was assassinated just after six p.m. as he stood on the balcony of his second floor room of the Lorraine Motel here in Memphis. A single shot was fired, hitting Dr. King in the neck. He died an hour later at St. Joseph's Hospital. Dr. King was only thirty-nine years old."

For a moment the four of them looked at each other for a sign of confirmation, a sign that they hadn't somehow misunderstood. When no one seemed able to speak, the reality of it sank deep into their consciousness, and the women began to cry the way one does when their heart has been split in two.

William and Jerome stood up, walked around the room aimlessly several times, and then sat back down.

"Dear God!" said William. "Why was this allowed to happen? Why were we robbed of one of the most heroic leaders of our time?"

"We have lost one of our dearest friends," said Jerome. "Is it even enough to say that we were fortunate to have known him? Let's go home, Esther. We will postpone our trip for a while. We will be there when he is laid to rest."

Jerome and Esther left in deep despair. William and Joanna sat in silence for the rest of the evening. On April 9, 1968, William chartered several buses, and every man, woman, and child at Langdon Plantation made the trip to Atlanta for the funeral of one of the greatest humanitarians the world would ever know.

History would mark a place for Dr. Martin Luther King Jr. beside that of President Abraham Lincoln, for it was

President Lincoln who broke the chains of slavery; it was Dr. King who broke the chains of segregation.

Long live equality!

Epilogue

The history of the United States is a fascinating story filled with bravery, sacrifice, tenacity, and a devout trust in Almighty God. From the beginning there have been numerous individuals whose destiny it was to shape our government, our religious convictions—our American way of life.

However, the entire story does not read like a fairytale; all was not well from the first day of our nation's birth. Included in the myriad of complications was the inception of a *free* country that contradicted its own Constitution by practicing slavery.

It has been clarified many times over the years by professing that those who held African Americans in bondage were able to do so with a clear conscience because they did not recognize their slaves as being quite human. Therefore, the white race concluded that they were superior in the sense that God is superior over all creation, and the black race was theirs to do with as they saw fit.

But God created different forms of the same thing, and so a red rose is a flower as is a white rose despite the variance in color. It is for broader minds to ponder just how it is possible to become accepting of the notion that members of the same species are not necessarily equal. It is even more audacious for any one form of that species to proclaim themselves the undisputed master of all others.

Fortunately, there has always been a minority within the majority, which has not suffered from such narrow mindedness nor do they succumb to false teachings, possessing the vision to clearly tell right from wrong.

It is from this minority that the abolitionists of the 1830s, men like William Loyd Garrison and Elijah Lovejoy, sprang upon the evils of slavery, pursuant to their own destinies.

Although freedom is the one inalienable right that no human would ever peacefully relinquish, freedom lacking the particular rights thereto, is as satisfactory as music with no sense of hearing.

For that reason, the situation necessitated the establishment of the civil rights movement in America, which once again called for those capable of leading the way to rise to the occasion.

Sadly, evil must be allowed to exist as an extremely difficult force to overcome in order to challenge the good Christian to a lifetime of adversity, proving that Salvation is their just reward.

Consequently, the struggle for equality was neither brief nor lacking in pitfalls.

While it is true that the Langdon family of Macon, Georgia is fictitious, they remain a fine example of goodwill and obedience to God's expectations when He said, "Love your fellow man as I have loved you."

In every possible way, they not only comply with His wishes but do so without question or reluctance. So open are their hearts that for generation after generation they instill in their children the same sacred principals in the hope of spreading an influence that will someday smother racism like a fire submerged in sand.

Through the years of victory and defeat, they are keenly aware that in the end, competent jurisdiction may reward their efforts with constitutional equality for every citizen. But they also understand that only a change of heart and a desire to follow the example of Jesus Christ will purify the meaning of humanity.

About the Author

James Gilbert, an author since November of 2012, has done extensive research on the American Civil Rights Movement. A true supporter of human equality, Mr. Gilbert has completed a trilogy on the subject titled, the Langdon Trilogy. Raised in the fifties and sixties, Mr. Gilbert witnessed the televised events during some of the most turbulent times in Black America's struggle for equal rights. It is the memories of those times and his love of history that inspired his literary work.

A native of Gettysburg, Pennsylvania, Mr. Gilbert now lives in Littlestown, Pennsylvania with his wife of thirty-five years. He works part-time as a residential electrician, continues writing, and enjoys spending time with his children and grandchildren.